Balancing
Act

Books by Fern Michaels

Published by Kensington Publishing Corporation

FERN
MICHAELS

Balancing
Act

ZEBRA BOOKS
KENSINGTON PUBLISHING CORP.
http://www.kensingtonbooks.com

ZEBRA BOOKS are published by

Kensington Publishing Corp.
119 West 40th Street
New York, NY 10018

Compilation copyright © 2013 by MRK Productions
All She Can Be copyright © 1983 by Fern Michaels; copyright © 2013 by MRK Productions
Free Spirit copyright © 1983 by Fern Michaels; copyright © 2013 by MRK Productions

Fern Michaels is a registered trademark of First Draft, Inc.

All Kensington titles, imprints and distributed lines are available at special quantity discounts for bulk purchases for sales promotion, premiums, fund-raising, educational or institutional use.

Special book excerpts or customized printings can also be created to fit specific needs. For details, write or phone the office of the Kensington Special Sales Manager. Attn.: Special Sales Department. Kensington Publishing Corp., 119 West 40th Street, New York, NY 10018. Phone: 1-800-221-2647.

Zebra and the Z logo Reg. U.S. Pat. & TM Off.

ISBN-13: 978-1-4201-1156-9
ISBN-10: 1-4201-1156-6
First Mass-Market Paperback Printing: April 2013

eISBN-13: 978-1-4201-3182-6
eISBN-10: 1-4201-3182-6
First Electronic Edition: April 2013

10 9 8 7 6 5 4 3 2 1

"All She Can Be" was originally published by Ballantine Books in March 1983.
"Free Spirit" was originally published by Ballantine Books in September 1983.

Printed in the United States of America

Contents

All She Can Be

Chapter One

*S*oft night sounds and cool, whispering breezes at last persuaded her thickly lashed eyes to close in slumber. Stars shone in the black sky, and a mellow sliver of moon watched over the earth like a lonely sentry, protecting the lovers in the magic hush of the desert darkness.

Morganna lay quietly, listening to the slow, even breathing of the dark-eyed, raven-haired man beside her. From time to time she gently touched his cool skin to reassure herself that he was real. He was hers, totally hers, for now, forever, for all eternity. Nothing save death could take him from her.

He stirred, extending a muscular arm to bring her closer. She sighed contentedly as she laid her dark head on his broad chest, feeling the thicket of fine fur soft against her cheek. Imperceptibly

*his arm tightened and Morganna nestled closer,
whispering soft words of endearment. She felt
warm lips caress her bare shoulder and then
heard her husband's soft murmur as he breathed
her name. "Morganna . . . Morganna . . ."*

*"Hush." She placed gentle fingers upon his
face, and he turned his head to press his mouth
against her sweetly scented wrist. Her skin was
smooth and warm, and even in sleep he was
drawn to that place where her pulse drummed in
a contented rhythm. "I am here, I'll always be
here," she whispered. "Sleep, my love." The soft
moan of her name on his lips drew her back to
their lovemaking of a few hours past. . . .*

It was all there. Every last word, every last
emotion. A little of her life's blood, a lot of
sweat, and far too many tears. Her editor would
genuinely like it, her publisher would find it salable, and her agent would pretend to love it for
the fat advance payment. Her readers would not
be disappointed; this was what a Rita Bellamy
novel was all about. Love. Passion. Romance.

"I'm the one who's disappointed," she muttered sourly. Her eyes dropped to the last page
still in the printer. It was good. Over the past
twelve years Rita had become a best-selling author of romantic novels, progressing steadily
from obscure little Gothics to historical novels
of national notice. It had been said that in a Rita
Bellamy novel there was a sense of soul touching. She knew her public speculated on what
kind of woman their favorite novelist was, what
erotic sensual delights she had tasted, what deep

and meaningful relationships she enjoyed. Only Rita herself knew that her life was empty, had been empty, and that her soul had never been touched.

Rita ripped out the paper with a fierce jerk of her hand. It was all a sham, a farce, this living through her writing. Six more chapters and *Passion in Paradise* would be finished, right on schedule. Two weeks until she met her deadline. She was a pro; she would do it. She couldn't disappoint her editor, her publisher, her agent, and her readers. What did it matter if she disappointed herself?

Now that the love scene was finished, she owed herself a breath of fresh air to shake away the shadows her characters had created. When she returned she would get into the confrontation between the hero and the heroine before the "happy ever after" ending. One of these days she was going to write a book and leave the ending hanging in the air. Just like real life.

Leaning back on her hard, wooden chair, she looked around the cottage. It amazed her that she could write in such a dreary place. Without the aid of her thesaurus the only other adjective she could come up with to describe it was "dismal." Brett had taken everything, had demanded everything, at the time of the divorce. *The* divorce or *his* divorce, never *their* divorce or *her* divorce. Those were terms she had not come to grips with in the two years that had passed. Brett demanded the divorce, wanted to be free. He had found *love*, he declared, total all-consuming love. But his charged emotions didn't cloud his thinking where salvaging material assets was concerned. He traded on Rita's insecurities as a woman and the pain of her rejection, which he masterfully inflicted. Wounded, feeling a failure and guilty into the bargain, she had stood numbly by while he packed up the gleaming decorative copper, the antique wall hangings, the colonial furniture that was so homey and comfortable. He had even taken the plaid draperies and the huge, oval, hooked rug she had slaved over one winter while she had been trying to prove her domesticity at a time when her professional life seemed to revolve around finances and bigger and better contracts. Now everything was gone but her pottery collection. It would be a long time before she would forget the disdainful look in Brett's eyes when he passed over her treasured one-of-a-kind pieces of earthenware.

Rita rubbed her aching temples. God, why was she still feeling guilty after two long years? The dust had settled and she was on her own, making a living at something she loved. Maybe it wasn't so much guilt as the sense of failure. If she chose to see herself as the heroine in one of her books, she would have lost patience with the character before chapter three. How tragic and besieged could a character be without becoming tiresome?

She lit a cigarette, her fifteenth, or was it the sixteenth in six hours? She looked with disgust at the littered tin pie plate that served as an ashtray. Brett had taken the dishes as well as the ashtrays. It didn't matter, she told herself, for the thousandth time. The hell it didn't, she reconsidered, inhaling a lungful of smoke. She exhaled a steady stream, hating herself and her need to pacify herself with a cigarette. After two years the melancholy was wearing off, the anger setting in, and suddenly things that hadn't mattered before mattered now.

It was a two-bedroom cottage set back four hundred feet from a gigantic natural lake in the mountains of Pennsylvania. She loved it and had fought to keep it as well as her home in Ridgewood, New Jersey. "I'll buy your share," she had said to Brett. "Mostly for myself, but for the kids too. Take what you want, but I keep the houses." Brett's lawyers had kicked up a fuss, wanting everything sold and split down the middle. But she had held out.

This was the first time she had come to the cabin since the divorce. She should do something with this place. Two years was a long time to leave it empty and now she was literally roughing it with her sleeping bag and camping utensils. Besides, she had come here to work, not to play at camping. The two sawhorses with the old door laid over them served as a desk, and her computer had been transported in the trunk of her Dodge SUV.

Crushing out her cigarette, Rita poured coffee from her thermos into a heavy mug. Fortified, she stared into space and contemplated her future and her past. Why couldn't she pick up the pieces and put the divorce behind her? Other women did; why couldn't she? Lately the wall she had built around herself was beginning to crumble. She knew it was time to get on with her life. To make a stand, to make decisions. But how?

"I just don't know you anymore," Brett had said, accusing her when he had demanded the divorce. That was another thing—he hadn't asked, he had demanded. He was in love. God, that had been almost funny, and it was a pity she couldn't have laughed. Instead, she had cringed, hating herself, feeling a failure, wondering where she had gone wrong. She had failed Brett. Reluctantly, she had agreed to the divorce, believing there was something definitely wrong with her, that in some way she alone was responsible for Brett's sagging ego and his midlife identity crisis. If she were a better woman, a true woman, Brett would never have sought a divorce.

Trouble had been brewing for some time. The financial rewards of her writing were a measure of her success, and she had naturally welcomed it. More than a measure of her success, her growing bank statements were a yardstick of her independence. This was something Brett couldn't deal with—or, apparently, live with. It had occurred to Rita after some revealing statements made by Brett that men equated money with power. If a woman had a dollar that wasn't given to her by her husband, she was exactly one dollar more powerful than he wished her to be. When a woman made thousands of dollars more than her husband and really had no need to ask him for anything, that made her thousands of dollars more powerful than he. Brett had been almost calm when he told her he did not need an over-the-hill forty-year-old writer of steamy sex in his life.

Her career had cost her her marriage, but she had not offered to give it up. She had paid her dues for over twenty years, and when she had finally succeeded in achieving something, becoming a person in her own right, he had no business to expect her to give it up so he could soothe his sagging ego. What about her ego? What about her wants and desires? What about her goddamned soul? Did he even know she had a soul and how it ached to be touched?

The cigarette scorched her fingers, reminding her that it was time to stub it out. Brushing her short, chestnut hair back from her forehead, Rita walked out to the back patio and surveyed her country home. It was beautiful. The Pocono mountains loomed above her, and the fragrant smell of pine and hemlock delighted her senses. She breathed deeply, savoring the pungent aroma. The acre and a half of pine-studded land and the cabin were all hers. Her name alone was on the deed. One of these days she would have to see about attaching the children's names on the crisp, legal paper. But not now. For now it was hers alone. Her eyes were dry when she looked at the brick barbecue she and Brett had built so long ago. And the clothesline with the rusty pulley. They had rigged that together too. A small outcropping of rock covered with dwarf pines and red maples made her draw in her breath in admiration. This wasn't exactly God's country, but it was damn close.

If the weather continued as it had, she would

still be able to swim in the lake. The days remained warm, the breezes soft, the water only a shade colder than "bracing." Summer was over; the neighbors had already left for home taking their children with them. The beauty and the solitude were all hers, shared only by the man who was renting the Johnson cottage at the bend of the lake. Taking her light Windbreaker, she made her way down to the edge of the lake, her sneakers scuffing at the pebbles on the walk.

If work went well today, she would go into town tomorrow and order some furniture. Rita's clear blue eyes widened at this thought. It occurred to her that this was one of the few conscious decisions she had made in the last two years that had nothing to do with her children or her work. She smiled; it was time to lay old ghosts to rest. Time to see to her own needs and comfort. Rachel, her youngest daughter, would be coming up to the cottage soon, and she wouldn't like sleeping on the floor. Not modern, liberated Rachel.

She stopped herself from lighting another cigarette as she slowly walked along the shoreline. Perhaps she should jog. Rachel was always saying it was the best thing in the world for a thick midsection. Rita pinched her own waistline. She knew Rachel looked at her with critical eyes and had intended her remarks about exercise and running for her mother. A slight woman and considered quite attractive, Rita had taken to hiding her thickening waist with overblouses and casual shirts. Exercise was just too time-consuming. One of these days she would shed those extra fifteen pounds and firm up—if and when she felt she was ready. Her thick, curly, chestnut hair was her pride and the envy of most women. Rita considered it her one redeeming feature. To hell with blow dryers and curling irons. A professional haircut and a shampoo and a good shake of the head and it dried to perfection, framing her softly rounded face and accentuating her clear, blue eyes.

The sun felt good. Her eyes dropped to her watch. She'd been working since seven and it was now past one. She deserved the break. Walking out onto the rickety boat pier, she inched her way past the missing planks. She wondered what Brett was doing with his new wife right now. She wasn't quite resigned to the fact that he had married a twenty-two-year-old. The lake, christened Lake Happiness, sparkled a deep, azure blue in the bright sunlight.

Sitting down on the end of the pier, she hugged her knees. See that, Rachel? Old Mom can still get her knees up to her chest. It had been a good day. She had managed to write the love scene she had been postponing. These days, she couldn't seem to find the heart for love and romance. Her own life was so barren, so indecisive and unfocused. She laughed aloud, a soft, throaty sound. Perhaps she should try her hand at science fiction? Yes, it was a good day. She had made a decision to buy furniture for the cottage, and she even thought she knew what she would choose. Not colonial. She didn't want a reproduction of what the cottage had been when she shared it with Brett. No, this time it would be something lighter, yet substantial. Not wicker; that always seemed so temporary to her. Something contemporary. Hefty pillows, eclectic decorations, bright colors with tinted glass and chrome. The kind of things she couldn't become attached to—nothing resembling family heirlooms. Bright, light, and crisp. That was the way to go.

When she went back to the cottage, she would complete the chapter, make herself dinner, and start the new chapter. Yes, it was a good day. Tomorrow would be better and the day after that better still. Slowly, she was coming out of her stupor and taking a good look at the world she lived in.

Twigg Peterson shoved his papers into an untidy pile and pushed back his chair. He had worked most of the night and again this morning, and he needed a shave and a shower. Reddish-gold hair stood on end like furbishes on a Valentine card, and he ran a long, slender hand through it, absently trying to smoothe it. The one thing he hadn't counted upon when he signed the lease for the cottage was loneliness. The owner had tried to tell him that summer was over and hardly a soul ever came up here during the fall and winter, but he had ignored the advice and signed the lease. There were times, like this, when he regretted his impulse to be alone, but he was sick of sand, sun, surf, and string-bikinis. By nature he was a social animal and gregarious. He missed having someone to converse with, to share a dinner with. He had taken a two-year sabbatical from the college where he was a professor of marine biology to study the relationship between killer whales and dolphins. He had spent eighteen months in the field, traveling from the blue of the Pacific to the black waters of the Indian Ocean. Now he had six months to write his reports as well as three articles he had promised to *Marine Life* and *National Geographic*. He wished he had a dog or a cat, someone. Something. Hell, at this point he'd settle for a goldfish!

Twigg Peterson had never been a creature of discipline; he preferred doing things when the urge came over him rather than waiting for someone else's schedule. Except, of course, when he was due in the classroom. Expressive green eyes and a winning smile made him a favorite with his students, and rarely did he ever have to ask for their attention. He was tall, athletic, and sapling slim. At thirty-two he felt he knew who he was and where he was going. He wore his self-confidence like a Brooks Brothers suit. One of his students, a precocious coed who had the hots for him, said he had a grin that made a girl just want to cuddle and snuggle with him. He had shied away from her after that, as well as several others whose interests were more for the instructor than the course. It wasn't that he didn't like aggressive women; he did. But "Betty Coeds" were hardly women as far as he was concerned. They were little more than girls, all giggles and Pepsodent smiles.

Twigg's eyes went to the cluttered kitchen with its seven-day supply of dirty dishes. He was going to have to do something about the mess or he wouldn't be able to eat without risking food poisoning. And, he was out of clean dishes. Baked beans out of a can only required a fork, and it was better than slugging into town and losing precious time from his writing. What he needed now was some exercise before he hit the sheets for a nap. A couple of laps along the lake would get his adrenaline flowing. Then a shower and a shave and he'd be a new man. Starting the iPod and adjusting the ear set, he hooked the modular miracle onto his belt buckle and left the cabin at a slow trot. He picked up speed as his feet left the rough, pebbled walkway.

Twigg was concentrating so intently on the music piping through the earphones that he didn't see Rita until he was approaching her as she sat on the far end of the pier. A human being and a woman at that! Not that Twigg wasn't aware Rita occupied the neat cottage with the long, sweeping, raised decks of aged cedar that encircled the house. He had known of her existence, but whenever he had seen her she had seemed so unapproachable, so distant, that he had been reluctant to make contact.

Rita watched the jogger approach her with some nervousness. She had seen him before, jogging at an energetic pace along the lake. With unsettling recognition, she realized that she had admired his tall, whip trim body and his easy loping grace to such an extent that the hero in her book was taking on some of his attributes. Whenever she needed to describe him, she had only to think of this man who jogged outside her cottage with the sun burnishing his hair to glinting auburn. Right now, she realized this stranger was approaching her with deliberateness. No, go away, she wanted to tell him. Don't stop, don't talk to me. I want to be alone and that means no companionship, no outside interests, not even a casual acquaintance. She debated if she should get up and pretend she was just leaving or sit and wait to see what he did. She knew she would look clumsy if she tried to get to her feet, so she opted for staying where she was.

"Terwilliger Peterson, professor from Berkeley, here on a sabbatical to write a series of articles on dolphins and whales." A wry grin split his features. "Call me Twigg, everyone else does." He sat down next to Rita and held out a hand. Rita blinked as she shook it.

"I'm Rita Bellamy. I'm a . . ."—she had been about to say a housewife—"I'm a writer and I'm here to finish my latest book."

"Jesus, I'm glad to meet you. I was beginning to get cabin fever."

"I won't bother you," Rita said hastily, wishing the man would leave. He was sitting too close and he was acting as though she was his long-lost friend. She wasn't ready for friends like this one. Out of the corner of her eye she took in his appearance. He looked like he had slept in the trunk of his car and then got rained on.

"Bother me! Bother me? I'd kill for a kind

word at this moment. Tell me, what are you thinking right this moment. The truth."

Rita flushed. Rachel would know what to say to this brash young man. The truth. He wanted the truth. "I was thinking you look like you slept in your trunk and then got rained on. You do look rather . . . untidy."

Twigg threw back his head and roared with laughter. Rita looked up at his long, slender throat. How wonderful his laughter sounded. She hadn't heard anyone laugh like that in years and years.

"Rita Bellamy, you are a writer, I can tell. Untidy, huh? I'm a goddamn mess. I worked all night and have had these clothes on for two days. I'm what you could call gamey right now. I promise though that the next time you see me I'll be spruced up to the nines."

Rita flushed again. "Oh, I didn't mean . . ."

Twigg's face grew serious. "Yes you did. You said what you meant. I always tell my students to say what they mean and not beat around any bushes. Makes for less misunderstanding later on." Twigg stared into her blue eyes and was startled to see the fusion of warmth and intellect that enhanced her femininity. He blinked and mentally backed off. He wanted to sit and talk to her. Talk to her for hours. Get to know her. But this wasn't the time. Instead, he got to his feet and stood looking down at her. "I'm staying in the Johnson cottage."

Rita frowned. "I know." She didn't know if he

knew where she lived and didn't offer the information.

"Nice meeting you, Rita Bellamy," he said, picking his way back toward the sandy beach. Rita nodded, grateful he was leaving.

Rita sat for another fifteen minutes wondering what Camilla and the children were doing and wondering who made the top three on the *New York Times* Best Seller List. Wondering about anything and everything except her recent encounter with Twigg Peterson. She should go back and get a letter off to Charles, her youngest son. Charles still wasn't handling the divorce the way she had hoped he would. At eighteen he could certainly make his own bed, and store-bought cookies were every bit as good as her own. Why couldn't he accept that she still loved him and would always be there if he needed her? Instead, he put obstacles in her path, daring her to fight back with him. How he resented the cleaning woman who now did the cooking and the baking and the ironing. Was that all she was to Charles . . . Chuck, as he now wanted to be called? Someone to clean and bake and see to his immediate needs? The typical stereotype picture-book mother? Time was what he needed. She needed time too; couldn't any of them see that? Camilla, the oldest with three children of her own, said she understood and didn't blame her mother. Blame! Rita's spine stiffened. Blame her! When it was Brett who married a girl younger than Camilla. Brett who couldn't wait for the ink on the divorce pa-

pers to dry. No matter what Camilla said, Rita
knew she blamed her in a way. That she was
somehow less than perfect, less than . . . those
two words, "less than," haunted her twenty-four
hours, a day. They had all hung guilt trips on
her, and she accepted them because she truly
believed in some way she was *less than*. It didn't
compute. Here she was, a successful author,
making pots and pots of money, and she still felt
less than.

It was Rachel who surprised her the most,
Rachel who accepted the divorce with a shrug
of her shoulders. Rachel who encouraged her
mother to "go for it" whatever "it" happened to
be. Get out, Mom, meet men, do your thing.
You're your own person, you aren't an extension of Daddy.

Rita tried to check the troublesome train of
thought. Why was she thinking about all of this
now? Now she had to get back to work. Or maybe
she should take a ride into town and order some
furniture and have it delivered as soon as possible. She didn't want Ian to see her primitive living conditions.

Ian Martin considered himself the man in
Rita's life. Middle-aged, attractive, he was her lit-
erary agent and business manager, deftly handling Rita's career. He doled out advice in large
doses and saw himself as her protector. She had
come to depend upon him and she respected
him. It was nice to have a man in her life, she admitted, and though Ian hoped for a more meaningful relationship, Rita was as undecided about
her feelings toward him as she was about almost

all other aspects of her life. Ian was coming to the lake to pick up her completed work and take it to a skilled typist in the city. She knew he expected her to ask him to spend the night. Pushing that thought from her mind, she concentrated on making preparations for his arrival. Groceries, furnishings.

That's what she would do. Pick up some food and a couple of bottles of wine. She would make the effort for Ian. Without realizing it her eyes circled the lake and sought out the Johnson cottage. There was no sign of the tenant.

Chapter Two

Rita entered her spartan cottage and for the first time was truly faced with the quiet and emptiness. Living like this was ridiculous. She deserved more and had certainly earned it! Why was she constantly trying to prove herself, to punish herself?

Quickly she washed her face and hands and changed to a clean blouse. Making a shopping list, gathering her credit cards and checkbook, she prepared to leave the house. There was no need to make an inventory of the refrigerator; the only thing it contained was a half dozen eggs and a can of evaporated milk for her coffee.

Willie Nelson warbled on the MP3 player in the SUV, and she hummed along with his reedy voice. It was the only recording of his she owned, bought impulsively despite Brett's comments about country western music appealing to vacant intellects. He had always been taking jabs at her intelligence near the end of their marriage, trying to shake her belief in herself and even in those things she enjoyed. "Sing on, Willie, honey," Rita spoke to the voice coming out of the speakers. "Your secret listener is coming out of the closet. She's a little afraid of the light of day after all this time, but she's coming out anyway."

In Maxwell's Furniture Store, Rita went up and down the aisles with the amazed salesman. She had first ascertained that delivery could be made the next day. She purchased entire display rooms, everything down to the accessories. Tables, lamps, modular pieces, and area carpets. As she made her choices, she felt the strain lightening between her shoulders. Everything was light, contemporary, gleaming and new. Nothing even remotely resembled the formal colonial cherry and bright chintzes that had previously occupied the cottage, and Rita worried that the house might not lend itself to this sleek style. But when she thought of the smooth varnished oak floors and light sandalwood paneling and floor to ceiling windows looking out on the open air decks, she realized it was actually contemporary in spirit. Besides, she didn't want to restore the cottage to what it had once been. She didn't need reminders.

"And send me those silk palm trees over there in the corner," she said, writing out a check for the full amount of her purchases. She had just spent eleven thousand dollars without a blink. Writing out the check made her feel good. She had worked for the money, earned the right to spend it in whatever way she wanted. There was no one to ask now, no cajoling, no reasoned arguments. She wanted it and that was reason enough. She now had four and a half rooms of new furniture that would be delivered by four o'clock the next day.

Her next stop was Belk Department Store. In the linen department she selected coarsely woven tablecloths, bright place mats and napkins, kitchen dish towels, bath towels, sheets, blankets, bedspreads. The salesgirl thought she was an hysterical housewife as she pointed and picked, but Rita smiled and whipped out her credit card. Lastly, she bought curtains for the bedroom and simple roll-up blinds for every other window in the house. They were easy to hang, needing only a few nails to secure them to the frame, and they would offer privacy in the evening. Privacy, not self-imposed exile, Rita smiled to herself.

At the grocery store the first item on the list was a kit of hair color, some body lotion, and a huge container of bubble bath. She filled two shopping carts with groceries for the freezer and empty shelves. Last on her list was a stop to the garden department and the purchase of six hanging baskets of flowers, two containing feathery ferns. One would go over her sink in the kitchen and the other next to her desk. If she had to be indoors, she could at least look at something green. She wondered if Twigg Peterson liked plants. Researching whales and dolphins, he was definitely an outdoor man. And a Ph.D. at that! She felt heat at the base of her throat and immediately switched her mind to the characters in her novel. Only thing was, the hero was beginning to look exactly like Twigg in her mind.

Driving up the scenic road leading to her cottage, Rita passed the Baker cottage and was surprised to see Connie's prized Jaguar sitting in the drive. Connie Baker and she had been friends for what seemed a lifetime, yet somehow as often happens they only really saw each other up here at the lake. God, it was two years since she had seen her friend! So much had happened in those two years, so much to talk about.

On impulse, Rita almost swung into Connie's drive but at the last instant thought better of it. She just wasn't in the mood right now to hash and rehash the defects and failures of the divorce. Soon, she promised herself, she would call Connie.

Deep into the history of the Dutch East India Company, Rita almost decided not to answer the phone that pealed insistently. The instant she picked it up she was sorry. It was her oldest daughter, Camilla, and if there was one thing she did not need right now this minute, it was to listen to Camilla trying to coax her children into saying "hello Grandma" despite the certainty that they would cry and scream. The least Camilla could have done was to wait until the kids were quiet before she made the call instead of trying to quiet them while Rita was on hold.

"Mother, I need a favor from you," Camilla

said breathlessly, a hint of emergency in her voice covering the imperceptible whine that was always present when she knew she was about to ask the impossible.

Rita clenched her teeth. "What is it, dear?"

"You sound as though you're going to refuse even before I ask," Camilla complained, immediately putting Rita on the defensive.

Rita shifted into what she called neutral and tried to concentrate on what her daughter was about to say. "I'm in the middle of a very important scene, Camilla. You know I came up here to work, and I did ask all of you children not to call unless it was an emergency."

"Yes, Mother. But this is an emergency. Tom has to go to San Francisco over the weekend, and he said I could go along if I could find a sitter for the children. I've already asked Rachel, but she said she had a big weekend planned. You always used to go with Daddy when he went away on business," she said accusingly. "No, Jody, you can't talk to Grandma right now. She's very busy talking to Mommy! Mother, Jody wants to say hello. Here, talk to him, won't you?"

For the next few minutes Rita carried on an infantile conversation with three-year-old Jody while little Audra cried in the background, *I don't need this! I really don't need this!* Rita was telling herself over and over even while she cooed and crooned to Jody. She was ashamed of herself. They were her grandchildren! She loved them! What kind of grandmother was she that she resented this intrusion? On another level of her brain, Rita was formulating excuses to decline babysitting. Camilla finally returned to the phone.

"What do you say, Mother? I really need a break from these darling demons. San Francisco would be such fun at this time of the year, and Tom and I need some time together." The tone of Camilla's voice was conclusive, as though Rita had already agreed.

"Darling, it isn't as though I haven't babysat for you in the past. You know I love the children. . . ."

"Good! Tom and I plan to take the six thirty out of Kennedy tomorrow evening. I'm so excited! I haven't been to California in over a year, and it was no easy trick getting my reservations at the eleventh hour."

Camilla had booked even before asking Rita. This chafed. There was starch in Rita's voice when she replied. "I'm very sorry, dear, but this weekend is definitely out. I must finish to meet my deadline. I've never been late and I don't intend to start being unreliable at this stage. Why can't you hire a babysitter?"

"Motherrr!" Camilla's tone was aghast. "Tom won't allow just anyone to take care of the children! You know how he is about that! You just don't know how important this is to me! There is more to life than laundry and children, you know. I remember how you used to go off with Daddy . . ."

"Yes, Camilla, I did go off with your father many times. But it was never at the last minute, and I always made preparations ahead of time.

You are being unfair, dear. I don't like to refuse you, but I do have to finish this book . . ."

"Where would you have been if *your* mother put a career ahead of you?" Camilla accused. "Grandma would always drop everything to come and stay with us and you know it."

"Camilla, my mother was a wonderful help to me and she loved her grandchildren. But that hardly applies here. Grandma was alone in the world without ties or a job and she looked for ways to make herself useful. Darling, it isn't as though I haven't helped you in the past. Only last month . . ."

"That was last month." Camilla's voice was cold. "I need you *this* weekend."

"I'm sorry, Camilla, I just can't see my way clear this weekend."

"Mother, you don't even have to come back to the city. I'll drive the kids up to you. Tom and I thought we'd stay on in San Francisco for a few days. Four at the most. I need you, Mother."

Rita clenched her fist around the receiver. She almost capitulated, but something stiffened within her. "No, dear, I simply have no time for the children this weekend. If there's nothing else, I must hang up now. Say hello to Tom for me."

Rita hung up as her daughter was saying, ". . . your own grandchildren, I can't believe . . ."

When the receiver was back in the cradle, Rita sat down, nearly collapsing. Her forehead was damp with perspiration and her hands trembled. She felt guilty and angry at the same time. God, why did they do this to her? Why couldn't they leave her alone and manage for themselves? Better yet, why hadn't Camilla called upon her new stepmother for assistance, or even her father?

The clear blue eyes misted over. They think I just play at this, that I have nothing else to do. None of them had ever taken her career seriously. Wife, mother, cook, laundress, seamstress, confessor, mechanic, baker, chauffeur . . . she was never Rita Bellamy, author. Rita Bellamy, person. No, they only thought of her in direct relationship to themselves and their own needs. They looked upon her writing as a competitor, alienating her from them. Even now, when she was alone, without a husband, needing to make a living for herself, they only considered themselves.

Damn, now her mood was broken. The Dutch East India Company would have to wait. For exactly two seconds she had been proud of herself in refusing Camilla and then the guilt had set in. Undoubtedly Camilla would report to Brett that Rita had refused to care for the children. She could almost envision him shaking his head and sighing in silent condemnation.

Food. Always eat and add to the midriff bulge when you're unhappy. She could certainly do that. She had spent two hundred dollars in the supermarket and could make a gourmet meal if it pleased her. A five-thousand-calorie meal. Poking about in the fridge, she decided on sausage and peppers so that she would have something left for lunch the next day.

The headache came on with blinding force as

she started to chop the onions and peppers. The sausage was simmering in a stainless steel pot along with some tangy tomato sauce. She swallowed three Tylenol and went back to the chopping board. It always happened this way. The moment the guilt set in, the headache arrived, and before she knew it she had a three-day migraine. She didn't need the migraine any more than she needed her grandchildren for the weekend. Her movements were awkward, as if being performed by a stranger as she dumped the peppers and onions into the fry pan for a few quick stirs before adding them to the sausage to simmer. She couldn't wait to get to the phone to call Camilla back. Anything to get rid of the headache, the damnable guilt. Anything.

Her trembling hand was on the receiver when she heard a voice call her name. "Rita, it's Twigg Peterson. I hate to be a bother but I let some oil bubble over and now the burners won't light. Could I impose on you long enough to fry some hamburgers. God, that smells good, what is it?"

Rita stared at the tall man through the screen door. She had to do something, say something. "Come in" was the best she could manage.

Seeing Rita's white, drawn face and the trembling of her hands, he asked, "Is anything wrong? I'm sorry if I'm intruding. I can eat them raw."

"Raw?" Rita asked, not understanding. "No, it's just that this headache came on so suddenly and it's brutal. Of course you can use the stove. What else did you ask?"

"I asked what you were cooking, it smells so good."

"Sausage and peppers. I didn't know quite what to make, so I settled for that." Damn, why did she feel the need to explain? Why was she always explaining? She'd be damned if she would apologize for the emptiness of the cabin.

"Rustic," Twigg said enigmatically. "I like sausage and peppers especially on a hard roll. Are you having hard rolls? I'll bet you are."

In spite of herself, Rita laughed.

Twigg stared at the woman and grinned. He hadn't realized how attractive she was down by the pier when she was squinting into the sun. Very expressive eyes, good features. No makeup. Natural. He bet she was a knockout when she was made-up. Late thirties, early forties, he judged. "How bad is the headache?" he asked with real concern in his voice.

Tears of frustration gathered in the blue eyes. It had been so long since anyone asked how she felt, or showed concern at what she was feeling. A stranger out of nowhere suddenly appears and I fall apart at the seams, she thought. "It's a bad one. Usually leads to a migraine and I can't afford a three-day lapse."

"Then allow me." Before she knew what was happening, Twigg was behind her, massaging her neck and shoulder muscles. She winced and closed her eyes. He had strong hands, capable hands. Was it her imagination or was the pain lessening? "Okay, now hold still and then relax. I'm going to snap your neck. On the count of three." Rita did as she was told. She heard her neck snap, crack, and then the gentle pressure was back. "There, that should do it."

The blue eyes were confused when she stared up at Twigg. "It really works. Can you guarantee it won't come back?"

"Absolutely."

"You just saved me from making a phone call that I would regret. Thank you. You wanted to use the stove, you said." He was unnerving her with his close scrutiny.

"Right. That's what I said." He held out a plate with a brown glob on it.

"What is it?" Rita asked as she stared down at what looked like a cross between hamburger and dog food.

"Actually, it's chopped meat that I think has seen better days. I should probably throw it out."

"That would be my advice." Rita smiled. The headache was gone. Thank God she hadn't called Camilla. "How would you like some of my sausage and peppers? It'll be done in a few minutes. We'll have to eat outside on the picnic table though."

"Lady, I thought you were never going to ask. I'd love to eat with you, and if you have a beer to go with it, I'll be in your debt forever."

"Oh, do you like beer with your sandwiches? So do I," Rita confided. How comfortable she felt with him. There was no fear, no anxiety. It seemed like she had known him for a long time. Such gentle fingers.

Twigg watched her as she set about making

the sandwiches. She was at home in a kitchen. He wondered if there was a Mr. Bellamy and what she was doing living in an empty cottage. He craned his neck to see if a wedding ring was in sight. He almost sighed with relief when he saw her bare hand. Maybe she didn't like rings. He liked the way she moved, the way she handled the kitchen equipment, the way she spooned the rich sauce over the sausage and then closed the roll tight so it wouldn't drip. He noticed that she made three sandwiches. His eyes asked the question. Rita laughed. "Two for you and one for me. You bring the beer. The glasses are in that cabinet over your head."

"Bottle is okay with me. How about you?"

"Okay with me too. Napkins are over there. Bring a handful. Now that you're dressed to the nines, I wouldn't want you to drip on your clean shirt."

"You noticed." Twigg grinned in mock pleasure.

"I noticed." And she had. She had noticed the tight fit of the worn jeans, the designer sneakers with their frayed laces. And the six freckles he had on his left hand. It was because she was a writer and observant, she told herself as she bit into the sandwich.

They ate in companionable silence. Twigg finished first and asked if he could have another beer. Rita nodded.

"Bring me one too," she called after him.

"How long are you going to be here?" Twigg asked.

"As long as it takes to finish my novel. A week,

two, I'm not sure, and then I always need a week to unwind. There's no hurry for me to get back home, so I may stay a little longer. How long will you be here?"

"I rented the cottage for six months. It's going to take at least that much time to collate my notes, draft the research reports, and then write the articles."

How many times she had sat on this same bench and watched the sun set with Brett and the kids, but she never enjoyed it as much as she did this minute. "I love the sunsets here," she said quietly.

"The end of the day. Tell me, what are you writing? Or don't you talk about it. I heard writers are scary people and are afraid someone will wander off with their ideas."

Rita laughed. "I'm past that stage. I write romantic novels for women."

"Oh, you're *that* Rita Bellamy. I thought there was something familiar about your name. When I was doing my dolphin research, several of the biologists were reading your books. They said you were good."

Rita was pleased with the compliment. "I try. I write what I like to read."

Twigg's gaze was puzzled. "Do you put any of yourself into your novels?"

Rita contemplated her answer. "Not myself exactly. Perhaps my longings, my yearnings, some of my secret desires," she said honestly. Somehow, anything less than an honest reply to this strange new friend—and he was a friend, she could sense it—would have been cheating.

"I guess I understand that. How does your family feel about what you write?"

"They tolerate it." Damn, this man was making her talk, making her see and feel all the things she wanted to forget. Honesty again in her reply. "The children are more or less on their own. Charles is away this summer doing camp counseling and then he goes to Princeton in the fall. Camilla has her own family, and Rachel is living in an apartment in the city. They all have their own lives."

"What happened to Mr. Bellamy?" Twigg asked bluntly. He had to know and what better way than to ask outright. He held his breath waiting for her reply.

"Mr. Bellamy is remarried to a young lady, a very young lady, who is one year younger than my oldest daughter," Rita said in an emotionless voice.

"Is that bitterness I hear in your voice?"

"Yes, dammit, it's bitterness you hear. I haven't exactly come to terms with it, but I will. Any more questions?" she snapped irritably.

"Not on your life. Look, I'm sorry, I didn't mean to dredge up old wounds. Hell, yes I did, I wanted to know about you. Because I want to know you better. I've never been one to dance around something. I'm sorry if I upset you."

"It's all right. I shouldn't be so defensive. It's been two years now and time enough for me to adjust." The phone shrilled in the kitchen saving her from further explanations. "Excuse me, she said, getting up.

Twigg sat back, leaning against the rough

redwood table. He tried not to listen, but Rita's intense voice carried clearly. It sounded brittle and defensive.

"Tom, how are you? You know I'm always glad to talk to you but I'm afraid you can't make me change my mind. I have commitments and I intend to honor them. . . . No, Tom. It's out of the question. . . . Of course, I love my grandchildren. Pay someone, Tom. There are all sorts of reputable agencies with people who take care of children. . . . No, Tom, bringing them here will not make me change my mind. I explained my deadline to Camilla this afternoon. . . . Of course, I realize how important your job is, I just wonder how important you think mine is. I try not to depend upon anyone to do things for me, Tom, and I think you can take that as good advice."

Rita listened to Tom's voice coming over the receiver. He had no right, no right at all. She listened for a few more minutes, but when he began calling Jody to the phone to ask Grandma to let him come for a visit, Rita became incensed. That was playing dirty. "Tom, that's not fair and I cannot understand why you and Camilla refuse to accept my answer. If it had been another time, even next weekend . . ." Damn, there she was making excuses again. What she needed was another beer and a course in assertiveness training. Why? She had absolutely no trouble dealing with those outside her family. Secretaries, publishers, editors, publicists, smart people, important people, demanding and exacting, and yet here she was practically pleading for Camilla and Tom to understand why she could not babysit for them and allow her care of the children to interfere with her writing.

"Tom," Rita said in a cool, controlled voice, "I would not make the drive up here if I were you. I have given you my answer and it stands. You must make other arrangements for the children this weekend. Have you tried Brett and his wife?" Lord, she was doing it again, trying to solve their problem for them.

"Yes, Rita, we did call and they both have colds. Besides, as Camilla says, you are their grandmother. And there's no one the children would rather be with than you."

"That's very sweet, Tom, however this weekend it is just impossible." She put conviction into her voice. The last thing she needed this weekend was the children. What with the delivery of furniture, Ian coming . . . no, it was just impossible.

"Rita," Tom lowered his voice to a level of confidence, "Camilla is quite upset. You know how she admires you, even tries to emulate you. You are disappointing her terribly. We don't understand what's come over you. You've never refused before."

"Then why is it so terrible of me to refuse this one time? No, Tom"—her voice hesitated; she had almost apologized again—"it's impossible this weekend. You are an intelligent man; I've every confidence you'll solve your dilemma. Give my best to Camilla and the children. Good night, Tom."

Twigg winced when he heard the receiver

slam down onto the cradle. He had gotten the gist of the conversation and had intuitively surmised Rita's conflict over refusing to babysit. He heard the slight tremor in her tone, the apologetic manner. When at last she had curtly ended the conversation, he found himself rooting for her, cheering her on. Atta girl, Rita! That took some doing, can tell, but if it's what you want, then good for you!

"Don't ask me to explain that conversation to you," Rita said, setting a fresh bottle of beer in front of him. Great God! Had she actually stood up to Tom and Camilla? No doubt she would be punished for it, and they would probably keep the children away until the next time they needed her. Realizing she was neglecting her guest, she smoothed the grim line from her mouth and directed her attention to Twigg. "Why don't you tell me about what you're writing? Are dolphins actually as intelligent as I've heard?"

"I spent eighteen months in Australia researching and studying the habits of whales and dolphins and it was fascinating. As a matter of fact, I only returned to the States a few weeks ago and found the Johnson cottage through a Realtor. My eyes got hungry for the autumn colors. Change of seasons and all that. Who knows when I'll get another chance like this." Twigg was encouraged by the genuine interest Rita displayed, gazing at him intently with those remarkable blue eyes of hers. "There was one dolphin we called Sinbad who literally took my breath away. The species has developed a sophisticated sonar system. They can hear up to one hundred forty kilocycles; that's eight times higher than a human. They can dive to almost a thousand feet with no decompression problems and use eighty percent of their oxygen to the fullest advantage."

As he spoke, describing the seas, the animals, and their habits, the conversation with Tom was already fading from Rita's mind.

"The females are more playful than the males, actually. Sinbad was an exception to the rule. The female is also the aggressor in courtship; the males don't mature sexually till they're almost seven years old. It takes eleven months for a calf to be born, and the mothers are very protective of their young."

"Most mothers are," Rita said quietly, thinking of her own role as a mother and the failures and successes she had achieved.

"I suppose so," Twigg answered. "Time for me to be getting back to work. I'll return the dinner invitation as soon as I wash my dishes. Thanks again, Rita."

"It's a beautiful evening. I'll walk along with you as far as the pier."

At the pier they said their good nights, and Rita watched him lope away down the sandy beach. She liked him, liked being with him. He made her feel good about herself. He hadn't asked any questions concerning the phone conversation with Tom nor had he given any indication that he had an opinion one way or the other about what she had done.

Twigg started off down the beach. He didn't want to go home but instinctively knew Rita needed some time to herself to mull over the unpleasant phone call. He didn't want to work on his articles; he wanted to be with Rita. He turned, making his way back to her. She was still standing on the edge of the pier. "I forgot something," he shouted, that lopsided grin lifting the corners of his mouth.

"What did you forget?" She was puzzled at the expression in his eyes as he drew close to her.

"This." His arms drew around her, holding her close to him. She realized how tall he was, towering over her, lifting her chin with the tips of his fingers to look down into her eyes. His lips, when they touched hers, were soft, giving as well as taking, gently persuading her to respond. His arm, cradling her against him, was firm, strong, but his fingers still touching her face were tender, trailing whispery shadows over her cheekbones. Having him kiss her seemed to be the most natural ending to an enjoyable evening. It was just that. A kiss. A tender gesture, tempting an answer but demanding none.

"Good night, pretty lady," he said huskily, his tone plucking the strings of her emotions. And then he was gone, leaving her standing alone while she watched him retrace his steps.

Rita moistened her lips that were so recently kissed. Soundly kissed, she would have written if it were a scene from one of her books. She had been licked by the flame of remembered passions, good lusty feelings she had thought were lost to her. Twigg Peterson was good for the ego. "Pretty lady" he had called her, and suddenly she did feel pretty and just a little bit more excited than she would have liked.

Back in his cottage Twigg faced the blank page on the computer. He had wanted to kiss her and he had. Wanted to kiss her almost from the moment he had introduced himself to her earlier that day. There was something vulnerable about Rita Bellamy and something strong too. How good she had felt in his arms, how sweetly she had returned his kiss. There was no need to sit here and ponder what she had thought of him, if he had offended her. With Rita, everything was up front. Black and white. She either liked you or she didn't. And that was good too. Emotional games were for children and more often they hurt rather than gave pleasure. The white page glared accusingly under the goosenecked lamp and he began to work.

Chapter Three

Rita lay deep in the sleeping bag, snuggling for warmth. It was early, still dark outside, probably no later than five A.M. Soon the birds would begin their incessant chatter. Rita groaned aloud. She wasn't ready for this particular day. She would not think about Twigg. No, she absolutely would not think about the long and lingering kiss that had reached something so deeply buried within her that she hesitated to put a name to it. Instead, she would think of something else. Camilla popped into her thoughts. She had always felt closest to her oldest child, and she did not like the rift coming between them.

It had always been Camilla who emulated Rita. Playing house, caring for her dolls, liking tedious household chores, always being the first to help with the dishes. Now there was an unspoken hostility between them, and Rita didn't quite know how to mend the fences. What had she done besides refuse to immerse herself in Camilla's life? It would seem that the girl had everything she had always wanted: a home, a successful husband, children. What could she still possibly want from her mother?

Children. She wondered if she had made impossible demands on her own mother. If she had, she had never known it. Yet, before Rita's mother had died hadn't there been a distance between them? In the end, when she was so sick, her mother had decided to go to Chicago to stay with Rita's brother and his wife, as though she was loath to impose upon her only daughter. Mother, too, had resented Rita's writing. Going out to Ted in Chicago had been meant as a slap in the face, and Rita had felt it. Was that what Camilla was feeling? As though she'd been slapped? No, impossible. Yet, Rita's mother had resented the fact that her only daughter had drifted away into a professional world, no longer validating her own lifestyle by devoting herself to family and home. Just before she had died they had talked about it, openly, honestly. Was it possible that Camilla, who had always identified so closely with Rita, was feeling abandoned and invalidated?

Camilla, who had always sought to be like her mother, to be a wife, a mother, now felt Rita to be a different person entirely. A divorcee, living on her own, making decisions and involved in the world of books and business. She was still demanding that Rita set the example and prove out the rewards of a domestic life, still wanted her to validate the life she had chosen for herself.

Rita shrugged off the depression that was descending over her thinking about Camilla. There were still Charles and Rachel. She hadn't written that letter to Charles yet . . . Chuck. She must remember. Chuck. And she must call Rachel and find out exactly when she planned to arrive so she could cook something special for her. The only time the model-thin Rachel ate decent food was when Rita cooked it for her.

Why should I care if Rachel eats or not? She's certainly old enough to take care of herself. And that was another thing. If she didn't remind Rachel and Charles about dental appointments, they would have a mouth full of decay. Not only did she have to remind them, she also had to make the appointments, often telephoning several times to fit their schedules.

Ian often offered to find her a secretary to see to the tedious arrangements of life, but Rita wouldn't hear of it. She did not want anyone to know what a slave she had become to her family. Ian only suspected half of her commitment to her grown children, and he doled out advice in choking amounts as to how she should deal with it. A widower with grown children of his own, he often pointed out how independent his offspring were. He would not accept that children always became independent of their fathers long before they were willing to separate from their mothers. It was an entirely different situation, she knew, but somehow could not convince Ian.

Dear, sweet Ian. Always looking out for her, protecting her, willing to take on the burden of any and all decisions if she so desired. Dependable Ian in his double-breasted suits and sparkling white shirts. A decent man, her mother would have called him. And good-looking in his middle years. Rita's eyes flew open. She was middle-aged. Ian was middle-aged. She knew there had been a smirk in the thought. She also knew if she encouraged him he would ask her to marry him. He wanted to take care of her as though she were a homeless waif needing his counseling, his protection from the big, bad world. Good, kind, safe Ian.

Perhaps she had needed protection in the beginning, just after the divorce when her emotions were like raw sores. But now she suspected she needed adventure. The sores had scabbed over and only a few of them were still terribly tender. She was just learning to enjoy this new freedom. She could eat when she wanted, do the dishes when and if she felt like it, go to bed, get up when she wanted, shop and buy whatever pleased her. She was beginning to learn to deal with mechanics and repairmen. She had even engaged a gardener in Ridgewood so Charles would be free for tennis and all the sports he loved. She wasn't even lonely anymore, except at night, and then a good book could ease even that. She was coping after two long years. *Twigg was too thin.*

Rita snuggled deeper into the sleeping bag. How warm and comfortable the thick down was. It was going to be a brisk day, she could feel it in her bones. A day for a sweatshirt and warm slacks. The weather in the Poconos was always temperamental. *His hair needed trimming.*

Her thoughts hopscotched to her ex-husband. He had always been an early riser; like herself, and had liked sex in the morning. She felt no shame when she wondered how he made love to his new wife. Probably with all the ardor he had shown on their own honeymoon twenty odd years ago. In many respects Brett had nesting instincts, something usually reserved for women. He liked a comfortable, cheery home. Good, home-cooked meals that took hours to prepare, shirts that had to be ironed, all fourteen of them, every week. He liked his slippers and pipe and his *Business Week* and *Wall Street Journal.* He liked the fireplace and his old sweater. Sometimes she wondered how he had managed to become as successful as he was. He had no imagination, no interest in anything outside his home and business. He had been a moderately good father, she supposed, going to the dancing recitals and the Little League games. *For God's sake! Twigg was only thirty-two years old, ten years her junior!*

She wished she had a cigarette. She should get up and make some coffee. Decaffeinated of course. Fry some bacon and eggs. Maybe pancakes. Or French toast with cinnamon and powdered sugar. Did she buy syrup? She rolled over on her stomach and reached for a cigarette and drew the ashtray closer. She counted the cigarette butts. Twenty-two. Two more than a pack. The kids were always on her back about her smoking. Even Camilla had gotten little Jody to make comments. She was an adult, capable of reading and understanding the Surgeon General's medical warning. The bottom line was she liked to smoke and she had no intention of stopping. Certainly not for someone else. When she was out in mixed company she never lit up without asking if anyone minded. The cigarettes were her pacifier, her security blanket. If and when the day ever came when she didn't need them, it would be because she had made the decision. *The tobacco Twigg smoked was aromatic. Her cigarettes didn't seem to bother him.*

Rita slid back down in the sleeping bag just as the first early bird chirped. Was he sleeping or was he awake too? Would he amble by today or would he ignore her after last night? She *knew* he would be back, if not today then tomorrow.

She laced her hands behind her head and felt her stomach go taut. You couldn't see the excess flesh when you stretched out. A pity she couldn't remain in a supine position so that she would look trim and fit. Maybe she should diet and start some moderate form of exercise. Was middle age too late to take it off? Three healthy eight-pound deliveries had added unsightly stretch marks. She had read somewhere that one could never get rid of those unless one had cosmetic surgery. That was out; she wouldn't go under the knife for stretch marks. Or would she? She liked him. She liked his up-front attitude and the way he was in touch with his own feelings, his confidence, his gentleness. She wished she was half the person he was. She had so much to learn, so far to go till she could be like that. Each step was new, alien, and she had to think twice before she moved in any one direction.

The word "affair" bounced around in her head. She didn't like the word. "Relationship" sounded better. Brett had had an affair. She wondered if an affair ever turned into a relationship. She didn't think so. Brett wouldn't have given it time. An affair and then marriage. What was her name? Sometimes she couldn't remember. Oh yes, Melissa. The children pretended they didn't like her but they did. She could tell. Charles walked around with a smirk on his face after seeing his father and stepmother. Camilla was forever talking about Melissa's apple pies and lamb stew. Even Rachel said she had to respect Melissa and her "go-for-it" attitude. The fact that she "went" for her father didn't seem to bother Rachel at all. They all accepted Melissa and the new marriage and then took out their hostility on Rita in small, picayune ways. Hurtful ways, degrading ways. They blamed her and were still blaming her that the family wasn't intact.

She knew in her gut that they, all three of them, resented her career. Resented that she spent time on something that was not only creative but lucrative. They made cutting remarks about her television appearances and her magazine interviews.

Rita rolled over and lit another cigarette. Of course, when Camilla needed a ten-thousand-dollar loan, interest free, to build a swimming pool, Rita's money was more than welcome. And

Charles had no compunction about accepting nine thousand for a new muscle car. Rachel gladly took the "loan" for her new apartment security and three rooms of furniture. Rita didn't expect to get the money back, didn't want it. But it hurt that they hadn't asked their father, that they had assumed she would be more than glad to help out. There hadn't been one word about repayment. She would have demurred but it would have been nice to hear.

"All I wanted was a little respect, a little recognition for what I was doing. Goddamn it, why did it have to come from strangers'? Why can't my own family see that I'm a person? I was a wife, a mother, and a writer. They had no right to force me to make a choice," she said bitterly to the empty room. Actually, the choice had been forced on her by Brett. *Thirty-two years young.*

Rita crawled from the sleeping bag and padded to the curtainless window. A low-lying mist crept across the ground like the swirly hem of a chiffon gown. In the lavender dawn she could see the diamond dew sparkle on the grass beneath the bedroom window. *Was he up yet?*

Rita turned the heat up and then made coffee. While it perked she showered and dressed. Another casual outfit of jeans and a navy blue sweatshirt. She stood in front of the mirror and then turned sideways. She sucked in her stomach and then released it. She winced. It had been a long time since she stared at herself so clinically. She had put on weight. Her new jeans with lycra were deceiving. As long as the zipper went up, she had ignored the pounds. She wondered how far the zipper would go if they were one hundred percent cotton. She made an ugly face at herself in the mirror. Then she laughed. "Who are you fooling, Rita Bellamy?" she asked her reflection.

"No one, not even myself," came the reply. "I'm almost to the top of the mountain now, and I don't intend to slide back. I worked too hard." Satisfied with her comment, she tugged the sweatshirt into place around her less-than-firm derrière and headed for the kitchen. She was who she was; it was as simple as that.

Two scrambled eggs, three strips of bacon, two slices of toast, three cups of coffee, and several cigarettes later, Rita felt ready to start her day at the computer. It was six fifteen. She could work till the furniture people arrived and then she would take a break. Once everything was settled in, she would start dinner simmering on the stove and work for the rest of the afternoon. She allowed no time for visitors, for phone calls or meandering thoughts. She had to work, wanted to work. And there was the letter to write to Charles and the phone call she intended for Rachel. She could do both things while the delivery men carried in the furniture. Rachel was always on the run.

Before she sat down to start the day's work she walked to the door and flung it open. She made a pretense of staring down at the lake and the surrounding grove of pines. The sandy beach and pier were deserted as they should be at this hour of the morning. She let her eyes go to the bend in the lake and on to the Johnson cottage.

There was no telltale stream of smoke wafting upward. He was probably sleeping or working. She wondered if he had anything in the house for breakfast. She stood a moment longer, delaying the time she had to start to work. She didn't realize how intense her gaze was till her eyes started to water. She was forty-three years old and would be forty-four in another month.

Rita wrote industriously, lost in her work for the next four hours. The knock, when it came, startled her. "Come," she called as she finished typing a sentence.

"Your furniture, ma'am," a man called through the door.

An hour later all the furniture was in place. For an extra twenty dollars the men assembled the bed and hung the ready-made drapes on the windows. Rita offered coffee and beer. The men accepted and they talked about the weather for a few minutes. When they left, Rita hastily made up the bed with the new sheets and bedspread. She stood back to admire her handiwork. Very colorful. She had chosen a king-size bed; she didn't know why. The old bed had been a double four-poster. The sheets she had picked from the linen department had brown and orange butterflies flitting here and there. Very fitting, just like me—free, free, free. The bedspread picked up the deep autumn colors and lent character to the knotty pine walls. The thirsty, designer sheet towels were hung in the bathroom adding still more of her own personal tastes, her preferences, her own identity.

The giddiness stayed with Rita till she sat

down to write to her son. First she filled out a check for two hundred dollars. She knew it was too much, knew that Charles would view it as a buy-off and smirk to himself. One of these days she would grab him by the scruff of the neck and slap him silly, regardless of the fact that he was almost nineteen years old. She stared at the check for a long time. Finally, she drew a big *X* over it and wrote another one, this one for twenty-five dollars. He was Brett's son too; let him share the expenses.

She could have written an entire chapter in the time it took her to compose a carefully written letter to her only son. Charles picked everything apart. Once he saw the check he would pour over the letter looking for ways to "zap" her. Certainly, he would expect mention of the football game the day after Thanksgiving. How she dreaded it. Brett would be there with his new wife. It would be her first meeting with the new and second Mrs. Bellamy. Charles expected her to be there and she had promised. Still, she dreaded it. Charles would smirk; Brett would be oblivious to everything and anything except his new wife. Melissa would preen beneath his adoring gaze while she tried to look away to hide her anger and hostility.

It took seven sheets of paper before Rita was satisfied with her draft. She copied over the one-paragraph letter and signed it "Love, Mom."

Instead of feeling strange and unfamiliar among the new furnishings for the cottage, she was exhilarated. Here was the proof of her first decision in too long a time. The contemporary style had been bought on impulse, on the opposite end of the pendulum from the cozy colonial she and Brett had chosen. Or had it been Brett?

Her computer now sat on a burled oak desk, and she sat on a chrome and beige director's-style chair that rolled easily on shiny ball casters. Tabletops were bronze tinted glass, and the upholstered pieces were modular, accommodating themselves to different arrangements in the rectangular room. Beiges, browns, startling touches of turquoise and cream. The roll-up blinds were perfect, mobile contraptions to control the light and her need for privacy without yards and yards of dust-collecting fabric. Geometric area rugs brought the pieces together in groupings, and she took delight in the oak-veneered three-piece étagère for holding her books and knick-knacks. Rita decided she had done the wise thing in purchasing entire rooms right off the display floor. She had no time for selective buying, and she knew that it was more than possible that faced with hundreds of little choices for the cottage she might have made none.

The second bedroom for Rachel was completed, even to the pressed silk flowers framed in brass and hanging over the low double bed. Splashes of orange and deep brown for the spread, rust and beige for the rug near the bed. She realized now that she much preferred it this way: clean, almost stark, color substituting for bulky furniture. Even the small dining table just off the kitchen, with its cane and chrome chairs, was perfect, utilitarian, and yet giving the illusion of space and sleekness because of its glass tabletop. Arc lamps and two or three startling oriental-flavored pieces, such as the vase holding tall pussy willow branches and the mural-sized picture to hang over the hearth, complemented the decor. Satisfied, more than satisfied, Rita took a tour of the cottage, appreciating everything she had bought and applauding her decision to at last make the cottage her own. Already her head was buzzing with items she would purchase when she next went to town. There were those long-stemmed glasses she had admired in Rose's, and the florist in town would create something wonderful for the dining table. Perhaps next spring she would look into getting new porch furniture. Something really colorful . . . that was next spring. Before long, winter would set in up here at the lake and snow would cover the ground.

Reluctantly, her mind went back to those times when she and Brett had escaped for those long, intimate weekends to the lake, leaving the children in her mother's care. Those had been wonderful times, much needed times to reacquaint them with each other. Too often the pressures of Brett's job in advertising would be overwhelming, and the routine chores of children and home would put a distance between them. Those long, lovely weekends. Brett would sleep late, and she would have breakfast ready for him when he awoke. Those were the best times, making love in the morning, going back to bed in the early evening with the gentle snow falling against the window.

Rita frowned. Perhaps she had been too quick

to refuse Camilla and Tom. She remembered how important those times alone with Brett had been and how they had restored their love for one another until again the pressures would build and they would run away together like naughty schoolchildren playing hookey. Her eyes swung to the computer and then to the phone.

No. Not this time. And if she really took a good, honest look at it, those runaway weekends hadn't been all that terrific. Had they freed her from the humdrum chores it took to keep a home? Hadn't she just traded one kitchen for another? And before leaving, it was she who had stripped the beds, collected the towels and the laundry to take back to New Jersey. She still had the cooking, the shopping, the laundry, and the feeling that the time spent away from home was more for Brett than herself. It was because of *his* need to get away, the pressures of *his* job that had to be relieved. Her job had been the same regardless of where they went.

Still . . . she looked at the phone again, already mentally dialing Camilla's number. Determinedly she sat down at the computer and began working. This was *her* time now, and she was doing what *she* wanted. Wasn't she?

Rita was so deep into her novel she failed to eat lunch and kept working straight through the afternoon. Once she got up for a bottle of diet soda and a quick trip to the bathroom. She rubbed her aching shoulders as she stared out the front door. Again she stared down at the lake and the empty pier. There was no sign of life from the Johnson cottage. She didn't really expect to see any signs at all. Last night was over and done with. It was the soft, dark night and the three beers that made Twigg take her in his arms. It didn't mean anything. It was only women who conjured up feelings and emotions when there were none. She was forty-three and should know better.

Thirty-two was so young to be a full professor. Thirty-two was young, period. Forty-three was middle age. Downhill on greased sneakers. Forty-three was the respite before the onset of menopause, a time for face-lifts and night creams, a time to sit back and take stock, a time to stare at the rocking chair and realize it was the enemy. A time to cover the gray hairs, time to buy a chin strap, time to lay aside old ghosts.

She had literally been going down for the count until last evening. With a huge mouthful of air she had surfaced. It was a beautiful world out there, and she wanted to be part of it. And she would, in time. But time could be the biggest enemy of all. Time. Time. Time to call Rachel before she got back to work. She should call Ian but she had nothing to say. Let him call her.

It was late afternoon when Rita pulled the phone toward her and dialed Rachel's number. Rachel finally answered the phone. Rachel was a textile designer and worked at her apartment three days out of the week. "Mom, how's it going? Almost finished?" She sounded interested, like she really cared. Rachel understood deadlines.

"Fine, honey, almost done, another week and it will be ready. How are you?"

"Just great, Mom. I met the sweetest guy. I'm going to Miami with him this weekend. He's in advertising and already has an ulcer at twenty-nine. You'll love him."

"Does that mean I finally get to meet one of your young men?" Rita asked caustically. Rachel talked a lot but usually didn't do what she'd promised.

"Depends on how it works out. He's not Mr. Perfect. I may move in with him or vice versa to see how compatible we are. Again, I might not. I'll let you know after the weekend. Anything exciting going on up there?"

Rita listened and felt the vague stirrings of a headache. It was impossible to follow Rachel. This had to be her fifteenth or sixteenth man. "Not much going on here. Rather cool today. The chipmunks are out in full force. I ordered new furniture and it was delivered this morning. It looks nice," Rita volunteered.

"Mom, Camilla called me last night after your talk with Tom. She was simply beside herself. Mom, she repeated your conversation word-for-word."

There was a ripe giggle in Rachel's voice. She approved. "Way to go, Mom. I'm proud of you. She would have dumped those kids on you like she always does and go off and have a good time. That's why I said no. I take the pill. Camilla should take the pill. It was her choice and now that she has those nasty children, let her take care of them. Mom, I didn't know you had it in you."

"Neither did I," Rita said softly. "What's the young man's name, Rachel?"

"What young man?"

"The one you're going to Miami with."

"Oh, him. I had to think for a minute. Patrick, I think. Why, is it important?"

Rita bristled. "Of course it's important. How can you go away with a man if you don't even know his name?"

"Mom, don't spin your wheels. It's Patrick. Patrick Ryan. I'd like to talk longer, Mom, but Jake is coming over to work on a new design. We'll probably work through the night. I gotta go now. I'll see you Thursday."

"Rachel, I thought Jake moved out."

"He did, but we're still friends. This is a working arrangement. If he wants to sack out, that's okay. Not to worry, Mom. I can handle it. Give my regards to the chipmunks."

Rita stared at the receiver in her hand. If she didn't control herself, she was going to get a headache. If Rachel could handle it, then that let her off the hook. She didn't have to play mother and worry. Rachel was old enough to take care of herself. She wished she knew if her second daughter had any bouts with VD. Evidently not or she would have confided the fact to her mother. Rachel confided everything. Nothing was secret as far as she was concerned. Rachel was right; she was spinning her wheels for nothing. *Nada.* There was nothing she could do. Nothing she *wanted* to do. "Headache, go away," she muttered as she scanned the papers scattered on her desk. She wondered what the thirty-two-year-old professor would think of her children if he ever met them. Somehow she didn't think he would be impressed. She wasn't impressed either. Had she failed them in some way? Was she guilty of untold atrocities that would come out later when they all went through analysis? That was all in the future. This was now. She had to get through the *now* before she could worry about past and future. She liked curly hair, especially with red and gold mixed. Green eyes went with that particular shade of hair. Usually only women were lucky enough to be green-eyed. Twigg Peterson was probably the first and only man she had ever met who had green eyes. She tried to remember the color of Ian Martin's eyes. She could barely remember what Ian looked like, much less the color of his eyes.

Something strange was happening to her. She was thinking. She was feeling. The process was similar to a sleeping hand coming back to life. Pinpricks of awareness were making her alive again. She had to put Rachel from her mind and concentrate on work and dinner. Dinner. She might as well get it ready now so she could continue to work.

Stew. Stew would be good. The evening was going to be cool, and a good, hot meal always worked wonders. It could simmer for hours, needing no care, no basting, no checking. She refused to admit to herself that she was purposely making stew so there would be something left over to take to her new neighbor. What kind of middle-aged fool would do a thing like that? "My kind," Rita snapped to the empty kitchen. She switched the satellite radio on and heard Willie Nelson singing the lyrics to some country western tune.

Her step was light as she moved about the kitchen to the beat of the music. The dredged beef cubes sizzled in the hot fat along with the sliced onions and celery, making a tantalizing aroma. She loved the smell of frying onions. Quickly, she rinsed off the vegetables and chopped them. She added water and waited for it to boil before she adjusted the heat and covered the pot. She glanced at her watch and then set the timer so she would remember to add the vegetables. A loaf of crusty, French bread was set on the counter to thaw, along with a stick of butter. There was nothing worse than trying to spread hard butter on hot bread. She wished she still had the microwave oven, but that was one of the first things Brett had carried out to the car the day the movers came. She could always get another one. There had been a time when she lived to eat; now she ate to live, she deceived herself. Food was almost secondary at this stage in her life. Binges didn't count. Everyone went on food binges at one time or another. Unconsciously, Rita tugged at the navy sweatshirt to make sure it rode down over her stomach and buttocks.

From time to time Rita sniffed the aromatic air and then glanced at her watch. She really didn't expect him to stop by. He hadn't said anything about seeing her today, had he? She couldn't remember. Her raw, new emotions kept getting in the way of her remembering.

Chapter Four

It was ten minutes after seven when Rita's stomach growled ominously. She turned off the computer and tidied her desk. Useless draft pages were shoved into one of the new desk drawers. She missed using the old door on the sawhorses. There had been miles of room for all her scattered research notes. This way she would have to hunt and fish for everything she needed.

She sat down to her solitary dinner at seven forty. The French bread was browned perfectly. The stew was hearty and yet tangy. It was the tablespoon of horseradish that gave it a special touch. She ate ravenously, topping off the meal with two cups of black coffee. Lighting a cigarette, she decided to walk off the heavy dinner with a stroll down to the pier. She was almost afraid to open the front door, hating the thought of seeing lights in the Johnson cottage. Lights meant Twigg was there and hadn't wanted to see her. If she took the stew over as was her original intention, he might think she was ready to initiate something. Better to leave it behind and just take her walk down to the pier as planned. The Johnson cottage was dark. The only light came from a street lamp on the other side of the lake and was so faint and yellowish it was barely distinguishable. Maybe something happened to him. Perhaps she should walk around and knock on the door. That's what she should do, what she would have done a week ago. It was the mothering instinct in her. Rita caught herself up short. Twigg might be younger, but there was nothing motherly about the way she felt last night or right now for that matter. Tomorrow would be time enough to see if he was all right. A grown man of thirty-two could pick up the phone and ask for help if he needed it. She was listed in the phone book. Perhaps he went into town and hadn't gotten back. Anything was a possibility and she, for one, certainly shouldn't be worrying.

Rita walked out to the end of the pier and stood staring across the lake. She shivered in her light jacket. She suddenly felt the loneliness for the first time and wished Twigg were here if only to talk about the dolphins and killer whales. She liked the resonant timbre of his voice, the lazy, confident way he moved. She liked to watch his slender hands that he waved about to express a point. How well she remembered the feel of those hands on the back of her neck and the way they stroked her cheeks. He was a gentle man, of that she was sure. He was Twigg Peterson, marine biologist. Why couldn't she say she was Rita Bellamy, writer? She sat down on the edge of the pier. I'm an ex-wife, a mother, a best-selling writer, she mused to herself. She stared across the water and it hit her like a bolt of lightning. Those are things I do, not who I am. I'm Rita Bellamy. Me, Rita, the person.

Something strange was happening to her, had been happening to her since she arrived. She was looking at things differently, feeling things.

She felt comfortable sitting here on the pier thinking about her life and where it was going. For the first time in nearly two years she felt comfortable with herself. She felt comfortable with her wants, and right now she wanted to talk to Twigg Peterson. She debated going back to the cottage for the stew and realized it was nothing more than a prop. She didn't need a prop. She didn't want a prop. She slithered sideways and got to her knees and then to her feet. There were still no lights on in the Johnson cottage.

Rita lengthened her stride and almost ran to the cottage. She rapped loudly and waited for some response. When none came, she knocked a second time, this time so loud her knuckles smarted. There was still no answer. Without hesitating, Rita opened the door and peered into the dimness. There was no sign of anyone. God, what if he was in the bedroom with a woman? She swallowed hard. There was only one way to find out. She reached for the wall switch and the living room came to life. Carefully, she tip-toed to the bedroom and inched the door open. Twigg lay sprawled across the bed fully dressed in the clothes he had been wearing the night before. Was it possible he had slept through the day? She had to know if he was all right before she left. She inched her way over the polished plank floor and dropped soundlessly to her knees. Satisfied that his breathing was deep and regular. She was getting to her feet when a long arm snaked out and reached for her. Caught off guard she floundered and then fell on top of a laughing Twigg. "I may be a heavy sleeper, but not that heavy. I was aware of you the minute you walked in the door."

"I wanted to be sure you were all right. I didn't see any lights and I thought . . ."

"That your sausage and peppers made me sick." Twigg grinned, his grip on her arm secure.

"No. I just wanted to see you and talk to you," Rita said honestly.

"Talk," Twigg said, rolling over on one elbow. His grip never lessened as he brought his face within inches of her own. Rita could smell his warm, sleepy breath as he stared into her eyes. She felt an exultant thump of warm delight as she saw the glowing, ardent look in his gaze.

Rita tried to inch back a bit. "Now that I know you're all right I have to get back to work. Why don't you come over for lunch tomorrow if you're not too busy?" Rita asked impulsively as she struggled to withdraw her arm. Damn, she had forgotten how long his arms were.

"You're a damn beautiful woman, Rita Bellamy," Twigg said quietly.

Positioned half on the bed and half off, Rita felt awkward and flustered. She had always found compliments of any kind hard to handle. Certainly, no one had ever called her beautiful, not even Brett. She became more aware of her surroundings, the double, maple, four-poster and the man staring at her. But more than that she was aware of her thumping heart and her fast-beating pulse. She had to say something to this man who wanted more than she was prepared to give. She tried to pull away. His grip was firm.

"I want you in this bed next to me. You know that, don't you?" Twigg said quietly. "I think I want you more than I've ever wanted a woman before." Twigg was shocked at how true the words were. He did want her. He did desire her. Goddamn it, he *liked* her and that was something he couldn't say about too many women in his circle of friends.

Rita met his unflinching gaze. "You barely know me. Twigg, you're thirty-two years old. I'm forty-three years old, ten years older than you. Why, you're not that much older than my children." Had she responded correctly? She had come here to talk, maybe have him kiss her again. She had no intention of playing games or teasing. Did women still tease men, she wondered.

"Age is a number. I have a number and you have a number. So what. We're people with feelings and desires. Lady, I have very strange feelings where you're concerned and I sure as hell do desire you."

"A number. Yes, you're right. Age is a number but my children . . ." she broke off lamely.

"Your children have nothing to do with this, with you or me. This is something that is strictly between you and me. Don't clutter up the issue with children."

"I don't know if I can do that. I want to be friends with you. I do feel something for you, but I . . . this is new to me, and I just don't think I'm ready to . . . to . . ."

Twigg studied her. There was no pretense about this woman. Tricks, schemes, maneuvers, and all the deviousness that made for beguilement were not part of her. He released his hold on her arm and she jerked it to her side. "Look, Rita, I'm no skirt chaser, and I'm a far cry from being a womanizer. I met you, I like you, and this is more or less a natural progression of events. Dammit, I really am tuned into you for some reason. It hit me the minute I saw you on the pier. I'm being honest with you."

"And I'm trying to be honest with you," Rita said softly.

"Come here, I want to tell you something. Look at me," he commanded gently. "I take my relationships seriously. I want you to understand that I am not what the kids call a jock. I agree I haven't known you all that long, but I want to get to know you better. My body is telling me it wants to go to bed with you. I think your body is telling you the same thing. That's physical. We can deal with that when it's time. I promise I will not take advantage of you or try to trick you unless it's to get you to feed me. I'm a lousy cook. I can't be any more up-front than that."

There was a slight misting in Rita's blue eyes. "I think I can accept that," she said lightly. "Come on, I made some stew. I was going to bring it over with me, but I thought you might think I was using that as an excuse to see you. I realized I didn't need an excuse. I wanted to see you so I came. But, it's time to go back."

They walked arm in arm back to her cottage, laughing and kicking at stray pebbles. "How's the book coming?" Twigg questioned.

"Fine. My agent is coming up tomorrow evening to take back what I've finished. He'll be spending the night. In the spare bedroom," she said hastily. "I got some furniture today."

Twigg spun Rita around till she was within inches of him. "You don't owe me any explanations. I don't want you to sound defensive when you talk with me. Agreed?"

"Agreed," Rita said. They went inside and she turned the burner on under the stew.

Later, Rita sat across from Twigg, drinking a cup of coffee while he finished the last of the stew. "I think you're a hell of a lady, Rita Bellamy, and a good cook in the bargain. Let's take a walk around the lake so I can work off all that French bread."

The quarter-moon bathed the sandy beach in a silvery glow as Rita and Twigg strolled along, her arm linked in the crook of his arm. She felt happy, alive, but a bit apprehensive. Conversation was casual, beginning with the contrary weather of the Poconos and going on to Twigg's sleeping an entire day, to Rita's children. She started off with Camilla and eased into Charles, leaving Rachel for last. Rachel always needed so much explaining.

"Whatever Rachel is or isn't, you are not to blame. She's her own person, Rita. For some reason you seem to blame yourself and I can see the guilt all over your face. All of them are adults now, even your son," Twigg said lightly. "You have to cut the strings, Rita, and when you cut them, let them stay cut. They have lives and you have a life of your own. You must be very proud of yourself," he said, easing out of the painful subject of her children.

"I am. I think I'm what you call a late bloomer. I'm doing something I love doing and getting paid while I do it. As they say in encounter groups, I think I'm 'realizing my potential.' "

They were on the way back and nearing the path that wound beneath giant hanging hemlock trees that, if followed, would bring them up and around to the back of Rita's cottage. It was eerie in the darkness, but down the center of the path was a white flood of moonlight. Prickles of electricity raced down Rita's arms as she tightened her hold on Twigg.

His embrace was neither expected nor unexpected. It was natural. Rita felt herself melting into his embrace as though she had been doing it for hundreds of years. He felt good. He felt right. His arms tightened, bringing her closer to him. No words were spoken, none were necessary. Gently, she felt his lips in her hair, on her cheek and throat. Tenderly, his fingers lifted her chin, raising her lips to his own. He was pressing her closer to his chest, crushing her breasts against him. His body was hard, muscular. Rita's arms encircled his back. Without reason or logic she felt safe and secure in his embrace, and she faced her tumultuous emotions with directness and truth. She couldn't help it, she wanted this man.

Their eyes met in the moonlight and without a trace of embarrassment she was aware she could drown in that incredibly dark gaze and emerge again as the woman she wanted and needed to become.

Seeing her moist lips part and offer themselves to him, he lowered his mouth to hers, touching her lips, tasting their sweetness, drawing from them a kiss, gentle, yet passionate. As the kiss deepened, searing flames licked her body, the pulsating beat of her heart thundered in her ears.

When he released her, his eyes searched hers for an instant, then time became eternal for Rita. From somewhere deep within her a desire to stay forever in his arms, to feel the touch of his mouth upon hers, began to crescendo, threatening to erupt like fireworks. Thick, dark lashes closed over her blue eyes and she heard her own breath come in ragged little gasps as she boldly brought her mouth once more to his, offering herself, kissing him deeply, searchingly, searing this moment upon her memory.

She kissed him as she had never kissed another man, a kiss that made her knees weak and her head dizzy. She knew, in that endless moment, that somehow this man belonged to her in a way no other man could ever belong to her, for however brief this time together would be. She had found him, a man who could make her feel like the woman she always knew she was.

Twigg's fingers were gentle as they danced through her hair. He sensed what she was feeling. There are needs of the soul that go beyond the hungers of the body. His voice was deep, husky, little more than a whisper. "Will you come with me so that we can make this a night for all eternity?"

He waited for her answer, wanted to hear her say it, commit herself to it. Wordless agreement would not do for him, he realized, not with this woman whose skin was so soft and fragrant beneath his lips and whose eyes were lowered with shyness. "Tell me, Rita. It can be wonderful between us. I know it can and I want to show you."

He felt her indecision, was aware that a part of her had withdrawn from him. Intuitively, he knew that she had not been with another man since her divorce and that she felt his touch was strange and alien. He was tapping at the walls of her insecurity and he did not want to rush her, did not want to frighten her away, yet his own burning need for her prompted him to persuade, to insist. "Tell me, Rita," he murmured against the hollow of her throat, sending little tremors vibrating through her.

"Yes, yes," she whispered huskily. Was that voice her own? A voice deep and singing with desire, a woman's voice. "Twigg," she murmured against his lips, feeling them soft and moist on her own, "I want you to make love to me."

Twigg was excited by her admission, each sensation heightened because she wanted him to love her. He captured her mouth with his own, entering with his tongue, feeling the velvet of hers. Together they knelt and fell into a soft bed of pine needles where she offered herself to him, allowing his hands to move over her body, exciting her, matching his hunger with her own.

Mindlessly, she surrendered to his touch, barely aware that he was methodically stripping away her clothing. The chill night air did not touch her, not in his arms, with his body sheltering hers, giving her the warmth she so desperately needed. She grew languorous under his touch as his hands possessed her breasts, the soft tenderness of her belly, and the smoothness of her inner thighs. His mouth gently opened hers, his silken-tipped tongue exploring, tasting, caressing with a fervor that sent her senses spinning.

When his hand moved between her thighs, rising upward, she moved against his touch and she heard the response to her passion in the catch of his breath and the deep, deep sound that came from his throat. "You're so beautiful, Rita. So beautiful. I love the way you want me to touch you." His voice was softer than a will-o'-the-wisp, and she wondered if she only imagined it.

He tore away his clothes, eager to be naked against her, wanting the warmth of her touch on his body. Rolling over onto his back, he took her with him, trailing his fingers down the length of her spine and returning over and over again to the roundness of her bottom. He invited her touch, inspired her caresses, always watching her in the dim moonlight, reveling in the heavy-lidded smoldering in her eyes. He wanted her to take pleasure in him, wanted her to find him worthy of her finely tuned passions. Did he please her, he wondered as she smoothed the flat of her palms over his chest, her fingertips gripping and pulling at the thicket of hairs. Her mouth found his nipples, licking, tasting, lowering her explorations to the tautness of his belly and the hardness of his thighs. He reveled in her touch, in the expression of her eyes as he took her face in his hands and held it for his kiss.

Putting her beneath him once again, he kissed the sweetness of her mouth, her eyes, the soft curve of her jaw. Her breasts awakened beneath his kisses; she arched beneath his touch.

She sought him with her lips, possessed him with her hands, her own passions growing as she realized the pleasure she was giving him. The hardness of his sex was somehow tender and vulnerable beneath her hand as she felt it quiver with excitement and desire . . . for her. His hands never left her body, seeking, exploring, touching . . . she wanted to lay back and render herself to him, yet at the same time she wanted to possess him, touch him, commit him to memory and know him as she had never known another man. Instead of being alien to her, his body was as familiar to her as her own. She felt her body sing with pleasure and she knew her display of passion was food for his.

Rita was ravaged by this hunger he created in her. She wanted him to take her and bring her release. "Take me," she breathed, feeling as though she would die if he did not, yet hating to put an end to excruciating pleasure.

He put himself between her opened thighs, his eyes devouring her as she lay waiting for him. Her soft, chestnut hair reflected the silver of the moon, her skin was bathed in a sleek sheen that emphasized her womanly curves and enhanced the contact between their flesh. Sitting back on his heels, his gaze locked with hers as his hands moved over her body. Rita met his eyes, unashamedly, letting him see the hungers that dwelled there and the flutter of her lashes that mirrored the tremblings in her loins. His hands slipped to her sex and she cried out softly, arching her back to press herself closer against his gently circling fingers. "You're so beautiful here," he told her, watching her eyes close and her lips part with a little gasp.

He gentled her passions, fed her desires, brought her to the point of no return and smiled tenderly when she sobbed with the sweetness of her passions. She climaxed beneath his touch, uttering her surprise, whispering his name. His hands eased the tautness of her thighs, kneading the firmness of her haunches and smoothing over her belly.

When she thought the sensation too exquisite to be surpassed, he leaned forward, driving himself into her, filling her sheath with his pulsing masculinity. Her body strained beneath his, willing itself to partake of his pleasure, to be his pleasure. The fine hairs of his chest rubbed against her breasts. His mouth took hers, deeply, lovingly. His movements were smooth and expert as he stroked within her, demanding she match his rhythm, driving her once again to the sweetness she knew could be hers.

Her fingers raked his back, feeling the play of his muscles beneath his skin. She found the firmness of his buttocks, holding fast, driving him forward, feeling him buried deep within her. He doubled her delight and she climaxed again, and only then did he raise up, grasping her bottom in his hands and lifting it, thrusting himself into her with shorter, quicker strokes.

Her body was exquisite, her responses delicious, but it was the expression on her lovely face and the delight and pleasure he saw there that pushed him over the edge and destroyed his restraint. The total joy, the hint of disbelief in her clear blue eyes, the purity of a single tear on her smooth cheek, were his undoing. He found his relief in her, her name exploding on his lips.

They lay together, legs entwined, her head upon his shoulder as he stroked the softness of her arm and the fullness of her breasts. His lips were in her hair, soft, teasing, against her brow. "You're a beautiful lover," he breathed, tightening his embrace, delighting in the intimacy between them.

Rita was silent, enjoying this aftermath to

their lovemaking. He had pulled her light jacket over her shoulder to ward off the chill, and his long, lean leg was thrown over hers. She was as snug as a bug, she smiled to herself, breathing in the scent of him and nuzzling her nose against the furring on his chest. His hand played with her hair as he told her how incredibly soft it was, almost as soft as her skin.

"It hasn't been this way for me in a very long time," she told him sincerely. For a moment he was so quiet she thought he had fallen asleep. Wasn't that what men did immediately after making love? Leaving the woman filled with emotions and thoughts and no one to share them with?

"I know it hasn't, Rita." She liked the way he used her name rather than the impersonals of "honey" or "sweetheart." "I knew we could share something wonderful."

Rita tilted her head, looking up into his face. "Was it wonderful for you, Twigg? Oh, that's silly. I sound as though I'm fishing for compliments and that's not what I mean at all."

He looked down at her, smiling. "Yes, it was wonderful for me. How could you think otherwise? Oh, I see," he said, suddenly comprehending. "I'm the one with all the experience, the free lifestyle, a part of the new morality. And I got all this experience while you were busy being faithful to your husband, and hence, I must have had sexual experiences more wonderful than tonight."

Silently, Rita nodded, burying her face against his chest; she could not meet his eyes. That was exactly what she had meant. It was still a marvel to her that he had wanted to make love to her at all. She had never considered herself a beauty nor particularly desirable. Oh, perhaps when she was young, but certainly not since her marriage to Brett had fallen apart. The beauty and sensuality she should have felt about herself was instead imparted to the heroines in her books.

Turning over until he was looking down into her face, Twigg gently touched her cheek with the tips of his fingers. "You are beautiful, Rita, and tonight was wonderful. So very wonderful," his mouth claimed hers, softly, tenderly. "I could make love to you again and again and again," he told her, chuckling. "Only I don't know if I'll ever get these pine needles out of my behind. What say we run up to your place and try out that new bed of yours? I want to hold you in my arms all night long, Rita Bellamy. I don't want to leave you until you're sleeping, otherwise I might never have the strength to leave you at all."

Laughing, they ran up to the cottage, dropping shoes, leaving behind jackets and picking pine straw out of their hair. And Twigg was as good as his word. He made love to her again, tenderly, lovingly, making her feel beautiful, truly beautiful. And only when she slept did he leave her to her dreams of him, a soft, slow smile lifting the corners of her lips.

Chapter Five

Rita awakened, stretching languorously beneath the butterfly sheets. Her first conscious thought was that something so good had to be right. As he had promised, Twigg hadn't left until she was asleep, nestled in the comfort of her own dreams. She lay quietly, allowing her thoughts to soar back to the night before. A warm flush worked its way up to her face. Making love in the woods in the middle of the night with a man she had known less than three days. In pine needles, no less! That was something Rachel would do!

She touched her flushed cheeks, felt how warm they were. Then she explored her nakedness beneath the sheets. Were her breasts fuller somehow? They were certainly more sensitive. She felt warm and wet between her legs. That was different too. She had just been starting to think of herself as "dried up," a term she had often heard her mother use after menopause. Menopause! Christ, she wasn't menopausal yet! And she wasn't on the pill! "Oh, no," she moaned, turning her face into the pillow. What was it her mother had said? Only the good girls get caught. The bad ones are too smart. Another moan of horror. Rita had always thought of herself as a good girl. No. She wasn't going to think about it, but she wasn't going to be a fool either. She liked making love with Twigg, and if he'd have her again, she'd gladly share her bed with him. She would do what the big girls did, what Rachel had been doing since she was seventeen years old. Birth control. Sensible. Easy. Certainly practical.

Squeezing her eyes shut against the morning light, she threw her arms up over her head. Practical! If she had been practical, she never would have become Twigg's lover.

Lover! Was that what she was now? She blushed. Imagine me, Rita Bellamy, a lover!

Her body felt a renewed bite of desire as she remembered the night before in Twigg's arms. He had loved her, totally, completely. Seeming to enjoy it. No, not seeming. He had enjoyed it! She knew from the way he touched her, kissed her, loved her. Why should she doubt him now? Just because he had admitted to her that he was finding staying in the Johnson cottage intolerably lonely? There were plenty of girls in town, and with his charm and good looks it wouldn't be difficult to persuade someone to share his

bed. Girls. Is that how she had thought of herself, just for an instant? The Women's Libera-
tion Movement would be aghast to know that
she, Rita Bellamy, nearly forty-four years old,
had thought of herself as a girl. As they would
have it, from the age of five on, the members of
the female sex were supposed to think of themselves as women.

That was just plain stupid. Of course she was
a woman, but was it so wrong to admit, even for
a moment, that within her nearly forty-four-year-
old breast beat the heart of a sixteen-year-old
girl? That she could feel a hunger for a man just
by remembering the feel of his hands on her
flesh and the sound of his voice in her ear as he
told her how beautiful she was, how desirable
he found her? No, it wasn't stupid, it was delicious, and she was going to enjoy it for all it was
worth.

For the entire time she was in Twigg's arms
she forgot about the age difference and the midriff bulge and the not-so-firm breasts. But now,
suddenly, in the full light of day, those same
fears came back to punish her. What was Twigg
thinking, feeling? She wished she knew. She
groaned and rolled over in the bed. How empty
it was. A smile tugged at her mouth. She would
take a bed of pine needles any day of the week.
If he had said she was lovely, desirable, then she
was. Period. And she wouldn't spoil it all by
thinking she had made a fool of herself. All she
wanted to think about was how his eyes had
greedily devoured her and how his hands and
body had reminded her she was a woman.

She moved beneath the sheets, feeling the ache and soreness in her thighs. It was a good ache, a good soreness, proof that she had not dreamed last night but had actually lived it.

Touching herself, she smoothed the flat of her hand over her belly and downward. He had said she was beautiful there. His words came back to her, his voice, the sound of his whisper, shooting new thrills and excitement through her.

He had stayed awake, caressing her, loving her, until she had been the first to fall asleep. And she had slept in the crook of his arm, feeling completely at ease as though it were the most natural thing in the world.

The ticking of the clock invaded her reverie. Glancing at the clock, she realized it was nearly nine o'clock! There was a spring in her step when she bounded out of bed and headed for the shower. That certainly was a positive. She hadn't bounded out of bed since Charles was seven years old and had croup in the middle of the night.

No breakfast this morning. Quickly, she towel dried herself and dressed in dark slacks and a shirt of watermelon cotton. She had invited Twigg for lunch. She was behind in her work and Ian was due this evening. God, she was going to have to hustle if she was to get anything done. Tuna for lunch. If it was good enough for her, it would be good enough for Twigg. She fished around in the freezer for a package of chicken and set it to thaw on the sink. Ian liked broiled chicken in lemon and butter.

Cigarette in one hand, coffee in the other, Rita stared at the computer screen. Don't fail me now, she pleaded. Don't make me regret last night. With all her willpower she forced her mind back in time to the seventeenth century and the Dutch East India Company and the trouble she had created for her characters. Today she was going to have them set sail for Sumatra and be hijacked by marauding pirates. She had to concentrate and make sure there were no loose ends anywhere. Imagination, go to work, she ordered as she turned the computer on.

Nearly two hours later she broke for a cigarette and another cup of coffee. Work was going well. She could spare the ten minutes to shift into neutral and rub her aching shoulders. She could feel the tenseness and the expectation as the hands on her watch crawled closer to the time Twigg would arrive for lunch. One o'clock she had said. It was barely eleven now. She had plenty of time before she had to make up the tuna salad.

Lunch was enjoyable. They sat in Rita's copper and brick kitchen with the new hanging fern in complete contentment. There was none of the awkwardness that Rita had feared, no gaps in the conversation. Instead, there had been smiling eye contact, shared laughter, and hearty appetites. It was Rita who glanced at her watch and signaled that lunch was over. Twigg obliged by getting up, kissing her soundly on the mouth. "I have to know something, Rita," he said seriously. "Was there any time last night when you thought about those twelve years? The truth now."

Rita grinned. "Not one minute. If you find yourself at loose ends tonight and want to take a break, why don't you come by and meet Ian? I'm sure he'll enjoy meeting you and you'll have lots in common. Maybe he can even find a market for your articles. Don't feel you have to come; it's an invitation, pure and simple."

Twigg loped back to his cottage, his steps springy and buoyant. Damn, he felt good. Rita made him feel good. At lunch she had been so helpful when he discussed his work with her, suggesting he might approach the article from a different point of view.

Perhaps he would walk over to meet Ian Martin, if only to see what he was like. In his gut he knew the friend-agent had more than a professional interest in Rita. It was obvious the way she talked about him. Yes, he would like to meet the man. Ian Martin would have to be a blind fool not to see Rita for the woman she was: talented, interesting, beautiful.

Leaning against the porch rail, his tall, lean frame striking an angular pose, Twigg tamped and lit his pipe. She had the clearest blue eyes he had ever seen. And she loved the sea, she had told him. And talking to her, discussing things with her, was enlightening, challenging. That was one lady who had an opinion, but unlike others he had known, she was also willing to see the other side.

Drawing on the pipe, the pungent smoke filling his mouth, his thoughts went back to the night before, as they had through most of the day. Rita Bellamy, woman, writer, beautiful lover. She had a way of making a man feel cherished. He laughed. It even sounded silly to him that a man would need cherishing; that was something women said they wanted from a man. But a man needed it too, needed to feel important and worthy. He could still almost feel the tenderness of her soft arms as they surrounded him, bringing him to her, welcoming him. There was an honesty about her, sharp and clear, with none of the calculating withholding he had experienced so many times before. She was exciting and stimulating and downright sexy. And yet, she was vulnerable too, and he supposed that was what made her seem so young to him, with a special brand of innocence that was lost to most women before they hit twenty.

Twigg frowned. He was thirty-two years old, and to all intents and purposes, completely alone in the world. He had friends, certainly, but no family of which to speak. It had occurred to him that a wife and children would ease this particular sense of aloneness, and yet he knew it was not the answer. Not for him, at any rate. He had never met a woman he wanted to marry, and he never considered his bloodline so superior that he wanted to propagate it. His work, his friends, and now Rita. That was all he needed. Good, better, best.

* * *

Ian Martin arrived shortly before seven o'clock. Rita heard his car in the drive and quickly switched off her computer. He would have no complaints with the work she was to deliver to her editor. She had caught up, for the most part, and if she started early in the morning, she would definitely meet her deadline.

Ian Martin was a tall and distinguished-looking man in his early fifties. A widower with married children. He carried a bottle of wine, a briefcase, and a bedraggled bouquet of daisies.

"They were fresh when I left the city." He laughed as he kissed Rita lightly on the mouth. He stood back to survey his client and felt a frown pucker his face. She was lovely, vibrant, with a new and curious glow about her. She wore her beige silk blouse open at the neck, all the way down to the shadowy cleavage between her breasts. The taupe skirt was cut slimly with a daring slash halfway up her thigh. Heeled shoes, sheer hose, and jewelry! He smiled at her a trifle nervously, wondering what she had done to herself. Where were her blue denim jeans and sweatshirt and run-down sneakers? The uniform she had adopted these last two years. He hadn't seen her looking this smart since before her divorce.

"It's good to see you, Ian. How are things back in the big city?" she asked warmly as she embraced him.

"Not much different from the last time I saw you. Life does go on in publishing. My firm has taken on several new clients, and we have great hopes for a movie deal for one of them. I also brought your last royalty statement with me. It's a good one and I banked the money for you."

Following her through the living room into the kitchen where he struggled with the cork in the bottle of wine, he was surprised when Rita turned to him, touched him on the arm and said softly, "Ian, you've been an excellent friend and business manager, but it's time for me to begin handling my own affairs."

He looked shocked, his hazel eyes narrowing as though trying to see through to her reason. Gently, she calmed him. "Ian, dear, please don't misunderstand. It is simply that I believe it's time for me to involve myself in my own finances and certainly time I involved myself in life again. I want to try my own wings." She laughed, quickly softening the statement. "Of course, I would always hope you were waiting to catch me should I begin to fall. I've become too dependent on you, and in many ways I've taken advantage of you. I don't want the time to come when you begin to resent me as a burden."

"Rita, darling," he murmured, pulling her into his embrace. "As if I could ever resent you. Surely, you know how much you mean to me. I love doing for you."

She was aware of the scent of his expensive cologne, the smoothness of his cheek as he pressed it against her brow. He must have used his battery-powered electric shaver on the drive up. Dear, fastidious Ian. So concerned with outward appearances. "Have I told you how lovely you look this evening," he said in a deep, intimate tone. "It's time you came out of that shell you built around yourself and remembered the woman you are."

Deftly, Rita extracted herself from his embrace, making a great fuss of selecting glasses for the wine. "You're right, Ian, it is time I crept out of my shell. That's one of the reasons I feel I must take over my own affairs." She meant her words to be strong, but she heard the softness in her tone, the vaguest hint of a whine and cajoling. She hated herself for it. Damn, wasn't she entitled to make her own decisions concerning the money she earned? She would like to try her hand at a little high finance, as Brett called it. Why did she always need someone to do it for her?

"Remember that tax-free fund I told you about several months back?" Ian poured the wine as he spoke; she watched the bold onyx ring on his pinky finger reflect the light. Hadn't he heard what she had said? Was he going to ignore her?

"I remember," she lied. Several months back she was hardly interested in tax-free funds or anything else, for that matter

"The time seemed right to buy and I did. Several more opportunities like that and you'll make a handsome living just from the interest you earn."

Rita was puzzled. "How . . . I mean, wasn't I supposed to sign something?"

Ian laughed, amused, as though she were a little, precocious child. "You don't have to bother your head about things like that. Remember, that's why you signed a power of attorney over to me. That tax-free fund was quite a coup, I can tell you that. . . . What's the problem, Rita? Am I mistaken or did you not tell me you had no interest in financial matters?"

"No, you're right, Ian. I did tell you that." Soberly, she sipped the wine, finding it tasted acid on her tongue. She had told him she wanted nothing to do with the financial end. Suddenly, she realized why. It wasn't that she didn't consider herself capable; after all, throughout her marriage she had been the one to manage the checking account, pay the bills, sock away a little fund for vacations. No, it wasn't that she felt inadequate. After all, Ian's prestigious firm had not always been her agent. She hadn't signed with the Ian Martin Agency until she was a fully established author. In the beginning she had been the only one to decide upon contracts, payments, royalty rates, always keeping her eye on the market and delivering books that were salable and in keeping with the readers' wants and likes. She had decided whether or not she could devote periods of time, her life, actually, to fulfill a contract. And if it happened to be the wrong choice for her, she had lived with it anyway and learned from it.

Rather, her sudden dislike for finances coincided with the trouble in her marriage. In a roundabout way she blamed her income for the distance between Brett and herself. It was almost as though she were ashamed of it. Brett had certainly made her feel that along with her increased income she had also taken to wearing the pants in the family. His words, not hers. At the end it had been such a bone of contention that she had simply turned away from such things and cheerfully deposited the responsibility with Ian.

Ian's hazel eyes blinked and his face ruddied against the stark white of his shirt collar. What had happened to the woman he had sent up here to finish her novel? He had left a trembling, insecure woman and now he found a different woman entirely. Oh, she had the same face, same name, but she wasn't the Rita Bellamy he knew, and it rankled and displeased him. Not that he ever wanted to feed on her insecurities and indecisions, but he had to admit it was certainly nice being needed and admired by an intelligent woman. Women weren't the same any longer, not since that ridiculous Women's Lib, at any rate. They all pretended to be fiercely independent, self-sufficient. What happened to those simple, endearing women who depended upon a man? Even the talented ones, like Rita, who knew their own limitations and admitted them?

Rita Bellamy was one of those old-fashioned women a man could depend on to boost his ego and see to his comforts. Maternal, loving, quietly deceptive because he knew that within her beat the heart of a very passionate woman. She stirred his blood, flattered his ego, and was so damned pretty. He liked her tremendously and would marry her if she would have him, but Rita always shied away, content to keep things on a professional level. Although there were times when he had thought she was softening to him.

Like now, inviting him up to the cottage. He had even packed his silk dressing gown.

Ian had always been Rita's confidant and protector, taking care of her when the breakup in her marriage occurred. Hadn't he been the one to find her the lawyer and consult with him so that ingrate husband of hers wouldn't rake her over the coals? Now she wanted to handle her own affairs. She had no right to go and change on him, Ian's temper flared, no right at all! Taking a swallow of wine, he soothed himself. Perhaps it was only this change of life he was always reading about. Rita couldn't possibly actually mean she intended to take up the reins and make her own decisions.

"We're having broiled chicken and salad for dinner, just the way you like it," Rita called from the kitchen. "The daisies are lovely, thank you, Ian. I'll keep them near my desk to cheer me up."

"You don't appear to need cheering, darling," he told her tartly. He had thought he would spend a long evening quietly comforting her and telling her she should come back to the city as soon as her book was finished. He wished someone would comfort him; he had this strange feeling as though the rug was being pulled from under him . . . an inch at a time.

"So tell me how it's going?" He had to know what was making her look like this. He had never noticed the lilt in her voice before or the sparkle in her eyes. She had always seemed like a wounded puppy. Oh, she smiled and even laughed, but she had been so defenseless that he wanted to crush her to him and tell her it would be all right, that *he* would make it all right. That he would share his life with her. After all, their children were grown and neither of them had to account to anyone. He wondered vaguely if the ten-year difference in their ages made a difference. When he was seventy-four she would be only sixty-four.

As they sipped at the wine and made small talk, he was more than ever aware of the change in her. She was still gentle, she would always be gentle, and the sensitivity still showed, but she was different.

"When do you think you'll be coming in to the city?" Ian asked over the rim of his wine-glass.

"I'm not sure," Rita said vaguely. Maybe never, she thought. Maybe when Twigg left. Maybe before. Maybe she would stay through the winter. She didn't have to make a decision now. She could drift with the days and make up her mind when she was ready. With Charles in college there was no need to rush back, and she deserved a respite between books.

"I thought your intention was to stay only till you finished the book." He tried to keep the snap and churlishness out of his voice but realized he was unsuccessful. Rita didn't notice.

"I know, but I like it here. I'm surprised, Ian, that you didn't notice my new furniture. As you can see, I'm quite comfortable here. I think I write better up here. It's certainly going well.

There's nothing pressing for me back in town, and we both agreed that I wasn't going on tour for this book, so really, my time is my own. It won't cause a problem, will it?" Her voice asked a question, but it clearly stated that she didn't care if it did make a problem. "What about the children. The grandchildren?" Ian asked sourly.

Again, Rita failed to notice his tone. "What about them? Ian, they aren't babies. Camilla is a responsible adult and has a husband to look after her. She's a wonderful mother and she has her own friends. Even when I'm home I talk to her on the phone, but I don't see her that often. As for the grandchildren, of course, I'll miss them but they aren't my responsibility. Their mother can tend them or get a sitter. I'm sure that you must have noticed that for some reason we've grown apart lately."

"Yes, of course. It saddens me. You've always said that Camilla is closest to you, the one most like you in so many ways."

"Perhaps that's the problem. She was too much like me when we were all a family and growing. Things have changed. I've changed and Camilla has changed. She has a stepmother who is a year younger than she is. She doesn't like my career. Over the past months I've sensed that there isn't a lot Camilla does like about me. I'm sure that in her heart she blames me for the divorce. The word divorcee is not something Camilla has come to terms with. I'm sorry, but there isn't anything I can do about it. Brett forced me into this position and I intend to grow from it, not backpedal and languish in an empty house. I'm just a late bloomer getting on my feet."

"Rita, you're surprising me. I've never seen this side of you. Whatever you want is fine with me. I'm just concerned that you don't make . . . make . . ."

"A fool of myself? Say it, Ian. Don't talk around it and up and down it. If I do make a fool of myself over something, anything, then I'll have to take the responsibility for it. It will be my decision, my choice. I may do things wrong, make a mess of certain things, but I'll learn from my mistakes. I can live with that. Everyone else will have to live with that too."

"And Rachel and Charles?"

"Rachel is Rachel. She accepts me as I am. She has never made demands on me, and I sincerely believe she's the only one who doesn't secretly blame me for the divorce. She's been after me for over a year to 'get with it,' as she puts it. I think she'll encourage me in my independence. Charles, I'm not sure about. He still needs me, but in a limited way. He wants to know that Mom is there when he wants her. He may never physically need me, but it's important for him to know that he can at least count on me. He's going to start growing on his own now that he's in college. If we're very lucky, we can grow together. If not, one of us is going to have to take some lumps."

Ian finished the last of his wine and poured some more from the bottle. "Rita, I hardly know you anymore," he said softly.

Rita smiled. Now where had she heard those

words before? "I think our dinner is ready. You're a good friend, Ian. I hope you won't endanger our wonderful relationship by censoring me for *anything*. Let me try my wings. But don't catch me if they get clipped. Deal?"

What could he say? "Deal," he said morosely.

Rita chattered happily all through dinner. She might see Twigg soon. She hoped she could carry off the visit so that Ian wouldn't suspect anything. Ian was astute and tuned in. The warm feeling stayed with her when she realized she didn't really care if Ian knew. It was just that everything was so new that she wanted to keep it to herself for a while. Later, much later, she would decide if the children needed to know, and if so, how she would handle it. Probably not well, she thought with a sinking feeling in the pit of her stomach.

Rita came out of her cocoon long enough to sense there was something bothering Ian. "Is something bothering you, Ian? Something you want to talk about? I didn't mean to offend you before. I think it's time that I started doing and thinking for myself. I could have written you a letter, but I thought it would be better if we discussed it between ourselves." She didn't want him to know that she had come to this decision suddenly. As suddenly as she had decided to take Twigg for her lover. Her lover. Just the thought brought pink to her cheeks.

Ian brushed at his salt-and-pepper hair. He knew he was an attractive man, well groomed and polished. He had never considered women a problem for him, not even during his marriage to Dorothy. When he was younger he had to literally beat them off, and his wife, rest her soul, had never been the wiser. He wasn't a complete cad, after all. A few indiscretions, an occasional affair, but always he had been considerate of the woman who mothered his children, protecting her from any knowledge of the lapses due to his randier nature.

No, he had never had to force himself upon a woman, and it annoyed him that Rita seemed impervious to his charms. He didn't like it. At all. He stared at Rita, knowing she expected an answer of some kind. He wasn't certain he loved her. Wasn't even certain he was capable of love at his stage in life. He did know he desired her and was certain that if he could get her into bed he could please her sexually.

His feelings for Rita were more complicated than mere loving. It was something deeper, more essential to him. Need, perhaps. She made him feel needed and he responded in a basic, masculine way. The feeling that he must protect her, shelter her from hurt and disappointment, was sometimes so overwhelming it took his breath away. Together, they could live a quiet, comfortable life, mutually benefiting one another.

Over the past years he had seen flashes of this independence she was right now wearing like a badge of honor. Those times in the past they had been quickly squelched, first by Brett and later by Camilla and Charles. Guiltily, he realized he could have encouraged her to find her own strength. But he liked it when she came to him for advice and he basked in her compliments for his astute business dealings on a particular contract. Most of his other clients lived their lives in the fast lane, and they sometimes resented what they called his interference. Once a contract was signed, they didn't want to see or hear from him again unless he had a check for them.

Jesus, he didn't even like the hokey garbage Rita wrote. But garbage or not, she was an established author with a huge following and even more potential than some of the "artists" who turned out a book once every seven years. Rita's earnings stunned him, and at times he chortled all the way to the bank. "I'm sorry, Rita, my mind was elsewhere. What were you saying?"

Rita smiled. Ian appeared tired. If Twigg didn't show up soon, Ian would go to bed and that would be the end of that. "It wasn't important. Don't feel you must stay up with me just because you're my guest. You have a long drive in the morning. I might work a little longer and since it's going good I'm getting ready to wind it down. I don't want to skip over any loose threads in the plot."

"It's the difference in our ages, isn't it? You've just realized that I'm ten years older than you are. I know you're young and vital, but I think I still have a lot of good years left in me."

Rita was about to light a cigarette. She stared at Ian, stunned at what he had just said. Her voice was brittle when she spoke. "Difference in our ages in regard to what?"

"Us. You and me."

"Ian, there is no you and me. You're my agent

and I'm your client. We're friends. I didn't know that you . . . what I mean is, you never said . . . am I interpreting all of this right?"

Ian nodded. "I didn't want to rush you. The divorce and all. The children like me. You like my children. We're both grandparents. We do have a lot in common. I thought you sensed . . . perhaps, I should have spoken sooner." His voice was sober and solemn and sent a chill down Rita's spine.

"Ian, I had no idea. I'm sorry. I'm flattered, even honored, that you think of me in that way." A week ago, a month ago, she probably would have fallen into his arms and never realized that he had not mentioned the word "love."

Ian was saved from defending his statement by a knock on the door.

"Come in," Rita called happily. She wanted to laugh and throw her arms around Twigg's neck. His unruly, curly hair was still damp and clung in tight corkscrew ringlets about his face. She could smell his woodsy aftershave and it made her light-headed. For the occasion he had put on a clean, wrinkled shirt and jeans that molded his slim hips and long legs. His sneakers defied description.

"Twigg Peterson," he said, holding out his hand to Ian when he noticed Rita was just staring at him. It could have become an awkward moment.

"Ian Martin," Ian said in surprise. His eyes went to Rita and clearly said, *I thought you said no one was here but you.*

"Twigg is doing a series of articles on dol-

phins and killer whales. He's staying in the
Johnson cottage around the bend in the lake."
She wondered if Ian realized he was glaring at
Twigg.

Twigg, on the other hand, had eyes only for
Rita. "I'd like a beer, if you don't mind. Don't
get up, I can get it myself."

"Get it himself," Ian mouthed the words to
Rita's smiling face. She nodded as she leaned
back in her chair and lit a cigarette. Ian would
never understand a man who could do for himself when a woman was around and available to
do for him. It never would have occurred to Ian
to get his own beer. That's what wives and house-
keepers were for.

Ian sat down heavily and Twigg returned, sitting down across from Rita and beside Ian. Rita
watched the two men for a moment. With Ian's
announcement and Twigg's arrival, she felt as
though she were tumbling backward to square
one, uncertain of herself and dreading the conversation that was to follow. Looking uncomfortable, even angry, Ian sipped his wine, draining
the glass and placing it on the coffee table. His
eyes shifted to Rita as though he expected her
to hurry and refill it for him, or at least ask if he
would care for another glass. Twigg seemed oblivious to Ian's discomfort as he drank his beer.
"I managed eight hundred words today," he announced proudly.

"That's wonderful! Looks as though you're
coming to terms with the assignment and it won't
be long before you can put it behind you." Easily, she entered into conversation with him. With

Twigg it was always so easy. Occasionally, he directed his questions to Ian who found himself joining in the light repartee.

Soon, Rita suggested that perhaps Ian might find another market for Twigg's articles, and it was the agent who expressed interest in seeing something on paper.

"It won't mean much without the pictures to accompany it," Twigg told him. "The assignment I'm doing for *National Geographic* naturally required photos, and they're damn good if I say so myself."

Ian seemed immediately interested. This was a man with high qualifications. An assignment from *National Geographic* was something to boast about, and he'd heard recently that one of the major publishers was looking for subjects to print into what Ian liked to call "coffee table books."

Relieved that the two men seemed to be getting on so well despite the uncertain beginning, Rita quietly excused herself and went into the kitchen to start the dinner dishes. A little while later Twigg came in for another beer, followed by Ian carrying his empty wineglass. The conversation had now progressed to having Twigg send Ian a portfolio of his photos and text.

As though it were the most natural thing in the world, Twigg took up a dish towel and began drying as Rita washed, still continuing his conversation with Ian. If the older man was a little surprised by this action, he said nothing. When it came to business, Ian was a dynamo, and the last in the world to alienate a prospective and profitable client.

It was past midnight when Ian stood and announced he was going to bed. Rita offered to call him at five thirty so he could beat the rush-hour traffic on Interstate 80.

"Good night, Ian," Rita said softly, refusing to meet those accusing hazel eyes that asked when, if ever, she was going to abide by propriety and send this young rascal, Peterson, home.

"Good night, dear." He kissed her perfunctorily on the cheek and warmly shook hands with Twigg. "I'll be watching for your stuff, Peterson. Don't wait too long to get it together. I have a saying 'strike when the iron's hot.' "

"I'll do that," Twigg assured him, sitting down on the floor beside Rita's chair.

"You certainly handled him efficiently," Rita complimented after Ian had left them alone.

Twigg raised a brow. "Efficiently, is it? That's succinct and descriptive. I'll have to use that myself."

Rita laughed. Twigg knew exactly what she was talking about only he didn't think it worth discussing. Ian had been prepared to dislike Twigg and instead had offered to help him find a market for his work. Amazing. She liked the way Twigg had handled himself. Self-confident without seeming to be too brash and cocky, at least to the slightly stuffy Ian. She knew Twigg would fit into almost any group of people, being well liked as well as admired. Just look at the way he had charmed her!

Silently, Twigg drank his beer, covertly watching Rita. He wanted to drag her off to his bed, to hold her, touch her, hear her whisper his name as she tumbled over the edge of pleasure. She had lovely legs, he had noticed. Slim, gracefully turned, and teasingly revealed by the slit-hemmed skirt she wore. He had been conscious of the deep, open neck of her blouse all evening and of the shadow of cleavage it revealed. He wanted to bury his face between her breasts, breathe in the scent of her. Tenderly, her hand touched his head, running her fingers through his hair.

"Penny for your thoughts," she said softly.

Turning, he looked up into her face. "I was just thinking I'd like to throw you over my shoulder and carry you down to my cottage and make mad, passionate love to you."

For an instant, Rita's eyes glanced in the direction of Ian's room. Then, turning back to Twigg, her eyes smiled down at him. "What are you waiting for?"

His smile was dazzling, his gaze smoldering, and she was lost to her own building emotions and desires. He rose to his feet, drawing her up into his arms, dipping his face to bury it in the hollow of her throat.

Chapter Six

He carried her into his darkened cottage, completely sure of his movements through the darkness. Rita nestled her face into his neck, hurrying him with playful touches of her tongue against the faint stubble of tomorrow's beard. She loved the way he smelled: spicy, musky, and most of all, masculine.

I'm like a girl again, she thought, delicious tremors racing through her body. I never thought I would feel this way again, all quivery inside, a little nervous in my stomach, more than a little light-headed. She had thought those sensations were left far behind her, that a woman her age would be too old, too knowledgeable about why her blood pressure rose, to respond with any spontaneity. It wasn't so, she rejoiced. There was no such thing as "too old." Here, inside her, were those old but never forgotten feelings: the skittishness of a new colt, the wild flutter of wings, the desire, no *need*, to please and be pleasured. In his arms she was as smooth and supple as that sixteen-year-old girl within her. Her hair was as dark as walnut, her skin as white as alabaster. She felt beautiful and, feeling it, became beautiful.

He took her into his bedroom and gently placed her on his bed. She was aware of his scent in here—aftershave, soap and dampness from the adjoining bathroom, leather and tobacco. All aphrodisiacs to her senses.

Twigg flicked on the night table lamp; it glowed dimly, filling the room with a cozy glow. "I want to see you, Rita. I want to watch you when I make love to you." There was a huskiness in his voice, a seductive look in his eyes, that set her pulses racing. She watched his hands as they came down to undo the buttons on her blouse, slowly lifting it off her shoulders and kissing the newly bared flesh and the top of her breasts.

She was mesmerized by his movements, a little frightened, very much aroused. Whispers filled her head as he kissed and petted her, telling her how much she pleased him, how very much he wanted her. One by one her garments came away under his hands, and always he abated the sudden chill of skin bared to cool night air with the caress of his hands and the touch of his lips. The sound of his voice, deep, throaty, brought echoing vibrations from somewhere deep within her. She responded to him totally, entirely, allowing him to be the aggressor, the maestro.

She heard herself moaning with pleasure as his lips ignited tiny flames of fire she had thought were long cold and dead, swept like ashes in a winter wind. He was murmuring his pleasure in her, telling her she was beautiful, womanly, desirable.

Rita wanted to be beautiful for him. Wanted to bring him pleasure, make him happy. At the center of Twigg's pleasure she would find her own, waiting for her, exciting her, making her fully aware of herself as a woman. Standing before her, he began to undress. He was gold from the sun, slender and hard muscled. His chest was broad, his long arms powerful, his hips sleek and narrow. Gilt hair bloomed on his chest and threaded over his belly to thicken again in a darker grove between his thighs. His legs were long and lithely muscled, but it was to the darkness between his thighs that her eyes returned. His desire for her was evident in the proudness of his sex, and she reached out to touch him, her hands lovingly holding his maleness and falling between his thighs to that special fragility that was a man's. His hands were in her hair, his eyes closed, head thrown back on the thick column of his neck. "I love how you touch me," he told her softly, so softly, she might have only imagined he'd uttered the words.

Her arms opened to him, taking him into her embrace as he slid down into the bed, sliding his nakedness against hers and reveling in the contact between them. She was electrically charged. His mouth against hers demanded her willing response. His hands heated her flesh, finding each womanly curve and claiming them for his own. Her abandoned movements against him provoked deep sounds of delight that left him breathless. He found the roundness of her breasts and she trembled as he sought them with his mouth, kissing and teasing.

Reaching down to take him in her hand, she stroked him, her fingers wandering to the secrets between his legs and the rough surrounding hair that so enticed her fingers. She felt the waves of bliss that emanated from him as he surrendered himself to her caress. Propping herself on an elbow, she raised herself up, tasting the freshness of his skin, nuzzling in the golden furring of his chest, trailing her lips lower, lower, until buried in the thicket surrounding his sex.

Laying back, he yielded to her, his hands never leaving her body, availing himself of the nearness of her hips, the roundness of her bottom. She captured him with her hand, drawing him to her, her mouth finding him, and she took her reward from the sound of his indrawn breath and the sudden arching of his hips.

He slid her lower body toward him, stroking the line of her back and following it over the curve of her haunches to the shadow between her thighs, parting them to avail himself of the center of her. His lips and tongue teased the sensitive flesh, his hands held her hips firmly, driving her closer to him. His mouth tasted her, devoured her, arousing echoing paroxysms in her caresses to his own body, doubling their excitement in one another, multiplying their desires.

Drawing her up beside him, he covered her mouth with his own, allowing her to taste herself on his lips, tasting himself on hers. Rita's body undulated beneath his touch as his hands strayed along her breasts, her back, between her legs. There was not an inch of her left untouched, unloved. He tantalized her, teased her, bringing her so close to the gates of her release only to deny her entrance. A fire burned in her belly and her need for him to take her grew into a hunger all-consuming. Her world was filled with him, her needs were for him alone. Only he could bring her the triumphant joy she could know as a woman.

Greedily, she took his rigid, throbbing maleness into her hand, frantically bringing it against her, rubbing it against the wetness of her yearning body. "Please, have me," she whispered, pleading, imploring, "have me now!"

He rose over her, taking her into his arms, covering her mouth with his own, his silken-tipped tongue coming in to touch and devour hers. She opened herself to him, demanding he come into her and fill this pulsing emptiness he had created within her.

He watched her face, exhilarated by the rampant lust he saw there, by the need for fulfillment she had allowed him to create within her. Lovely, so lovely. Lips parted to reveal the tip of her velvet-lined tongue; head thrown back and eyes closed with the weight of her passion. He entered her, feeling her warm, satiny sheath close and ripple around him. He wanted to bury himself in her, become a part of her, know her as he had never known another woman. Soft, kittenish sounds of pleasure fell on his ears as he moved within her, thrusting gently, becoming more insistent as his own restraint began to fail. He plunged into her, becoming one with that honeyed flesh, feeling her meet each thrust with a lift of her hips, holding fast to him with her arms, her legs, taking him deeper, wanting him deeper.

At the point of no return, Rita's eyes flew open, staring up at him, a smile lifting the corners of her kiss-bruised mouth. He felt himself falling into those clear blue depths, turning over and over, down and down, rushing toward that magical and mysterious melding of their souls that made the mating of the flesh an insignificant interlude compared to the full and total joy of loving and being loved.

Rita nestled her head against Twigg's shoulder.

"Sleepy?" Twigg murmured. Rita nodded. "I'll watch the clock for you if you want to sleep. I don't own an alarm but my watch is trustworthy."

"Hmmm," she purred contentedly, "just like you are."

"Me? Trustworthy? Why, madame, haven't you noticed that I've just ravished you?" She liked the sound of his laughter.

"You, sir, have been reading too many romances!" she pretended to scold, lightly pulling his chest hair.

"I haven't been reading romance, Rita, I've

been living one. Since the day I met you." There
was a deep note in his voice that started a shudder between her shoulder blades. "You, darling,
are the most romantic woman I've ever known.
Sweet, sensitive, womanly. Without false cha-
rades or devious facades. I like you, Rita Bellamy, very much."

His words warmed her as his embrace tightened around her, holding her close to him.
He's good for me, she thought, so very good.
Time spent with him was exciting and at the
same time soothing. Her work was going well,
and he didn't intrude himself upon her and
make demands. He had work of his own, and he
understood how difficult it was to restore a neb-
ulous train of thought.

"Admit it," he whispered into the soft cloud
of her hair, "you'd completely forgotten about
Ian, hadn't you?"

"Rascal! How did you know?"

"By the look in your eyes when I was making
love to you. I was the only man who existed for
you. Wasn't I? Admit it!" His tone was teasing,
joking, but there was an underlying note prompting her confession.

"All right, I admit it. Yes, you were the only
man who existed for me. You filled my world
and I loved it. You touched me, Twigg, here, inside." Her hand covered her breast and her words,
meant to be light and noncommittal, suddenly
became her truth.

"You make me feel special," he told her,
rolling over to press himself against her. His lips
worshipped her breasts, the pulsing hollow of

her throat, and his hands began a ritual of possession, awakening hungers she had thought satisfied. "I want to love you again, Rita. And I'm not certain I'll ever stop wanting to love you."

He took her mouth, possessed it suddenly, intently, and she felt the quickening of her response. Yes, she thought before she surrendered herself to their shared ecstasy, this is a kind of loving. If it wasn't "till death do us part," it was still a very special kind of loving.

Rita sat staring at the phone, tapping the eraser end of her pencil against her teeth. It was just after nine in the morning and Ian was long gone, sent off splendidly with a "good, old-fashioned breakfast," as he liked to call it. Coffee, bacon, eggs, juice, and a special treat of hash browned potatoes. Mountain air was invigorating, he told her as he polished off his second piece of toast and perused her downloaded pages.

Ian was not an admirer of historical romances, Rita knew. He considered them slightly better than trash and had once, to her horror, referred to the explicit but gently written love scenes as "soft-core porn for the ladies." She had immediately set him straight on that fact, and he had never mentioned it again. He was always encouraging her to begin work on a contemporary novel, and there was a nucleus of an idea roaming around in her head. But how could he expect her to bring her head out of the seventeenth century, or thereabouts, to begin work on something modern when there was still another book due on her present contract? Impossible. Yet she had found herself dallying more and more with this particular plot line and had even sketched in some of the characters. She sighed. Perhaps after completing the next book she would take a stab at it.

Ian had not mentioned his declaration of the night before. It was painfully obvious to him that Rita was not romantically inclined in his direction. No, it would seem her interests lent themselves to much younger men. Peterson must be in his early thirties, he told himself as he gulped his coffee. He was fully aware of the fact that shortly after sending himself off to bed Rita had left the cabin with that Peterson fellow. He was already awake when she crept back into the cottage to awaken him at five thirty as she had promised. Ian didn't care for the situation at all and believed Rita was riding for a fall. A hard fall. But he didn't suppose there was much he could do about it, unless, of course, it was affecting her work. That was why he was perusing through the pages she had delivered to him. Everything seemed to be in order, he found to his dismay. The dialogue was sharp and clean and uncluttered, and her concentration on visual description was typical Rita Bellamy, playing out the action as though it were being projected on the wide screen. Here he had been all set to gear himself up to a paternal talk with her, chastising her for her amorous activities. If Rita would no longer allow him to see to her financial affairs, he knew she would at least listen to advice concerning her work. But there was no fault to be found, and, disgruntled, he had choked down the last of his coffee and made his departure.

Rita had been glad to see him go. Ian was a dear, a good friend, but his declaration last night and her suspicions that he knew she had not spent the night in her own bed made her uncomfortable. Go! Go! she thought. I don't want you here. I don't want anyone here. I want to explore and discover this new person I'm becoming. This new woman.

Now, sitting before the telephone, Rita had her directory opened to the number of a local gynecologist. She was being silly. She was a grown woman with three children and certainly familiar with birth control methods. But still, it all seemed too contrived. So cold and calculating.

Buck up, Rita old gal! she thought. Face it. The real dilemma comes *after* you discover you're pregnant! Use your head!

Her finger traced the line of names in the phone book. Neither she nor Twigg had spoken of birth control, but then it wasn't as though she were a sixteen-year-old schoolgirl. She was a grown woman, for God's sake, and it was natural that Twigg expected her to know how to take care of herself. Even Rachel had been on the pill since she was seventeen years old. Why, then, had it been so easy for her to come to terms with the fact that her seventeen-year-old daughter was sexually active but not with herself? Brett had always seen to that part of their relationship, using condoms or practicing coitus interruptus. Birth control was something Rita Bellamy had never given a thought to pertaining to herself. And now here she was, faced with it.

Don't be a Dumb Dora! she told herself. If a child of seventeen can think about protecting herself from an unwanted pregnancy, certainly her mother can! Almost viciously, she dialed the phone and hastily made an appointment to see the doctor. She nearly choked when she told the nurse she needed an immediate appointment, and it was for a birth control device. The voice on the other end remained cool and business-like. God, did they always get emergency phone calls from forty-three-year-old women demand-ing birth control so their lovers wouldn't get them pregnant? Four o'clock. Today? Tomor-row? No, today. Rita's palms became sweaty and she could barely speak. It was unthinkable she was actually doing this! Cold. Contrived. Hell no! She finally breathed relief. The word was *smart. Adult. Responsible.*

There was a little discomfort and cramping after the insertion of the IUD, but the doctor had told her to expect it and it didn't worry her. It had occurred to Rita as she sat in the nearly empty waiting room that if she had been home in New Jersey, no amount of frantic calling would have gotten her a same-day appointment with her own doctor. Thank heavens for small towns.

She was to refrain from sexual activity for at least twenty-four hours, the physician had said sternly, and she had felt herself blush. Did he know? Did it show that she had an ardent lover who was only thirty-two years old and very impetuous?

Twigg was coming for dinner, and Rita wondered what she would do if he wanted to make love. One did not just come out and announce to one's lover that a crazy loop of plastic had been inserted into one's vagina that was meant to prevent the embarrassment of an unwanted pregnancy and forbid one from indulging oneself that particular evening. Did one?

It was over the salad that Rita blurted out her news. Twigg sat there, fork in midair, and stared, astonished. Suddenly, he burst out laughing. Her innocence was amazing, and he was amused by it. But he was also deeply touched, for two reasons. First, that she thought enough of him to confide something so personal. Second, that he knew he was her only lover, something he had not dared ask.

Standing up, he went to her quickly, putting his arms around her and kissing the back of her neck in an impetuous gesture. "Rita, sweet, I think you're wonderful."

"Do you? Even though I sit here and confess my naivete, I'm having growing pains, Twigg, and they hurt. I've been so protected all my life, and now I know I must face the fact that I'm a grown woman and accept responsibility for it."

"That's what's so wonderful. That you'll let me stand around to watch and share it with you."

Later that night, when all the world should have been asleep, Twigg held her in his arms, smoothing his hands over her naked body and just holding her. They talked, they laughed and shared secrets. They touched and caressed and kissed, but the fires of their passions were banked and kept to softly glowing embers. She knew he wanted her, he told her so, and the hard evidence of his desire was pressed between her legs. She learned there were other and very meaningful ways to express tenderness and passion without the act of intercourse. And all of them left her cheeks pink and lips ruddy and feeling completely loved. Twigg's brand of loving.

It was late in the afternoon when Rachel pulled up the driveway, horn blaring to herald her arrival. Rachel never did anything without noise and fanfare, and the more the better, Rita smiled to herself. Only that morning Rachel had called to say she was making a "surprise" visit before she winged off to Miami with "whatzizname."

Rita shut down her computer when she heard the Jaguar sports car in the drive. She enjoyed Rachel's outrageous company, and while she might secretly disapprove of some parts of the girl's lifestyle, she would never condemn her own child.

Rachel was a striking young woman, sable-haired and model-thin, with soft feminine curves in only the right places. The slinky blouse and the painted-on jeans with designer label made Rita's eyes bulge. How did she walk and bend in them? Carefully, Rachel giggled.

"How goes it, Mummy dear? Slaving away in the boonies with no one but the chipmunks to keep you company?" Not waiting for a reply, she asked, "What's for dinner? Spaghetti. I knew it. It smells delicious, as always. I could eat spaghetti seven days a week."

Rita poured two glasses of orange juice, wondering if she was pleased that Rachel had decided at the spur of the moment to come up to the lake. Worse, and contrary to all she thought maternal, she wondered exactly how long her daughter intended to stay. Not that she would ever ask her to leave. Everything would simply have to be put on a back burner for the present, or at least while Rachel was here. Everything included Twigg. Rita wasn't ready to reveal that relationship to her offspring, if she ever would be, not even to high-flying, free-winging Rachel.

Mother and daughter were settled next to the fireplace sipping their juice. "I really love what you've done to the cottage, Mum. Did you have a decorator come in and do it for you? It's a glad and far cry from your usual stuffy choices, Mum. Did I ever tell you I never liked chintz and antiques and overstuffed chairs? And I always hated those ridiculous tester beds you had in the room Camilla and I shared at home."

Rita looked blankly at her child. She had always thought she had furnished their home with love and comfort. A fine time to discover that her child had never appreciated the furnishings and had actually hated the beautiful antique beds she had refinished and stained especially with her daughters in mind. Rachel was so opinionated, had always been, even as a child, and Rita couldn't help but wonder what else Rachel had disliked and hated while she was growing up. Something else to go on the back burner, she supposed, deciding not to pursue the subject. But it hurt terribly, to know that her efforts had not been appreciated. "How is everything, Rachel? Have you seen Camilla and the children?"

"Mother, you know Camilla is pissed with me. I knew you were going to ask, so when I stopped for gas on the way up here, I called her, from a phone booth. She was cool, very cool. I asked about the monsters and she said they were fine. Tom is fine. The dog is fine. What that means is the dark stuff hit the fan when you refused to babysit. Not to worry. Camilla will come around. She has to pout first. I'm surprised at you, Mum, Camilla was always your favorite, you should know how she does things."

"Rachel, that's not true. I have no favorites among my children. I've never shown favoritism and you know it."

"Mum, it doesn't matter. We're each our own person. Camilla is a dud. Charles has potential, if you don't smother him. Daddy, well, Daddy wanted something and he went for it. Now you, Mother, are another brand of tea."

"When are you leaving for Miami?" Rita asked, trying to change the subject. It was because Camilla was the oldest. A parent sometimes felt something special for the firstborn. It didn't mean the other children were loved any less.

"Tomorrow, the plane leaves at five ten. I'll

be back Monday morning. Mom, they picked my designs for the new trade show. A hefty bonus. That means I can start paying you back. Will one hundred fifty dollars a month be okay to start? If I pick up the top prize, I can pay you back in one lump sum."

"Fine. Whenever. Don't cut yourself short. You know I was glad I could help you. More than that I'm proud of you and appreciate your effort to repay me. Have you seen your father?"

"No. But I talked to him a week or so ago. He doesn't call. I do my duty and try to call once every ten days or so. He really has nothing to say to me. I think he's embarrassed. I asked him if he heard from Charles and he said no. Camilla calls him every day and makes sure the kids get on the phone. I just know Daddy is thrilled to be reminded that he has three grandchildren when he just married a twenty-two-year-old chick."

"Rachel, that's no way to talk about your father."

Rachel's wide, blue eyes were innocent. "Why?"

"I really don't want to go into it now. Why don't you take a walk around the lake or go outside and rake some leaves for me? I want to finish something I'm working on, and then we'll have dinner. We can spend the evening together. Ian was here and he brought me some new books."

"Sounds good to me, Mummy. Are you cooking the long spaghetti or the shells?"

"Shells. Two boxes of them so I can put on another five pounds." Rita grinned.

"You *are* getting a little hefty. Must be all this

good clean living up here. You just sit and work and then sit and eat, right? That'll do it. You're at that age where it all goes to the middle. You should give some thought to working it off. Join an exercise class! It's bad enough being a grand-mother at forty-three, but a fat grandmother is a no-no. By the way, I think you need a touch-up. You don't want to be a fat and gray-haired grandmother. I'll do it for you tonight, if you like. Okay?"

Rita nodded as she sucked in her stomach. "Dinner is in an hour. Don't get lost."

"That's what you used to say when I was a kid. How can I get lost? This place is about as big as a penny and I know it like the back of my hand. Listen, I saw smoke coming out of the Johnson chimney. Are they here?"

Rita swallowed hard. "No, they have a ten-ant." Leave it to Rachel; don't ask questions, she prayed. She turned her back on her daughter and turned on the computer. Her shoulders were tense as she tried to work with her stomach sucked in.

Two hours later Rita glanced down at her watch. Rachel should have been back by now. It was almost dark outside. From the bedroom window she had a clear view of the lake and the Johnson cottage. She would not spy. She would not look out that window to look for her daugh-ter.

Bustling into the kitchen, she busied herself with the sauce and setting the table, laying out napkins, putting water on to boil for the maca-roni. She cleaned the coffeepot and measured out coffee. Mixed a salad and slit the Italian garlic bread and stuck it in the oven, only to take it out again. Where was Rachel?

Another half hour crawled by as Rita drank two cups of steaming coffee. She would not spy. She could throw open the front door, walk out onto the deck, and shout Rachel's name as she had when Rachel was a child. No, she wouldn't do that either. Rachel was all grown, a woman, used to making her own choices and decisions.

Unconsciously, she sucked in her gut and marched into the living room. She felt angry. And guilty. What if Rachel had walked up to the Johnson cottage and knocked on the door and introduced herself? That was Rachel's style. What if they were both inside, laughing and talking? What if Rachel was telling tales about her childhood, making it perfectly obvious to Twigg that Rita was really too old for him? Rachel was spontaneous and charming and totally disarming.

This is ridiculous! Rita snapped to herself. Twigg knows exactly how old I am . . . no, that wasn't what was eating her. The truth was, she felt threatened by her own daughter who was young and lovely. And her maternal pride was prompting her to think Rachel was everything and more a man like Twigg would find to his tastes.

Chapter Seven

The front door opened and Rachel walked in, Twigg behind her. Rita's heart flopped and then righted itself. She forced a smile to her lips. "Hello, Twigg. I see you've met my daughter."

"I've invited him for dinner, Mother. He said you were friends so I didn't think you would mind. When you make spaghetti, you make lots. Twigg was sitting on his front porch when I walked by. He thought I was you. I don't know how he could have made such a mistake." She laughed, a derisive note in her tone. "I don't *look* anything like you!" Rita sucked in her stomach again.

"That's nice. I hope you like spaghetti, Twigg." How brittle and dry her voice sounded. "Love it." Did his voice sound apologetic? Again, Rita tucked in her stomach.

"Can I get either of you something? I have a few more things to do in the kitchen. Coffee, beer, wine?"

"Nothing for me," Twigg said quietly.

"Me neither, Mummy. I was telling Twigg about your grandchildren on the way over. Tell him I didn't lie, that they really are called 'the monsters.' "

"They're mischievous, like most children," Rita said defensively. Why did she have to call her a grandmother in front of Twigg? *Because,* an inner voice responded, *she doesn't know you slept with him, and she is only saying what she would say under any circumstance. You're nitpicking, Rita.*

She attacked the salad greens with a vengeance as she chopped and sliced them into a large wooden bowl. She wondered what they were talking about in the living room. It sounded too quiet. Knowing Rachel as well as she did, it didn't have to mean they were talking. They could be doing other . . . She sucked in her stomach again as she bent down to take the garlic bread from the oven. She set it on a rack to cool before slicing. Waiting impatiently for the pasta to boil, she had a feeling she wasn't going to enjoy dinner. Rachel was so young and beautiful. God, she couldn't be jealous of her own child, could she?

She called them for dinner and sat down. Twigg was opposite her, and Rachel was at the end of the table.

Rita picked at her dinner not wanting to eat

the heavy pasta. She stirred the salad around on her plate and ate a piece of lettuce from time to time as she listened to Rachel and Twigg talk about the tennis match at Forest Hills. "As far as I'm concerned, Djokovic has great form, do you agree?" Twigg nodded as he wolfed down the meal.

"I think Federer has about had it—he's such a show-off. Mother, you aren't eating, how come? Don't tell me I really got to you with that business of getting too fat. I was just teasing you."

Twigg stared across at Rita, his eyes wide and thoughtful, even puzzled. She hadn't said much, not that her loquacious daughter gave her much of a chance. "How did the writing go today? I don't mind telling you I had a hard time," he said enthusiastically. "I have to admire you, the way you can string words together. Two words at one time is okay, but give me three or four and I have to rewrite."

"It will get easier as you go along. Don't be so quick to discard what you write. Usually, the first thing you do is the best. You just spin your wheels after that. That's the way it works for me, anyway."

Rachel stared from her mother to Twigg. A glimmer of comprehension appeared in her wide-eyed gaze. Her mother was uncomfortable. Twigg was at ease and concerned with Rita's silence. He was going out of his way to include her in the dinner conversation. And the way he got up and opened the refrigerator, as though he knew just where everything was.

Hating to be ignored, Rachel interrupted the

conversation. She was aware that her mother was annoyed with her and that Twigg had forgotten she was there. "How long are you staying at the lake, Twigg?" Rachel asked pointedly.

"I'm not sure," Twigg replied evasively.

"Mother?"

It took Rita several moments until she realized the one word was a question.

"I haven't definitely decided. It depends on how soon I finish and if there are going to be any further rewrites. There's no reason for me to hurry back with Charles away at college."

"But, Mother, it's going to be getting cold. You don't like the mountains in the winter. You know how you like to snuggle in with your woolly bathrobe early in the evening."

Rita almost laughed as she met Twigg's eyes. His bright green gaze said he could offer other ways to keep warm.

Rachel felt her eyes narrow. "You won't mind then if I come up to keep you company after the trade show, will you? I'll have some time off before I have to get back into the swing of things. It's the week of Charles's big game."

It was on the tip of Rita's tongue to say yes, she *did* mind, she minded *very much*! If there was one thing Rachel had never done, that was to spend more than one day in her mother's company, becoming definitely antsy to get back to the city and her own lifestyle. She shrugged. "If I'm still here, of course you can come up. However, you don't like the mountains in the winter either."

"Mother, how can you say that! I ski every winter. Do you ski, Twigg?"

"Some," Twigg answered as he pushed his plate away. "I go to Tahoe a couple of times a year. Do you ski, Rita?"

Rachel laughed. "Mother ski! Mummy's idea of exercise and sports is to watch it on TV. Right, Mother?"

Rita forced a smile to her lips. Rachel couldn't be doing this deliberately, or could she? The thought of the two snowmobiles she had bought on impulse anticipating wondrous hours of her and Twigg skimming over the snow nearly choked her.

Her tone was light, casual, when she replied. "Rachel's right. I'm a creature of comfort. I don't do any of the things you *young* people do." She bit back the urge to mention her secret of the snowmobiles. "Why don't you take your coffee and go into the living room. I'll clear away here and join you when I'm finished."

"I'll help you, Rita. It's the least I can do after such a good dinner."

"I can see you don't know Mom very well. If there's one place you stay away from, it's her kitchen. C'mon, we'll do what she wants. If you leave them we can do them later, Mother, while I'm dyeing your hair," Rachel called over her shoulder.

"I changed my mind, Rachel. I decided I like the little bit of gray I have. Go along, I can finish up here."

Twigg's eyes frantically sought hers in apology for the second time. Rita smiled before she turned to the sink to run the water.

The minute the door closed behind them, Rita wanted to smash something. Hot, scorching anger engulfed her. She couldn't ever remember being so angry. Angry at herself, angry at Rachel. But never angry with Twigg.

Rita washed and dried the dishes slowly, delaying the time when she would have to go back into the living room. She cleaned the coffeepot and got it ready for the morning. She carried out the trash and put a new liner in the wastebasket. She swept minuscule crumbs from the floor and then washed off the dustpan; she didn't know why she did it. She looked at the yellow plastic scoop and grimaced. Whoever heard of washing a dustpan? There was nothing else to do but light a cigarette. So far she had killed thirty-seven minutes.

She almost bumped into Twigg when she pushed the swinging door that led to the living room. He was so near, so close, she thought she could hear the beat of his heart. It was probably her own. "Sorry," she muttered.

"I've got to be going, Rita. I want to transcribe some tapes and I promised myself an early start in the morning. Thanks for dinner." He squeezed her shoulder intimately before he left. Rachel waved good-bye and Rita walked to the door and opened it for him. "Good night, Twigg."

"See you tomorrow."

"See you tomorrow," Rachel mocked after the door closed. "Mother, is something going on

here I don't know about?" Not waiting for a
reply to her ridiculous question, she rushed on.
"He's fascinating. Wouldn't you know I had to
come to the woods to find a really titillating
man. He's not married either. How old would
you say he is, Mom?"

"In his early thirties I would imagine."

"Just right." Rachel grinned. "If you're serious about not dyeing your hair, I think I'll turn
in. I'm beat. Don't forget to wake me early.
Night, Mom."

"Good night, Rachel."

Rita walked back to the kitchen for a wine-
glass and a bottle of wine. She sat in front of the
fire drinking steadily. He skied, he played tennis. He was thirty-two. He didn't take vitamins
with extra iron like she did. He was lean and fit.
He was only a few years older than her children.
He was young. God, thirty-two was so young. A
set of tennis would kill her. Skiing would make
her a basket case.

Rita nursed the bottle of wine until she was
tipsy. "Drunk!" she admitted rebelliously. Her
last conscious thought before she fell into bed
fully clothed was that it wasn't fair. Nothing about
any of this was fair—from Twigg, to Ian, to Rachel,
to herself.

It was early morning; Rita could tell from
the filtered light coming in between the drawn
drapes. She half heard Rachel when she poked
her head into the room to announce, "It's a
good thing I have my own built-in alarm or I
would still be out. See you soon, Mother. I'll call
you when I get back from Miami."

"Regards to Patrick," Rita mumbled as she slid beneath the covers.

"Who? Oh, Patrick. Right! See you, Mom. Say good-bye to Twigg for me."

The golden idyllic days of autumn were upon them. October had fulfilled the promise of an Indian summer—warm, balmy days and cool, crisp nights. The landscape became a tapestry of golds, oranges, and reds, wild and abandoned color to match the abandon of Rita's emotions.

Her novel was completed and she knew it was good. Via Ian, it had been sent to the copy editor with no revisions due. Time was her own and she reveled in it. Until the first of the year she had only to research and set up her next outline.

Twigg was still busy with his project and hoped to be finished before Christmas. Christmas! Had another year rolled nearly to the end? Neither of them could believe it. Had it only been just after Labor Day that they had met? Only weeks ago, really. How had they come to know one another so well, learned so much about the other? Concentration, Twigg had laughingly said.

Writing was new to him. Theses and papers published through the university came easily enough, writing for an audience of students and biologists already quite familiar with his subject of marine life. However, preparing for a larger, less-informed audience was totally different, and he had come to depend upon Rita to review his work, encouraging her to be free with her criticism and she was, boldly. Her point of view was valuable to him, and she would not diminish it with flattery instead of honesty. Recognizing this, Twigg followed her advice where she suggested he clarify certain passages.

Rita liked helping him this way, instinctively knowing he never would have asked if she were still busy with work of her own. It was another side of their relationship and their growing dependence upon one another, and she enjoyed it immensely.

She was learning she could allow herself to be dependent upon Twigg for companionship and fun and a sharing of interests. Yet it was a new kind of dependency that required nothing of her, only her desire to be with him and he with her. There was none of the feeling that he might begin directing her life, press his opinions upon her, or try to protect her the way Ian had done. And when her opinion differed from his, there was none of the bitter derision there had been with Brett. With Twigg, Rita could be together with him, feel he was a part of her life and she of his, and yet remain an entity herself.

The day after Rachel's departure, Rita had contemplated her life. She had thought about Twigg, her children, and her grandchildren, but, mostly, she had thought about herself. This alone was a breakthrough as far as she was concerned. Too often for too many years she had shirked the effort of coming to know herself the way she was today, now, instead of remembering herself as she had been twenty years before when her role in life was clear-cut and simple. Wife and mother.

She attempted to decide if a diet and weight loss would make her happy. If so, would she be doing it for herself or for Twigg's approval? Then she made the decision to diet and watch her weight because it was what *she* wanted. Her cigarette habit was consciously cut in half, going down to less than a pack a day and switching to a low tar brand. Soon, with effort and willpower, she planned to kick the habit altogether. She lived with her decisions for several days before she started her new routines, wanting to be certain she was comfortable with what she was doing. She made no mention of it to Twigg nor to her children when she spoke with them on the phone. She believed her decisions were wise and healthful and would benefit her in the end.

It was Twigg who invited her to come jogging with him, and at first she demurred, claiming it was too rigorous. But she did take walks, long ones, while he worked on his articles, and she liked the fresh bloom of color that was returning to her cheeks. Often, when he noticed her through his window, he would join her, silently urging her to quicken her pace. Now, four weeks later, she was actually jogging with him a quarter way around the lake and seeing her reward on the bathroom scale.

The pretense of separate living quarters had been abandoned by mutual consent. Twigg used the Johnson cottage for work and had moved into Rita's cottage with her.

It was delicious waking in the morning and

finding herself in his arms. It was heaven to no longer eat dinner alone. Reading, watching TV, or just sitting by the fire talking, everything was wonderful with Twigg.

Their lovemaking had reached new heights of intimacy and freedom. He encouraged her to be the aggressor when the mood struck her, and yet he never took her for granted. His delight with her seemed to increase and take on new colorations. His lusty demands in bed left her feeling desirable and every inch a woman. He told her he couldn't get enough of her and proved it by his ardor and attention.

They had gone into the city together three times. Once for Rita to lunch with her publicist and twice for Twigg to meet with Ian and an interested publisher. Each time Rita had seen and appreciated another side of him. She liked the way he put people at their ease, thoroughly enjoying their conversation and learning about their interests outside their work. He fit in. Simply put, but true. The young female publicist had winked surreptitiously at Rita, and the publisher, known to be a hard-nosed, opinionated man, had been charmed by him. Twigg easily won respect and a handsome publishing contract into the bargain.

Rita poured another cup of coffee when she saw Twigg running up the path after a morning's work. "You're invited to dinner tonight," he told her, carefully sipping the steaming brew. "My place around six. Nothing special, steaks and salad, I suppose. I'll run into town and pick everything up. I'm having some guests, good

friends of mine, and I know you'll enjoy them."
Suddenly his eyes locked with hers, concern
wrinkling his brows. "You will come, won't you?
It's short notice and I know my cooking isn't the
best . . ."

Rita laughed delightedly. "Of course I'll come,"
she assured him, rewarded by his smile. In-
wardly, there was a note of alarm. She wasn't
quite certain she was ready to share him with his
friends or to have their solitude invaded. Because of this, she had tried to keep her own children away, and in Camilla's case it was met with
sullen disappointment.

"You'll like them, both of them. They live in
New York and they'll probably stay the night because we're known to stay up to the wee hours
talking. It's sort of a celebration for the publishing contract. Both of them are eager to meet
you, especially Samantha, who proclaims herself
to be your most ardent fan."

"You've told them about me?" she said weakly.

"Of course. You're my lady, Rita, and very important to me. I want my friends to meet you, to
know you. I would be selfish to keep you all to
myself." His hand reached over the table, cap-
turing hers. "They're very good friends, and very
discreet. I promise you. But if you're uneasy
about meeting them or having them know about
us, I'll call them back and tell them it's off." He
spoke quietly but without a trace of judgment.
He was simply concerned for her feelings and
would sacrifice an evening with his friends if it
was what she wanted.

Feeling terribly selfish and yet somehow

proud that he had admitted to his relationship with her, Rita grasped his fingers and squeezed. "You're very sweet, Twigg, and terribly sensitive to my feelings and I appreciate it. Truly. Certainly want to meet your friends, especially if one of them is a fan."

"Samantha said she was getting all her books together to have you autograph them." He laughed. "You'll find her somewhat exuberant but altogether charming. Is there anything I can get for you in town? Would you like to come with me?"

"No, on both counts. If you're going to have guests, I'd better give my hair a wash. I can't disappoint my public, you know."

Twigg kissed her soundly, telling her they'd have time for their walk when he came back from town. Then, in a teasing and seductive voice, he said, "Of course, if you can think of some other kind of exercise while I'm gone, I want you to know I'm open to suggestions."

A delicious shiver ran up her spine. It was heaven being wanted by this man, and she was drunk with the power of her own sensuality.

After he left, Rita allowed herself to frown into her coffee cup. She was presented with the problem of what to wear that evening. Slacks, skirt, jeans? If she knew who these friends were, how old they were, she would know what to wear. There it was again, the age problem. She had every reason to suppose that Twigg's friends were as young as he, younger even. And the name Samantha brought to mind a young, slim girl with long blond hair and not much on her mind. That was unfair! And ridiculous! Here she was picturing a flower child of the sixties just because of the name Samantha. If Twigg had thought his friends would not like her or that she would be uncomfortable with them, he never would have invited them up to the lake. You've got to begin trusting, Rita, my dear, she chastised herself, both yourself and others.

At five after six Rita knocked on the door to the Johnson cottage. Twigg's friends had arrived, she knew. Their car was parked beside his in the drive. She could hear the sound of voices from within. Earlier that afternoon, Twigg had returned from town and they had taken their walk. When she offered to help him with dinner or straightening the cottage, he had refused, telling her to take the time to make herself beautiful. After a long leisurely bath Rita had decided upon gray slacks and a bulky turtleneck sweater of banded pastel colors from beige to pink to lavender. Her chestnut hair gleamed in soft, collar-length waves, and she carried a bottle of Twigg's favorite wine. It had taken all of her courage to overcome her sudden shyness and actually walk the path to his cottage.

Twigg himself opened the door, smiling approvingly at her and kissing her lightly in thanks for the presented wine. He made informal introductions to Eric and Samantha Donaldson.

"You've seen Eric on the six o'clock news, Rita. That's why he looks so familiar. Samantha used to teach pottery and ceramics at the university; that's how I came to know them."

Immediately, Rita was brought into their fold.

Eric was a handsome man, dressed casually in slacks and a hand-knit sweater, and when she commented on it, Samantha smilingly took the credit.

Samantha, Rita was glad to see, was a far cry from the "flower child" she had envisioned. A tall, slim woman with Titian hair and an obvious flare for fashion, Rita liked her immediately because of her charming smile and warmth.

"I'm so pleased to meet you," Samantha said brightly, without gushing as so many did when meeting a renowned novelist. "I so enjoy your work and want you to know it."

Rita was pleased to know this stylish and graceful woman liked her work. She spied several of her older titles on the coffee table and remembered what Twigg had said about Samantha wanting them autographed.

"Twigg has been telling us about you," Eric supplied, smoothing a hand over his iron-gray hair. "He admires you greatly."

"That's my stuffy, news commentator husband for you, Rita." Samantha smiled. "We've been looking forward to meeting you since Twigg first told us about you, and you're everything he said you were." There was an embarrassed moment. What had Twigg told them? How much had he said? Twigg slipped his arm around her shoulders, pulling her against him, easing the awkward moment.

"We're going to sit right here while the *men* fix the dinner," Samantha announced. "If you need help, don't call us, call Betty Crocker," she told them as she pointed them in the direction of the kitchen. "And whatever you do, do it quickly. I'm starved!"

Sitting beside Samantha, Rita felt herself relax. Samantha was a friendly and talkative woman, enthusiastic and knowledgeable. It wasn't long before they were discussing acquaintances they had in common in New York and favorite recipes for spaghetti sauce. As an artist in ceramics, Samantha was familiar with the antique pottery Rita collected and was impressed with the author's knowledge of early American pottery houses.

"It was something I stumbled upon while doing research for one of my books," Rita explained. "I found myself intrigued and began a modest collection. However, I must admit I frequent a shop in the city and pick up pieces from a favorite potter of mine. The name is Jeffcoat, and I particularly like the banded shades of blue she uses and the mottled browns. Have you ever heard of her?" she asked Samantha.

"Heard of her!" Eric laughed as he came from the kitchen carrying a tray with two glasses of wine. "You are speaking to Samantha Jeffcoat Donaldson. Jeffcoat is Samantha's maiden name."

"How trite that sounds," Samantha complained. "Maiden name, posh! It's my name, sweetheart. Donaldson is your name! You distinguish yours and I'll distinguish mine!"

Everyone laughed when Eric complained some of Sam's brainstorms were right out of the pages of *Ms.* magazine. "Except the floor wax advertisements and laundry powder ads. Sam does discriminate against anything to do with house-hold chores," he said good-naturedly.

"Oh, hush, Eric, I want Rita to stroke my ego by telling me how she loved my work! It will make me feel so much better about asking her to autograph her books for me and allow me to present her with that little hand-thrown bowl I've brought along for her!"

Dinner was delicious and afterward Twigg threw more logs on the fire and they all congregated near the hearth. There was an unforced camaraderie, and they all basked in one another's company. Eric and Sam were easy people, sensitive and discerning. Listening to them speak on a wide range of subjects and enthusiastically offering her own opinions and having them respected was good for her ego. But it was when Eric and Sam asked after some friends they had left behind on the west coast that Rita realized Twigg traveled in a varied circle of people. Some of them artists, some in the media, academics and even what Sam called "Hollywood types." Twigg made eclectic choices in his friendships, and yet their varied backgrounds seemed to blend harmoniously in his life. Apparently, somewhere, there were "flower children" with whom he associated, but he did not restrict himself to types when it came to making relationships.

It was nearly three in the morning when Rita made a move to leave, and the Donaldsons begged off to go to bed. Twigg walked her back to the cottage and kissed her warmly at the front door. "I told you you would like them. And they adore you, especially Eric. I saw the approving glances he was throwing at you all evening. I should be jealous, but I'm not. I know Samantha is the only woman for him."

Returning his kiss, Rita expected him to return to his cottage, but he opened her door and stepped in behind her. He took her into his arms. "I love you like this, all sleepy and warm from the conversation and the wine. I want to make love to you, Rita Bellamy, and then I'm going to hold you in my arms all night long." And he made good on his promise and never once did Rita worry what the Donaldsons were thinking when Twigg didn't return.

Chapter Eight

The days slid by, each more beautiful and wonderful than the day before. Two and a half months had passed since she had met Twigg Peterson. Two and a half months that were probably the happiest of her life.

It was ten days before Thanksgiving and Charles's important football game. Rita had promised to attend and attend she would. Somehow, she had managed to lose ten pounds and had also whittled off several inches in crucial areas. Her breathing was less labored because she had cut her smoking in half. One of these days she hoped she could give it up entirely. But not yet.

The only blight on her happiness was that Twigg would be leaving the day after Christmas. She knew she would have to deal with that when the time came.

Rita got up, stretched luxuriously, and then added more logs to the fire. It felt like snow. It even looked like snow. She hoped so. She had never been marooned before and would enjoy it. It was a known fact that this area of the Poconos was the last to see a snowplow, and it was not unheard-of to remain snowbound for as long as four or five days.

The phone rang, jarring her from her thoughts. "Hi, Mother. It's Rachel. I'm calling to make sure you're still in residence. If you want I'll bring the turkey. Talk to me, Mum."

"Yes, I'm here, Rachel. It feels like snow so you better bring your boots and warm clothing. When are you planning on coming up? I appreciate your offer, but I'll take care of the turkey."

"Thursday. I'll stay through the weekend after Thanksgiving. By the way, is your handsome neighbor still there? If it snows, maybe we could go skiing together."

Rita drew in her breath. "Yes, he's still here. I'm not sure if he has skis. Perhaps you should bring Charles's if that's what you want to do."

"Good thinking, Mum. Okay, see you Thursday."

Rita replaced the phone. She could have told Rachel not to come, that she was knee-deep in work. That she couldn't holiday on Thanksgiving and lose time if she intended to be at Charles's game the next day. Why hadn't she? The question punished her, demanding she admit the truth. "Because," she blurted aloud, "because I'm challenging Twigg to find my young, vivacious daughter more desirable than me. I'm testing him and I hate myself for it, but God help me that's what I'm doing."

Now she was in a funk. All the old insecurities flooded through her. All the old guilts. And jealousy. She was jealous of her own daughter. Twigg had been more gallant after Rachel's last visit. Neither of them had discussed her child and her tactless comments concerning Rita. As long as she was keyed on self-destruct she might as well call Camilla and then Charles.

Rita waited patiently while Camilla quieted the children. "Mother, I can't believe what you're telling me. Are you saying Charles's football game is more important than spending Thanksgiving with your grandchildren? I spoke to Rachel last night, and she said she was going up to see you and said there was the most interesting man there that she wanted to get to know better. Why is it always Rachel, Mother?"

"Camilla, I promised Charles when he started the semester that if he made the team I would go to the Thanksgiving game. I can't go back on my word. Surely, you can understand how important it is to your brother."

"Are you planning on leaving Rachel there at the cottage with the new, interesting man? Mother, I can't understand you anymore. You seem to have changed. Anything goes, anything Rachel does, no matter how outrageous it is, is okay with you. Mother, ever since you started that . . . that career of yours, you've . . . never mind. I think you should know that Daddy is going to the game too. He's probably going to take Melissa. Are you sure you're ready for that?"

Rita cringed. Not at the words but at Camilla's bitchy tone. "As ready as I'll ever be," Rita said, forcing a light note into her voice.

"You're so different, Mother. Everything is so different. I'm sorry if I sound like I'm ticked-off. You don't seem to care anymore. Do you realize you've been gone for almost four months. We've missed you, especially the kids."

"I didn't call you so we could get into a hassle. I wanted you to know about Thanksgiving in plenty of time. Besides, Camilla, this year it's your turn to have dinner with Tom's family. Maybe you think I've forgotten, but I haven't. This is your year for Christmas with Tom's family too."

"Mother, does that mean you aren't coming back for Christmas?" Camilla shrieked.

"I'm not sure. More than likely, I'll stay here. Charles will want to come here so he can do some skiing. We have plenty of time for all of that. I hesitate to remind you, but you do have a father."

"Oh, Mother, he's so wrapped up in Melissa, he has no time either. The whole family is falling apart. Rachel is so flaky and you never know where or what she's going to be doing from one minute to the next. Charles is away and he never writes or calls. I feel so alone."

"Camilla, you have your own life, your own little family, and it's going to be whatever you make it. I'll always be here if you need me, but I do have my own life to lead, and I intend to lead it the way I see fit. I won't allow you or Rachel or Charles to dictate to me."

"All you think about is your books, your royalty statements, and your super-duper business deals. You have no time for us anymore, Mother."

"That's not true, Camilla. What you mean is I'm not at your beck and call anymore. You also resent that I now do something other than housework. That I've become my own person and am no longer an extension of your father."

"There's no point in discussing this anymore. I can see I can't get anywhere with you. Do you want to speak to the kids?"

"I'd love to talk to them if they aren't screaming and crying. I can't see paying long-distance rates for me to listen to you yell at them and then all they do is scream more."

"Forget it, Mother, just forget it. Tom isn't going to believe this. Oh, yes, he will, he still remembers the last conversation he had with you. Good-bye, Mother."

"Give my regards to Tom and the children. Good-bye Camilla."

One ten-minute conversation with Camilla was enough to drain one's life's blood. Now, for Charles.

Rita listened to some good-natured banter while she waited for Charles to come to the phone. "Hey, Bellamy, there's some chick on the phone for you" made her grin from ear to ear. She had to remember to tell Twigg.

"Charles, it's Mom. How are you?"

"Mom, wow, why are you calling? Is something wrong?"

"Good heavens, no. I just wanted to see if you were all right and if you got your allowance."

"Got, it and spent it. The guys had a beer party and I had to put in my share. I'm okay. Hey, you still coming up for the game?"

"I'll be there, you can count on it."

"Uh, Mom, you do know Dad is coming, don't you? Do you think it will be a problem? I think he's bringing Melissa. I didn't know what to do so I just sort of ignored the whole thing."

"I think we're all adult enough to handle it."

"There is something I need to talk to you about."

Need. He had said *need*. He needed her. How different he sounded. How grown up. "Yes, Charles, what is it?"

"With the situation between you and Dad as it is, I thought there might be a problem about Thanksgiving dinner. About who to have dinner with, I mean. So what I thought I'd do was accept an invitation to Nancy Ames's house for dinner. She doesn't live far from here, and she said I could bring you along. What do you think, Mom?" he asked anxiously.

Oh, God, oh, God, her baby was worrying about her. He was making decisions for himself and for her. He cared about her feelings being hurt.

"I think that's wonderful, but you go alone. Rachel is coming up to the cottage for Thanksgiving so I won't be alone. I was worried about you. Is Nancy your girl?"

"Almost. I haven't clinched it yet. You know, given her my high school ring. I'm working on it though. Do you think it would be all right if I brought her up to the cottage the weekend after Thanksgiving?"

"I sure do. I'd like to meet her." She suddenly wanted to see Charles share his happiness and his new sense of himself.

"One more thing, Mom. Is Dulcie still staying in the house, or did you let her go when you moved to the cottage?"

"No, she's still at the house. Someone had to stay there to make sure the pipes don't freeze. Charles, I didn't move to the cottage; I'm only staying here between books. Why did you want to know?"

"Do you think she could make me a batch of brownies and send up my gray sweatsuit? Ask her if she'll fish around for my Izod socks, the black and gray ones."

Rita smiled. "Charles, I have some free time, I could make the brownies for you."

"Thanks, Mom, but I think I'd rather have Dulcie's. No offense."

"None taken."

"What time do you think you'll get to the game?"

"Just about game time if the weather is okay. Do you need anything else?"

"Nope, that about covers it."

"Okay, I'll see you a week from tomorrow."

"Bye, Mom."

She felt pleased with herself when she hung up the phone. Charles was going to be okay. Nancy, whoever you are, you have my blessing and my thanks. Her baby worried about her. It was wonderful. Everything was wonderful. Well, *almost* everything; the thought of her daughters popped into her mind.

Twigg arrived back at Rita's cottage, his face glowing with excitement like a small boy's, "Have you looked outside?" At her bewilderment, he led her away from her desk where she was making notes for her next book and brought her to the panoramic windows in the living room. "Look!" He pointed to the lightly falling snow as though it were something he had conjured up especially for her. "It's snowing. Our first snowfall," he murmured, wrapping his arms around her and burying his face in the back of her neck.

His words touched Rita. Was there something in his voice that promised this was only the first of many snowfalls they would share together? Inexplicably, her heart broke rhythm. Somewhere in the back of her mind she had been preparing herself for the day when he would no longer be a part of her life. No, that was wrong, Twigg would always be a part of her life, a most important part. But nothing had been said about their relationship after the coming Christmas when he planned to return to California. It was almost as though she were living each day to its fullest and after that future point in time everything seemed dark and hazy.

His arms tightened around her, his breath warm and soft on her skin. So warm, warmer than the fire's glow, which shed the only light into the afternoon's dimness. She felt his desire rising firm and hard against the swell of her buttocks and the insistent caress of his fingers upon the tips of her breasts. He turned her into his embrace, finding her mouth with his own and possessing it with soft and myriad kisses that deepened imperceptibly and aroused her senses to beat in tune with his own.

He drew her down onto the geometric carpet before the hearth; the fire's heat seemed cool and distant in comparison to the warmth he imparted to her flesh as he tenderly stripped away her clothes, leaving them in a heap mingled with his own. His hands caressed her tenderly, tracing the sweet hollows of her body and rounding over the supple, womanly curves of her breasts and belly, wandering in teasing, erotic touches to the moist, warm valley where thigh met thigh.

Her clear blue eyes closed then, heightening her perception of his lovemaking. She moved against his fingers and mewed in delight when his lips followed where his hand had explored, tracing her contours with delicate ardor.

Twigg began to tremble with the force of his desire. He reveled in her responses, knowing he had found the woman who could both give and take, who needed this sensuous contact of his flesh upon hers. He wanted to wait, to double her pleasure and watch her rock beneath him with the force of her climax. But the sight of her half-parted lips beckoned to him, tempting him, sounding an echoing note in his very center. Her vulnerability, so much a part of her, deepened his emotions for her while her responsive body appealed for the complete fulfillment she could only share when his flesh entered hers and he claimed her for his own.

His mouth descended upon hers as he parted her thighs and he felt her warm, pulsing flesh welcoming him. Her arms wrapped around his neck, clinging to him, making herself a part of him and he a part of her. He loved to watch her face smile up at him, her mirror blue eyes seeming to fill themselves only with him.

Rita's eyes opened to see him looking down at her, his eyes dark with seduction and passion, the line of his mouth softening and forming the shape of her name. He came to her and took her, this marvelously loving man who had filled her life even more sweetly than he was now filling her body. She did not know if she loved him, did not know if she wanted to love him. Would she ever trust herself to that emotion again? Love demanded so much, it seemed. There were no demands here, only a sharing and a needing and giving. Love had too many sharp edges, able to cut through the soul like a razor, unlike this that seemed to be more a melding and a joining of the heart and the body.

The lines of her body seemed to perfectly match his, meeting him thrust for thrust and driving him closer and closer to the edge of that abyss where he would carry her with him into the shattering void. Her arms held him tightly, her mouth yielded beneath his and she took him into her again and again, deeper, closer, ca-

ressing him in undulating waves until he heard
the sound of his own pleasure in his ears and
she clung to him as they toppled over the edge
of carnality into the wondrous garden where
soul touched soul.

The world filtered back into consciousness;
the flicker of the fire, the soft fall of snow against
the window. They had held each other following
their simultaneous release, closing their eyes
into the shared oblivion, warmed by their pleasure and astounded by the force of their passion.

When she turned, Twigg was looking down at
her, watching her through lowered lids. His
mossy-green eyes answered all her unasked
questions. There was no need to talk about the
magic that happened between them.

Sighing, she nestled against his chest and he
cradled her close to him, imparting his warmth
and stroking her skin. There was so much he
wanted to tell her, but he knew she was still skittish as a colt and so very, very vulnerable.
There's a place in my life for you, my love, my
friend. Could you find a place for me?

Rachel arrived with the first snowfall of the
year. Without Rita having to mention it or to
ask, Twigg had removed all his personal belong-
ings from her cottage: his razor, his toothbrush,
items of clothing, and notebooks. With each

possession he dropped into the paper sack, Rita had become more resentful of her youngest daughter's intrusion.

Looking beautiful in her scarlet parka trimmed in white fur, Rachel was the perfect snow bunny, Rita thought, pushing away her selfish resentment.

Rachel lugged in two sets of skis and poles. "Mom, you wouldn't believe how bad the roads are. If this keeps up through the night, we should have a good surface tomorrow. I came in the back way and they were preparing the ski lift. You have Twigg's number, don't you? I want to make sure he's up for skiing." Rita felt herself flinch but turned and made a pretense of reading the number from the small address book on her desk.

Rita went into the kitchen to make a hot toddy for Rachel. She didn't need to hear the conversation between her daughter and her lover. Didn't want to hear it.

"Thanks, Mummy. I'm going to drink this and hit the sack. Twigg said he was raring to go and would meet me at seven. Don't worry about getting up to see me off. This is one date I won't be late for."

Rita lay in her empty bed aware of a deep loneliness. Twigg should be there with her, just within reach of her hand. She remembered how long it had taken her to become used to sleeping alone once Brett had left. At first, with Twigg, it had taken some doing to get used to sleeping with someone again. Now she was back at square one. Rolling over, she pounding the pillow. Get used to it now, she told herself. Once Christmas comes and goes, this is the way it's going to be. Lonely.

She ached. She resented. She almost hated. Sleep was fitful and there was no sense in tossing and turning and bemoaning the loss of her lover because Rachel had arrived. Rachel was innocent, and why shouldn't the girl expect to spend some time with her own mother? Rationalizing didn't help. Better to get up for some hot tea and read until she felt drowsy.

Rita scanned her shelves for the new titles Ian had brought, looking for the new Patricia Matthews novel. By page two she was hoping to immerse herself in the story. She admired the author's style and her remarkable ability to capture a character's essence.

Rita turned the page, then realized she hadn't the faintest idea what was happening. Rita's mind, seething with frustration and jealousy was simply incapable of concentration. Her big plan, her wonderful surprise, was dashed. The two snowmobiles in the garage were meant to surprise Twigg. She had purchased them weeks ago with the intention of barreling up to Twigg's cottage and inviting him for a ride. Her plan was to skim the snowy mountains for hours, letting the wind whip their cheeks and then come home for hot soup and fresh bread in front of the roaring fireplace. They would make love and lie in each other's arms. They would talk about everything and nothing, have long, comfortable silences, and then make love again, until the fire died and they crept into bed to lie spoon fashion against one another.

Laying her book aside, Rita pulled the belt tighter about her now slim waist and walked into the cold garage. She stared down at the two shiny machines. All gassed and ready to go. The keys hung on a nail by the garage door, still shiny and unused. She hardly felt the cold as she walked over to peer down at the padded seat with its safety strap. It would have been a wonderful memory.

The snowmobiles would make a smashing present for Charles and Nancy Ames when they arrived after Thanksgiving. If anyone was going to have a wonderful memory, she was glad it was Charles.

Back in the warm living room, Rita shivered. She added another pine log to the fire and sat down on a mound of pillows. She sipped at her lukewarm tea. She couldn't let Rachel's visit throw her into a tizzy. She had to do something, get her act together, as her daughter put it. Wasn't Rachel the one who always said "Go for it"? Did she really want to put up a fight for Twigg? She hated the term "fight for him." If whatever they had between them wasn't stable enough to withstand Rachel's arrival, then she didn't want any part of it.

Eventually, she dozed and woke early when Rachel tiptoed through the living room. "Sorry, Mom, I didn't know if I should wake you or cover you with a blanket. You're going to be stiff and sore from sleeping in that position. Couldn't sleep, huh?"

"I haven't been here all that long, an hour or so," Rita lied. "Can I make you some coffee or something to eat?"

"I already plugged the pot in. I have to meet Twigg in fifteen minutes. How do you like this new ski suit? I just had it made. I wanted to impress the great Tahoe skier. I designed the material myself. What do you think?"

Rita eyed the sky-blue pattern and nodded. "It's beautiful," she said honestly.

Rachel gulped at the scalding coffee. She handed it to her mother. "You'll see me when you see me. Have a nice day, Mom." She was gone.

Rita sighed and headed for the bathroom. She was about to step into the shower when she heard squeals and laughter outside. She parted the curtains in the bathroom and looked out. Twigg was pummeling Rachel with snowballs, to her daughter's delight. Rachel ducked and grabbed Twigg below the knees. Both bundled figures toppled into the snow. Laughing and shouting, they got up and trudged toward the ski lift.

The driving, needle sharp spray did nothing for Rita's mood nor did the brisk toweling. The scented bath powder annoyed her as did the fragrant lotion she applied to her entire body. She dressed and made herself a huge breakfast, which she threw away. She was settling down with the Patricia Matthews book when the phone pealed to life.

"Rita? This is Connie Baker. My kids told me they thought they saw you in town the other day. If you aren't doing anything, why don't you come over for lunch and we can spend some time together. I can have Dick pick you up in the Land Rover. What do you say?"

"I'd love to come over. Don't bother sending Dick. I can use the snowmobile. I can leave now if it isn't too early."

"Are you kidding. Yours is the first human voice I've heard except for these kids since I got here. If you have any good books, I'd appreciate a few."

Should she leave a note or not? She sat down at the computer and typed out a brief note:

Rachel,
Took the snowmobile and went visiting. I don't know when I'll be back.

She signed the brief note and propped it up on the kitchen table between the salt and pepper shakers.

She liked Connie Baker with her down-home approach to life. She was a spunky farm girl from Iowa who, according to her, married a city slicker with more money than brains. She hadn't seen Connie since the divorce, so there would be a lot of catching up to do. A lot of telling on Rita's part. Maybe it was time for her to talk, to confide in someone, and who better than Connie?

Rita felt twelve years old as she skimmed over the hills and fields that led to the Baker property. She brought the whizzing snowmobile to a smooth stop in back of the sprawling ranch-style house and beeped the horn that sounded like a frog. She had forgotten how much fun it was to ride on a snowmobile. She wondered what Brett was going to do with the machine he took from the garage when he moved out the contents. Maybe add a sidecar for Melissa so they could ride down Fifth Avenue on a snowy Sunday morning. She giggled at the thought and then laughed out loud.

There were kisses, hugs, fond looks, and tight grips on each other's shoulders as the two women stared at one another.

"Should we lie to each other now or later how neither of us has changed and we didn't get older, just better?" Connie grinned.

"Why don't we pass on that part and get down to serious talking." Rita laughed. "Tell me, what are you doing with yourself?"

"You know that big ox I married, the one who had more money than brains? He decided life was passing him by and he wanted to taste some of that young stuff out there. We divorced last year, and I'm happy to say that I took everything. Now, I understand his ladylove has taken a job in a drugstore to help pay the rent." Connie laughed, but it was a brittle sound and totally without mirth. "Don't feel sorry for me, Rita, I'm doing the best I can to be as happy as I can. Ask the kids!"

Why should I ask anyone? Rita wondered why Connie thought she wouldn't be believed.

"Hell, being forty-six going on forty-seven is

like being born again. Second time around, that kind of thing. Enough of me, tell me about yourself."

Rita sat down with a cup of coffee, propped her stockinged feet on a maple table, and proceeded to fill in her friend on her life during the past year. "I don't know how to handle it, Connie. Rachel is my daughter. How do I deal with that?"

"Just like she was any other woman. She's no kid, Rita. She knows exactly what she's doing. So, you're really caught up in this fella, are you? Tell me what this Twigg Peterson is like."

"He's terrific. Warm, sensitive, loving . . . all the good things I like in a man." Connie heard her friend's voice become soft and shy. Like a young girl's, she thought. "You would like him, Connie. Everyone seems to like Twigg," she said proudly. "I watch him with his friends, my friends. They respond to his sincerity and his concern. He treats people with respect. In some of those unconcerned and impersonal New York restaurants, I've seen waiters respond to his smile and courtesy. No small feat, I can tell you. There's genuine caring between his friends and himself. I saw this one night when he had the Donaldsons stay overnight at his cottage. He has a knack for making everyone feel special. . . ." Rita broke off in midsentence, running her fingers through her shining chestnut hair. "I'm running on like a schoolgirl."

"And you almost look like one," Connie said, eyeing her friend's slimmer waistline and pink, glowing skin. "God, if this guy of yours could bottle that magical rejuvenation he's given you, he'd be a millionaire."

"God, Connie, is that all you think about? Money?"

"It keeps a girl warm at night. Sure, what's wrong with thinking about money?" She said it lazily, offhandedly, but she watched Rita closely. If for one moment this Peterson man was thinking he had found himself a meal ticket, Connie personally would go down to the lake and kill him. When all was said and done, when all the looks were gone, what else was there besides a woman's children and financial security. She would never say this aloud to Rita. Being too much of a romantic, Rita never considered the practical side of life. How else had Brett managed to walk away with so much? Deciding she should steer the conversation along other lines, Connie asked, "Are you thinking of marriage?"

"It's never come up. . . ."

"I didn't ask if this Peterson proposed to you. I didn't even ask if it was something the two of you talked about. I asked if you were thinking about it."

"No . . . that is . . . I just don't know. I only know I don't want to be hurt again."

"Do you expect to be hurt?"

Rita looked at her friend, a claw of anger nicking at the back of her brain. "What kind of question is that?" she demanded.

"Hey, don't go getting your back up. I merely asked if you *expected* to be hurt."

Rita jumped to her feet, pulling her sweater down over her hips. It was a habit acquired from the time when the bulge around the middle needed hiding. "Dammit, Connie! I'm hurting right now!"

"How does this Peterson guy feel about you?" Connie pressed, disregarding Rita's obvious pain. If it was going to be painful, better it be here and now when there was someone to comfort her. Connie was too familiar with lonely, empty bedrooms where there was no one to hear the tears or hold back the loneliness.

Rita pulled a cigarette from Connie's pack and lit it, her hands shaking perceptibly. "I don't know how he feels," she said abruptly, exhaling. "No, that's not true. I *think* he loves me. He acts as though he loves me. Sometimes, when he makes love to me, he calls me his love. But what the hell does that mean, anyway? Men say all kinds of things when they're making love."

"I see. And, of course, you know this from your wide and varied experience, right?"

"Oh, shut up, Connie. No, don't shut up. I need you to help me." It was a cry, a plea, a dependency on an old friendship.

"Do you love him, Rita?"

"Yes, dammit. As much as I'll allow myself." It was the first time the question had been put to her and her own answer stunned her.

"But?" Connie asked quietly.

"But. Yes, there's always a but, isn't there? It's the age difference. I saw Twigg and Rachel having a snowball fight this morning. They both looked so young, so carefree. So young. My God,

Connie, he's only a few years older than Camilla!"

"By my calculations, he's nearly ten years older than Camilla. Quit being a martyr to your age, Rita. It snatches the hope away from the rest of us who've had their fortieth birthdays. And why do you consider the ten years between Twigg and Camilla so negligible and yet the ten years between Twigg and yourself seem so monumental? What's so earth shattering about a little difference in age?" Connie demanded.

Rita plopped down again on the sofa beside her friend. "Okay, you've got something to say. Say it."

"Look at Brett with his twenty-two-year-old wife and look at my ex with his younger-than-springtime girl. In a way, I do admire them. They went for it, as the saying goes. They didn't let me or you or their kids stand in their way. My ex is living on the poverty level with his drugstore queen, but they're happy, damn them. They're happy. Jake came over to see the kids one day, and he confessed that his lover has made him feel like a man, that she didn't care if he was rich or poor. That as long as they would be together they could live anywhere. And he bought it. This is coming from a guy who slept on silk sheets and drove a 450SL Mercedes, who didn't bat an eye at spending a fortune for a vacation. It was hard at first, but I discovered I can live without him and with his money and enjoy it. I wouldn't take him back for anything in the world. I like myself now, who I've become.

There's a whole world out there, Rita, a world we never knew about. I can see a difference in you too. You look like you're a person instead of someone's mother or someone's wife. Don't get me wrong, I'm not knocking marriage or mother-hood. I think marriage should be like a driver's license, renewable every few years, before it gets to the point we were at a couple of years ago."

"Have you really become so jaded? What about commitment to one another? What about love?"

"What about it? Commitment, I mean. If having a commitment means suffering, I don't need it and neither do you." Rita felt herself come under Connie's frank stare. "Wasn't that essentially what you were saying before? That you expect to be hurt?"

"No . . . yes . . . Christ, I don't know! I only know how I feel when I'm with him. How I feel when I'm in his arms."

Connie reached over to pat Rita's hand. "Then enjoy it, friend. Enjoy every minute of it and quit trying to play the odds. Be truthful and honest with yourself and him. Don't pretend to be something you're not. If you win, you'll have the satisfaction of knowing you've done it on the fair and square. If you lose, you'll have nothing to regret, wondering if you should have done this or said that. Games are for children, Rita, and they play by childish rules."

They sat for hours talking about their lives, their dreams and expectations. They discussed mutual friends, Rita's career, their grandchildren, and Connie's man-friend who had a lot of brains and absolutely no money. "He's a tree surgeon." She laughed delightedly. "And I want to tell you he's one hell of a hunk in bed. I get orgasmic just thinking about him. He actually listens to me when I talk. He respects my opinions and he thinks I'm as poor as he is. He thinks this place is my uncle's and the big house in Scarsdale belongs to my parents. I know my money would scare him off. He's a fine man, Rita, and I love him. You want to hear something crazy, something really off the wall?" Rita nodded. "I'm toying with giving my ex his money back and getting myself an apartment someplace and starting all over. The kids are all in college now or married. They're leading their own lives so I should be leading mine. I have a good job with the same advertising agency, and there's talk of making me a partner. With a lot of hard work I can make it. Joe thinks I can, anyway. If you know anyone who needs trees cut, let me know. He's fully insured so there's no problem."

Rita stared at Connie and then doubled over laughing. She laughed till the tears flowed. Connie joined in and then they were both rolling on the floor, laughing and crying hysterically.

"And those smart-ass kids of ours think we don't know where we're coming from," Connie gasped, wiping at her eyes.

"Or where we're going," Rita said through peals of laughter. "What time is it? I should be getting back."

"Why?"

Rita laughed again. "Beats me. It seemed like the thing to say. We've covered about all of it."

"How about a hot buttered rum before you start out? You'll freeze your tushy off if you go out there without being fortified."

"You got it. Don't spare the rum."

Rita looked at her watch. Her eyes widened in shock. It was three ten. Where had the time gone? Who cared; she'd had the time of her life and didn't regret one minute of the time she'd spent with her old friend.

It was two minutes after four on her digital watch when she drove the snowmobile into the garage. She was climbing out of the seat when the door opened. Twigg stood outlined in the doorway, Rachel beside him.

"Mom, where in the hell have you been?"

"Didn't you get my note?"

"Of course I got your note, but you didn't say where you were going!" Rachel said accusingly.

"You keep reminding me of my age, Rachel, and at my age I don't think I have to check in or out with you unless you want to show me the same courtesy."

Twigg and Rachel stood aside, but not before Rita saw the look of relief in his eyes. He cared.

"You smell like a distillery," Rachel snapped.

"Really. I suppose hot buttered rum will do that," Rita said by way of explanation.

"Where did you get those snowmobiles? I thought Dad took ours."

"I bought them. They belong to me. Any other questions, Rachel?"

"I was worried about you. I didn't even know we had snowmobiles."

Twigg's voice was soft, concerned, but not accusing. "Glad you got back in one piece. This child here wouldn't let me leave till you got back. I tried to tell her you were okay, but she wasn't buying."

Rita's eyes thanked him. She wondered if he had kissed Rachel. Or if Rachel had kissed him. It wasn't important. "Thanks for staying with Rachel."

"Any time. I've never been on a snowmobile. Would you mind taking me for a spin tomorrow and showing me the ropes?"

"Love to. What time?" Rita called over her shoulder as she made her way to the bathroom.

"Noonish, if that's okay with you. I have a little research I want to do in the morning."

"Sounds good to me," Rita called back as she closed the bathroom door.

Rachel's voice carried clearly and distinctly. "Hey, what about me?" she wanted to know.

"No sidecars. Guess you'll have to ski. Rita doesn't ski," Twigg said casually.

The silence was thunderous with the closing of the door. Rita switched the bathroom fan on and stripped down. The hot, steamy shower left her squeaky clean. She felt satisfied, even smug. She had really carried it off!

Chapter Nine

A state of undeclared cold war existed in the Bellamy cottage over the next few days. Rachel was in turns sullen and then ecstatic when Twigg spent time with her. Her eyes would fall sharply on her mother when she went out with Twigg to the ski slopes or the resort lodge for a few drinks and dancing. There was a gleam of triumph in Rachel's eyes when Twigg would ask Rita to come with them and she would automatically refuse. "Isn't he polite?" Rachel said on more than one occasion, and Twigg's eyes would fall on Rita with dark questions in their depths.

At these times of Rachel's brutal tactlessness, Twigg would watch Rita's face pale and see a shard of pain pierce her eyes. He would feel the impulse to take her in his arms, to kiss away the hurt. He could easily find excuses not to spend time alone with Rachel, but was that really Rita's answer? He didn't believe it was. Rita had to learn to trust him and to believe in herself as an attractive, desirable woman. If she saw younger women as her competition, she must learn to deal with it even if one of those young women was her daughter. To ignore Rachel or to pretend to dislike or be bored by her would be a lie and unfair. He could only hope that the next time he invited Rita to join them she would accept his invitation.

Rita's pain was sharp and acute and there was nothing to do for it. She took to insulating herself by cooking and cleaning and going to town with the laundry. Rachel knows, Rita guessed intuitively. She knows I've been sleeping with Twigg and she knows I care for him. And yet, it doesn't deter her from flirting with him, almost seducing him right under my nose. Don't do this to me, Rachel, she thought. Don't force me to a choice, because right now, I don't think I like you very much. Your "go for it" attitude should not include "going" for Twigg. Especially if you suspect he's become my lover and is very special to me.

The fault was not Twigg's. Rachel usually got what she went after. The captaincy of the cheerleaders, the big man on campus, the right job, the right friends. Once Rachel set her sights, there was no stopping her. How could Twigg be blamed? Rachel was young, vital, and exciting. And so very, very determined.

On Thanksgiving Day Rita was peeling carrots for dinner by the kitchen sink when she lifted her head and looked out the window. At the end of the property was a small gully. When the children were little they used to ride their sleds down the hill and then squeal with delight when they toppled into the gully. Rachel, cherry-red parka brilliant against the snow, was sledding down the hill, knowing full well she would topple over. Twigg was still on top of the hill, head thrown back, laughing.

As predicted, Rachel toppled, Twigg fast behind her. It was inevitable that he would lift her to her feet and that his lips would find hers. Or was it Rachel who leaned into Twigg's embrace? She stared a moment longer, her eyes misted, and she quickly moved away from the window. She didn't see Twigg push Rachel away, nor did she see him lift his eyes in the direction of the kitchen window. She wasn't sure what she felt, was uncertain as to what she should do. When in doubt, do nothing, she told herself. That's nothing, as in zero. Zilch.

"Why did you do that?" Twigg asked Rachel, anger ripping his voice.

"Do what?" Rachel feigned innocence.

"You know. Why did you kiss me like that? I like to decide who and when I'm going to kiss someone."

"For God's sake. You almost sound like my mother," Rachel pouted.

"Your mother happens to be a wonderful woman and a beautiful person and I value her friendship. In short, Rachel, I happen to like your mother, a lot more than I like you!"

Rachel was shocked; no one had ever said they preferred someone else to her. Much less her own mother! Not even her father, who adored his youngest daughter. "Have you been sleeping with my mother?" Rachel demanded. "You have, haven't you! I thought so! It's written all over her. Dear old Mummy. I can't believe it! God, you aren't much older than I am. What would you want with her?"

Twigg seized Rachel's arm, shaking her furiously, his face set and murderous. "Don't you talk about her that way. Why don't you open your eyes and see her for the lovely woman she is rather than just seeing her as your mother? She's been a friend to you, Rachel, and you've betrayed her, and I hope to God she never knows. What your mother and I mean to one another is no concern of yours. Is that clear?"

"Very clear," Rachel hissed, the fury of rejection beating wild within her. Was it true what he said? That her mother was lovely and wonderful? How could it be? Rita was already in her forties! She was old! *She was her mother!*

"Why can't you see her for the person she is, Rachel? Oh, I know you think you're a grown woman, but you are also a selfish child. Perhaps you are woman enough to give of yourself to someone you love deeply. But all of us remain children, selfish children, where our parents are concerned, making demands for complete love and total attention, forgetting that our parents are people first and parents second. Think about it, Rachel."

Rachel was humiliated. She didn't need this

man to tell her how to feel about her parents, much less how to feel about her own mother! "Very well, O lord and master, I will think about it!" she snapped, bowing from the waist in mock respect. "But before I do, tell me. Has my mother been properly grateful for the attentions of a young stud like you?"

At the rage suffusing his face, Rachel stepped backward. She hung her head in shame for her coarse remark. She liked Twigg and she loved her mother. It was only that she had never been rejected this way before, especially not in favor of her mother. Mothers were supposed to be self-sacrificing and interested only in their children's happiness. They weren't supposed to reach out and take that happiness for themselves.

"What you need, Rachel," Twigg was saying, looming over her, "is a good swift kick in the ass. A pity someone hasn't done it before now."

"C'mon," Rachel cajoled, "we were having such fun. Why spoil it? So okay, I'm sorry I got you in a clinch. I'll even tell old Mummy it was me who trapped you. She saw us, you know. She was standing by the kitchen sink. Probably spying."

"She wasn't spying. Rita would never lower herself. That's something you would do, isn't it, Rachel?" His tone revealed his total disgust.

"If it was important to me, yes, I would!"

"What about trust and faith?"

"You've gotta be kidding. The man hasn't been born a woman can trust and believe. Look what my father did to her. Even my own father!

And you call me a child, Twigg Peterson. You have some growing up to do yourself."

Twigg clenched his fists. He wanted to push her down into the snow and rub her face in it till she screamed for mercy. "If men are like that, Rachel, it's because of women like you. One more thing, if you so much as say one word about this incident to Rita, I swear you'll have to deal with me. Make certain you understand; Rachel. I mean it. I won't have Rita hurt."

Rachel stared into his challenging green eyes. What she saw frightened her. "Okay, staunch defender of middle-aged women. Now that you've spoiled the day, I think I'll go back to the house and read a book. A good book! None of that unrealistic crap my mother writes."

"Why are your mother's books so unrealistic, Rachel? Because she writes about relationships? Real people and their emotions and their love? Yes, I can see where that would seem unreal to you."

Twigg flopped down onto the Magic Flyer and wrapped his arms around his snow-covered knees. He stared at the kitchen window for a long time, willing Rita to materialize. He felt there was a large hole in his stomach that was gradually sucking up his chest. Whatever he felt for Rita Bellamy was stronger than any emotion he had ever felt for another woman. She was warmth. She was comfort. She was intelligent and loving; she was Rita Bellamy. His love. A part of himself that could not be denied. They had searched for, found, and touched each other. Was that love? He grinned. Yes, he was in

love, did love. This special, fragile woman whom
he yearned to protect and yet realized he admired. He wanted her to fulfill herself as a
woman, as a person. He wanted her to remain
in charge of her own life; he only wanted to
share it with her. There was no way around it.
He wanted to love her.

It was a small word, according to Rita. It didn't
take much space on a page, yet it was awesome.
It was a word capable of changing two lives, shap-
ing the destiny of both.

Twigg dusted off his pants and then picked
up the sled. He tramped up the hill toward the
Bellamy cottage. He wasn't sorry for the way he
had spoken to Rachel. It was time someone set
her straight. He leaned the sled against the side
of the garage. He opened the kitchen door and
shouted. "I'll see you later, Rita."

"Okay," she called back from somewhere deep
in the cottage. A sigh of relief escaped him. She
sounded fine. Trust and faith. She trusted him,
believed in him regardless of what she had seen
through the window. That was what it was all
about.

While the turkey basted itself, Rita curled herself into the deep love seat by the fire and
started to read. She was surprised, after an hour
or so, that she was really comprehending what
she was reading. She wasn't engulfed in the
scene she had witnessed.

Rachel walked into the room carrying two

cups of coffee. "When are we eating? I'm starved!" she complained.

"Then eat something. We're not going to eat till around seven. That's the time I told Twigg to come over."

"Why did you invite him anyway?" Rachel snapped.

"I invited him because I wanted to invite him. The two of us certainly cannot eat a thirteen-pound turkey. Thanksgiving is for sharing or have you forgotten?"

"It depends on what you're sharing." Rachel snapped.

"Is that supposed to mean something in particular?" Rita asked evenly.

"It means whatever you want it to mean," Rachel almost snarled.

Rita felt the most uncontrollable urge to slap her daughter and send her to her room. "Rachel, don't talk in riddles. If you have something to say, I suggest you say it and get it over with," Rita said levelly, her gaze keen and direct.

Rachel dropped her eyes. "For two cents, I'd leave and go back to the city, but the road to the highway is closed."

Rita made a mental note to call Connie and ask her to have her son plow her out to the main road. Nothing must keep her from Charles's game the next day.

"Why don't you take a nap till dinner is ready. I'll call you so you can mash the turnips."

"Call me after they're mashed. Let your friend Twigg do it, after all he's freeloading, isn't he?"

"No, he isn't freeloading. I invited him. However, if you want to get into technicalities, I don't recall inviting you. You called and announced that you were coming. Either keep a civil tongue in your mouth or don't speak. I mean it, Rachel. I've had enough of your sly innuendos. If you want to say something, now is the time to say it. If not, stay off my space."

Rachel stared at her mother, stunned at her words. She turned and fled as though a dog was snapping at her heels.

Exhausted, Rita fell back onto the couch. Damn, she hated confrontations. Especially with Rachel.

Twigg arrived early, eager to help with the last-minute preparations for dinner. He worked beside her in the small kitchen, sipping his wine and making small talk. Lord, how she enjoyed being with this man. She glanced up, seeing the window through which she had seen Rachel and Twigg kissing. It was dark now, mirroring Twigg and herself working happily side by side. Strange how the same window could look out to a hurt and look inward to a pleasure. Twigg followed Rita's gaze, meeting hers in the dark glass. As if knowing what she was thinking, he wrapped his arms around her, pressing his lips against her hair. "They look happy, don't they, that couple in the window. How lucky we are to be inside looking out."

She leaned back against him, feeling his warmth and recognizing the sweet, fruity aroma of the wine on his breath. Is that what we are, she asked herself, a couple? Is that how he thinks of himself and me? She looked again, seeing them reflected there. He was tall, leaning over her, holding her. She fit into the circle of his arms so naturally, so willingly.

"It's Thanksgiving, love," he murmured against the side of her neck, "and we have many blessings to be grateful for." His embrace held her fast and his lips found hers.

Yes, she thought, sighing, leaning against him, catching sight of the window again, there are many blessings, and the most precious one is you.

Dinner was delicious and enjoyable. Rita and Twigg talked animatedly, their eyes meeting and lingering. Rachel picked at her food, her mind otherwise occupied. From time to time Rita looked at her daughter and forced her into polite conversation.

Whatever had happened between Twigg and Rachel out there in the backyard, Twigg seemed to have handled it. Rachel was subdued and thoughtful but not hostile. At least not hostile or angry toward Twigg, Rita thought disdainfully. I'm another matter entirely. Somehow, I've disappointed her and I'm not certain how. She wondered, not for the first time, does Rachel guess that Twigg and I are lovers? Is that the source of the disappointment? That my morals are somehow lacking, unworthy of a mother? How easily these young people decide what's right for them and at the same time deplore and condemn the same values in their parents. It doesn't matter. Not really. Rachel, being Rachel, will soon come to terms with it. While the girl has never displayed prolonged loyalty or interest in any one person or thing, she also doesn't harbor ill feelings and anger. Whatever, it's Rachel's problem and she'll have to deal with it.

The conversation drifted around to the football game the following afternoon. "Why don't you go with Mother?" Rachel asked Twigg snidely. "I'm certain she'd love taking you with her and introducing you to all the family."

Twigg's eyes met Rita's. "In the first place, I have not been invited. Secondly, I have work to do." Silently, he told Rita that he realized it would complicate things if he were to go with her. She needed this time with Charles and her own feelings.

Wordlessly, Rita thanked him.

"How about a game of chess, Twigg?" Rachel asked as he took his pie plate to the sink.

"Later. I want to help Rita with the dishes. I know those three-inch nails of yours don't get themselves into dishwater," he teased.

Not for the first time Rita was aware that he usually referred to her by her name instead of saying, "I want to help your mother with the dishes." She was Rita Bellamy, to Twigg. Not Rachel's mother. How nice, just to be herself.

Later, Twigg played chess with Rachel while Rita busied herself with her needlepoint. She would feel his eyes fall on her, and when she lifted her head she could read the message they spoke.

*   *   *

When Rita awoke the next morning she looked outside. Connie had been as good as her word. Her oldest son, Dick, had arrived sometime during the wee hours and plowed the road.

Rachel could go back to the city now, if she chose. Yet Rita knew her daughter would still be in the cottage when she returned. Perhaps she herself would spend the night in a motel rather than make the long trip back on the same day.

Twigg was waiting for her when she drove the car around the bend. Rita rolled down the window. "What are you doing up so early?" she asked, laughing at his rumpled hair and the stubble of beard on his chin.

"I couldn't let you go off without telling you to drive carefully and to hurry back. You're very special to me, lady, I hope you know that."

Interstate 80 was free of snow, and Rita felt her shoulder muscles relax. It would be a good trip. She switched on the radio and heard Kenny Rogers singing "Lady." She grinned, remembering Twigg's departing words. She was glad he had kept it light between them. She didn't want any declarations of love and promises that couldn't be kept. Being "special" could mean so many things. It didn't necessarily mean love.

"Do you expect to be hurt?" Connie had asked her. Rita pulled her thoughts away from Twigg. She should be thinking about Brett and what she would say when she saw him. It had been a long time. Because of the tickets Charles had sent them, they would be sitting next to one another all through the game. Somehow, she would face it when the time came. She wouldn't worry about it now. Instead, she concentrated on Kenny Rogers and wished he would sing the song again.

Stopping at a restaurant for lunch, Rita delayed and lingered over coffee so she would arrive at the stadium just before game time. There was no point in arriving early and bearing up under the strain of spending all her time with Brett and his new wife.

Walking outside into the chill after the warmth of the restaurant, she was glad she had worn her mink jacket and high, fleece-lined boots. She wished Twigg was with her so the two of them could cheer for Charles. Twigg would like her son, and Charles would like Twigg. Perhaps, at first, there would be some resentment, but later they would learn to appreciate one another. She laughed uneasily. Whatever gave her the idea there would ever be a "later"? Now, and only now, was all that was important.

It was like old home week when Rita took her seat in the crowded college stadium. Surprisingly, Camilla and Tom were there. Brett hadn't yet made his appearance. Camilla wrapped her arms around her mother. "Tom said we had to come and root for Charles. We had a devil of a time getting tickets though. We're two rows ahead of you."

"I'm so glad you came, honey. Charles will be so happy to have all of us here. He has a girl," Rita whispered. "He's bringing her up to the cottage next weekend."

"We had our dinner with Tom's folks. I'm glad I came, Mom. Family is, and should be, very important." Rita steeled herself for Camilla's diatribe on family closeness, complete with charged and veiled statements concerning one's duty to family solidarity. Instead, she heard her oldest daughter say, "The kids miss you, Mom. Let's not be angry with one another. Maybe one of these days I'll understand and I'll handle it better. Just hang in there with me, okay?"

"Okay," Rita said softly, hardly daring to believe her ears. "You'd better take your seat. I'll see you later. They're tuning up for the 'National Anthem.' "

Tom put his arm around Camilla and looked at her approvingly. He leaned over from his tall, rangy height to plant a kiss on Rita's cheek. "Do you know how wonderful you look?" he asked.

She laughed; the sound was carefree and almost girlish to her own ears. "I feel wonderful, Tom."

"Daddy isn't here?" Camilla complained.

"He will be, don't worry. He probably had trouble getting a parking space. Are you warm enough? I brought a blanket."

"We did too. Keep it, it must be all of ten degrees."

There were three minutes to play in the first quarter when Brett arrived with his wife. Rita's eyes widened in surprise as he ushered Melissa past pairs of knees. "Rita," he said pleasantly, "this is Melissa."

"Hello." Rita smiled at the young, dark-haired woman. How young, was her first thought. How pretty and wholesome, was her second. How very, very pregnant, was her third! It was a shock, but not unpleasant. Funny, Camilla had never mentioned Melissa's pregnancy. Did she think her mother would be devastated by the news? Truthfully, Rita knew that only months ago it would have sent her into a panic and a depression. Now, since Twigg, she had gained a different perspective.

Brett looked happy. Happier than she had seen him in years. Contented. A contentment and excitement that she had once been responsible for, when she was young and hugely pregnant. And Brett looks younger too, she thought, softer and somehow more mellow. He's not fighting for his identity; his ego is intact. How awful it must have been for him when he was so insecure and uncertain of his place as her husband, of his masculinity and position as head of the household. Her career and its rewards had stripped him of that, she knew. Money was freedom and, according to Brett, possessed a masculine gender. Freedom was for men, just like power. She was glad to see he wasn't shattered by the changes she had wrought in his life. He had been and still was very important to both her and their children.

Melissa glanced up at Brett when he tucked a thick blanket around her knees. She adores him, Rita saw. Did I look up at him that way? Of course I did, when all I wanted from him was love and security. As soon as I wanted more, like support and understanding and respect, that's when he began to balk. Men like Brett revered women, they didn't respect them—there was a difference. Like gallant, white knights their image of themselves only shines through a woman's adoring eyes.

A sudden thought stunned Rita. Brett hadn't deserted her after all! He hadn't divorced her because he had found her lacking. No, to the contrary, he had found Rita, the young, adoring, dependent Rita all over again in Melissa! His new wife was probably the same person Rita had been at the same tender age!

Pleased with her realization, Rita sat back and watched the playing field. How nice to know that Brett had loved the life he had shared with her enough that he had actively sought to duplicate it. She had not been so much a failure as a wife and mother if he sought the same things in Melissa. Brett was positively beaming, proud as a rooster and just a little pathetic. What would happen, Rita wondered, if Melissa proved to be a "late bloomer" as she was?

"Are Camilla and Tom here?" Brett asked. "Where's Rachel?"

"Camilla and Tom are two rows ahead of us. Rachel is still up at the lake. She wants to do some skiing." She saw Brett's eyes go to his wife and her chattering teeth. Poor thing, her coat barely covered her stomach. She must be freezing. Rita removed the heavy plaid robe from her knees and nudged Brett. "Here. Give this to Melissa. She's cold."

Brett rewarded her with a smile. How well she

remembered those smiles. They used to light up her life during those early years. When had smiles ceased to be enough?

Melissa seemed a bit wary of taking her husband's ex-wife's blanket. "I'll just go down and squeeze in between Camilla and Tom," Rita said. "It was nice to see you, Brett. Very nice. Melissa, much happiness with your new baby." The young girl nodded and tried to smile, pulling the blanket closer around her. "Brett, why don't you take Melissa home? This is no time for her to get sick. I'll explain to Charles. He'll understand."

"If you think he'll understand, okay," Brett said, relieved.

"Before you go, can you spare a minute for Camilla and Tom? They'd like to say hello."

Brett looked at Rita, thinking how wonderful she looked. Fresher, more confident . . . something he couldn't put a finger on. There was a style about her, a certain flair . . . a man. It was a man! The thought saddened him. Rita had so much to offer a man, this he knew from experience. Warmth, tenderness, loyalty. Why hadn't she been able to offer him those things when they were married? Why had she insisted on pursuing that silly career? Melissa was holding on to his arm to keep her balance. No matter, Brett thought with certainty. He had Melissa now, and this time he was going to be certain *this* wife didn't get crazy ideas!

Camilla was stunned when she looked up at her father and stepmother. Her father hadn't said a word about the baby. Clearly, talking on the phone every day and seeing were two different things.

Melissa and Camilla hugged and Brett and Tom shook hands. It was obvious to Rita that they all shared warm feelings for one another and she realized she was glad. Brett had divorced her, not the children, and it would be unfair to expect them to take sides against their father. Brett lovingly assisted Melissa up the stairs to the exit, a protective arm about her. Camilla approached Rita excitedly. "My God, Mother, my kids will be that baby's nieces and nephews. Tom, say something!" Her husband grinned at Rita and went back to watching the game.

"Mother, say something."

Rita laughed. "Camilla, your father is deliriously happy. Let him enjoy it. You may feel uncomfortable for a while, but eventually you'll get used to the idea. Now watch your brother; he has the ball."

After the game in the Knife and Fork, the campus coffee shop, Rita waited along with Camilla and Tom for Charles and his girl, Nancy.

"I wonder what she's like," Camilla speculated.

"I'm kind of curious myself." Rita smiled.

"If I know Charles, she's probably centerfold material. He always goes for the flash." Tom grinned.

Charles walked in, his hair damp and slicked back. A young girl in a heavy jacket with a hood was beside him. How big he looked. How tiny she looked. There was an air of protectiveness about Charles when he gently pushed the girl forward. "Mom, Camilla, Tom, this is Nancy Ames. Nancy, this is my family. Where's Dad?"

Rita quickly explained. She dreaded the look on her son's face. Instead, she saw it split in an ear-to-ear grin. "You're kidding! That's great. Maybe it'll be a boy and I can take him under my wing."

Nancy slid into the booth. "I've read all your books, Mrs. Bellamy. I think they're super. All the girls in the dorm read them. We don't pass them around either; we each buy our own."

"That's so nice to hear." Rita smiled. Charles preened. His girl read his mom's books and liked them. Hell, what more could a guy ask for?

Was she mistaken or was there a new note of respect in Camilla's eyes? "Are we all set for this weekend, Mom?" Charles asked.

"All set. I even went out and bought two snowmobiles. His and hers, so to speak. That snow is going to be around for a long time. I'm glad you're coming up, Charles. I have a friend I want you to meet. His name is Twigg Peterson. I think you're going to like him." The statement bubbled out of her and she realized how good it felt to say those words. Charles and Twigg would like one another, and the thought pleased her. She wanted her children to know the man in her life. Seeing Brett again with her new confidence and this sense of herself had relieved her of the burden of the past. She could be free of old memories and ancient hurts and could look to the future. She could believe in herself and could trust in love. Twigg's love.

"I'd like to spend more time with you, but I have a long drive ahead of me. Camilla, call me next week. Remember, any time you want to come up, the door is open. Tom, take care of her for me. Nancy, it was nice meeting you. When you come up, I'll have a copy of the bound galleys for my new book. Perhaps you'd like to see what a book looks like before it gets to the bookstore."

"Charles, do you need anything?" she whispered in his ear as she hugged him.

"I'm okay, Mom. Dulcie sent the brownies. In fact, she sends a batch regularly now. I'll see you on the weekend. This Twigg guy, is he the one Rachel bent my ear about?"

"One and the same." Rita laughed.

"She struck out, huh?" Charles whispered in her ear. Rita shrugged. "You always were a class act, Mom." He kissed her soundly on both cheeks and then walked her to the door. "Drive carefully. It's supposed to snow again this evening."

"I'll be careful and, Charles, I like your girl."

"I knew you would. See you, Mom."

"See you, son."

Chapter Ten

Rita swung the car onto the interstate, hoping she could reach the lake before it began snowing again. It had been an enlightening afternoon, and she was glad she had gone to Charles's game. Seeing Brett and Melissa had relieved her of those last vestiges of guilt, and she felt lighter now, as if she had shrugged off a heavy cloak. Oh, she knew it wouldn't always be that simple; one just didn't wipe away over twenty years of marriage. But she was making a good start. The guilt she had carried for not being the wife Brett wanted and the mother her children expected was unfair and unjust. She would have nothing more to do with it. She hadn't traded her family and those she loved for the glory of a career or pursuing her own selfish interests. She was neither wife, nor mother, nor best-selling author. "Those are the things I do," she said aloud as though to reaffirm her decision, "those are things I do and not who I am."

Who am I? The answer came easily. I'm a woman who loves a man. I love Twigg. I'll fight for him if I must, even if my adversary is my own daughter. Twigg understood. She loved him and, more, she trusted him. Even with her innermost and tenderest of feelings.

Perhaps Connie had known what she was asking of Rita. "Do you expect to be hurt?" At the time, Rita had missed the point. The truth was that she did. Always had.

She'd expected to be hurt by her children just because they were all growing as people, no longer babies to be cuddled and burped. That was a rough one, letting go. If the fact escaped her before this, she now faced the truth. She had sold them short, each one of them, Camilla, Rachel, and Charles. She had sent out unspoken but clear signals that cried, Need me! I'm your mother! I'll always be here for you! Only Rachel had struck out on her own, becoming independent. And because Rita feared losing her altogether, she had catered to Rachel, refusing to censor, even silently, the girl's most selfish and promiscuous behavior.

Making loans she never expected to be repaid, buying expensive gifts, becoming an easily available babysitter . . . it all amounted to the same thing. She had demanded her children prove their love by remaining dependent upon her. And when she had had enough and withdrew, they naturally resented it. The whole pattern was destructive, both to them and herself. Thank heavens she had seen it before it was too late! She might have destroyed her children, sacrificed them to her own needs. And in the end when they turned on her, and they would have, she would have seen herself as their victim! Just the way her own mother felt victimized when Rita turned away from her.

Victim. It had an ugly, unpleasant sound. Was that what Connie had meant? Did she realize Rita expected to be a victim? Did she expect to be hurt?

Rita had expected to be hurt when she saw Brett again. Instead, the meeting had given her new insights about who she had been and who she was now. Was it her image of herself as a victim that kept her from admitting her love to Twigg? Was that the real barrier and not the difference in their ages?

The snow was falling steadily, thick, heavy flakes freezing to the windshield.

Rita kept her eyes glued to the road. She was a fool to start out in such weather conditions. God, where were the plows, the snow trucks with their ashes and salt? Home, eating leftover turkey, she answered herself. Annoyed with the radio, she switched it off. She didn't need to be reminded that driving conditions were hazardous. If there was anything to be glad about, it was that her car had front-wheel drive.

An hour to drive under normal conditions, two with this weather, possibly even three before she would make the Whitehaven turnoff.

She blessed the tiny red lights in front of her.

They were like a beacon for her and helped her
stay on the road. God, how her eyes ached. Her
shoulders were hunched over as she strained to
see through the driving, swirling snow. Fear-
fully, she noticed the sluggishness of the windshield wipers. Not ice, please God, not ice. If the
wipers froze, she was in real trouble.

A low rumble behind her made her look into
the rearview mirror. A snowplow. She inched
over as far as she dared to let him pass her.
Once the ash was spread, she could follow him,
providing he was going past Whitehaven. Surely,
he was just ashing the interstate and not the
turnoffs or side roads.

The wipers were freezing badly now and
needed to be scraped. Visibility, however, was
better as the glow from the truck's taillights pro-
vided her with a small beacon to follow. At least
she was staying on the road with the ash for trac-
tion.

It had been a long time since she prayed. Far
too long. To do so now seemed like cheating.
Instead, she blessed herself and said her children's names over and over. For the life of her
she couldn't remember the names of her grandchildren. For sure she would never make "Mother
of the Year." Mother of the Year would remember her grandchildren's names.

She couldn't see, the red lights in front of her
were now barely visible. Her back window was
full of snow and the side mirror frozen stiff with
ice and sleet. She had to stop and pray that if
there were anyone behind her, he would stop in
time.

Her fingers were numb in their thin leather casing as she tried to chip and pry at the frozen wipers. Tears gathered in her soft blue eyes and instantly froze on her eyelashes. There was no point in trying the passenger side. She did the best she could and climbed back into the car. The twin red lights were specks in the distance. She accelerated slowly and caught up to the snowplow. Her grip in the sodden leather gloves was fierce, and her shoulders felt as though she was carrying a twenty-pound load.

She drove steadily for what seemed like hours. The huge road signs were covered with snow. God, how was she to know when she reached the Whitehaven turnoff? There was something there, but what was it? A marker, an identifying mark of some kind. If only she could remember. A campground sign, that's what it was. She had to watch for a turnoff with a double sign. She switched on the radio and got nothing but static. She turned it off and felt like crying. How stupid she was. What if she had an accident and died all alone out here on an interstate highway? When would she be found? Who would mourn her? What would Twigg feel? What would he say? If only she knew. Crazy, wretched thoughts filled her mind as she continued to follow the ash truck.

She was so intent on planning her own funeral she almost missed the sign. A sob caught in her throat. She maneuvered the car slowly off the road and up the curving ramp. She turned right and saw the lights for the truck stop. Inching her way down the snowy road, she turned into the well-filled lot where the lights gleamed and sparkled like Christmas lights.

The warmth and steam from inside hit her like a blast furnace. She looked for a vacant seat and sat down. A beefy trucker moved his heavy jacket and looked at her sympathetically. "Bad out there, huh?" She nodded and ordered a cup of black coffee from the waitress. The young, friendly girl looked at her, took in the mink coat and designer boots. "Is your name Rita?"

"Yes, why?" Lord, she didn't need another fan tonight.

"Some guy's been in here six, maybe seven, times looking for a woman in a mink coat. You match his description. There's somebody out there looking for you, lady. He's like a phantom; he comes and goes on a red snowmobile."

"He's been riding up and down the interstate," the trucker with the heavy jacket volunteered.

"Said for you to wait if you got here before he got back. I wish my boyfriend would worry about me like that," the waitress said, placing the cup in front of Rita.

"Jody, and David, that's their names," Rita said triumphantly.

"Whose names?" the waitress asked, inching away from Rita.

"My grandchildren. What time was the man with the snowmobile last in here?"

"An hour at least, wouldn't you say?" the waitress asked the trucker.

"Yeah, a good hour. He's about due. We got bets on him around here."

"I bet you do. I have a kind of bet myself."
Rita smiled.

"He your husband?" the trucker asked curiously.

"No," Rita said quietly.

"Oh, one of those."

"Yeah, one of those." Rita grinned.

"Nothing wrong with that." The trucker grinned back.

"My sentiments exactly," Rita said over the rim of her coffee cup.

The door opened. Rita's head jerked up. Her world stood in the doorway.

"Hi, I heard you were looking for me."

"Didn't have anything to do. Lady, you scared the goddamn living hell out of me," Twigg said, sitting down next to her. His eyes never left hers. "You okay?" Rita nodded.

"You look like you're frozen," she said. She couldn't tear her eyes away from his.

"Frozen! I'm too numb to feel it if I am. They got bets running on me here, did you know that?"

"I heard. Drink this coffee," she said, pushing her mug toward him.

"The roads are impassable. I think we can both ride the snowmobile. Tight fit."

"I like tight fits," she said, her eyes still on his.

"So do I." His voice was husky and there were shadowy secrets in his eyes. She took his hands, warming them in hers. Her head fell against his shoulder and she felt his lips brush her hair.

Twigg heard her sigh, felt the treasured weight

of her head on his shoulder. She was quiet, so quiet. "Penny for your thoughts, love."

"I was just thinking that maybe it's time we talked about that small word," Rita murmured.

"Are we talking about that small word that's so awesome? You mean 'love'?" The shadows in his eyes lifted and he gazed at her sharply, steadily. There would never be a backing away with this man. His honesty would prevent it.

"That's the one."

"You ready to talk about it?" he questioned.

"I think so." Rita grinned.

"Don't think, Rita, my love. With me, you've got to know for certain."

"I *know* so. Let's go home."

"Your place or mine," he teased, that familiar, seductive glint visible in his eyes.

"Yours. I have a guest."

They laughed with each other, standing to leave the diner, eager to be alone with one another. Impetuously, Twigg took her into his arms, lifting her chin to kiss her softly on the lips. Rita was oblivious to the eyes and stares from the others in the diner; she only knew she was in Twigg's arms, being kissed by him, being wanted by him.

He hurried her out into the cold night. Their night. The snow was falling steadily, silently. Breathless, exhilarated by his nearness, Rita found herself once again in his embrace. She lifted her face for his kiss, unashamed to ask for it now, and she felt his lips trembling against hers.

He held her in the circle of his arms; she felt

him strong and tall against her. This was her love. He had waited for her to learn about herself. He had trusted her to do so. She now knew she didn't need to be a perfect, stereotypical mother. She did not need to feel guilty for wanting to be more than a wife and homemaker. What she did need, Twigg offered: to be a woman with him, the lover who touched her soul and knew her for the woman she was and not for the roles all women must play.

I love him, for all I am and for all I can be.

Free Spirit

Chapter One

Only the rustling of their bodies against the sheets and the soft sounds of their murmurings broke the silence of the night. She nestled against him, burrowing her head into the hollow of his neck, the silly strands of her pale blond hair falling over his shoulder. She breathed the scent of him, mingled with the fragrance of her own perfume. Her fingers teased the light furring of his chest hairs; her leg, thrown intimately over his, felt the lean, sinewy muscles of his thigh.

They were like light and shadow—she silvered, the color of moonlight, and he dark, like the night. He held her, gentle hands soothing her, bringing her back down from erotic heights.

It was the best of all times, this moment after making love, when all barriers were down and satiny skin melted into masculine hardness. This closeness was the true communion of lovers who had brought peace and satisfaction to one another.

Dory Faraday burrowed deeper into the nest of Griff's embrace. He drew her closer and she smiled. She loved this hunk, as she liked to call him. He was good for her in every way—understanding her and accepting her for the person she was.

"Want to talk about it?" Griff asked softly, as his fingers traced lazy patterns up her arm.

"I suppose we should. It's just that this is such a perfect moment, and I hate to tamper with perfection." She felt his smile through the darkness. They had discussed Griff's leaving New York for months, but now that the time had almost arrived, Dory was finding it hard to accept. Washington, D.C., was only forty-five minutes away by air, but this knowledge did not bring her comfort. Holding tightly to Griff, Dory whispered, "This is our last day. I'm going to miss you until it's time for me to join you. Up to now, everything has been so perfect. We had our work, our careers . . ." She stopped to dab at her eyes with the hem of the lavender-scented sheet.

"Shhh. Don't cry, Dory." His touch was comforting as he wiped away her tears with the tips of his fingers. "It's only a few weeks. D.C. is only minutes away, and we can talk on the phone in the evening. You said you understood." His wasn't an accusing tone, but Dory felt compelled to move and struggled to prop herself on one elbow to face him.

"I do understand, Griff. It's a golden opportunity for you and you had the idea long before you met me. You deserve this chance. You'll broaden your horizons and do the work you like best. It's just that I'm going to miss you. Simple as that. I also have a few qualms about telling Lizzie I want a leave of absence."

There was an anxious note in Griff's voice, and he reached to touch the silky strands of Dory's hair, rubbing them between his fingertips. "You aren't anticipating any problems, are you?" If he had been in a less romantic position, he would have crossed his fingers. How he loved this long-legged woman with the lithe cougar walk and one hundred sixty-two pairs of shoes. When she offered to take a leave of absence to join him in Washington, he had been more than pleased, but he was also apprehensive. Was it selfish of him to agree that Dory give up her prestigious position at *Soiree* magazine? He admired her independence and didn't want to infringe on her career. Life in D.C. would be different for her but, as she explained, it would also present new opportunities. That had made him feel better, but now he wished, for the thousandth time, that she would accept his proposal of marriage instead of opting for a live-in arrangement. At least he would see more of her in D.C. than here in New York, where Dory lived in her small but stylish apartment while he continued occupying his loft. If things worked out with his new partnership in the veterinary clinic and if Dory could find challenging work, perhaps she would change her mind. Marriage was what Griff really wanted.

"No, honey, I'm not anticipating problems with Lizzie. She's fair and I've worked hard. The magazine can hardly refuse me a leave of absence to pursue my doctorate, can they?" She rushed on, as though not wanting to entertain for one instant the possibility that her request might be refused. "I can do all the freelance work I want from Washington. Contrary to popular opinion, Griff, New York is not the *only* city in the world where a woman can find work. Meaningful work. Even if we live in Alexandria or Arlington, school and work won't be a problem." Her tone was only a shade less anxious than Griff's, and if the room weren't darkened, he would have seen her vivid green eyes cloud with questions. "You aren't having second thoughts, are you, Griff?"

"Good God, no!" He ran his fingers through his thick, chestnut hair, the soft waves falling over his wide forehead. "I just want you to be aware of what you're getting into. I'm going to be up to my neck in work for the first couple of months, and our long, lazy weekends are going to come to a screeching halt. The clinic is going to consume me, love. Rick and John are going to be just as busy, so you'll have their wives to keep you company. You're going to be pretty busy, too, going to Georgetown University and keeping house and freelancing. I'll help as much as I can, but I think we should find house-keeping help right off the bat. Don't you?"

Dory pondered the question. "Not right away. Let me settle in and then decide what I can and can't handle. It's going to work out, Griff. Let me take care of the domestic end of things and you concentrate on the veterinary clinic and your partners." She leaned down and found his mouth, delighting in the feel of his lips against hers and the slight abrasiveness of his mustache.

"I should be getting back to the loft." He stretched and squinted at the radium dial of the bedside clock. Three ten. His eye fell to the floor and the persimmon froth of her discarded nightgown. A lazy look veiled his expression as he lay back down and felt himself stiffening beneath the sheets. What the hell, he could just as easily leave an hour later. This was now and there were some things that would always be more important than sleep. Griff Michaels's Law. He smiled indolently, turning to gather Dory in his arms and nuzzle the softness of her neck.

Dory sensed his immediate mood change and allowed herself to be carried with it. One moment his arms cradled her, soothing her, the next they became her prison, hard, strong, inescapable. She loved him like this, when the wildness flooded his veins and she could feel it beating through him. It brought her a sense of power to know that she could arouse these instincts in him. She yielded to his need for her, welcoming his weight upon her, flexing her thighs to bring him closer.

His hands were in her hair, on her breasts, on the soft flesh of her inner thighs. He stirred her, demanded of her, rewarded her with the adoring attention of his lips to those territories his hands had already claimed. And when he pos-

sessed her it was with a joyful abandon that
evoked a like response in her: hard, fast, then
becoming slower and sweeter.

She murmured her pleasure and gave him
those caresses he loved. Release was there, within their grasp, but like two moths romancing a
flame, they played in the heat and postponed
that exquisite instant when they would plunge
into the inferno.

Dory rolled over and stretched luxuriously,
feeling vibrant and alive. Griff's vigorous lovemaking always left her ready to conquer worlds
and build universes. There was no point in going back to sleep now. She might as well shower
and get to the office early after a leisurely breakfast.

A wicked grin stretched across her lips as she
watched Griff dress. "You look better in those
jockey shorts than any Calvin Klein model. Griff,
how about doing a layout for *Soiree*?"

Griff laughed. "And have every female who
reads that racy magazine lusting after me? I
have all I can do to handle my bills, let alone
tons of fan mail. Besides, how would it look to
old Mrs. Bettinger when she sees it? God, she'd
never bring her cats to me again."

"Nerd. She isn't going to be bringing her cats
to you anymore. You're moving, remember? A
head shot? How about a beefcake layout?"

"I can see the headline now: 'Stud Michaels,
his own best endorsement.' "

Dory giggled. "It would be something to show
your grandchildren."

Griff frowned. She hadn't said "our" grand-

children. Immediately he erased the frown. Time.
Time would take care of everything.

His kiss was long and lingering. Dory clung to
him with a feverishness that surprised him.
"Don't forget we're going to the theater with my
aunt tonight."

Griff smacked his forehead. "It's a good thing
you reminded me. I forgot all about it."

"You're going to love Aunt Pixie."

"The question is, will she love me?"

"She's going to adore you just the way I adore
you. If there's one thing Pix is good at, it's sizing
up a man. You'll pass muster."

For a moment Griff wore a frazzled look.
"Dory, all those outrageous things you told me
about her. Were they true or were you putting
me on? It's not that I care, it's just that I want to
be sure to say the right thing to her. I really want
her to like me," he finished lamely.

"Don't worry. She's going to love you. And,
with Pixie you could never do or say the wrong
thing. She is outrageous. I used to think everyone had an aunt like her, but she's unique. I
don't know what I'd do without her. Anytime I
have a problem, she's there. She's been more of
a mother to me than my own mother. Look, if
you're really worried we could meet in a coffee-
house for a visit before going on to the theater.
Would that make you feel better?"

Griff nodded.

"Okay, I'll give you a call when we're ready to
leave. Now go home and stop worrying. Or are
you putting me on and what you're really worried about is this big change in your life?"

Griff grinned. "Lady, you know me too well. Of course I'm concerned. This is a major step in my life. I want it so bad I can taste it, but I still have butterflies when I think about it."

"Go home. Think happy thoughts," Dory said impishly as she pushed him from her. "See you tonight."

He was gone. For a brief moment it seemed as though the walls were going to close in on her, but she recovered quickly. He was gone but it wasn't the end. In more ways than one it was a new beginning. She felt confident, sure of herself and her new choices. Options were something she liked. Options were a part of her life.

Her nakedness was something else she was comfortable with as she padded out to the kitchen to prepare the two-cup coffeepot. She would soak in a nice warm tub and work on her checkbook while the coffee perked. Some French toast for sustenance, and she would be ready to face her day.

The warm, steamy wetness worked its magic as she deftly computed the numbers in her checkbook. It looked good. This month she had an even two hundred dollars left that she could invest. She was pleased with the way she had handled her finances. All her bills were paid, money was set aside for the next three weeks for lunches, cab fare, hairdresser, even a new pair of shoes if the mood struck her. She calculated her airline fare into her totals and still she was ahead. Her small portfolio was looking better and better as the months went on. She could exist for an entire year on her savings account alone if she suddenly found herself jobless. Not bad for a career girl who just turned thirty-one.

Dory attacked her breakfast the way she did everything, with energy and gusto, savoring each mouthful. She enjoyed everything about life, more so now that Griff was a part of it. An important job at one of the most prestigious magazines in the country, a wonderful relationship, money in the bank all gave her the confidence she needed to be part of the active life in New York.

She would miss it. But nothing was forever. Now the important thing was being with Griff and taking the proper steps to finish her doctorate.

While the breakfast dishes soaked, Dory poked through her walk-in closet. It was bigger than her tiny living room, and the main reason she had leased the apartment. She finally selected a fawn-colored Albert Nipon original. She loved the feel of the exquisite silk that was one of Nipon's trademarks. She scanned the specially built shelves holding her shoes. The sexy Bruno Magli strap shoe was the perfect choice.

When she left her apartment an hour later she was the epitome of the successful New York career woman. Her lithe cougar walk, as Griff liked to call her long-legged stride, drew more than one admiring glance. She was not unaware of her image, and she reveled in it as she slid gracefully into a cab, returned the driver's smile, and gave the address of *Soiree*.

Dory leaned back and closed her eyes for the ride uptown. Her thoughts were with Griff. Until he came into her life six months ago, she had been so busy carving out a career and seeing to her financial future that she dated rarely, preferring casual relationships that wouldn't get sticky. But all her good intentions fell by the wayside the moment she met Griffin Michaels. It was at a cocktail party given by Oscar de la Renta, and Griff had been dating one of the designer's models. He had looked so elegant in his Brooks Brothers suit and shoes that she had smiled. Loose was the only word that came to her mind at the time. He didn't exactly fit in with that crowd, yet he did. He wasn't impressed, of that she was certain; in fact, he seemed to be bored by all the surface glamour and sophistication. She had taken the initiative and introduced herself. Things progressed rapidly; within the hour he made his apologies to his date, who was hanging onto a male model, and he and Dory left together to have a drink at a small cocktail lounge.

It was a wonderful old-fashioned courtship. Long walks in Central Park, weekend dates that always ended at her front door at midnight or shortly thereafter. Delicious, searing kisses that left her breathless and wanting more were a way of life for six weeks until he finally seduced her. Or had she seduced him? It didn't matter now. Now they were truly together.

They found they had much in common. They both knew the words to all the Golden Oldies and often danced in her small living room to the beautiful songs. They loved the same writers and laughingly compared books. He loved walking in the rain as much as she did and regarded snow as the most wondrous thing in the world.

He never crowded her, never asked for more than she was prepared to give. He was patient and understanding, and Dory loved him all the more for it.

Wonderful, short, intimate phone calls from Griff in the middle of the day were something she treasured. Her penchant for sending Snoopy cards delighted Griff. He was pleased that Dory would take time out of her busy schedule to shop for just the right card and mail it at just the right moment. Both had laughed in embarrassment when they admitted that not only had they been thumb suckers but blanket holders as well when they were toddlers. Snoopy and his pals were a joy to read about in the Sunday comics over a long, lazy breakfast in bed.

The mutual concern they shared was Dory's most prized possession, if emotion could be considered a possession. She adored the tall, loose individual she called Griff. She was never sure how that adoration had turned into love, but one day she woke and looked at the man sleeping beside her and realized she loved him with all her heart. "For all my life," she had whispered softly, so as not to wake him.

Griff proposed after three months. She refused. She wasn't ready to commit herself to something as awesome as marriage. It would have to wait for a while. Griff said he understood, and smiled when she said she didn't want to move in with him or vice versa, not yet. She needed her own space, and so did he, didn't he? Again, he said he understood.

Her friends told her she was a fool. Here he

was, handsome as sin itself, a successful veterinarian with his own practice, money, no strings attaching him to someone else, great potential. But what did they know, with their on-again, off-again romances that left them teary-eyed and neurotic? Thanks, but no thanks. Time was on her side, or so she thought. Griff had been honest with her from the beginning, telling her that he would be giving up his New York practice to open a clinic in the Washington, D.C.–Virginia area with two partners. As soon as the clinic was ready, and he estimated the work would be finished within four months, he would be leaving. His practice was sold and he was staying on only until the new vet got the hang of things. He had been up front all the way.

"Here you are, miss," the driver said, leaning over the seat. Dory gave him a second dazzling smile that made him grin. "You have a nice day now, you hear," he said in a fatherly tone. Damn, he wished he was thirty years younger. He also wished he had more fares like her. Made your day when a pretty woman smiled. And this one didn't just smile, she beamed. A meaty lady in slacks two sizes too small huffed and puffed her way into his cab. He shrugged. You win some and you lose some. "Where to, lady?"

Soft early-morning sunshine washed across Dory's desk. The stark white paper stood out against the buff-colored blotter. Her request asking for a leave of absence. She still had an hour before her meeting with Lizzie Adams, the managing editor of *Soiree*. Was she gambling with her future? Was she doing the right thing? Or was following Griff to Washington the wrong thing? That was a negative question and negative thoughts had no place in her life. She hadn't gotten where she was by entertaining negative thoughts. The word "no" was one word she simply refused to recognize. She was a positive person all the way.

Dory stood up and met her reflection in the smoky-mirrored wall. She was attractive by some standards, beautiful by others. Chic, elegant, fashionable were compliments paid to her by the staff. But it was those people closest to Dory who realized that her beauty came from within. Serenity, confidence, success were the traits that made Dory Faraday beautiful.

She straightened the soft silk at the neckline of the Nipon dress. Any designer would have gladly dressed Dory just for the pleasure of seeing his creations shown off to perfection. Bruno Magli would have been pleased to see his soft kid shoes worn on such pretty feet. There was no need for jewelry at the long, slender throat, nor elaborate makeup and a styled hairdo. Dory was naturally lovely. In the world of slick sophistication and cosmetic beauty, Dory Faraday was one of a kind.

The hazy gray mirror lost the reflection as Dory turned to scan her surroundings. She was going to miss this peaceful, charming office where she spent so much of her time. Decorated in earth tones with splashes of vibrant color, it lent itself to the serenity that was Dory's trademark at *Soiree*. Emerald ferns graced the corners of the office, wicker baskets and tubs held flowing greenery. Everything in the room, including Dory, blended like a chord in a symphony.

In the space of fifteen minutes Dory took three phone calls, penciled corrections on a lipstick layout, and nixed a model's see-through blouse. She sat back, her hands folded on the desk while the model ranted and raved about the desirability of the tasteless blouse. "The blouse goes," Dory said crisply, "and so do you if you don't wear the one your ad man sent along with your folio. Take it or leave it."

"Okay, okay," the model snapped as she grabbed the offending article from Dory's desk. "You aren't the last word, Miss Faraday," she shot over her shoulder as she made her way to the door.

"I am if you ever want to do another ad for this magazine." There was no mistaking the ring of steel in Dory's voice. The model hesitated a second and then raced from the office. Dory sighed.

"I heard all that," Katy Simmons laughed as she sailed into Dory's office. Katy was Dory's right hand—keeper of the files, confidante, mother hen, provider of low-calorie brownies. She had been with *Soiree* from Day One and was fond of saying that Dory was the only person she could get along with because Dory knew what she was doing and didn't let people walk all over her. "How's it going today? Never mind, you look like someone gave you the moon and the stars for a present. I hate people like you," she grumbled good-naturedly. "Just tell me how the hell you manage to look so gorgeous at eight thirty in the morning with no makeup. It takes me hours and hours and then I always look like I slept in a park and got dragged by a stray dog."

"You're being too hard on yourself, Katy. And I'm not so dumb that I don't know you're fishing for a compliment. Yes, you have gorgeous eyes and, yes, you have a wealth of hair that I would kill for. Now, does that make you feel better?"

"Sort of." Katy sniffed. "Want your schedule?"

"Why not. I just pretend to work around here."

"First, you have a meeting with Lizzie. I allowed forty-five minutes for that. She wanted an hour but I said no way. You're having lunch with two digital-advertising execs and are they something. Hunks, both of them. Look sharp. You have a two-hour meeting after lunch so don't be late. A layout presentation after the meeting. Somebody from Dior is having a bash, and it would be a good idea if you made an appearance. It was Lizzie's idea—she can't go. She's all booked up with out-of-town clients who are demanding more space but don't want to pay for it. Some new models are downstairs, modeling jeans. They want you to take a look-see and give them your opinion. I told them you wouldn't be caught dead in jeans but they wouldn't listen. I picked up the two new profiles for the spring issue and they need your pencil and approval. Whenever is okay. Today, if you can. And, if you have any extra time this evening, I have tickets for the theater that some turkey sent here for you. He said he'd meet you in the lobby at curtain time. I guess that's about it. Now, what do you want *me* to do today? I have this headache and one of my corns is killing me, so take that into consideration when you unload on me."

"Cancel the turkey with the tickets. I'm already going to the theater tonight. Go back to the lounge and take a catnap. I can handle things here. Send Susy in and she can send some e-mail I didn't get done yesterday. That's an order, Katy."

"Yes, Ms. Faraday," Katy drawled as she left the office.

The door opened and a breathless young girl breezed through as though blown on the wind. "Gee, Miss Faraday, do I really get to help you today? Katy said she was too busy. I love that dress and those shoes are out of this world. You're just gorgeous, you really are. Everyone says so. They all talk about you out in the front office."

Dory smiled when the girl finished. "Do you know you said that all in one breath? Amazing. Thanks for the compliments, and you can thank the girls in the office for me too. This is what I want you to do." Quickly she outlined the work, ending with instructions to water the plants and make coffee. "I have a meeting with Lizzie and I know she could use some about now. Refer all my calls to her office. Why don't you work here at my desk while I'm gone."

There was reverence in Susy's eyes. Wait till the girls outside heard she was not only working at Dory Faraday's desk but also watering her plants and making coffee. She'd be the talk of the office for a week. Someday she was going to be just like Dory Faraday. She could feel it in her bones.

The plaque on the door read LIZZIE ADAMS, MANAGING EDITOR. Dory rapped softly and opened the door. She held the stiff paper in her right hand at her side.

"Dory, come in. Coffee?" She looked around vaguely as though expecting it to materialize out of nowhere.

"I told one of the girls to bring some up. It should be ready soon. I've got a full schedule today, Lizzie, so I'll get right to the point. I would appreciate it if you would give me a leave of absence." She laid her written request on the dark green blotter and waited for Lizzie to say something.

Lizzie was a chunk of a woman. From the neck down she was all one size. Pudgy, she called herself. But people never seemed to notice her size; they kept looking at her face. She had eyes the color of warm chocolate and the thickest eyelashes Dory had ever seen. A flawless complexion and perfect white teeth. Hair that was clipped short and blown back from her face. She looked sixteen while, in fact, she was thirty-six.

"Why?" It was a question, a demand, a don't-give-me-any-crap answer.

Dory swallowed hard. "I want to work on my doctorate."

"Just like that. No warning, no nothing. You just walk in here and ask for time off. I asked you why? How much time?"

Dory stared at Lizzie, not understanding her attitude. They had always gotten along. Why was she being so dogmatic about this? Dory's stomach churned. Lizzie would understand about the doctorate but she would never understand Dory wanting to follow Griff to Washington. No one at *Soiree* would understand something like that. The doctorate really was her main reason for the leave of absence. The timing was perfect; she could live with Griff.

"I told you, Lizzie, to pursue my education until I complete it. That's the best answer I can give you. If you can't hold my job, I'll understand."

Lizzie leaned across the desk. "Does this have anything to do with Griff? Level with me, Dory."

"I'm going to move in with him. I'll be studying at Georgetown, so it will work out all around."

"You think so, do you? If you thought that, why aren't you getting married?"

"I'm not ready for that kind of commitment yet, Lizzie, This is what's best for me right now. For me, Lizzie. No one else."

"What if I told you I was leaving here in six months and planned on having you step into my job? What would you say to that?"

"I'd be stunned," Dory said truthfully, her green eyes widening in surprise.

"Then look stunned. You know, open mouth, insert foot, raise your eyebrows and all that."

"Are you serious?"

"Damn right I'm serious. Who did you think I would pick?"

"I never thought about it. I didn't know you were leaving."

"Jack and I finally got the adoption agency's approval. They said they would have a baby for us in six months. I can't work and raise a baby too, so that puts my job up for grabs. You're the logical person to take over. Now you floor me with this. Are you sure you know what you're doing? Six months, that's all I can give you. I'd like five with a firm commitment but I'll settle for the six."

"Lizzie, this will be my last chance to go for my doctorate. If your offer holds and I take the job, I could bring new focus to the position. You know I never do anything halfway. Do you want an answer now?"

"I think you're capable of giving me an answer now. That's why I hired you in the first place. I've never regretted that choice, Dory, not once. You've proved yourself time and again. You're like me. You can make a decision and live with it. I have to know and I have to know now so I can start scouting for a replacement. Six months. You can finish that degree at Columbia, can't you? And, just so you don't get too wrapped up in this live-in relationship, I think you should consider doing some freelance work in the meantime. Take a look at this. It came down from on high today."

Dory scanned the printed words and then laughed. "You're one shrewd fox, Lizzie. That's called covering your tail, in this business."

"Look, Dory, I think I've known all along that you were planning this move. You're right. This might have come down from on high, but it was my idea. Who better than you to do a few profiles on eligible, handsome senators and congressmen? Pay's good too. Top dollar. A person could live a full year on what you'd make, say on just four of them. Quality, of course. Standout casual pics, that sort of thing. Say you'll take it so I can let my ulcer rest."

"Okay, but it means I'll have to work like hell."

"Dory, when do you plan to leave?"

"I'd like two weeks, but if you need three, I can handle that. That should be more than enough time to break in Rachel Binder and Katy will be there to take up any slack. You do agree with Rachel as the logical choice, don't you?"

"No question about it. Two weeks it is. Will that give you time to sublet and handle all the mundane details of moving?"

"I can manage. Weekends I'll be going to D.C. to help Griff and find some place to live. Lizzie, I'm grateful, I truly am. I was hoping you'd be fair, but *generous* and fair is something I didn't count on."

"Listen, I'm being selfish too. I might want to come back here someday and I don't want to burn any bridges. You're good, Dory, and there will be no qualms around here. I'll feel right turning it over to you if that's your choice. I want you to promise me something. I want you to call me in three months and tell me how it looks from where you're standing. You owe me that."

"That's fine with me. I'm afraid I've been lax in not congratulating you on the adoption. I know how long you've waited for this. Jack must be delighted."

Lizzie laughed as she toyed with a pencil. "He's got the room painted and decorated. He bought a rocking chair and is sanding it down. Supposedly, it's some kind of antique and hundreds of years old. Can you just see me in a house with antiques?"

Dory laughed as she looked around the starkly modern office. Chrome and glass were everywhere. "Give it time, you might learn to like it. I'm going to miss this place. You've all been good to me. It's hard to say good-bye."

"It is just temporary, isn't it, Dory?" Lizzie asked in a pinched tone.

"I don't know. I'll call you in three months and that's a promise."

"Here's our coffee. Put it here on the desk, Susy."

Lizzie poured, then blew softly into her cup, watching Dory over the rim, her eyes full of unasked questions. "Damn it, I want to know more, Dory. Call it curiosity, concern or just plain nosiness. Somehow I didn't think you were the type for a live-in relationship. I'm not saying it's wrong. For me, sitting where I am, it just doesn't compute. And going back to school. That's a mind-bender, right there. Do you have any idea of what size chunk you're biting off? You're leaving the city and your job, you're going into a live-in relationship, and you're going back to graduate school. It's a goddamn mind-bender is what it is. I always knew you had guts and if anyone can do it, you can. I just hope that you've looked at all sides of it. I don't want you to have regrets later. Consider me a sister now and not your managing editor."

Dory leaned over the desk, her face earnest and sincere. "I have thought about it. I have to admit I had some doubts. I still have a few but I have to take a shot at it. I love Griff. That's my bottom line. As for marriage, maybe I love him too much to marry him right now. I never do things halfway, you know that. And you know how important my doctorate is to me. I can't keep putting it off forever. I'll give it my best shot and go on from there."

Lizzie sipped at the hot coffee. "This stuff is mud. My ulcer is going to complain. I like you, Dory, I always have. Everyone here on the staff thinks highly of you. None of us would stand in your way. Hell, what I'm trying to say is if for some reason things don't work out, don't wait six months. Saving face is not an American trait."

Dory smiled. "I'll remember that. It's nice to know the door is open. But I can't make any promises."

"You're really sure you need that doctorate? How long will it take?"

Dory flinched. She really didn't want to talk about going back to school. Not now anyway. "I only have another year to go. When I copped out that last year and came to work here it was the right thing to do at the time. I'd had enough of school and working part-time. I cheated myself, I know that now. I've always been sorry I never finished. I'll handle it."

Lizzie looked at her sharply but dropped the

subject. "I wish you the best, Dory. I hope things work out the way you want them to. We'll keep in touch."

"Thanks, Lizzie, and my best to you too."

Lizzie stared for a long time at the chair where Dory had been sitting. Blunt fingers with squared-off nails tapped at the smooth surface of her desk. The conversation ricocheted around her brain. The blunt fingers tapped faster. Suddenly the fingers stilled and a wide grin split her features. Her money was on Faraday.

Back in her own office Dory closed the door behind her. For some reason she felt cold and clammy. An interview, a conversation really, with Lizzie shouldn't be having this effect on her. Lizzie was on her side. What more could she want or expect? She slid into her chair and leaned her head back. Why was she feeling so light-headed? Taking a deep breath, she lowered her head to her knees. Another deep breath. Her mouth was dry, as if she'd eaten too much peanut butter. She didn't like what was happening to her. Was this some kind of warning? Surely it couldn't be an anxiety attack. Only people like her mother had anxiety attacks. Why would she have one? Things were going smoothly. Everything was falling into place. She almost had the world by the tail. Her breathing was almost regular now. Paper bags. People used paper bags when they hyperventilated. Was that what was happening to her? Was that the same thing as an anxiety attack? What did you do if you didn't have a paper bag? Exactly what she was doing. Nothing. A picture of

herself carrying a brown grocery bag in her
purse made her smile. "Just take the bag out of
my purse and put it over my head." God, what if
she had to say that to some stranger? Never! Get
it together, Faraday, she told herself firmly. Pick
up your head and wipe off your hands. Handle
it. *Take control.* Don't *lose* control.

It was a good ten minutes before she felt normal. Now she leaned her head back and closed
her eyes. Managing Editor. Jobs like that only
came around once in a lifetime. It certainly was
something to think about. It was also something
to keep to herself for the time being. She wouldn't
share it with Griff now, especially when he was
just getting started in his new job. What a long
way he had come from the days when he worked
for the ASPCA. She wouldn't do or say anything
that could put a blight or a shadow on his confidence or happiness. For now, Griff had to come
first. Would her successful career be as appealing if Griff were not in her life? Would a life with
Griff but without a career for herself be appealing? She didn't know, wasn't sure. For now, she
could have the best of both. She was a reasonably intelligent woman and she should be able
to handle both the man in her life and her career. It was something she really wanted, to return to school and finish her degree. But was
that really true? Or was she using school as an
excuse to go with Griff? The thought bothered
her. It was the perfect time and the perfect opportunity. But was she really ready to go back to
the academic life? *Really* ready? She shrugged. It
felt right and that would have to be good enough.

If it proved to be the wrong decision, she would handle it. Griff seemed to sense how important her doctorate was to her. Could that have something to do with her decision to go back to school? *She didn't want to disappoint him.* He found it admirable for a woman to pursue education, and she believed it brought their relationship to a more equal level. He already had his degree in veterinary medicine; she would soon hold a doctorate in the humanities. No, she couldn't disappoint Griff. It had to be Griff and Dory. Equals.

By the end of the day news of Dory's plans had spread through the entire fifteenth floor. She knew this had been engineered by Lizzie who, by showing her approval, sanctioned all the good wishes and congratulations of Dory's colleagues. David Harlow, the editor of *Soiree*, stopped by to congratulate Dory and offered her drinks and dinner at Le Bernardin the following day. In essence, this was an open declaration that *Soiree* would always welcome Dory back with open arms.

Dory was overwhelmed by Harlow's offer. In her eight years at *Soiree* she had rarely been in the man's presence. Several wild and exhilarating Christmas parties and one summer picnic hardly counted. David Harlow was a commanding, dynamic man who generated office gossip concerning his private life. Two wives and twice as many mistresses were attributed to this rather short, nattily dressed man with the bruised circles under his eyes. Because of the authority and timbre in his voice a person forgot about the road map of veins in his cheeks and nose and the beginning of ponderous jowls.

"I'd like that, Mr. Harlow," said Dory as she accepted his invitation. Although she wasn't eager to spend an evening with this man, she realized it would be inopportune to refuse. Especially for Lizzie's sake. Dory's replacing Lizzie as managing editor would require Harlow's blessing and now was as good a time as any to pave the way.

He didn't smile or brighten at her acceptance, nor did he ask her to call him David. One didn't call Mr. Harlow David. Ever.

Jewel-bright eyes flicked over Dory's attire; he seemed to register satisfaction. "Fine," he told her, his voice conspiratorially muted, "I'll stop by around seven tomorrow and we can catch a cab from here."

Dory sat quietly for a few moments considering the brief exchange of words. For some reason she felt vaguely disgruntled. Katy always said it would take an act of Congress to make the big guy step down to the fifteenth floor to chat with the underlings. Was her leaving and the offer of Lizzie's job equivalent to an act of Congress?

The late afternoon sun slanted into the spacious office, turning the plants into shimmering green jewels. Dory looked for dust motes but could see nothing but the band of light that seemed to laser through the wide window. She suddenly felt claustrophobic—as though she were trapped in a paperweight, the kind she had when she was a child that snowed tiny flakes when you turned it upside down. An overwhelming urge to talk to Griff washed over her. She drew in her breath, not understanding the feeling.

Katy bustled into the room, jarring Dory from her deep thoughts. She closed the door behind her and flopped down on the chair next to Dory's desk. With the door closed they could indulge in familiarity. "I'm impressed. So is everyone on the damn floor. God, do you have any idea of the stir you just created? By the weekend, according to rumor, you'll either be having a raging affair that's been going on for years or going off on a 'business trip' with Big Daddy Harlow. Le Bernardin, no less. Mr Harlow's secretary told Lizzie's secretary who told Irma who told me. What do you have to say about that?" Katy grinned.

"With a network like this who needs AT&T? I was as surprised as you are. I've only spoken to him once or twice and both times it was at a Christmas party. He's being nice. Don't give me problems, and for God's sake shut the girls up, will you? You know how I hate gossip."

"I'll do my best but it's going to be a lost effort. Wouldn't you rather assign me to something else?" Not waiting for a reply, Katy rushed on. "I was going to invite you over to the house for dinner, but I can't come close to Le Bernardin in decor or food. So enjoy. We'll get together before you leave. How did it all go today?" Her question was serious and Dory, long used to Katy's moods and questions, fell into the called-upon role.

"Good. Lizzie really surprised me. It's going

to take some getting used to, I can tell you that. It's a chance of a lifetime, but so is going for my doctorate. I won't deny that I have a lot of thinking to do. Did you know about the adoption and the offer?"

"I had an inkling. Lizzie's secretary spread the word that an adoption agency has been calling Lizzie for several months now. That was something no one wanted to discuss because if it didn't come through for Lizzie we would all have been devastated. You know how badly she wants a baby. And who but you is capable of stepping into her job?"

"They could have brought someone in from outside. I was stunned. I had no idea whatsoever. This has been a day to end all days."

"The day isn't over. You still have dinner and the theater, and then there's tomorrow—dinner with the big boss. You will tell me what it was like, won't you? I won't sleep a wink tomorrow night, worrying about you."

"For heaven's sake, Katy, why would you worry about me having dinner with Mr. Harlow?"

Katy pursed her full lips till they resembled a rosebud. "Because Mr. Harlow was just divorced and divorced men get lonely and for God's sake, Dory, do I have to tell you that men, important men like David Harlow, sometimes bring pressure to bear on lowly employees to get . . ."

"My sexual favors?" Dory laughed. "Don't worry. I'm sure it's nothing like that. This is strictly business, I can feel it in my bones."

"That's what Cassie Roland thought," Katy mumbled.

"Okay, who's Cassie Roland?"

"Cassie Roland is the girl in the publicity department." Her voice dropped to a whisper. "They say Harlow lured her back to the stacks after closing time and had her bloomers off in the wink of an eye."

"Katy, I'm surprised at you for repeating such gossip. Did they get caught?" She giggled.

"Why do you think he was just divorced? Where in hell have you been for the past eight years? Everyone knows you can't get a job in publicity unless you sleep with Harlow."

"I never pay attention to rumors like that," Dory said. "Where's Cassie Roland now? Did she get a promotion?"

Katy doubled over. "She sure did. She lives in the Dakota and is driving a Mercedes S550. She *says* she's doing freelance work."

Dory's stomach churned. "I'll handle it."

"Will you be going to D.C. this weekend?"

"I'm going to leave early Friday. Griff's partners' wives have been lining up apartments for us to look at. Griff will be staying with John for the time being. He hasn't even left yet, but I already miss him. Just knowing he won't be here in the city after tonight gets to me."

"And yet you say you aren't ready for marriage. I don't understand you, Dory. You're obviously crazy about the guy, yet you won't marry him. A live-in relationship could get sticky. You know, everyone isn't as liberal as we are. How much do you know about his partners' wives and the other women you're going to be associating with? Not much, right? I'd hate to see you get hurt, Dory, or dumped on, for that matter. I suppose you're sophisticated enough to handle it all, but is Griff? He seems like such a sweet guy, and he's going to be hanging out with some pretty influential people if he goes into equine medicine. You're talking about political clout, old money. Look, I'm talking to you like a mother, now. You can't just think about your-self—you have to think about Griff. Don't get so involved you can't walk away. I want to make sure that whatever you do you do for the right reasons."

"It will be for the right reasons, believe me. I've been honest with Griff and he's been hon-est with me. He says he understands and will wait for me to make my mind up. I didn't jump into this. I've given it a lot of serious thought. For me now, at this point in time, this is my best move. I'll deal with later when later comes. All I know is I love him and I love my career. I have to find a way to combine the two of them, and going back for my doctorate is the first step. It's the best I can do for now. Everything is up front. Neither of us would have it any other way."

"Okay, I can buy that," Katy said, sinking deeper into the leather chair. One shoe slipped off and she sighed with relief. "If I could just take off about twenty-five pounds, I know my feet wouldn't hurt so much." She grimaced. "How you manage to walk around in those three-inch heels is beyond me. What's the shoe count this month? I picked one hundred sixty-six in the pool. Just tell me if I'm close."

Dory laughed. At first she had been less than

amused when she found out the girls in the outer office were running a pool on her shoes. Then she had been flattered when they continued the practice. "No way. Pay your money and take your chances like everyone else."

"Much as I'd like to chitchat some more, I have to clean up my desk, run down to copyediting, and then it's home for me and the love of my life. I'm referring now to my cat, Goliath, not my husband. We're not speaking. It was his turn to do the laundry last night and he copped out. He said his back hurt. He's starting to give me that 'women's work' routine. It isn't sitting too well with me."

"That's because you make more money than he does. I told you, every dollar you earn above his is a dollar's worth of power. Guess you're going to have to turn down your next raise. You're due next month, aren't you?" Dory's voice was light, teasing, but there was something in her eyes that made Katy think twice before she answered.

"I would never turn it down. I would, however, do some serious reevaluation of my marriage."

Dory said nothing, but her eyes were sympathetic as she watched Katy bend over and struggle to slip her swollen foot into her espadrille. She winced and Dory looked away. "I'll see you in the morning and thanks again for the invitation."

"Any time," Katy said, limping from the office.

The end of another day. For some reason Dory felt saddened at the thought. There weren't too many days left. She couldn't start thinking wishy-washy thoughts now. The die was cast; she was leaving. Maybe she would return and maybe she wouldn't. For now she had an evening with her aunt and Griff to look forward to. His last night in town and he was generously offering to share it with her and her aunt. It pleased her that he was going to the theater after a busy day and all the last-minute details that had to be taken care of before he could leave in the morning. That was so like Griff. He really put out for her in more ways than one. And, in her own way, she did the same thing. It was give and take. Griff wouldn't exactly "suffer" through the play but she knew he would rather be doing something else. Thoughtful, kind, wonderful Griff.

Dory straightened her desk as she made her brief call to Griff to arrange their meeting in the coffee shop. He was agreeable as always. "Love you," Dory said softly.

"Yeaaaaaah," Griff drawled.

Dory knew when Pixie walked into the coffee shop, even though she couldn't see her. Pixie's entrance had created a hush. Dory smiled. There was no doubt about it. Pixie was an attention getter. She stood up and waved. "Over here, Pixie."

"My God, you look stunning, Dory. You do take after our side of the family. I'm not late, am I?" she asked, looking around. "Where's Grit? He is coming, isn't he?"

"Of course. He'll be here any minute now. Good Lord, wherever did you get that outfit? Is that a new wig? Those aren't real diamonds, are they? Is that cape really lined with ermine?"

"One thing at a time. You wouldn't believe me if I told you. Yes, the wig is new. I always wanted a black wig. I had to take this one because all the others made me look like Cher. I'm as skinny as she is but there the resemblance ends. I had to glue it. There's a high wind out there. Of course these diamonds are real. Your mother would give her eye teeth for them. I needed a cape and this was the only one I could find. What difference does the temperature make? The theater will be air-conditioned. You can wear ermine any time, any place. What are we having to drink?"

"Coffee. Here comes yours."

Pixie looked around to see if alcoholic beverages were served. Seeing nothing but a coffee urn, she rummaged in her bag and came up with a silver flask. She faked a sputtery kind of cough and poured liberally for the waitress's benefit. "Medicinal purposes."

"If that's your story, it's okay with me," the waitress said wearily.

"Smart-ass." Pixie grimaced.

Dory stifled a laugh. "Here's Griff."

"You didn't tell me he was this good-looking," said Pixie. She held out her hand to Griff. "Be continental and pretend you're kissing my hand. I do so love attention. Look at these poor starved souls in here. This will be something for them to talk about for days."

Griff swallowed hard as Dory made the introductions.

"It's all right, young man. I usually have this effect on people. Isn't that right, Dory?"

"Absolutely," Dory said.

"I always wanted to be a household word. You know, famous, that kind of thing," Pixie said, yanking at the black wig.

"In Mother's house you're a household word," Dory said as they sat down. "She called me today and told me you went for your annual checkup. How did it go?"

"The doctor was dumbfounded. He couldn't find anything wrong with me. Your mother seems to think I'm senile. I sent her an e-mail saying I would live. That should ruin her day tomorrow when she gets it. The doctor was amazed when he took my history and found out I had had so much repair work done. He said it was astonishing that a woman would go under the knife so often and for so little results. He also told me I should get a cat or some other dumb animal for my twilight years. I let him know what I thought of that in quick order. Grit, would you like a belt of this?" Pixie held out her flask. Griff shrugged and took a swig.

"Jesus, what is that?" he croaked.

"Some people call it white lightning. Others call it shine. I have a whole barrel in my kitchen. It was a legacy from one of my husbands. Right now, I can't remember which one. But it will come to me."

"Those gloves are certainly elegant," Dory said, peering closely at her aunt's hands.

"I only wore them because my hands are smeared with Porcelana. I do hate those damn liver spots. No one really believes they're giant freckles except your mother," Pixie said fretfully. "Shouldn't we be leaving? It's not nice to walk in after the play starts."

"I guess so. Why so quiet, Griff?" Dory asked.

"No reason. Here, let me help you . . . Pixie." He looked wildly at Dory and mouthed the words. "What should I call her?"

"Of course you should call me Pixie. Everyone else does," Pixie said, craning her neck and knocking the wig off center. "Is it on straight, Grit?"

"Looks all right to me. Dory?"

"Perfect."

With a swish of the ermine-lined cape Pixie sailed down the aisle.

Dory almost choked on her own laughter when Griff pinched her arm. "She's wearing Puma funning sneakers."

"Guess her bunions are bothering her again. Don't worry, no one will notice unless she trips on that damn cape. Don't you just love her?"

Griff grinned from ear to ear as he linked arms with both women. "I'll be the envy of every man at the theater. Not one but two beautiful women. What more could a guy ask for?"

"Not much," Pixie snapped. "I like him, Dory. He knows beauty when he sees it."

"There's one thing I hate about the theater," Pixie whispered during the third act. "They don't sell anything for you to eat during the play. I like to nibble and sip."

Dory nudged Griff, who was dozing in his seat. She smiled. "He only came along because he knows I like the theater. He'd rather be home watching a ball game. Isn't he wonderful, Pixie?"

"Do you go to ball games with him?" Pixie whispered.

"No, we go to wrestling matches. I hate them but I go and scream like everyone else. After I'm there I don't really mind. Griff loves wrestling."

"One of my favorite husbands loved wrestling but I can't remember which one. This play is boring. No wonder he went to sleep. Did I tell you about my pen pal?"

"No. Male or female? Ooops, sorry. What's he like?"

"Smashing. I think. We're really getting to know one another. One of these days I plan to meet him. He writes delightful letters."

"What kind do you write?"

"What do you think? I lie my head off. No woman ever tells a man the truth unless she's a fool. Women my age, that is. You better wake your prince before the play is over. He might be embarrassed when the lights go on. He's a nice young man, Dory. I like him."

Dory let out a long sigh of relief. She had been waiting all evening for Pixie's opinion. Her two favorite people in the whole world and they liked one another. "I'm glad." Pixie knew how important her opinion was to Dory.

"I wasn't sleeping, merely resting my eyes," Griff said sheepishly. Pixie smirked. Plays were boring. She'd take the wrestling matches any day over Broadway.

"We'll put you in a cab, Pixie," Dory said. "I'd go along home with you but I have a big day tomorrow. And Griff has an even bigger one."

"You mean you and I aren't going for a nightcap? I thought we would go to Gallagher's and pick up some hunks and play around a little. Actually, I thought I would pick up a hunk and you could watch. Now that I met Grit I don't think you should play around. It doesn't hurt to look, though."

"Pixie, it's Griff, not Grit. Can I have a rain check? I know I'm missing out on hours of fun and I do love to watch you in action but I really do have a big day."

"You know me. Once I get a name in my mind it stays. To me he's always going to be Grit. Good name. Sturdy. Guts and all that. Of course you can have a rain check. Hang on to that guy, he's good stuff."

"I know," Dory laughed as Griff flagged down a cab and gave the driver the Dakota's address.

"Driver, ignore that address and take me to Gallagher's," said Pixie. "You know where it is, don't you."

"You bet." The driver grinned and winked at Pixie.

"Well don't just sit here, burn rubber, man," Pixie said, leaning back against the seat.

"You got it." The driver smiled to himself. He got them all. This night shift was something else.

It was really hard to say good night like this, but Dory and Griff had agreed to call it a night.

They hailed separate cabs and Dory sank back against the cushions. She was too tired to care. What a day this had been!

Griff listened with one ear to the chattering cabbie on the ride across town. His thoughts were with Dory, her lovable eccentric aunt, and the move he was making in the morning. At this time tomorrow he would be in a new environment and loving every minute of it. His dream was finally coming true. And in a couple of weeks his dream would have a big gold ring around it when Dory joined him. It still bothered him that marriage wasn't in the picture, but he was coming to terms with the whole idea.

"What'ya say, buddy, am I right or wrong?"

"Hmmmmmnnn?" Griff said absentmindedly.

"That's what I say. If some crazy football team wants to give you five million smackers, take the money and run I say. Hell, the kid can always go back to school later on. Best goddamn running back I've ever seen. Heisman winner to boot."

"Hmmmmnnn." The old lady was a pure delight. For some crazy reason she was everything he thought she would be. No wonder Dory was such a wonderful person. Imagine growing up with someone like Pixie. She had liked him, and approved, he could tell. And that flirty wink she gave him. He smiled to himself. She was okay in his book. But he cringed a little when he thought of his mother meeting Pixie.

The play wasn't bad, what he could remember of it. It wasn't that he minded going to the theater or to a musical with Dory, but if he had a choice he would pick wrestling. Dory was a good sport about going with him, even though he knew she didn't particularly care for sports.

"I think Georgia can get along without him. Don't you think Walker is doing the right thing?"

"Hmmmmnnn." Now that his big move was almost upon him he was more certain than ever that it was the right thing. The clinic had always felt right; it was the move with Dory that gave him jittery moments. He knew now it was right because it *felt* right, he told himself. And when he felt right it was all systems go.

"Driver, let me out here, I'm going to walk the rest of the way. Hell no, I'm going to run the rest of the way," Griff said, thrusting a ten-dollar bill at the driver. "Keep the change and you're absolutely right about Walker, he is the best goddamn running back I've ever watched."

"You got it, buddy." The driver grinned as he pocketed Griff's money. "See you around. Jersey is only across the river."

Running? Griff looked down at his evening clothes and his shiny shoes. Without a moment's hesitation he bent down and took off his shoes and socks. What the hell, it was only four blocks. No one in New York would give him a second thought as he raced by in his bare feet. Damn, he felt good. Tomorrow he was going to feel even better.

Chapter Two

Dory's stomach churned all the way down in the elevator as she stood beside David Harlow, feeling his shoulder brush insistently against her own. She had been aware of the speculating glances from the women in the outer offices as Mr. Harlow escorted her to the elevator. Word was out that he was taking her to dinner. She must have been mistaken, Dory cautioned herself; those same speculating glances couldn't have been touched with pity. Could they?

Mr. Harlow stood aside to allow her to walk through the revolving doors in the lobby. He walked too close and she resented the way he cupped her elbow in his hand as they walked to the corner.

"A taxi? Or would you rather walk?" Harlow asked.

"Let's walk. It's a nice evening. We could use the exercise after sitting in an office all day." There was no way she was going to sit in a taxi with David Harlow. If all the stories were true, and she was beginning to suspect they were, she had no intention of allowing him to paw at her.

They made small talk as they walked to the restaurant. She winced and tried to draw away from him when he put his arm around her shoulder as they waited to be seated. There was something possessive in his touch, something too deliberate, too firm, too certain.

"Drink?"

"Whiskey sour on the rocks," Dory replied smoothly. She wouldn't allow him to rattle her. And she wouldn't have more than two drinks with this man. She needed her wits. This was supposed to be a spectacular day! A day that held such promise for her future . . . if she wanted it. She wouldn't allow a man like David Harlow to spoil it for her. Why hadn't she made some excuse that she couldn't join him for dinner? She should have. But she had been so filled with herself, so confident, and he had approached her at the height of her ego trip. All through the afternoon she had had time to reconsider, but by then it was too late.

"The food here is excellent," Harlow said as he lifted his drink to toast Dory. "Here's to a long and fruitful relationship."

"I'm leaving, Mr. Harlow. How long and fruitful our relationship will be still remains to be seen." Her mouth was dry and she could barely get the words out of her mouth. She didn't like this man. Neither his reputation as a lecherous bastard nor his arrogance.

"You'll be back," Harlow said loftily. "I carry a lot of weight at the magazine. I have your future right here in my hip pocket, Dory. You and I could make an excellent . . . working team." Dory was fully aware of the pregnant pause in his statement. "I personally approved of Lizzie's choice to have you succeed her. I've already gone to the board of directors and read off your qualifications like a litany. They were as impressed as I. We're all looking forward to your return."

"I haven't even left yet. And, I didn't say I would be back. I haven't decided." Dory didn't like the turn the conversation was taking. "Why all this sudden interest, Mr. Harlow? You've never expressed interest in my career before this."

"Darling, a man of my position cannot offer his attentions to every little copy girl whom *Soiree* employs. I admit I am irrevocably attracted to executive women who share my station and power. Didn't you know, I'm an equal opportunity employer!" Harlow seemed to find this extremely funny, and as he laughed he firmly gripped Dory's hand. "I could be of tremendous help to you, Dory. The right word here and there, and you could make it all the way to the top. I could do that for you."

Dory cringed and tried to cover her distaste, hating herself for her pretended politeness and her reluctance to make an enemy of this man. She knew she should simply stand, excuse herself and leave him. To hell with David Harlow.

She didn't need this weasel . . . did she? Evidently, *he* thought she did. How slick he was. So certain she would seek his patronage. Dory forced what she hoped was a smile to her lips. "Are you saying I won't be able to succeed without your help? What about those qualifications you litanized for the board?"

"Dory, I'm not quibbling about your ability. Your ideas have always been creative and valuable to the magazine. All I said was I could help you make it to the top. Success requires a particular type of woman. A sophisticated worldly woman who knows where her allegiances lie. I believe you're that kind of woman."

"You didn't answer my question. What would I have to do to have you in my corner?" Her heart was pumping madly and she was certain the man across from her could hear it.

Harlow set his drink down and leaned across the table. Dory felt herself shrink back into her chair. He reached for her hand again. Swallowing hard, she steeled herself against the feel of his clammy hands on her. His flat white skin repelled her. Still, she didn't withdraw her hand. "We're both mature, consenting adults," she heard him say. "Don't play games with me. The only time I play games is in the bedroom. How good are *you* at games?"

"I manage," Dory said in a strangled voice. This couldn't be happening to her. She couldn't be sitting here, listening to this man threaten her integrity. She couldn't be letting him hold her hand. For what? For what, for God's sake? For a job? Was she actually compromising herself to this miserable excuse for a man? She had to do something, say something, get out of this somehow. "There are other jobs."

"Of course there are, my dear. This is New York. I think it's safe to say I know every editor-in-chief on every magazine in the city. I'm sure you could *apply* at any one of the magazines."

There it was, out in the open. She knew exactly what the words meant. If she didn't play ball, his way, she was out of a job and she wouldn't find it easy to get another one, not if he knew every editor-in-chief in the city. She could feel the bile rising in her throat. She withdrew her hand from his grasp and brought the glass to her lips. She gulped the sour drink and finished it in two swallows. She had to get out of here, back to her apartment. She would never come back to this sleazy city, with all its sleazebags like David Harlow. Griff. Think about Griff and a new life. She didn't have to sit here and listen to this weasel with his slick words and heavy threats. All she had to do was get up and walk out. Tell him to go to hell, drop dead, who did he think he was talking to anyway? This was sexual harassment at its worst. But if she did that, there would be gossip. Shameful things would be said. People would look at her and snicker. They'd talk about her behind her back. They'd say things and believe them, terrible, degrading things. Who would hire her with something like that hanging over her head? She had to do something, say something, get through this somehow.

"I'd like to order now. I have an early day tomorrow." After dinner she would make a graceful exit.

David Harlow leaned back in his chair and opened his menu. A smile played around his mouth. They were all alike. The woman hadn't been born who wouldn't climb in bed for the promise of money and some semblance of power. Words like *threat, coercion,* were not in David Harlow's vocabulary. This one was an easy piece. He wished he had noticed her earlier.

"May I suggest the lobster . . ."

Griff slid behind the wheel of the clinic van and stared at the ashtray full of plum pits. He grimaced. John's wife might look as if she'd stepped off a *Vogue* magazine cover, but she was the sloppiest woman he had ever come across. Tissues littered the floor and the stale scent of her perfume was embedded in the velour seat covers. He hated it. God damn, the van was for clinic use, not for Sylvia to joyride around in. That Sylvia might consider him to be joyriding didn't enter his mind. He was picking up Dory at the airport and then they were going apartment hunting. There was a difference.

There were times when he felt boxed in, almost trapped. For the past several days the feeling had grown stronger and stronger, making him uneasy and skittish. He had hungered for this chance for so long, had worked so hard toward this end that he didn't understand his discomfort. It must be the practice. Surely it had nothing to do with Dory. Or did it? He loved her. God, how he loved her. Maybe it was Dory he was really worried about and not himself. After all, it was Dory who was giving up her career. It was Dory who would have to make a new life for herself here in the D.C. fishbowl. Dory would be starting from scratch. He at least had a job, colleagues he liked and admired, and a purpose in life. Was he robbing Dory of the very things he was gaining? Was he being fair to her, to himself? Hell, Dory was a vibrant, go-for-it young woman with sophisticated savvy. Wherever she went she would take those traits with her. Dory was Dory and that was why he loved her. So why was he uneasy?

He liked New York, even loved it, but when opportunity knocked he had to respond. Everyone had to respond to a dream at one time or another. This move was a must if he was to get on with life and career. He knew in his gut that another opportunity like this wouldn't come along again. The timing was perfect and Dory was part of the dream; she belonged in it. But was this what Dory really wanted? Was he being fair to her? She said he was, and he had to believe her. She said it was right, felt right. And, she had added, it was the perfect opportunity for her to finish her studies. In the end the decision had been hers.

Griff sighed. If all this was true, then why did he feel so anxious? Why was he so skittish? What was really bothering him?

The mere fact that anything at all was bothering him made him mad as hell. He hated it when he couldn't solve problems, come up with the right answer and get on with things. He was never one to sit and ponder. Either the dream was right or it wasn't. He loved Dory and Dory loved him. The practice was a golden opportunity, a step onward and upward for his career. He was happy with his decision to move here. If it was possible to be delirious with joy that Dory was moving here with him, then he was delirious with joy. So what was the problem?

The lack of commitment on Dory's part, perhaps? Her decision not to get married at this time? That's what it was. It was too loose. Not exactly temporary, just loose. When things were loose they could go either way. Marriage was a big step, an awesome responsibility. Perhaps Dory was right in not wanting to take such a step yet. Giving up her job, moving to a strange place, going back to school were probably all the decisions she could comfortably handle right now. He should understand it and he did understand it. He just didn't like it. He wanted to marry Dory. He wanted her to be the mother of his children. She wanted those same things, but she didn't want them right now. He was going to have to accept that because he loved her. He felt better now that he had put words to his feelings. The bottom line to his edginess was the lack of commitment. He could and would live with it. He had no other choice.

Christ, he was tired. He hadn't realized how tired he was until he saw Dory step off the plane from New York. All he wanted to do was take her in his arms and fall asleep against her softness. No thought of sex entered his mind. The clean fragrance of her was a balm to his senses. They kissed, a long, hungry kiss that made his head reel, oblivious to the stares and smiles of the other travelers. National Airport was a great place for kissing.

"Don't tell me the smell in this van is from some poodle, because I'd never believe it," Dory teased.

"John's wife was using it till their car was fixed. Needed new shock absorbers or something. She isn't the neatest person, as you'll find out. I didn't think you'd want to stay with them so I took a room at the Airport Holiday Inn. What's your feeling on orange bedspreads and drapes? You don't mind, do you?"

"Mind? I adore the color orange. I love motels, if you go with them. Tell me, what prospects do you have lined up for us to see? Griff, you look tired. Are you sure you want to bother with apartment hunting today? I'll go alone and only bring you to the most likely ones."

"I am tired, but I'll be all right. We're going to look together and that's settled. Sylvia and Lily really knocked themselves out lining up apartments. I hope one of them pans out. By the way, we're having dinner with the four of them. I wanted you all to myself, but the sooner you meet them the better we're all going to be. The girls are dying to meet you."

Dory felt a little annoyed. What if she didn't like "the girls"? How would Griff react? How like a man to assume that just because he and John and Rick got on so well, she would get on equally well with their wives. She was tempted to put her annoyance into words but changed her mind. Griff had made it clear that he liked the two women. He would never understand if she didn't, so it was grin and bear it. She was probably worrying about nothing. Griff didn't include any undesirables among his friends. If Griff liked them, so would she. Think positive, she told herself.

"Hungry?" Griff asked.

"No. They served a bagel with cream cheese on the plane along with a copy of the *Wall Street Journal*. How about you?"

"I had some coffee and toast. We'll have an early lunch. I thought we'd start on the Virginia side and work toward D.C. I'd like to avoid the city if possible. Traffic in the morning is a bitch. First stop Arlington."

They spent the morning looking at cramped apartments with no closet space and outrageous rental fees. Dory vetoed all of them. The last apartment building was a complete disaster. Two of the three elevators had OUT OF ORDER signs on them with messages tacked below in green crayon, making it clear what the tenants thought. The lobby tile was grimy and artificial plants were heavy with dust, making Dory sneeze. The rent for a studio was thirteen hundred dollars and a bargain, the manageress said in a squeaky voice. She reeked of stale beer and garlic.

"We'll let you know," Griff said hurriedly, as he ushered Dory past a loathsome rubber plant and out a smeared glass doorway.

They both inhaled deeply and Dory laughed. "Griff, the main road we were on before we got to the second apartment, what was it called?"

Griff checked his map. "Jefferson Davis Highway. Why?"

"I saw some town houses that looked nice. Why don't we take a look."

Griff shrugged. "Okay, but I think those rentals are more than I can afford right now."

"I'd like to take a look. Really, Griff, what we've been looking at is barely big enough for you, much less me."

The Georgian-style town houses were set back from closely cropped boxwood hedges and wide borders of colorful flowers. Dory liked them immediately. She jabbed at the buzzer of the manager's office and waited. Griff rolled his eyes and whistled under his breath. Dory knew he was thinking the rent would be outrageous. Outrageous plus utilities. They were here, it wouldn't hurt to look.

Dory blinked at the man who opened the door. He was a jock of the first order. Skin-tight Stitch's jeans, ankle-high boots with a shine that any Marine would envy. From the looks of his arms and chest he pumped iron when he wasn't out jocking. His navy blue shirt had a sprinkling of dandruff on the shoulders. "Call me Duke, everyone does," he said in a phony Texas twang that was one hundred percent Brooklyn.

Griff seemed mesmerized by Duke's attire, so Dory took the lead. "We'd like to take a look at one of the houses if you have a vacancy."

"Well, little lady, I just happen to have two. A congressional aide moved out the last of the month and the place was just renovated last week. Two stews are moving out this weekend. It's a duplicate of the aide's with a different color scheme. Want to take a look?"

"That's what we're here for, pardner," Griff drawled in annoyance. He hated macho jocks almost as much as he hated politicians. Shady and slick, the lot of them.

"Is there a lease?" Dory asked.

"Two-year lease but it's not firm. We bend if you bend. Get my idea?" he said, nudging Dory playfully on the shoulder.

"Yeah, we get it. We pay off and it goes into your pocket, right, pardner?" Griff snapped.

"It's a mean, hard, cold world around here. This ain't the nation's capital for nothing."

"You're right. This is Virginia, not Washington, D.C.," Griff said as he ushered Dory through the doorway.

The smell of fresh paint assailed their nostrils. The place was antiseptically clean. The dove-gray wall-to-wall carpeting had been shampooed, the windows sparkled, and the fireplace with its Italian marble facade was a dream to behold. Dory loved it immediately, The kitchen was yellow and green, and she mentally hung green checkered curtains and added a hanging fern. A braided rug and some wrought-iron furniture would make it bright and cheerful. She loved it. The first-floor powder room was a soft plum color. She could decorate with blue, deeper plum or stark white. Upstairs, the master bedroom with fireplace made her draw in her breath. Griff did a double take as Dory walked into the huge bathroom, done in shades of beige and dark brown. A king-sized bed with a spread to match the lightning zigzag foil of the wallpaper would be perfect. Congressional aides certainly knew how to live. She knew that the wallpaper and carpeting were the aide's choices, not the management's.

"Where did the aide go?" she asked bluntly.

"Georgetown," Duke said in a belligerent tone.

Griff smirked. "How much is the rent?" he demanded.

"Nine hundred a month. Management pays all utilities. Look around some and if you're interested, come over to the office. This place will be snapped up by Sunday, so decide now. We require a two-month security deposit."

"Twerp," Griff snarled as Duke left the room. "Dory, I can see you love this place and I don't blame you after what we've seen so far, but there's no way I can afford it now. Maybe next year."

Dory's face fell. "But, Griff, there are two of us. I'll help with the expenses. How much were you willing to pay? You haven't said."

"I didn't want to look at anything more than six hundred. How are you going to help? You'll be going to school, and I wouldn't want to dip into your securities. I can't afford this, Dory. I'm sorry."

"Griff, I'm going to be doing some freelance work for Lizzie. Profiles of congressmen and senators. The pay is adequate, believe me. I can carry my share. Please reconsider. Look at this fireplace. Can't you just see us making love in front of it on some cold, snowy night?" Not waiting for him to respond, she rushed on, "You're going to want to do some entertaining, and this place is perfect. We could even have a small barbecue in the back. Each house has a patch of garden in the rear, I saw it from the kitchen window. Some yellow canvas chairs and a table to match. Griff . . ."

"Honey, I didn't plan on you paying or helping out. If I can't afford you, then I have no business asking you to share my life. It's my responsibility to care for you."

"Just for now, Griff, until you get on your feet. Later we can change the arrangements if you want. Let me help. It's fair. With your furniture and mine this place could be a knockout."

"What about your apartment?"

"I'll sublet. No problem. Apartments on the Upper East Side are like gold. Say yes, Griff."

Griff stared down at Dory. She was probably right, but it hurt his ego that he would have to rely on her to pay half the rent. "Okay. I can see how badly you want this place. It's yours. Let's go talk to Superjock and settle it now."

"Oh, Griff, thank you." Dory threw her arms around his neck. "How far away is the Holiday Inn?"

"About four and one-half minutes from this doorway," Griff laughed.

Twenty-seven hundred dollars poorer, Griff looked stunned when they left the rental office of the Clayton Square Complex. Dory was oblivious to his tight expression and tense shoulders. She had mentally decorated the entire town house, both floors, while Duke explained to Griff tiresome things like yard maintenance and the workings of the water heater and snow removal in the winter.

A fat, red-eyed pigeon wobbled down the walkway in search of his dinner. Two more joined him in the quest, making Griff step off the walk onto the lawn that brashly displayed the mandate, KEEP OFF THE GRASS.

On the short ride back to the motel Dory was eagerly anticipating the moment when she and Griff would be alone at last. It seemed months rather than days since he had left New York, and she had missed him dearly, especially that closeness they shared after lovemaking. Not since that first kiss at the airport had Griff attempted any intimacy with her. That sudden advance of hers in their newly rented town house didn't seem to count. That had been an impulsive move entirely her own and now, for the life of her, she couldn't remember if he had returned the gesture.

He's tired, poor dear, she excused him for his lack of ardor. Nevertheless, she was already looking ahead to the solitude of the motel room and Griff's embrace.

Immediately upon entering the room and locking the door behind him, Griff collapsed on the bed, one arm thrown over his eyes to block out the light from the wide windows. "Do you want to shower first, or shall I?" Dory asked, a bit annoyed. She assumed that Griff had missed her just as much as she had missed him, and when the door closed she waited for him to take her into his hungry embrace. Romantic, she accused herself. Give the guy a break. It's obvious he's worn out. Still, her charitable logic did nothing to lift her disappointment.

"You shower first, honey. I don't mind a steamy bathroom and used soap. Training from the Marines."

Dory sat down on the edge of the bed, her fingers ruffling through his dark, wavy hair. "We could always shower together," she whispered invitingly, "that way, no one gets to use a steamy bathroom . . ."

Even before she uttered the words, she realized Griff was already asleep. He looked so pathetically weary, so vulnerable. Quietly, Dory closed the drapes to darken the room and then carefully removed Griff's shoes. She stripped off her dress and crawled onto the bed beside him, pulling up the spare blanket at the foot of the bed. Nestling down beside him, she offered her warmth and tenderness. In response to her, Griff turned on his side and wrapped her into his embrace, holding her.

Dory lay quietly. She wanted to talk about her plans for the town house. She wanted to talk about their new life and what living together would mean to both of them. Instead, she heard the deep, sonorous breathing that indicated he was sound asleep.

John and Sylvia Rossiter lived in a large white and wedgwood-blue colonial house set back from the street. Natives of Virginia, they had occupied the same house for twenty-three years of their twenty-four-year marriage. Griff liked and re-

spected John Rossiter, and when he had made
his offer three years ago, Griff had jumped at
the opportunity. John had been in New York to
read a paper on equine medicine, and the two
had hit it off immediately and had been friends
ever since.

While Griff liked and respected John, he always felt a little nonplussed about Sylvia. Sylvia
was, as she put it, thirty-nine and holding. She
admitted that she liked to be considered a trend-
setter in fashion and often attired herself in out-
landish costumes that made Griff wince. Dory
might recognize the style and the cost of Sylvia's
wardrobe and be impressed, but secretly, he
considered his partner's wife to be a plastic creation, and he often wondered how she managed to dress herself at all with those three-inch
nails. He must ask Dory if she thought they were
real. Sylvia couldn't cook or clean house, and
John pretended to be amused by his wife's con-
stant references to domestic chores, saying if
God wanted her to be a domestic he would have
permanently attached a mop to one hand and a
broom to the other. The Rossiters' house had
more than a lived-in look. Griff sought the right
word and finally came up with "disaster." Satisfied, he rang the bell and grinned down at Dory.
"This is going to be one hell of an experience for
you. Just keep your cool and ride with it."

Sylvia Rossiter opened the door herself and
smiled widely as she offered a carefully made-up
cheek for Griff to kiss. Long, thin arms reached
out to draw Dory to her but not before her eyes
added up the prices of Dory's complete outfit,

right down to the shoes. Outrageous lashes fluttered wildly as she calculated. She approved.

Dory fought the urge to sneeze at the cloying
smell of Sylvia's perfume. Later, Griff told her it
always reminded him of a cross between Pine-Sol
and rose water.

"Darlings, darlings, darlings!" she cooed shrilly.
"Come along, we're all shivering out on the
patio. As you can see, I didn't get a chance to
clean today, or yesterday or the day before that."
Her tone indicated it was not something she
ever planned on doing. "We'll just get a few
drinks in you and you won't feel the chill. John
is already cooking. Dory," she trilled, "I just
know you're going to love it here, and you are
not to worry your pretty little head for one minute about what people will say. If I hear so much
as one word, I'll straighten it out immediately."

"She means it," Griff said. "She's hell on
wheels about justice and the American way." It
was Dory's turn to be nonplussed.

"That's a lovely outfit you're wearing," Dory
said, smiling as she, too, mentally calculated the
cost of Sylvia's outfit—the culottes with the tight
band about the knee, raw silk in the palest
shade of pink she had ever seen; a long, karate-
style coat with a three-inch-wide crimson obi.
Shoes to match the obi completed her outfit. It
didn't go for a penny less than seven hundred
dollars. Sylvia had four strands of jet-black beads
at her throat and a matching band of beads and
fringe worn low on her forehead. Dory felt awed,
not so much at the cost but at the sheer audacity
of the outfit.

"Darling, there is a story behind this getup. I had just bought it in Bergdorf's on my last trip to New York. There I was, carrying this outfit, walking down the street, minding my own business, wearing all my really good jewelry, when these four hoodlums started tracking me. I was more than a little nervous. I knew they were going to attack me any minute. Just any minute! I don't mind telling you I had to make one hell of a quick decision. It was either give up the outfit and jewelry or take a chance that someone might see me run into Lord & Taylor. God!"

"As you can see, she opted for the unthinkable. She went into Lord & Taylor," John Rossiter said, holding out his hand to Dory.

John Rossiter was a credit to his barber. His chalk-white hair and mustache were trimmed to perfection. His tailor had nimble fingers, as did the shoemaker who crafted his handmade loafers. The family genetic pool could take credit for the weathered golden-brown skin that contrasted sharply with his prematurely white hair. His eyes were nut brown, observant, and keen, and the laugh lines etched deep grooves at the corners. Dory liked him immediately.

"Come along and meet Rick and Lily." Dory dutifully followed but not before she saw Sylvia roll her eyes at Griff.

Seated away from the smoke of the open barbecue, Lily Dayton was breast-feeding a cherub of a baby. Her husband sat beside her, his eyes glued to his firstborn son. Dory's first thought was Madonna and Child. Griff had a strange look on his face as he watched the baby suck, making soft little sounds in the quiet of the patio. A spurt of grease shot in the air from the barbecue, startling Dory. She looked up; Sylvia stared pointedly at Lily and grimaced.

"Why you can't bottle-feed that child is something I'll never understand," Sylvia all but snapped. "She even does that in department stores," she said to Dory. Her tone became light and could almost be taken for teasing, but Dory knew better. She herself felt embarrassed for Lily, who was now propping the baby over her left shoulder, leaving her right breast exposed while she made him comfortable. "Disgusting," Sylvia hissed between clenched teeth.

Dory looked around. John and Griff, as well as Rick, seemed mesmerized by the large, swollen breast.

Rick, a tall, splinter-thin man, shook hands warmly. He reminded Dory of an intense young Anthony Perkins. A good surgeon, Griff had said. Sensitive hands, not a nerve in his body. Animals rarely had to be sedated while Rick examined them. "Welcome to our little group," Rick said softly. Everything about him seemed in place. He gave the impression that there was nowhere else he would rather be and that his life was in perfect order. It probably was, Dory thought, as her eyes went to Lily and the sleeping baby.

"Aren't you going to put him down now and button up?" Sylvia demanded.

"In a minute. I just want to hold him for a few

minutes. It's a shock to their little systems to be taken from the warm breast and then placed in a cold bed."

"This is Dory, Griff's live-in," Sylvia said brashly.

"I'm so happy to meet you," Lily said. "I hope you can come over and lunch with me some time. I have some wonderful recipes I can share with you. Just ask Rick. I made a carrot cake that turned him into a beast."

Rick bared his teeth to show that he agreed. "We brought one with us. Sylvia never serves dessert."

"I'd like that," Dory lied. Imagine her swapping recipes with this little mother. Somehow Dory didn't think Lily would be interested in her recipe for Alabama Slammers. This child didn't look old enough to drink, and if she did, it was orange squash or grape Nehi.

The evening progressed and so did the chill. When it became apparent that everyone was shivering, Sylvia called a halt to the party. "I have a seven A.M. golfing date, kiddies, so we better call it a night."

Dory was thankful that the party was over. For the past two hours since finishing the burnt steak, she had been afraid to smile for fear tiny bits of charcoal would be stuck between her front teeth.

Lily's sweet voice continued chattering. "Have you been having a problem with the water, Sylvia? Ours is so hard I'm afraid to wash little Rick's clothes in it. I can't get the rust stains out of the toilet either. Do you know what I can use? It's really upsetting me."

The look on Sylvia's face was ludicrous. "I thought it was supposed to be like that." Dory turned her head to avoid laughing. Not for the world would she open her mouth and tell them her own secret for removing rust stains.

As they walked through the living room, Dory could hear Lily telling Sylvia that she had tried baking soda, vinegar and Clorox and nothing worked, and, "Sylvia, you might get germs if you don't do something."

"For Christ's sake, let's get the hell out of here," Griff said, sotto voce, as he led Dory out the front door. "See you Monday," he called over his shoulder.

"Well, what do you think?" Griff asked anxiously as he started up the van.

"They all seem very nice," she replied in a noncommittal voice. She had to think about the lot of them before she made any statements that she might regret later on. Slow and easy for now.

Griff laughed. "When you get to know them, they don't get better, they stay the same. John is fantastic, as you know. Sylvia is Sylvia. She's into clothes. Spending money is her hobby. She plays golf and tennis and drinks more than she should. She can't cook worth a damn and you saw how she cleans house. She does get a cleaning crew, or wrecking crew, to come in twice a year to give the place a once-over and then she throws a party that would knock your eyes out. She's generous and friendly. You'll get along. Fashion is something you have in common."

Dory bit her tongue to keep from replying. She could see little that she and Sylvia Rossiter had in common, particularly in matters of taste.

"Lily Dayton is a lovely, sweet person, as you must have seen." Dory wondered if Griff was aware of how his voice changed when he spoke of Lily Dayton. "She's wrapped up in her baby and so's Rick. They really and totally live for one another. She loves to bake and cook and fuss in the house. She had a garden this summer that was mind-boggling. Rick said she canned vegetables and fruits for weeks on end. She has a cold closet in the basement where she keeps all the things she cans. It's remarkable," he said in an approving voice. "Rick said she knitted all the baby's blankets and sweaters last winter. Their house, while not as large and expensive as the Rossiters', is a showpiece. Lily refinished all the furniture herself, hooked the rugs, sanded down the woodwork, and repainted it. She has some priceless antiques that she's collected since she and Rick got married. I'll bet she can help you when you start decorating our place."

Our place. How wonderful it sounded. But he was wrong. Lily Dayton would have no part in her decorations. This was something she was going to do on her own. Imperceptibly, she moved a little closer to the door. She was annoyed. Did he have to be so damn complimentary where Lily Dayton was concerned? It surprised her and rankled that Griff had never even alluded to the fact that he admired homemaking. And babies. Maybe it was the baby that made him so agreeable and . . . just what the hell was it, she wondered. Was she jealous? Of course she was jealous. She wanted Griff to look at her the way he looked at Lily. She wanted to hear that approving tone in his voice when he spoke about her and her accomplishments. She inched still closer to the door. What could he say after he said, "Dory works for *Soiree* magazine in New York." Now he could say she was going for her doctorate. Big deal. She suddenly realized she would never get that reverent approval unless she singlehandedly canned eighty-seven quarts of string beans. Men! She didn't think she was going to like Lily Dayton.

"By the way. You were a knockout. Everyone liked you. Sylvia will be after you to find out where you get your clothes. You looked every inch New York and Fifth Avenue. New dress, huh?"

"Not really. It's three days old." Dory grinned. It was okay now. Now he noticed her and was paying her compliments. There for a minute she had felt like the forgotten woman. He approved of her and the way she dressed. He approved of her.

"When do your classes start?"

"I thought I'd come down early next Friday for final registration. I have Katy doing all the paperwork and making the phone calls. I don't anticipate any problems."

"Are you sure you're going to be able to handle the freelance work and school, not to mention the house?"

There it was again. Keeping house. Home-making. Was that what he wanted? A home-maker?

"Of course I can handle it. We're just two people, so how much housekeeping can there be? You aren't messy and neither am I. If we both pick up after ourselves, there shouldn't be much of a problem. If I must, I can engage a cleaning person once a week. I don't want you to start worrying about me and how I'm going to cope. You have enough on your mind without all of this. Let me handle this end of it, Griff." Even to her own ears she sounded so certain, so confident. But was she? If she were back in New York, at *Soiree,* among people she knew and places that were familiar, her confidence would be well founded. Here in Washington, everything was new—new people, new situations, the pressures of school, making a home for herself and for Griff . . . why, she didn't even know where the grocery market was or where to get a really fine cut of steak. Dry cleaners . . . Dory gulped back a wave of doubt. She would handle it, she must handle it. Smiling, she decided to cross those bridges when she came to them. For now, she'd concentrate on Griff. "What do you say we get back to that motel where we can be alone. Together?"

"She's a mind reader, too," Griff grinned in the darkness. "I really dislike bucket seats in automobiles. Wiggle closer, we can at least hold hands."

Dory reached for his hand and gave a little involuntary shiver. "Cold?" Griff asked. "The evenings always get damp this time of year, even here in Virginia. Autumn is hard upon us, gal, it's already the middle of September, or almost. Only seventeen shopping weeks till Christmas. Think you can handle it?"

Dory laughed. "Goon. Reminding me about Christmas when I'm still in the midst of setting up a home for us. And school . . ." Her tone softened, becoming a little breathless. "Christmas. Our first Christmas, Griff!"

"Home. Our first home, Dory," he mimicked her dreamy tone, teasing her. Then more seriously, "Would you mind if I invited my mother for at least a part of the Christmas festivities?"

"Not a bit. If you think she'd come . . ."

"Mom doesn't set herself up as a judge, Dory. You should know that. Mom would love to share the holidays with us."

"As long as you're talking family, I have this zany aunt who actually advocates the racier side of life . . ."

"It's settled then." Griff squeezed her hand. "We'll invite Pixie, too!"

Dory settled back against the seat, still holding fast to Griff's hand, resting it on the top of his thigh, feeling the roll of the muscles as he manipulated the gas pedal and the brake. It was nice to know that he was thinking ahead to Christmas and the holidays and that she was first and foremost in his plans. There would be a continuity to their lives, a kind of settling down, a comforting safeness. With Griff, she knew exactly where she would be for Christmas and exactly what she would be doing. No more jaunting off for winter holidays at the Christmas season. No more touring around the ski slopes or lying in the Bahama sun with others who also lacked a connection and permanency in their lives. With Griff she had gained a definition of time and place. In December, at the holidays, she would be here, with the man she loved, in their very own home. If the excitement of spontaneous, last-minute plans was a thing of the past, that was all to the good . . . wasn't it?

When Griff and Dory closed the door to their motel room, he took her into his embrace, biting lightly on the tender flesh beneath her ear. Dory heard herself laughing, delighted that Griff was once again the attentive lover he had always been. His hands impatiently moved to the tiny buttons at the back of her dress, hastily working the fastening, eager to bare the creamy skin of her shoulders and breasts.

Lips caressing, tongues touching, they stripped away the offending garments, exploring and kissing as though they had never made love before.

Dory's hands were hot and demanding, covering his flesh with eager deliberation. "Easy, love," Griff whispered in her ear. "We've got the rest of the night and I intend to spend every minute of it making love to you." His lips were pressed against her throat, his voice sending little tremors through her body. "Easy, love, easy."

In a graceful, swift movement, he lifted her into his arms and carried her to the bed, holding her against him while he threw back the spread and laid her gently down on the smooth sheets.

He stood beside her for a long moment, drinking in the long, sweeping lines of her body, traveling up the length of her slim thighs to the perfection of her small but sweetly molded breasts. The fire in his loins rose to his head, making him feel heady, knowing a deep, aching longing for her. She held out her arms to him, and with a sound that was close to a groan, he lay down beside her, entwining himself around her, drawing her close against him.

Dory's head was swimming with anticipation. Her body was ready for him, arching, needing, eager for his touch and for his ultimate possession of her. But he would not take her quickly, she knew; his would be a slow, artful exploration, giving, taking, claiming for his own. And when she would feel herself splitting into fragments, incomplete without him deep inside her, only then would he take her, filling her world and joining her to himself.

Their mouths touched, teasing little tastes of his tongue, while he held her so tightly that each breath was a labor. He anchored her body to his while her senses took flight, soaring high overhead until her thinking became disjointed, and her world was focused only on those places that were covered by his hands, by his lips.

Taking his dark head in her hands, she cradled his face, kissing his mouth, his chin, the creases between his brows. His mustache tickled and aroused, adding further sensation to the contact between their mouths, making his lips seem softer and warmer in contrast.

"Love me, Griff, love me," she implored, her voice deep, throaty, almost a primal cry of desire. The sound in the silent room made his passions flare. He covered her with his body, holding her fast with his muscular thighs, while he skillfully caressed her heated flesh. She drew his head down to her breasts, offering them. His lips closed over one pouting crest and then the other, nibbling, teasing, drawing tight, loving circles with his tongue. His excursions traveled downward to the flatness of her belly and the soft, darker recesses between her legs.

Dory felt herself arch instinctively against his mouth, her head rolling back and forth on the pillow as though to deny the exquisite demand of her sensuality. Her fingers curled in his thick, dark hair, her body moved of its own volition against the caress he excited against her. Release, when it came, was the ebbing of the flood tide, seeping from her limbs and the sudden exhaling of her breath. She was floating, drifting on a cloud, the whole of her world consisting of his lips and her flesh and the contact between them.

Still, his movements were slow, deliberate and unhurried, although there was a roaring in his ears that was echoed in the pulses of his loins. His hands grasped her hips, lifting her, drawing her against him, filling her with his bigness, knowing his own needs now and demanding they be met. His breathing was ragged, his chest heaving as though he had run a mile. Lips met, lingered, tasted and met again. He moved within her imprisoning flesh, insistently, rhythmically, bringing her with him to another plateau so different from the first yet just as exciting. He rocked against her, feeling the resistance she offered, knowing that as she tightened around him as though to expel him from her, she was coming ever nearer to that climaxing sunburst where he would find his own consolation.

Panting, Griff's body covered hers, calming her shudders and comforting her until their spasms passed. It was with reluctance that he withdrew from her and silently pulled the covers over them, taking her in his arms to cradle her lovingly. Contentedly, Dory rested against him, sweeping her hand down the length of his body and finding him moist from her own wetness. Curled together in a dream of their own, they murmured love words until at last they slept.

Chapter Three

The days moved swiftly but not swiftly enough to suit Dory. She concentrated on one thought: get to Virginia as soon as possible and be with Griff. She went through the motions at *Soiree*, but at the end of the day she wasn't certain she had accomplished anything. Her thoughts were on furniture, dishes, and lamps. Green plants and drapery fabrics were a close second. Her doctorate was almost an afterthought.

She packed with feverish intensity in the early hours of every morning. Boxes of books and her personal things would go with her in Griff's SUV when she bade her final adieu to the Big Apple. Subletting the apartment had been no problem, Katy's cousin's boyfriend's sister was delighted to take it off her hands at a hundred dollars more a month than she was paying. An extra hundred to decorate with, Dory chortled to herself, and then later, that hundred dollars every month would buy what she wanted. Shoes, new blouse, lacy underthings. Whatever.

Never more than a cursory cook, she now mentally planned nourishing menus that she would serve on just the right dishes with just the right place mats and real napkins that had to be ironed. She would make a centerpiece and an exquisite dessert. She would need cookbooks. Katy could take care of that for her with a phone call to her friends in the publishing houses. Dory could imagine herself poring over cookbooks in front of the fireplace while Griff studied his veterinary journals. Togetherness. Wonderful. Griff would sigh with delight and pat his stomach and look at her the way he looked at Lily Dayton. Homemaking would have its own brand of rewards. Candlelight. Dinner would always be by candlelight. She would make sure the atmosphere stayed romantic so Griff would have no cause to regret his decision to rent the town house. In the spring she would plant some pansies and tulips. Griff loved flowers and bright colors. Pots and pots of flowers. Maybe a few geraniums. Spring? Spring would be March. April. Six months away. Her stomach churned as she thought of the deadline she had promised Lizzie. She could play house for six months and get it out of her system, as Lizzie put it. Or she could settle in, marry Griff, and finish her doctorate. Or she could come back to *Soiree* and take on David Harlow and all the problems that would go with the job. Six months was a long way off. For now she couldn't think past Thanksgiving and Christmas. She would make it memorable for both Griff and herself. It would be their first Christmas. God, how she could decorate that place for the holidays. Just last year *Soiree* had done an in-depth interview on a wealthy woman who handmade Christmas decorations for the Fifth Avenue crowd. They had been exquisite and the prices had been mindbending. Somewhere in the bowels of the *Soiree* building were cartons of those decorations that she herself had packed up to be stored. She vaguely recalled the wealthy woman saying she could have them for the wonderful job she had done on the layout. Feeling guilty because all the office girls wanted them, she had packed them up and then forgotten about them. Now, she would add them to the boxes to be transported to Virginia in the SUV.

Dory fixed herself a cup of coffee and walked to the window. She certainly hoped she would sleep better once she was in Virginia. The past days, with only three or four hours of broken sleep, were doing nothing for her already impatient disposition. She wanted to be gone, to be with Griff in their new home. New home. How wonderful it sounded. How happy. A nice, warm, snug, safe place of their own. Decorated by her for Griff with loving hands. Griff couldn't help but approve. They were going to be *so-o-o-o* happy.

The heavy drapes swished open. To the east the sky began to grow light. A streak of orange-gold appeared on the horizon, dividing the space into two endless halves of smog and pollution.

The phone shrilled just as Dory finished making a second cup of coffee. She balanced the cup in one hand and cradled the receiver next to her ear. The voice on the other end of the phone delighted her. A wide grin stretched across her face as she carefully set the cup on the counter. "Pix! Talk about timing. I was just thinking about you. How are you?"

"Do you want the truth or an outrageous lie?"

"I'll take the truth. How's things in the Dakota where all the fancy people live?"

"B-o-r-i-n-g. But, yesterday I saw Yoo Hoo in the elevator. You know the one who wears the sunglasses and was married to that rock singer. Anyway, she took off her glasses when she saw me."

"You probably dazzled her with one of your costumes. What were you wearing and how many diamonds did you have on? By the way, where are you?"

"In the coffee shop downstairs. I thought I'd stop by to see you for a few minutes. Do you have the time?"

"Pix, for you I'll make time. Have you had breakfast?"

"Breakfast! Good God, Dory, if I ate breakfast it would kill me. I feel in the mood for Irish coffee and a bagel. Can you swing it?"

"Absolutely. I'll have it ready when you get here."

Dory opened the door at the sound of the buzzer. She stood back to view her aging aunt. For some reason she was always reminded of a rainbow when she saw Pixie. They hugged each other and giggled like two schoolgirls. "God, I'm exhausted," Pixie said, slumping down on the sofa. "It's a jungle out there in the morning."

"Tell me about it. I have to hack my way through it every day. What are you doing up so early? I thought you slept till three."

Pixie snorted as she gulped at her Irish coffee. "If you would just figure out a way to get your mother off my back so I can get on mine I could sleep till three. Ten days of celibacy is all I can handle."

Dory laughed. "Mom's at it again, huh?"

"I swear that woman has a private detective trailing me. I think I shook him this morning, though. She said I was becoming an embarrassment to her and she wasn't going to tolerate it anymore. Can you believe that?" Pixie snorted again as she straightened her silvery wig of cascading curls. "I think you put too much coffee in this cup. This is the way your mother serves it to the minister when he stops by to console her over my antics as she calls them. How do you stand her? I know she's my sister and your mother but she's missing out on all that life has to offer. She must spend at least twenty-one hours of every day worrying about what I'm going to do next."

"Well, what are you going to do?" Dory giggled.

"I already did it," Pixie said, filling her coffee cup a third time. "I put myself in the hands of the best plastic surgeon in the country and told him not to stint. You're looking at the results."

Dory frowned. "What did you have done?" She hated asking the question but she had to know. A sucker was born every minute. Not Pixie. Pixie wouldn't . . . or would she?

"I knew you were going to ask that. Not a whole hell of a lot. I got a boob job and a derriere lift. Doctor Torian, who by the way is a handsome devil, and a class act, said he was a skilled surgeon and not a miracle worker. My fanny is now featuring a silicone implant. It's so marvelous, I can't tell you. I can bounce like a rubber ball. I am disappointed in my boobs, though. I would have had a complete overhaul but the doctor said there was only so much he could do. So, I settled for this. But," she said, wagging a bony finger at Dory, "I know that when I walk away from someone I juggle. I mean jiggle. It was worth it," she grinned as she slurped the last of her coffee. "You used instant coffee, didn't you?"

"I'm impressed," Dory said in a hushed voice.

"So was your mother, that's why she has this detective on me. She says she wants me to be respectable. Can you believe that? What business is it of hers if I have my ass lifted?"

Dory watched in stunned amazement as Pixie literally leaped from the sofa. "See what I mean, I sort of bounce."

"You know Mom. She's . . . well, she's . . . what she is . . ."

"Dead from the neck down. I'll say it for you. You know I love her but she drives me nuts. I'm so horny right now I could scream. I don't dare do a thing with this cretin she hired to watch me. She had the gall to tell me that sex should be curtailed at fifty. Fifty!" Pixie screeched. "I could hardly believe my ears. Fifty! I sent your father a condolence card." Dory nearly choked on her coffee as she watched Pixie strut around the room. "I refuse, I absolutely refuse to be a geriatric casualty. You should do an article on the subject for that magazine you work for."

Dory's eyes grew thoughtful. "Pix, would you defy Mom and do a layout, baring all? Verbally I mean," she said hastily as she noticed a wicked gleam in her aunt's eyes.

"I thought you'd never ask," Pixie said, flopping down and then bouncing on the sofa. "Of course. Will it be in good taste? Even if it isn't, I don't care."

"Listen, Pix, if you're serious, I'll speak to Katy about it. If it can be done in good taste, you're our gal."

Pixie bounced up again and tugged at her wool sweater. "The talk-show circuit, residuals, commercials—will I get it all?"

"I wouldn't be surprised. Who's going to tell Mom?"

"He is," Pixie said, pointing to a man lounging next to a car on the street below. "I refuse to be a party to your mother's next anxiety attack. Aren't you going to be late for work?"

"I sure am. I have to get moving. Why don't you stay and finish off the coffee. Lock up when you leave."

"Would you mind if I stayed the better part of the day? I could do some entertaining while I'm here. I have this friend . . ."

Dory turned to hide her smile.

The talk-show circuit yet! Hot damn, it might be good for a story at that. There must be a lot of older women who have the same feelings Pixie has. What do they do? How do they handle it? Her mind started racing as she pictured the layout and the intimate shots they could do of Pixie. By God, it would be interesting! *Soiree*'s readership, if you believed the last poll, consisted of twenty percent over the age of fifty-five.

All the way to the office her mind clicked like a computer. It wasn't until midmorning that she realized she hadn't thought of Griff or the town house once. She sat down with a thump. She was giving it all up. Permanently or temporarily. Damn, Pixie would make a terrific story, and with the two of them working together it would have been super terrific. She sighed heavily. Someone else could handle it. Someone else *would* handle it. She would have to read about it like everyone else from now on.

Katy's eyes bugged out when Dory presented her idea. She jotted down Pixie's address and phone number. By the time Dory left the conference room the entire floor was buzzing with the news that David Harlow himself had given the okay to do a cover story with Dory's sexy old aunt. They were even toying with the idea of putting Pixie's picture on the cover, Katy said.

"Harlow said you were to be commended," Katy gasped. "Commended, mind you. Not congratulated, but commended. Jesus, Dory, do you know who you have to be to get your picture on the cover of *Soiree* magazine?"

Dory giggled. "You can't say I'm leaving quietly. Fanfare, style, that's my departing theme. You'll all remember me in the days to come. Why don't you get us some lunch and I'll tell you how I'm going to decorate the spare bedroom."

"Again? You told me that yesterday and the day before."

"That was the living room. This is Griff's den. The extra bedroom is going to be his study. I thought all earth tones with a few splashes of color."

"Where are you going to do *your* work, *your* studying?" Katy asked.

For a moment Dory looked blank. "Oh, I suppose I could use Griff's desk or the kitchen table. It doesn't make a lot of difference where I study, I'm adaptable."

"I can see that," Katy said sourly. Her eyes narrowed as she stared at Dory. "It's . . . it's . . . commendable what you're doing. Don't slack off before you start." Her tone was sour and Dory picked up on it immediately.

"It's just that I have so much on my mind. How could I slack off. That's the main reason for the move. Don't worry. When you see me next, I'll be on my way. Do you think you'll have any difficulty calling me Doctor Faraday?"

"Not a bit. By the way, I left a pile of information on your desk and all the cookbooks are stacked in boxes. One of the stock boys said he'd drop them off at your apartment after work. There's even one on microwave cooking."

"Katy, that's fantastic. I'll buy a microwave. It will make things easy for me when I start school. Thanks for mentioning it."

The going-away party for Dory was held in the office at three o'clock. There was champagne punch in plastic glasses and assorted canapés, made by the girls, on paper plates. A Coach leather briefcase was her going-away gift from the office staff. Lizzie and Katy had chipped in and added a matching overnight bag. David Harlow handed her an envelope she didn't have the nerve to open. His eyes were too readable, too knowing. Suddenly, she felt as though she were swimming upstream in shallow water.

Later, after all the hugs and kisses, Dory walked through the offices for the last time and opened the envelope. A pink check (why were they always pink?) in the amount of one thousand dollars made her blink. Bribe was the word that came to mind. And then a second: pimp. She swallowed hard. She didn't want the check. She stuffed it and the envelope into her bag; she'd think of it as a microwave oven. A microwave and three pairs of shoes. Or six pairs of shoes and an electric toaster-oven. Or a new outfit and some schoolbooks. Or, put it in the bank and let it grow some interest. Or tear it up and forget about it? She disliked David Harlow intensely. He was slick, unctuous. Hell, it was company money, not David Harlow's personal money. That made a difference. It didn't matter what she did with it. Tomorrow, when she drove down to Virginia, things would look different. One more day and she would be with Griff. Not even one whole day. If she started early in the morning, as she planned, she would be with him around noon. Perhaps they could even have lunch if he was free. She ached for him. Her eyes thirsted for the sight of him and her mouth hungered for his. It was just hours now. Hours till he took her in his arms and wiped away all thoughts of David Harlow and New York.

The Big Apple. She was actually leaving New York. In her wildest dreams she had never imagined living anywhere else. This was her city, her town, her people. Pixie lived here. Her parents lived here. Her job was here. Wrong . . . Her job used to be here. She didn't have a job anymore. Now she was a free spirit. Her feelings were so mixed that she wanted to cry.

As Pixie would say, this was fish-or-cut-bait time. All the decisions were made. Now all she had to do was follow through. She wasn't giving up her career entirely. She would be keeping her hand in, in a limited way. Freelance work would keep her active. School would definitely be an asset to her later. Perhaps a doctorate wouldn't actually help her career, but Ph.D. after a name never hurt. Doctor Dory Faraday sounded good no matter how you looked at it. The opportunity was here so why shouldn't she take advantage of it? Everything would fall into place once she settled into her new home. She could handle it all. She worked best under pressure, when things were at sixes and sevens. Long hours and rigid schedules had never frightened her. She could handle anything as long as Griff was in the picture. Anything.

Was she making a mistake by leaving the door open at *Soiree*? Shouldn't she have cut the cord completely? If she had resigned she wouldn't have anything to come back to if things soured between her and Griff. God, why did she have to think of something like that? She couldn't go off with negative thoughts to start a new life. She had to consider the temporary leave and the open door at *Soiree* as an option. An option she could either renew or cast aside. It would be her choice.

Damn it, she hadn't realized it was going to be so hard to leave. Her life was here. This was life. Dear God, don't let me be making a mistake, she prayed silently. No, it was the right thing to do. Griff was the right thing. She loved Griff. Happiness was being with Griff. A job was only a job.

A devil perched on her shoulder. If that's true, why aren't you marrying Griff? Why aren't you making it for life instead of this . . . whatever it is you're calling it in your mind? "Shut up," Dory said tartly as she shrugged her shoulders, hoping to dislodge the devil's unwanted voice that always irritated her when she was in turmoil.

It was time to leave. She *was* doing the right

thing. It felt right and that would have to be good enough. Griff *was* right for her. All the rest didn't matter. Not really.

Dory said her last good-bye to Sara, her next-door neighbor, promising to keep in touch. Sara handed her a thermos, saying she knew Dory would want to get to Virginia as soon as possible and not have to stop. Dory thanked her and was off, the SUV loaded to the top, the rear end noticeably lower than the front. Books were heavy. Thank God, Griff had flown to Washington and left the SUV for her.

Shortly after nine o'clock Dory uncorked the thermos and took a healthy swallow. She turned on the radio. Someone was shrieking about a love that lasts forever and ever and ever and then some. She switched the station and Willie Nelson warbled to life. She grinned. Griff loved the seedy, rambunctious Willie with a passion. He had every tape and record the man ever made and could sit and listen dreamily for hours on end. He said Willie was better than any tranquilizer for his animals and would probably make sure that his music was piped into the new clinic.

At eleven thirty Dory, guided the loaded SUV into her assigned parking space. Sylvia and Lily, pushing a stroller, walked around to the parking area with Duke, the manager, walking just a shade too close to Sylvia. Lily smiled happily and hugged Dory. God, Dory thought, eleven thirty in the morning and Sylvia looked as if she had

spent the entire morning in bed. There was no
mistaking the look on her face. Dory wondered
if John was responsible for the contented, rap-
turous look—or could it be Duke? She couldn't
help wondering. "How long have you been
here?" she asked.

"Darling, for hours. The phone people were
here at eight. They hooked up the washer and
dryer at nine thirty and the movers called to say
they'd be here at two o'clock. Your refrigerator
came awhile ago and it's plugged in and running."

Dory looked pointedly at Lily. "No, I'm a
slouch," she said. "I just got here. Little Rick
naps in the morning. I had to bathe him and
feed him and then he was hungry again. I
haven't done a thing. But I'm here now and I'll
be glad to do my share if little Rick can behave
himself."

Duke smirked as he swaggered over to the car
and offered to help with the heavy cartons. "Did
you ever see such muscles?" Sylvia whispered.

"Can't say that I have," Dory said, bending
over to take a box out of the car.

"I brought coffee and Lily brought some of
her homemade blueberry muffins," Sylvia volunteered.

"Where's Griff?" Dory demanded. "Why isn't
he here?"

"Darling, he's in McLean checking on some
senator's horses. John went with him. You won't
see him till late tonight or maybe tomorrow if
they have to stay over. This is a whole new ball
game for you, so you'd better adjust, darling." It

was clear that *she* had indeed adjusted. Dory wondered if John had any idea how well.

"You'll get used to it, Dory," Lily said softly. "If you had a bundle of love like little Rick, you'd hardly notice Griff's absence."

Dory's heart plummeted. She had been looking forward to seeing Griff, and now if what Sylvia said was true, she might not see him till tomorrow. She would have to spend her first night in the town house alone. There would be no one to carry her over the threshhold. Griff would have carried her over it, she was sure of it. He was romantic in so many ways. "Damn," she muttered. Lily's eyes flew to the baby to see if he had heard. She frowned to show her disapproval. Dory winced and made a note to be careful of her vocabulary from now on.

"Why don't we have those muffins so we can all gain five pounds? Lily uses pure butter, tons of it," Sylvia complained. "Maybe Duke will be good enough to let us heat the coffee in his apartment. You don't have any pots. I'll do it. You two go along and I'll bring the coffee as soon as it's ready." Before Dory could agree or disagree, Lily was pushing the stroller ahead of her and around to the rear of the building. Duke had made three trips to the back and now, with the exception of her luggage, the SUV was empty. Brawn certainly did have its merits. She couldn't help wondering how artful he was in bed. If Sylvia's Cheshire-cat smile was any indication, he performed admirably. Sylvia would never settle for less than the best. I wonder if

Griff knows, Dory muttered to herself as she trudged behind Lily, lugging two heavy suitcases. Sylvia's trilling voice and Duke's phony Texas twang grated on her ears. Damn, she wanted to see Griff. She didn't need Lily and her baby or Sylvia and her Saks wardrobe and alleycat appetites.

Inside the town house Lily was unpacking muffins wrapped in waxed paper, Saran wrap and tinfoil. She spread colorful checkered paper napkins to match the paper plates on one of the packed cartons. Dory fought the urge to tell her to leave. The phone shrilled to life and so did little Ricky. Lily tried to quiet the squealing baby as Dory strained to hear Griff's words.

"Oh, darling, it's so good to hear from you. I just this minute got here and Sylvia said . . . Sylvia said . . . When are you coming home, Griff?" she all but cried.

"Not till tomorrow. I just wanted you to know I'm thinking about you and I can't wait to see you. This will give you a chance to start your decorating without me underfoot."

"What did you say, Griff? I can't hear with the baby crying and all." She sent Lily a murderous look that went right over the young woman's head. The more she crooned, the louder little Ricky shrieked.

"He does have a good pair of lungs, doesn't he?" Griff laughed.

"What? Talk louder, I can't hear you."

"Never mind, darling. I'll see you tomorrow. Tomorrow, darling."

"God damn it to hell, Lily, that was Griff. Couldn't you keep that kid quiet for two minutes? I have no idea what he said to me," Dory wailed. She felt like throwing a tantrum to equal little Ricky's. Instead she sat down with her back against the wall and bit into one of the moist muffins. Lily waited expectantly for her comment. Evidently, Dory's sharp words about her baby had fallen on deaf ears.

"Good. Very good," Dory muttered. Lily frowned. "Delicious. Are they difficult to make?" she babbled. "Can you make them in a microwave oven?"

"Do you really think they're good? I spent all last evening making them for today. I brought enough for Griff too, so you won't have to worry about breakfast tomorrow."

Dory ignored her as Sylvia tripped into the kitchen on her three-inch heels. The skin-tight, lime-green coverall was made of silk and clung to Sylvia as though it had been painted on. Three strands of real pearls graced her throat. Dory would have parted with her eye teeth for just one of the strands. The pearls were worth at least four thousand dollars and the coverall around three hundred. She wondered how much John paid for his clothes.

"Here we are, kiddies, piping hot coffee. I'd like to stay and chat, but I have to go to the hairdresser and then I have an appointment for a pedicure. I'll give you a call tomorrow, Dory, to see how things are."

"You just went to the hairdresser day before yesterday," Lily grumbled.

"Darling, I refuse to look dowdy or matronly. It wouldn't hurt you to pay more attention to your own looks. You need a rinse and isn't it time you stopped nursing that child? You look positively . . . fat. You have to start thinking about your figure now."

"Why? Rick hasn't complained. I'll work on it when little Ricky is older. I want to enjoy every minute of him and nurse him as long as I can."

"You're a fool," Sylvia said curtly. "I love you, Lily, but you are a homemaking fool. Still, somebody has to do it." With a breezy wave of her hand Sylvia was gone, her heels clicking on the flagstone walkway.

"I just bet she slept with that . . . that . . . jockey," Lily said through pursed lips. "How could she?"

"It's easy, you take off your clothes and slip between the sheets. Isn't that how you got little Ricky?" Dory sniped. God, what was happening to her? Had she really said that to Lily? Evidently she had, for tears welled up in Lily's eyes. "Look, it isn't your business or mine. I'm sorry. Let's forget it. Why don't you take little Ricky home? I can manage and I'd like to be alone for a while. I'm also very tired."

"But Rick said I should stay and help you," Lily complained. "He'll be upset with me if I don't help you."

Dory lost what little patience she had left. "Then for God's sake don't tell him. The baby looks sleepy. You go along now and I'll manage very well. Thanks for thinking of me with the muffins. I would like the recipe, if you don't mind."

Lily's world was suddenly right side up. Her face lit like a beacon. "I'll call you as soon as I get home and give it to you. You're sure now that I can't do anything?"

"Not a thing. Go along now," Dory said in a motherly tone.

The moment Lily and the baby were out of sight, Dory locked the back door and sighed with relief. Now, damn it, she could cry. She could cry or bawl or stamp her feet and bawl at the same time. Instead, she rummaged in one of the cartons till she found a fat, silken comforter. She carried it upstairs to the bedroom. She spread it out by the fireplace and lay down. She had time for a short nap before the movers arrived. Tears clung to her lashes as she closed her eyes in sleep.

Dory felt as though she had just closed her eyes when the phone jangled. Thinking it was Griff, she crawled groggily across the room. "Hello," she said sleepily.

"Dory, it's Lily. I just got home and I'm calling like I promised, to give you the muffin recipe. Do you have a pencil?"

"Of course," Dory lied. Why me, she said silently, her eyes raised upward. She listened patiently while Lily read off ingredients and measurements. "Thank you, Lily," she mumbled between clenched teeth.

Sleep was out of the question now. She might as well get up, change her clothes and get to work. Maybe Griff would change his mind and make it home tonight after all. If she could entice the movers to set up the bed and place the furniture, she could get on with the unpacking.

It was late afternoon when she realized she was hungry. Dory looked around to survey her handiwork. She felt pleased with herself. She had definitely made inroads. Tomorrow, the drapery people would hang the curtains and the surprise chair she had purchased for Griff would arrive. Covered in a deep plum velour, it would give his study just the touch of color needed to make the room restful and yet attractive. He was going to be so surprised. She smiled to herself as she envisioned the way he would pick her up and twirl her around, his eyes laughing merrily. Then he would say, "How did you know this was exactly what I wanted?" And then she would say, "Because I think like you do and can read your mind." They would kiss, a long, searing, burning, mind-reeling kiss, and then they would go to bed and make the universe tilt the way it always did. If I don't get some food, Dory thought, I won't have the strength to kiss him, much less tilt universes.

She backed the SUV out of the parking spot and headed back toward Jefferson Davis Parkway. She drove till she came to Fern Terrace and Ollie's Trolley. It was a real trolley car, converted into a diner, and Ollie had the best chili dogs on the eastern seaboard. At least that's what his sign proclaimed. Dory tested his advertisement and agreed. Two chili dogs, one giant root beer and one envelope of greasy French fries made her burp with pleasure. "Ollie," Dory said as she paid her check, "you are indeed a prince among men. You deliver what you promise. I think these were the best hot dogs I've ever eaten."

The man named Ollie threw back his head and laughed. He had baby-fine hair that barely covered his scalp and an infectious laugh, and Dory found herself joining in. "I get people from all over. Secret is in just serving what you advertise. When you add to your menu, that's when you get into trouble. As you noticed, the French fries leave a lot to be desired, but I have to serve them. Kids demand French fries. You were lucky, I was just getting ready to close up. Good day today. I had two senators and the secretary of the navy sent his aide for a batch of my dogs. The Pentagon is my best customer. You take that Senator Collins. He comes here three times a week. He says he's never getting married as long as I stay in business."

Dory's ears perked up. "He's the young good-looking one from somewhere in New England, isn't he? A bachelor and the youngest man in the Senate, right?"

"That's the one," Ollie said, packing up his stained wrap-around apron in a plastic bag for his wife to wash. "Three days a week, huh?"

"Yep. Why, a person could just stop by, say around one-ish and you'll find him leaning against the trolley eating three dogs. Always has two root beers. Never touches the French fries. Says the grease gives him zits. He's always gettin' his picture took and he don't want no . . . blemishes marking up that good-lookin' face of his.

You new around here?" he asked, shoving his money bag into his plastic carryall.

"Just moved in today. I live over in the town houses on Jeff Davis Parkway. My name's Dory Faraday," she said, holding out her hand.

"Nick Papopolous, a.k.a. Ollie," Nick said, offering her a hand and arm as large as a railroad tie. "Come on, I'll walk you to your car. Lots of loonies around here." To prove his point, he withdrew a heavy-looking black gun and shoved it into his belt. He didn't bother to pull his shirt down over the weapon, preferring to let it show. "I got a permit for this," he said, pulling the door closed behind him.

Dory watched in awe as he tossed his plastic bag full of money and his dirty apron into the back of a Mercedes 380SL. The hot dog business must be good, Dory thought as she guided the SUV out of the parking lot. Drake Collins, the newest, the youngest, the sexiest senator on Capitol Hill. *Soiree* would love him. Unattached, brilliant, going far, eye on the governor's chair. What more could a girl want, especially an unemployed girl. Woman. Career person. *Soiree* reader. *Soiree* was aimed at the successful woman and was rated second only to *Time*. Collins was perfect for her first *Soiree* profile. She would definitely make it her business to lunch at Ollie's Trolley every chance she got. But first things first. She had to finish the house and start school.

For some reason she felt annoyed and out of sorts when she got back to the house. The boxes of books made her frown. She had to find a place for them until she could have some shelves installed. One more day to herself before she hit the classroom. Even though she was late, she would catch up. She would have to!

Dory made up the bed, showered and washed her hair. Wrapped in a cheerful lemon-colored robe, she gazed down at the bold geometries of slate grays and umber browns on the crisp sheets and pillowcases. Griff loved this particular set of sheets, saying they made him want to do wild, impetuous things to her. She was propping the pillows up so she could read when the phone suddenly rang. It had to be Griff saying good night. She smiled as she picked up the phone. Her voice was a low, sensuous purr. "I miss you, darling," she said, leaning back into her nest of pillows.

"You'd be in big trouble if it wasn't me on the phone," Griff laughed.

"Who else would be calling me after dark? I really don't want to complain but this bed is so big and I'm not taking up much room. I wish you were here."

"I do too, honey. But I've got my work carved out for me here. This was a golden opportunity that was too good to refuse. It just came at a bad time. I'm sorry. There's eleven thoroughbred horses in the senator's stables, and this afternoon I began inducing labor in one of his prize mares. By noon tomorrow she should drop a fine colt."

Dory bristled. Normally, she loved to hear Griff talk about his work. She loved animals too, but this . . . this was too much. She had just propositioned him over the phone, and he was telling her about a prize mare and eleven thorough-breds. Even as she thought it, Dory felt ashamed. Just because her needs weren't being met was no reason to get her back up. Griff had needs too.

"Dory?" his voice questioned. "Are you there?"

"I'm here, Griff."

"You're not angry, are you? Tell me you understand, Dory."

"I do, Griff. It's just that this would have been our first night together in our own house. I thought you would carry me over the thresh-hold and we could have some wine. You'd light the fireplace in the bedroom and we'd make long, lazy love. But it's all right. I understand."

Griff's groan was clearly audible. Dory felt smug. At least now he knew what he was miss-ing. "We'll do that tomorrow night and that's a promise. Now that you've churned me all up, I'm going to have to take a cold shower. By the way, did Sylvia give you a hand today? She of-fered to help."

Dory thought of Sylvia and then of Duke and the smitten looks on both their faces. "Yes, Sylvia helped," Dory said grudgingly. Helped herself is what she did, the nasty thought con-cluded.

"She's something. I think she's one of those people you can always count on in a pinch," Griff was saying. "Look how she hunted apart-ments for us."

"Hmmmm. I suppose." And look what the wonderful Sylvia came up with, Dory grimaced, thinking of that last especially unattractive apartment house complete with Sylvia's own brand of grime.

"Remember now, we have a date for tomorrow night. I'll give you a call sometime during the day if I get a chance. I love you, Dory."

It was on the tip of her tongue to give her usual response of "I love you, darling" but she didn't. Instead she said, "Me too."

Dory lay for a long time staring at the ominous jacket of Dean Koontz's latest book. Tomorrow wouldn't be the same. Tomorrow was tomorrow and this was now. Today. The *first* night. How could tomorrow possibly be the same? She felt cheated. Angry and cheated. And she didn't like it.

She opened the book with a dramatic flourish. And just what did one do for a horse in labor that took the entire night? Priorities. Order of preference. She came after a horse. And induced labor? The thought just struck her. If Griff had had to induce the labor, couldn't it have waited until tomorrow? He was setting the timetable, not Mother Nature!

Her eyes snapped and chewed at the words written by Koontz, not comprehending, not caring. Angrily, Dory leapt from the bed, the new book skidding to the floor. She ripped the geometric sheets from the bed and carried them to a white wicker hamper in the dressing room. She replaced them with a frilly set of lacy ruffled sheets and pulled them up haphazardly. These sheets were designed with a single woman in mind. Extravagantly feminine, too lush, too Victorian to make a man feel comfortable.

Sitting alone on her girlish bed didn't make her feel a hell of a lot better. Griff could have talked to her longer. He could have said more. Been more romantic. Groans didn't count. He could have asked her how her day went, how she had made the trip down from New York. How the house was coming. He could even have asked about his SUV! For all he knew, she could have had an accident. Sylvia. Horses. He was only allowing himself a precious few minutes to talk to the woman he said he loved, and yet he talked about a horse she didn't even know and a woman she wasn't certain she even liked.

She wouldn't cry. What was the point? To feel better? Would tears really make the hurt go away? Too bad she didn't have a Band-Aid big enough to ease the pain she was feeling. Was she expecting too much? Would she be feeling the same way if they were married and this happened? Griff had priorities, but so did she, damn it. If she could put him first, why couldn't he put her first?

What really hurt was the fact that she was disappointed in Griff. Not in the circumstances, but in Griff himself. Was it unrealistic to expect the man you love to come home on the first night and make love to you? No, and tomorrow wouldn't be the same. How could Griff think it would be? For God's sake, she wasn't sitting here waiting to be seduced. Their relationship was beyond that stage.

She felt as if she had been put through a mill

and had come out mangled and smashed. It was so damn easy to pick up the phone and make a call, sure in the knowledge that the other person would understand and forgive. Forgive, yes; forget, no. When you hurt you don't forget, she told herself. And when you're taken for granted, you don't forget that either.

Despite her resolution not to cry, the tears trickled down her cheeks. She wanted him to *want* to come home to her. She didn't care about priorities, she didn't want to think about them. All she wanted was Griff here beside her. She wanted him here telling her he loved her and it was right, this move to D.C. Goddamn it, she needed reassurance. Second fiddle to a horse. Wait till Pixie heard about this one.

Sleep would never come now. She should get up and watch television till she worked off her hostility. Or better yet, have a few snorts from the bottle of brandy Pixie had given her. Now, if she could just remember where she had put it, she could get pleasantly sloshed. Snookered, maybe. On second thought, three aspirins would be better, she decided. Besides, she had promised herself to save the brandy to toast Pixie's story.

Dory punched the pillow with a vengeance. She was angry, frustrated, *out of control*. The thought made her rigid. Eventually, she slept, her dreams panicked by a wild-eyed stallion carrying Sylvia on his back as he raced up and down Jefferson Davis Parkway. She woke exhausted.

Chapter Four

The draperies were hung and pinned by noon; the new chair for Griff's den was delivered. Both Lily and Sylvia called to invite her to lunch. She begged off, saying she had to do some grocery shopping and pick up a map so she could find her way to Georgetown University the next day. "I want to make Griff's favorite dinner, so I don't have all that much time," she told Sylvia.

"Are you going to freeze it?" Sylvia asked indifferently.

"No, why?"

"I just spoke to John and he said they wouldn't be home till late this evening. We were invited out for drinks and dinner, and now I either have to go alone or cancel. I don't suppose you'd like to go with me, would you? Griff suggested I ask you."

Out of control, out of control, her mind screamed as Sylvia rattled on about how she had told Griff Dory wasn't ready yet for the social scene and to give her time.

Dory floundered. "Well then, I'll just have a snack and get my things ready for tomorrow. First day of school. Thanks for calling, Sylvia. I appreciate the invitation, but some other time." She broke the connection, not waiting for Sylvia's reply.

Lily's phone call was an invitation also. She wanted Dory to come over and watch her make quince jelly, Rick's favorite. "I thought we could have tea and I'd make some fresh crumpets or scones. Little Ricky is so good in the afternoon, he just plays in his crib. We could have a nice long talk and really get to know one another."

Dory rattled off a list of real and imaginary things she had to do. When she hung up the phone she felt as though she had done ten laps in a whirlpool. Upstream!

She was on her way out the door when the phone rang a third time. Dory debated for four rings before she picked up the receiver. Her voice was controlled. It was Griff, a cheerful Griff, asking how she was and what she was doing.

"Not much. I was just going to the supermarket, if I can find it, that is. I understand you won't be home for dinner."

"I hope you don't mind. I should be home

around nine thirty or so. Just fix me a sandwich. Remember now, we have a date."

"I haven't forgotten," Dory said lightly. Damn, why did his voice sound so preoccupied? He was saying words but his mind was somewhere else. She could tell. "What kind of sandwich would you like?"

"What? Oh, anything. Pastrami and corned beef on rye would be good. Don't overdo, darling. Save some of your energy for this evening. I have to run now—the others are waiting for me. Love you."

Dory replaced the phone and stared at it for a long, mesmerizing minute. Day two and already there was trouble in paradise. No one had said it would be easy. Adjustments all the way. With her doing the adjusting. Lizzie had tried to warn her. Katy had been right on target when she said, "A woman gives ninety percent to every relationship. The man gives five percent and the dog the other five." Dory wondered what happed to the last five percent if one didn't have a dog.

All the way to the supermarket she told herself she was just feeling sorry for herself because she was alone with nothing to do. Nothing mental, that is. Physical work always frustrated her. She wasn't using her mind.

Tonight when she saw Griff things would be different. If they weren't different, this arrangement wasn't going to work. She would give fifty percent, maybe sixty percent, but that was her bottom line. She was getting off the track here.

It was time to restructure her thinking before something serious happened. So what if Griff had to work late and be away? It was his job and she had said she understood.

She was being selfish. Selfish and childish. It had been a long time since she had answered to anyone, if there ever had been a time. The only person she had to please or defend was herself. Now she was thrust into a new ball game where there was a second player and she was going to have to adjust and realize she couldn't have everything her own way. No snapping of the fingers and getting whatever she wanted. And what did she want? To be happy with Griff. To be with Griff. To share Griff's life. That was what she wanted. So what if she didn't like some of the adjustments? She could live with that. She could adjust. In her own way.

Dory felt better immediately. She would surprise Griff and make a late dinner. Something that could hold and not be ruined if he was late. She would put the little rosewood table that had been her grandmother's in front of the living room fireplace. The new place mats and napkins, of course, and she would wear her cashmere lounging robe and dab the new, exotic perfume she hadn't used yet behind each ear and into the deep V of her breasts. She would seduce him first with her dinner and then with her body. She giggled to herself as she walked up and down the aisles of the supermarket, tossing in items helter-skelter. She bought all the ingredients for a succulent lamb stew and the makings for bread. Now, all she had to do was go home and get out her cookbook. If all else failed, she could always call the obliging Lily.

Dory watched in awe as the totals came to life on the cash register. How could she have spent one hundred sixteen dollars on four bags of groceries? Cooking certainly was expensive. She whipped out her Gucci wallet from her Gucci handbag and paid the bill. She felt momentarily deflated. She could have bought a silk blouse at Bloomingdale's for one hundred sixteen dollars. She would talk to Griff about groceries when she got a chance. They would have to arrive at some manner of sharing the bills.

On the drive back to the house she let her mind race up and down an invisible column of figures. Drapes, the chair for Griff, the new sheets and towels she had bought at Saks before coming down here, the odds and ends from Macy's Cellar, the deposits for the utilities, the cost of tuition and registration, not to mention the books she would have to buy, and now this one hundred sixteen dollars. The invisible sum stunned her. A quarter of a new fall wardrobe; a down payment on a mink coat; twenty-eight pairs of shoes. This new life wasn't a mistake, was it? This was unusual for her, this vacillation. What was wrong with her? No one forced her to come here; it was her own decision. That was it, the word "decision." Was it the wrong one? She couldn't think about all that now. Now she had to think about cooking dinner: lamb stew with homemade bread. Peach pie for dessert. Coffee and then a drink in front of the fireplace. The congressional aide had left plenty of logs for her use. It was going to be perfect, and then tomorrow, bright and early, she would start her studies at Georgetown. Pursuing her studies had to take top priority. God, how she was beginning to hate that word. Nothing and no one was going to rain on *her* parade.

By five thirty the lamb stew was simmering, the peach pie was baking, and Dory was patting two loaves of bread into baking pans. She was smeared from head to toe with flour. This cooking was a bit much, in her opinion. She didn't see how women did it every day, three times a day.

While the dishes and pots and pans soaked she would change her clothes and put on her lounging robe. The worst part of the work was over now. She looked in dismay at her smudged and wrinkled shirt and flour-smeared jeans. Even her tattered sneakers from college wore a light dusting of flour. Her hair was tied back with a piece of string, and she looked a mess.

Novice that she was in the kitchen, Dory checked everything and set all the timers twice before she felt safe enough to fill the tub for a long, leisurely bath. Lord, she was tired. She should sleep like a log tonight. For more reasons than one, she smiled to herself as she made her way upstairs. She was halfway up when she heard a key in the lock. Wide-eyed, unable to move, she stood frozen on the steps and waited to see who it was that dared invade her new home.

"Griff!" It couldn't be Griff. It was Griff. He couldn't see her looking like this. But he was seeing her like this—and what was that strange look in his eye? Disbelief. By God, it was disbelief.

"Dory?" It was a question and a statement all in one.

Wild thoughts careered around in Dory's head. "Hi, darling. I was just going up to take a bath. Now that you're here, why don't you join me in a nice hot shower?"

"What I need is a drink, not a shower. Something smells good."

"Lamb stew, peach pie and homemade bread. I think it's the bread that smells so good."

"I bet you even churned the butter," Griff said lazily as he smiled at Dory's flour-smudged face.

"That's next week, " she grinned, rubbing her nose with the back of her hand. "I didn't expect you till later." She realized suddenly how stiff the words had sounded. Almost like an accusation. Was she always going to hear about Griff's schedule and plans first from Sylvia or Lily? Was it only an afterthought on Griff's part to call her and tell her himself? "I'm such a mess," Dory blurted, hoping the edge had left her voice. "Oh, Griff, I wanted everything to be so special for your first night at home. You've caught me at my worst."

"I thought we were having baloney sandwiches," he grinned, gathering her into his arms. Apparently, he hadn't noticed the recrimination in her tone.

"You said pastrami and corned beef. I thought this would be better." Dory snuggled closer into his embrace. "If you're going to work all kinds of crazy hours, you need good, substantial food. Also, you better enjoy it now because when I start school you *will* be eating baloney sandwiches. Kiss me like you haven't seen me for ten days."

"On second thought," Griff told her, rubbing his mustache on the tip of her nose, making her wrinkle it against the tickling, "maybe a nice warm shower would be a good idea." He picked her up in his arms and carried her up the stairs. "This is in lieu of carrying you over the threshold last night."

Contented, Dory cuddled in his arms, already anticipating the warm sting of the shower spray and Griff's warmer hands on her body.

Wrapped in her cozy, lemon-yellow terry robe, Dory sipped her wine while she watched Griff wolf down his dinner. His appetite would have to serve her as proof of his approval, for the words were not forthcoming. Even little promptings like, "I hope the stew is seasoned to your taste," and "don't you think the bread is a bit overdone?" only brought incoherent grunts that neither agreed nor disagreed.

This certainly wasn't the romantic evening Dory had envisioned. Their gymnastic lovemaking in the shower was rushed and somehow unsatisfying. The wine and candlelight, which should have been conducive to quiet conversation and romance, served instead as background for the TV news program Griff wanted to watch.

Dory glanced longingly at the stereo and the carefully chosen stack of mood-music records she had planned to play.

Competing with the television for Griff's attention, Dory tried conversation. "You never told me what kept you at the senator's farm," she said softly, compelling him with her green eyes to turn his attention away from the television. The plight of welfare mothers did not seem to fit in with the sumptuous meal she had prepared.

"Hmmm? Oh, well, our little colt was extremely shy about making his debut into this world. I think I told you the mare should have delivered before noon today. She didn't make her presentation until almost three in the afternoon. Then we had to fight the traffic back into the city. Fine little colt. The senator raises quarter horses, as well as thoroughbreds, and he has lots of friends with the same interests. His recommendations should be a boon to the clinic."

"How did your clinic get involved, Griff? Wasn't the senator happy with the veterinarians he'd been using?"

"Actually, it was Sylvia and some of her connections that pulled it through for us. I don't have to tell you, honey, breaking into any business in the D.C. area can be tough. There's so much competition. We have Sylvia to be grateful to for this little venture. Fortunately, everything worked out well for the mare and her foal. John and I were quite concerned that inducing labor at the wrong stage of pregnancy could invite a breech birth. Tough on the mother and the baby."

An unreasoning chord of jealousy struck Dory. Griff was so damn grateful to Sylvia. She was almost tempted to shatter his regard for the woman by revealing what she suspected between Sylvia and Duke. What's happening to me? Dory thought, aghast. I've never been greedy for petty gossip! I never make judgments and betray other people, especially with the intention of destroying their reputations. Dory was terribly disappointed in herself and was only glad she'd stopped herself in time to keep her suspicions to herself.

"Did Rick join you and John out at the farm?" Her inquiry was made in a shaking voice. Dory was having doubts about herself and her motives. The whole center of her values seemed to have suddenly shifted. Why? Before she could answer herself, Griff was speaking.

"No, Rick didn't come out to the farm. You see the way he is with little Rick and Lily. John and I thought it would be an unnecessary imposition on their family."

"Lily is certainly wrapped up in her 'two men' as she calls Rick and the baby. Do you think it's good? I mean, certainly a woman should have something else in her life besides mothering and blueberry muffins."

Griff dug heartily into another slice of bread, lathering it thickly with butter. He seemed distracted both by the bread and the news commentary, and he didn't answer Dory's question until he'd taken another sip of wine. "I'm not so sure, Dory. Lily is of that special breed who seems most a woman when she's making a home for her man. Rick certainly adores her, as you can tell."

"I'm not asking what's good for Rick, darling. I'm asking what's good for Lily."

Griff smiled, his eyes lighting, a silly smile spreading beneath his sexy mustache. "I *am* talking about what's good for Lily. That girl positively blooms. And didn't I already tell you how John and I relieved Rick of responsibility out at the farm so he could be home with Lily and the baby? If that's not good for Lily, I don't know what is."

Dory returned his smile somewhat sheepishly. She didn't want to spoil this night with a contest of opinions, but she couldn't help thinking that Rick and Lily had already had so much time together. They were already a family. But last night had been Dory's first night in her new home, and that didn't seem to cut any ice with either John or Griff. What was it about Lily that made the partners want to protect her and make her happy? Was it simply that she was the typical "little woman"? What was it about herself that seemed to make it unnecessary for Griff to take special consideration of her, that left him guiltless about spending what should have been a special night for them by nursing a pregnant horse? Did she give the appearance of being totally self-sufficient and understanding about career and responsibility coming first? Dory stood abruptly and began clearing the table. She didn't like herself very much this evening and she wasn't quite certain what to do about it. Why should

Sylvia be praised for being cosmopolitan and social climbing and Lily be idolized for being the
perfect wife and mother? What about her, Dory?
And when, if ever, was Griff going to comment
on her efforts to make a home for them?

The dishes clattered into the sink. Taking a
deep breath, Dory tried to rationalize. She was
an intelligent woman, but right now she needed
some focus to her life that was separate from
her activities of setting up a home. Focus. That
was what she was used to. Focus on her job, on
the people she worked with, on Griff. She simply had to get these things back into perspective. Tomorrow, she promised herself. School,
new people, new things to learn and study. Tomorrow, it would be all right.

Chapter Five

Griff left for the clinic early in the morning, kissing Dory good-bye as she put their coffee cups into the dishwasher. "Here's for luck your first day of school. Nervous?"

"You bet. It's been some while since I've sat in a classroom, don't forget. But I think there's still some life in the old gray matter," she laughed, tapping her head.

Dory was nervous, more than she cared to admit. After Griff left the house she found herself compulsively straightening cushions and smoothing the bed and giving another swipe of the dishcloth to an already clean white Formica counter. She walked through the house, trying to see the results of her efforts through objective eyes. The soft gray carpeting in the living room picked up the gentle pinks and buffered whites in the Italian marble fireplace. Most of the furnishings from her apartment in New York were already in place; only a few decorator items and knickknacks were still left to be unpacked. The chrome and glass étagère and end tables from Griff's loft added a striking note of contrast against her more formal traditional pieces of white velvet and damask. She could run into town today and see if she could pick up some toss pillows, a few in the same shade as the carpeting and others in that deep plum color she liked so well, Perhaps she could order several huge stack cushions in plum velvet to serve as extra seating. Her collection of crystal paperweights would look terrific on the glass table banked against the sofa.

Dory shook her head. What was she doing standing here decorating the living room when she should be upstairs this minute getting dressed?

Up the carpeted stairs and down the short hallway, Dory entered the bedroom, which, along with its accompanying dressing room and bath, comprised the entire second floor of the town house. There was still much work to be done here. New drapes to be hung, deciding on the accent colors, finding a love seat and easy chair to place before the fireplace. She must see about finding a wax or a finishing compound to bring out the best in the ornately designed andirons. Set with white fieldstone, the fireplace was built into a stuccoed wall and centered on the far side of the room. A really striking tapestry or rug would be just the thing to hang over the hearth.

Dory's eye caught the movement of the digital alarm clock on the bedside table. If she didn't hurry, she would be late for school. The city map she had bought made finding the university easy, but she still didn't know about parking or even how to find the buildings where her classes were to be held.

Rifling through her drawers to find underwear and stockings, Dory chewed her bottom lip with worry. She had had every intention of driving out to Georgetown yesterday to get the lay of the land, but somehow she hadn't done it. Why had she allowed herself to become distracted by household chores and preparing that extravagant dinner? Griff had told her he would be more than satisfied with sandwiches. She could have put her time to better use.

Rushing for the bathroom and turning on the shower, Dory berated herself for not making her priorities stand. She never should have let herself be sidetracked. She detested being late, and even judged others by how promptly they kept appointments. Stepping under the steaming spray, she pushed back the thought that perhaps her dallying around the house with her various chores might be an indication that she was not as eager to go back to school as she had thought.

Midway through the first day of school Dory had what Griff later described as an anxiety attack. It hit her when she was walking from one

building to the next shortly after the lunch hour.
She felt weak and her head reeled. The first
thought that ricocheted through her brain was
that she was pregnant. Then she realized how
ridiculous the thought was and felt worse. She
sat down on a bench until the dizziness passed,
her heart fluttering wildly. By the time she
teetered to her class she had herself diagnosed
and was making out a will in her mind. She was
to be cremated and . . . God, what would they
do with her ashes? Her parents might want
them or Aunt Pixie might find some use for
them. Griff wanting her ashes never occurred to
her. If she was going to die, why was she sitting
here in this damn dumb, stupid class trying to
convince herself and the instructor that she did
indeed want to get her doctorate? As the court-
room voice of the professor droned on, Dory let
her mind wander. Some inner sense told her
that there was nothing wrong with her, physically. It was nerves, it was all too much, too
quick, too fast. She hadn't adjusted yet. Time.
She needed time.

Time was measured by clocks and calendars,
things she had worked with for years. She had
always watched the clock, ticked off the days on
the calendar, made a schedule and stuck to it.
Now, she felt adrift.

When the class was over Dory hadn't the
faintest idea of what had been said or who sat
next to her. The instructor was almost out the
door before she got up from her seat. Thank
God, she had taped the class. She switched the
button on the small Sony recorder and slipped

it into her bag. She felt rotten. Not physically rotten. Just rotten. She glanced at her watch and wondered what Katy and the others were doing. If she really wanted to know, she could call up and find out. She didn't really want to know, she told herself as she walked down the hall looking for a student lounge. A cup of coffee would help. Maybe some crackers or something to settle her churning stomach. She was behaving worse than a child on the first day of school.

Dory suffered through a two-hour lecture on Chaucer's boyhood, watching the minute hand on her watch. The instructor walked up and down in front of the class, tapping a pencil against his fat, pink palm. It might have helped her concentration if he was handsome with good teeth. It was no fun to look at a middle-aged, balding man with baggy trousers. There was even a shine to his pants. For shame on his wife, Dory thought. His white shirt was polyester, and gray with repeated washings. Ring around the collar, no doubt. Lily would know how to make the shirt clean again. Little Ricky's bibs were so blindingly white they hurt the eyes. She wondered what Lily was doing. Where was Sylvia? She wished she was with Griff.

Her palms were starting to sweat again. By forcing herself to stare at the instructor's shirt-front she was able to control the attack of dizziness. Think about something pleasant, anything. A meadow of daisies. A clear, sparkling lake filled with jumping fish. Christmas with Pixie and a mound of presents. Damn it to hell, why wasn't it working? Why was her throat closing? My God, what if she collapsed? She tried clearing her throat and got an annoyed glance from the instructor. Her throat constricted again and she could feel the saliva building up in her mouth. Oh God, don't let me drool, not here in front of all these people. Was it her imagination or were people staring at her as she dabbed at her wet mouth?

To get up now and walk out would only call attention to herself. Better to sit still and try to concentrate on the lecture. Why was this instructor so damn long-winded? Didn't they cut classes short anymore? She wanted to cry when she felt her throat muscles relax. She drew in deep breaths and exhaled slowly. She felt a little better. Thank God.

Dory looked around at the other students. They all wore rapt expressions. None of them was having an anxiety attack or whatever it was she was having. None of their minds appeared to be wandering the way hers was. They seemed to be accepting the instructor regardless of his looks and clothing. What was wrong with her? How could she be thinking about such ridiculous things? Or was this one more indication that she wasn't taking her doctorate seriously? Intentions, good or bad, were one thing; following through was something else entirely. She had to give that theory a lot of thought.

Dory was the first one out of the room when the professor nodded his head in the general direction of the class. Dismissed. Thank God. If she checked the map, she might have time to

stop by the garden nursery she had noticed on
her way to school. Autumn blooms and some
plants for the house. There would be time to
arrange them and place them to the best advantage. Also time for making a pot roast. Griff
loved pot roast and so did she. Aunt Pixie always
said if you added apple juice to the gravy, you
had pure ambrosia.

She drove with the windows down. She felt
wonderful with the crisp fall air whipping at her
through the open window. She couldn't wait to
get home and out of the tight, clinging silk
slacks and Oscar de la Renta overblouse with
matching belt. She kicked the two-hundred-
dollar shoes off and wiggled her toes. She had
to remember to buy some foot powder for her
sneakers. And she needed more than one pair
of sneaker socks. Back in New York she had only
used the washers and dryers in the basement of
the building once every three weeks or so. Everything else went to the cleaners. Now there were
Griff's clothes to launder.

While the nursery man loaded the ferns, the
philodendrons, and Swedish ivy into the back of
the SUV, Dory stared at the colorful blooms of
the autumn flowers. To the right there was a decorative display of pumpkins and coppery colored chrysanthemums. On impulse, she bought
the biggest pumpkin and four pots of the bronze
flowers. Then she added one of the deep yellow
and another of rich lavender. There was barely
room in the car for herself. The owner was delighted with the check she wrote out for two
hundred thirty dollars. She didn't bat an eye. It

was worth it. Griff would love the flowers and
the pumpkin. Everyone needed a fern at the
kitchen window. Fireplaces always needed greenery on the hearth. Oh, what she could do with
that fireplace come Christmas.

Back at the town house her silken garments
slithered to the floor. The alligator shoes lay
lopsidedly beside them. A lacy froth of powder
blue bra found a home on the neat spread. Jewelry went back into the nest of velvet.

Dory stepped into faded jeans and a pullover
shirt of deep orange. She liked the feeling against
her skin. What a pleasure to go without underwear. A wicked grin split her features. If Griff
liked all that froth and lace, he would love bare
skin even more. She liked it when he ran his
hand up under a blouse or shirt. God, he had
such delicious hands.

The Coach case with its notebooks and cassette recorder landed with a thump on a coffee-
colored slipper chair. Dory grimaced as she
read her initials in gold lettering. Ostentatious,
she thought.

Time to put the pot roast on. While it was
browning, she would bring in the plants and
arrange them. But when she was finished she
felt disappointed. She should have bought
more. A tree, a big leafy tree was called for, and
she needed more fill-in plants. Damn, she had
been so sure she had enough. If there was one
thing she disliked, it was something that looked
unfinished. A glance at the digital clock told her
she had time to make a quick run back to the
nursery. But first she called the clinic to see what

time Griff would be home. He sounded annoyed when he said some time around seven. Dory barely noticed the annoyance as she calculated her driving time.

It was six o'clock when Dory backed the SUV into her parking space. She struggled with the bushy tree and had to drag it into the house. The second tree, reed slim with lacy pointed leaves, found its way to the living room. A second pumpkin and the three boxes of assorted fill-in plants sat next to the fireplace. When she was finished arranging them, she stifled the urge to call Lily to come for a look-see. Lily would love it. Sylvia would say, "Darling, it looks like a goddamn jungle and what do you mean, you wax the leaves?" Griff would be delighted and compliment her on making the town house look like a home. She decided not to mention that this batch of greenery had set her back another two hundred forty dollars. Trees were expensive but every leaf was worth the money. She would economize somewhere else.

Satisfied with her handiwork, Dory retreated to the kitchen to wash the greens for a salad. Fresh string beans and four ears of corn would complete their meal. Dessert would be fresh pears soaked in brandy. Griff was going to love it, just love it.

Griff's mind was on the interstate as he watched for the Arlington turnoff. John had to speak to him twice before he turned to look at the older man. "I'm sorry, John, what did you say?"

"I said Sylvia is going back to work at the beginning of the week. You know she likes to have her summers off for golf and tennis. It's not that she makes a fistful of money; actually, she uses up half of what she makes driving that gas guzzler of hers, but it makes her happy. I'm glad she's doing something for herself. It's important that women do things just for themselves. Makes them . . ." he sought for the word Sylvia had drilled into his head a hundred times. ". . . fulfilled. Of course, you know what I'm talking about. Dory is a career girl. And now that she's going back for her doctorate, you must be very proud of her, Griff. She'll definitely be an asset to you. Of course, Sylvia isn't anywhere near Dory's league, but selling cosmetics is something she likes, and Neiman-Marcus is a prestigious store."

Griff wondered why John sounded so defensive when he spoke of Sylvia and fulfillment. Dory as an asset. His eyebrows went up a fraction of an inch. "Dory is her own person, John. Always has been. I love her. I respect her intelligence. I admire her independence and the way she's climbed her way to the top of her field. I don't mind telling you I'm a little in awe of her now that she's going back to pursue her studies. She's probably the only person I know who is a 'whole' person. Capably whole."

John swiveled in his seat to stare at Griff. Was there a hint of something other than admiration in the man's voice? Surely, he couldn't be jealous of his . . . live-in. John always felt uncomfortable when he had to refer to Dory in a manner other than calling her by name. These live-in situations were not to his liking. In the end they always caused problems. Sylvia, with all her free-spirited ways, was probably even more suited to marriage than Lily. Sylvia liked being married. She preferred being Mrs. instead of Miss or Ms.

"I hope the girls hit it off and can do things together. Sylvia still has a lot of time on her hands. Lily has never managed to domesticate her, so it's up to Dory to take her in hand. Sylvia doesn't like to be pushy, if you know what I mean. She's going to stand back and give Dory room. You mark my word, those two are going to be good friends. You do think they'll hit it off, don't you?"

Griff noted the anxious tone of the older man. "I'm sure of it, John. But I do think we should let them pace it out themselves."

"Absolutely." John leaned back and closed his eyes. There was no sense in telling Griff that he was worried about Sylvia and the way she was spending her time *and* money. His money. It was nothing for her to drop two thousand dollars at the Galleria in one day. Even with wise and careful investing, he was going to have to draw the line with her. And, she was now annoyed when he asked her where she was and how she spent the day. He hated to use the word secretive, but, it was the only word that applied to Sylvia these days. He also wasn't going to tell either Griff or Rick that he had joined a men's health club. His blood pressure was up and he had willingly given up salt and spicy foods. It wasn't too late, he assured himself. There was still time to put that lift in his step and beef himself up a bit. He had never been athletic and his lean body seemed to be shrinking into a kind of old man's stringiness. Sort of like a tough, old rooster.

"I think I'll tell Dory to put whatever she cooked for dinner in the fridge and take her out to dinner. I could use some ambiance this evening. Dory started school today and I know she's not going to be in the mood for much of anything. A nice, quiet dinner, just the two of us."

"Sounds good to me," John drawled. He wondered if Sylvia was going to serve Swanson's pot pies or make soup and sandwiches. Someday he was going to figure out how many cans of Campbell's soup he had consumed since marrying Sylvia. Christ, how he hated what Sylvia called grilled cheese sandwiches. White bread with a slice of cheese on a paper plate warmed in the microwave oven. Low-calorie yogurt on a stick was dessert seven days a week. But he loved her, heart and soul. It never occurred to him to complain. Sylvia wouldn't like it if he complained. When he complained Sylvia turned away from him in bed and spent money faster than he could breathe. He wondered who was going to take care of him in his twilight years. He smiled. Sylvia would hire the best nurse possible to wheel him around. She would check on him three times a day. The thought made him want to gag. I'm counting on Dory Faraday to bring some stability to my marriage, he admitted to himself. If it didn't work out, naturally he would bring pressure to bear on Griff. He wouldn't like doing it, but if it meant saving Sylvia from whatever she needed to be saved from, he would do it. In his gut he knew she wasn't sleeping around. Sylvia would never do that to him. She respected her marriage vows. He was *almost* sure of it. But why was she so restless, so lacking in serenity? He hoped Dory could find out.

Griff dropped John off and headed north toward his own home. The goddamn plum pits were still in the van. Sylvia's stale perfume curled his nostril hair. He fought off a fit of sneezing and turned on the air-conditioning. It didn't help. Sylvia might be a class act, but she sure needed a lesson or two in the use of perfume. He wondered how John stood it.

The van slid in next to the SUV. Walking around the back, he noticed the spilled dirt and broken leaves and branches in the back of the wagon. He frowned. He'd always been meticulous about his car. What in the hell had Dory been lugging around?

"Hi, honey, I'm home. What say we splurge and go out to dinner this evening?" Griff called out to Dory as he walked down the hall to the kitchen.

Dory stared at the thickening gravy of the pot roast and then at Griff. Griff's eyes took in the set table, the bubbling pots and Dory's flushed face. "You did all this and went to school too?" he asked in amazement.

Dory nodded happily. "Pot roast, gravy, string

beans, corn on the cob and pears soaked in brandy for dessert. Do you still want to go out to dinner?" she teased.

"Hell no, only a fool would do a thing like that. How about a beer while I get ready to shower?"

"Go along and I'll bring it up to you. How did you like the living room?"

"Why, what did you do? I just headed straight down the hallway."

Dory uncapped a bottle of beer and trailed behind Griff. She couldn't wait to see his reaction.

"Honey, this is fantastic. How in the hell did you do all of this? I didn't know you were Superwoman."

"By working my tail off. I'm so glad you're pleased. Plants make all the difference. Tell me you like it, Griff."

"You did a great job, honey. Was it expensive?"

"Not really. I got some bargains and . . . the total was . . . around one hundred dollars or so," Dory lied.

"Fantastic. A bargain hunter too. I definitely approve. I knew I liked you for a reason. What time is dinner?"

"Dinner is whenever you finish your second beer," Dory said, kissing him lightly on the cheek.

Griff ate voraciously. He praised everything at least three times. Dory preened as he complimented her. She rattled on about the care and feeding of the plants and the amount of sunshine they needed, and how a grow light was a must. From there, she babbled on about the apple juice in the pot roast gravy and how she had, just by a stroke of luck, found the last corn of the season. Griff listened to every word, mesmerized by her excitement. "How did school go?" he asked when she slowed down to sip at her wine.

Dory frowned and told him about her dizzy spell. Griff stared at her with concern. "And you did all this when you got home? No more spells?"

"No. Never felt better. Nerves, I guess."

"Anxiety attack. Don't overdo, Dory. We have a year's lease. Take your time and don't push yourself. Promise me that if it happens again, you'll tell me and we'll get it checked out. I'm as sure as you are that it's just nerves, but it doesn't pay to leave anything to chance."

"It's sweet of you to be concerned, but I'm okay and I promise. Now tell me what you're going to do this evening? Do we watch television like an old married couple or do you have work to do in your den?"

"Honey, I have to go back to the clinic. We have a Kerry blue that had nine pups today, and they aren't doing all that well. Upper respiratory problems. They're such valuable dogs, I want to make sure we do everything possible for them. I'd do the same for a mutt, but these particular dogs belong to Senator Gregory. Politics, my dear." He grinned.

Dory's face fell. Her wonderful mood was shattered. Griff didn't seem to notice as he talked on about the Kerry blues. "I guess you'll have the den to yourself for studying. I shouldn't be too late. Around ten or ten thirty. I'll be back before you know it. By the time you get the kitchen cleaned up and do some studying, I'll be home, and then look out," he leered. "Say, why don't you call Sylvia? John told me she's about to go back to work at Neiman-Marcus. I know she'd love to hear from you."

"Okay, I'll do that," Dory promised as she started to clear the table. Griff pecked her on the cheek and left by the kitchen door. It was at times like this that Dory wished she smoked.

While the dishwasher sloshed its way through two rinse cycles Dory called Sylvia and chatted for a few minutes. "Darling, how nice of you to call. How was school?" Not waiting for a reply, Sylvia rattled on. "I always hated school. So Griff told you about my job. I just adore it. And," she said, laughing, "I get thirty percent off anything I buy. Let me know what you need. And, darling, when you have some free time and want to go shopping, just call me. I can show you the stores to stay away from. If Lily would just stop breast-feeding that tot and get a sitter, we could have some wonderful times. I don't know about you, but I'm mortified every time she unhooks her bra. That baby just . . . guzzles and Lily always has this stupid look on her face as though she's orgasmic. Disgusting. I'd love to chat longer, but John and I are playing bridge with some friends this evening. Call me now," Sylvia said airily. Dory stared at the phone for a minute and then hung up. So much for Sylvia. Thirty percent off. That was good. She wondered if it applied to anything in the store or just cosmetics.

Dory stared at the phone, willing Sylvia's animated face to appear. What made Sylvia run? What was Sylvia all about? A little dose of Sylvia went a long way. She thought she knew what the older woman's problem was, if it was a problem. She feared old age, suffered from a fear of being unloved and ending up alone someday. Fear was the crack in Sylvia's veneer. Dory could understand that fear. It was something every woman could understand. It was the way a woman handled that fear that made the difference. Tolerant . . . that's what she must be, with Sylvia.

Dory sighed. She might as well call Lily too. She felt as though she needed an excuse. Her eyes fell to the trash can and the blueberry muffins she had thrown out. "Lily, I just wanted you to know Griff loved the muffins."

"Oh, I knew he would. Men always love anything homemade. How are you, Dory? I've been thinking about you all day and how I admire you going back to school and all. I wish I had the stamina to do it, but I'm locked in here with little Ricky and big Rick. Did Griff tell you about the Kerry blues? Rick said they're all worried about them. Wouldn't it be awful if all nine of them died?"

"Yes, it would. Sylvia told me she's going back to work. Isn't that wonderful?" God, it was hard to talk to Lily.

"I'm not sure if it's wonderful or not. Sylvia just pretends to work. She spends most of her time making up her face for the customers. I hardly find that work. In fact, I think it's dull. I rarely use cosmetics myself, Rick doesn't like them. So when I do use them I use the organic kind."

"Somehow I knew you would." Dory's tart tone was lost on Lily.

"Dory, I'm starting to make quilt squares. I'm going to make a quilt for little Ricky. Quilting makes me feel so . . . so Old American, you know, like in Colonial times or something. If you want to do one, we could work on them together. I have the pattern and loads of material. I save everything, all kinds of scraps. I have so much we could each make three quilts and I'd have some leftovers."

"Lily, I'm all caught up in school and everything. It sounds . . . interesting. If I find the time, I'll be glad to give it a try. I better get going now, I have a lot of work to catch up on. I'll call you as soon as I have some free time."

"Any time. I'm always here. Now, don't you work too hard. Those old teachers are slave drivers. I remember what it was like."

Quilts. Quince jelly. Blueberry muffins. I bet she paints murals on little Ricky's wall too, Dory thought uncharitably as she turned off the kitchen light and headed for the den.

The tape cassette she had recorded in class was playing, but she listened with only half an ear. Curled up on the new recliner she had bought for Griff's den, Dory recalled her conversation with Lily and tried to figure out what it was about the young woman that irritated her.

She had known other women, her mother included, who concentrated all efforts, physical and emotional, to the making of a home. Lily's devotion to home and husband wasn't really that unusual, so what was it?

The remainder of the recorded lecture went unheard as Dory pondered her own questions. Finally, after much soul searching, she decided that Lily's capabilities and unswerving sense of direction made Dory feel inferior and inept. Rick seemed so content and happy due to Lily's ministrations, and Dory wanted to put that same gleam in Griff's eyes.

This was silly, Dory chided herself. Of course Griff was happy. What was there to be unhappy about? The niggling thought that she had refused Griff's proposal of marriage crept into the back of her mind. Was it possible that Griff really needed the stability and contentment of a legal, committed relationship? Was this arrangement of theirs somehow threatening? Why wasn't she able to commit herself to marriage? If she was happy with Griff, why shouldn't she turn in her resignation to *Soiree* and plant her roots here in D.C.? Did Griff suspect her of always needing a back-door escape out of a situation, and was he right?

The sudden, unwelcome thought of David Harlow sent a shameful shudder down her spine. It was true, she was trying to cover all the angles, even to the point of compromising herself to Harlow by not making it perfectly clear that she could never have more than a professional interest in him and that she resented his implying that she might. Compromised. She had walked into his trap with her eyes open, and now Harlow was sitting back in New York thinking that when she returned as managing editor there would be after-hours recreation. Fool! Fool!

The sound of a key in the door made Dory jump in alarm. Griff! How long had she sat here? Her eyes flew to her watch. It was after nine and she still hadn't listened to the recorded lecture.

"Hi, I'm home!" Griff called. Dory was on her feet and running out to the living room, throwing herself into Griff's arms.

"Hey, what's this?" he asked, holding her tightly, feeling the tremblings race down her spine. "What's the trouble, honey? Did something frighten you?"

Dory clung to Griff as if for dear life. That was the word—frightened. Scared to death. She wanted him to hold her and tell her it was all going to be all right, but she knew she couldn't express *what* frightened her. It was impossible to put it into words, or even to face the fears head-on. Right this minute, she only knew she needed Griff's strength, his love, his support. She wanted to hide herself away in him, have him protect her from the world and from her self-doubts. Safe. She wanted to be safe!

Dory buried her face in the crook of Griff's neck, wrapping her arms around him, wanting to dissolve inside him. She began kissing him, frantic little kisses at first, then longer, more seductive caresses of her lips and tongue contrived to evoke his passions and responses.

Griff was overwhelmed by this display of emotion, but his confusion was allayed and finally stilled by a more primal need that she stirred. Lifting her into his arms, he carried her up the staircase, taking her to their bed. Dory's insistent fingers worked the buttons on his shirt and the fastenings of his belt. She wanted him, she kept murmuring, breathlessly, almost desperately. Baring his chest to her hands, she caressed the smooth expanse of his skin, following her touch with moist, hungry explorations of her lips. Impatient with the confining fabric of their clothing, Dory practically ripped the garments from her body, turning back again to hurry Griff with his.

Feeling him against her, skin against skin, breath against breath, Dory stretched out beneath him, pressing herself into the strength of his embrace.

"Take me now, Griff!" she implored, thrashing wildly under his weight. "Please take me now!"

The desperate edge of her voice was disguised by the passion in her words. Griff covered her, rocking against her, feeling himself trapped in the grip of her thighs and the clutch of her arms. Her words echoed through his head; his love for her compelling him to satisfy her desires.

Dory tried to lose herself in the arms of the man she loved. She tried to hide in him, to make herself safe from those faceless shadows and self-doubts that pursued her.

Griff lay on his back, Dory's head resting

peacefully on his shoulder. Something told him that only her body was at peace; something was very wrong for Dory. "Want to tell me about it?" he asked softly, caressing her arm with the flat of his hand, much the way one would soothe a child. He waited for her response; it was so long in coming, he thought she might not have heard him.

"No," Dory whispered at last. "This is something I've got to work out myself." Her cheeks bloomed pink in the darkness. Griff knew her well enough to know that something was very wrong. She had initiated their lovemaking with wild and wanton behavior and then ended in surrendering herself to him. Whatever she had done, it was different than it had ever been before. They had always been equals as lovers, giving and taking, pleasing and being pleased, finding in one another that special sensitivity that nurtures love and shares in the responsibility for it. Tonight, Dory was ashamed of herself. Tonight, she had used Griff to hide from her insecurities. Her body was sated, but there was a lingering feeling of failure. Tonight was different. Not better. Dory knew it and Griff knew it too.

Chapter Six

September's exquisite Indian summer days gave way to a sharper October complete with a kaleidoscope of autumn colors. Dory went to classes on a hit-and-miss basis, preferring to settle snugly into the town house poring over decorator books and gourmet recipes. She studied when the mood struck, often leaving it until early Monday morning while she did laundry. Sometimes, late at night after Griff was asleep, she would creep downstairs to pore guiltily through her notes and read assigned chapters.

In the morning, Griff would find her asleep at the desk. He'd kiss her consolingly and bring her coffee, saying, "Poor baby, you're really carrying quite a load, aren't you?"

Dory would protest heartily, pretending to slough off his commiserations. Although she crept down to the den with full intentions of studying, her real reason for getting up was that she couldn't sleep, knowing how she was neglecting her schoolwork. But once settled in the den with soft music coming from the stereo, she would soon fall asleep. Nothing she read could penetrate the hateful malaise.

Griff was truly concerned. Dory had always been eager to share her life with him, telling him what was going on at the magazine and discussing new projects with him. Since coming to D.C. he'd noticed that she often became quiet, preferring to listen while he told about his day at the clinic and how business was increasing. It was tender and sweet, he decided, the way she listened so intensely to his recital of the day's events, and he had to admit he was selfish with her attention. But when he did ask her about her studies or her freelance projects for *Soiree* she would become quiet and introspective. He was quickly learning to shrug off Dory's lassitude. When he came right out and asked her if something was troubling her, she would look at him with that wide-eyed green stare of hers and offer denials. He might have pressed her further, following his instincts, if he weren't so involved and preoccupied with the clinic and his doubling patient file. That Dory was happy living with him, Griff had no doubt. She took pride in their home, was steeped in new ideas and color schemes, and she always sang or hummed tuneless little songs while she worked in the kitchen. Dory made their lives comfortable and cozy. It was just that she seemed to have taken on a burden—housekeeping, cooking, her studies, and her freelance work. When he thought of the subtle changes in her, a little frown would form between his brows.

Dory knew that Griff was concerned about her graduate work and her promised projects for *Soiree*. He always asked questions, which she took great pains to dodge. How could she tell him that she was already weeks behind in her reading and that she hadn't even made the first contact for her magazine articles? It was easier to avoid the subject entirely. Just yesterday, she'd received a phone call from Katy, telling her *Soiree* had contacted several promising subjects for her, giving her the names and data on each. But when Katy began asking how things were going in D.C., Dory found an urgent excuse to cut the conversation short. She had heard the puzzlement in her friend's voice and several times during the day she had been tempted to call Katy back, but somehow she lacked the courage to pick up the phone. It occurred to Dory that she was actually hiding out, pulling the ground over her head. How could she converse about what she was doing and how she was doing it, when in truth she was doing nothing? She was disappointed in herself, angry actually, and was constantly vowing to get a grip on herself. Each night when she crawled into bed beside Griff she would experience deep shame and self-loathing because today had been no different from yesterday. It was only when she was buried in Griff's embrace, feeling his hands on her body and hearing the little love words he murmured, that she felt good about herself. She could hide away, even from herself, while she surrendered her body and her soul to the man she loved.

Shopping trips with Sylvia left her teeth on edge. It wasn't that she didn't enjoy the trips; she did. But the older woman's preoccupation with spending money in the shortest time possible annoyed her. If she was hiding, then Sylvia was hiding, too. She hid behind designer labels, costly makeup and secret trysts in the late mornings. Dory knew that shortly, inevitably, Sylvia was going to confide in her, and she didn't want to hear those confidences or be a part of them. Little by little she inched away from Sylvia and leaned more toward Lily. Lily was safe. With Lily she didn't have to think. Sylvia's blatant independence and bravado made Lily roll her eyes in dismay. "She's the most dependent person I know," Lily had smiled at Dory over a casserole lunch on the day before Halloween. "If you took John away, she would cave in and wither up like an apple."

Dory decided she almost liked Lily. Tolerating the plump young woman wasn't as difficult as it had been in the beginning. Take today, for example. She hadn't winced when Lily invited her for lunch to make scarecrows for the doorway. Halloween was such fun, she had said. Dory agreed, although she couldn't remember ever having much fun on the children's holiday. "It's little Ricky's first Halloween and I made him a Peter Cottontail costume," Lily said. "I'm taking him trick-or-treating in the stroller so he can see all the children. You can't start early enough with the little ones. I want him to be a part of everything and that includes Halloween." Dory nodded agreeably. Griff was certainly going to be surprised when he came home this evening and saw her outdoor arrangement. She was handy and creative, as Lily pointed out. "You've changed since you got here, " Lily smiled as she stuffed straw arms into a plaid shirt.

"How so?" Dory asked.

"When you first arrived you were New York City from the top of your head to the tip of your toes. You were like Sylvia would like to be but isn't. Do you know what I mean? You had the clothes, the right hairstyle; by the way, would you like me to trim your hair? I'm real good at it. I always cut Rick's hair."

"Sure." She giggled to herself. She wondered what her stylist at Vidal Sassoon would say if he could see Lily "trimming" her hair.

"Anyway, as I was saying, now you're just like everyone else. You cook, you clean, you go to school, and you've come out of your shell. I bet Griff is happy with all you've been doing."

Dory frowned. Was Griff happy with the things she had done? Or was he tolerating her? She wasn't sure. He seemed to have changed too. The pressures of the new clinic and all, she told herself. He never seemed to want to go out unless it was to someone's house. Money, she told herself. It always came down to money. She hated to see the look of concern on Griff's face when he made out the bills. Perhaps she should have offered some of her money. Next month, she told herself. After all, she was buying the groceries and she had paid for all the decorating. Surely he didn't expect more. He seemed drawn and tense these days. And twice a day he quizzed her about school and how she was doing. She found to her chagrin that she was beginning to lie, telling him she went to class when she stayed home to trim the plants and feed and water them. Or just to sit and read *Redbook* all by herself. She always felt guilty when she did something like that and then would outdo herself cooking a gastronomical feast for Griff.

"Is he?" Lily prodded.

"Is he what?" Dory asked, coming out of her reverie.

"Is he happy with the way you've taken over and turned that house into a home?"

"I think so. Griff doesn't say much. Sometimes it's hard to tell, and you know all three of the guys are uptight with the clinic. He comes home some nights and falls into bed exhausted. But I think he's happy." Dory spoke with more confidence than she felt.

"Well, I know one thing for certain. Rick says Griff's so proud of you sometimes he gets on his nerves the way he talks about you."

"Rick said that?" Dory's eyes glowed like moonbeams at the words.

"That's what it's all about, Dory," Lily said softly. "Taking pride in one another's accomplishments. Griff is so pleased that you're going to school and that one day you'll hold your doctorate. He brags about you to John, too. Sylvia told me just the other day. By the way, what's wrong with her? She seemed out of sorts." Dory shrugged. She didn't want to get into a discussion of Sylvia.

Lily finished the torso of her scarecrow and watched as Dory followed her instructions. She admitted to herself that she hadn't liked Dory Faraday when she met her for the first time. She felt responsible for Dory's transformation, as she called it. She didn't feel at all guilty about subtly persuading Dory that her own lifestyle was far superior to Sylvia's gypsy, freewheeling attitude. Her patience had been rewarded; Dory had become domesticated. Yes, she liked Dory Faraday much better now, and she would like her even more if only she wouldn't withdraw at times into her own secret world. Meanwhile she would stand by and be the good friend that Dory needed. Who knows, she mused to herself, I may even talk her into marriage.

"I'm done, what do you think?" Dory asked as she propped her straw man next to Lily's.

"Perfect," Lily said as if she were talking to her prize pupil. "I want you to call me after Griff sees it and tell me what he says. Promise now," she said, wagging her finger in the air.

"Okay. I've got to run now. I'm going to make that apple pie you gave me the recipe for. I bought the apples at the stand where you told me to go. While it's baking I have some notes to transcribe. By the way, I took some cuttings from my plants. If you want them, you can stop by tomorrow. I'll make lunch this time."

"Wonderful. Now don't forget to use the large pumpkin instead of the small one. By the way, what are you and Griff doing for Thanksgiving?"

"I'm not sure. He hasn't mentioned anything."

"Rick and I would love to have you. We make a real big deal over the holidays. I'm having twenty people. We'd love it if you'd come," she repeated.

"I'll speak to Griff. If he's agreeable, what can I bring?"

"Pies," Lily said promptly. "Pumpkin, of course, and several of the apple quince I showed you how to make. A pecan one would be nice too, just to be different."

Dory bent down to dangle her fingers at the baby and then looked around. Lily's house was screamingly neat. She frowned. Something should be out of place. Some piece of lint on the carpet, something.

All the way back to the town house she thought about Lily and her neat house and about Sylvia who lived like the Queen of the Gypsies. The thoughts did nothing for her tense mood. She was getting a headache. She was getting a lot of headaches lately. And she had gained seven pounds. Seven pounds in all the wrong places. Griff had jabbed at her playfully and mentioned it. Womanly. She looked womanly. She banished the word matronly from her mind.

Griff sat in the clinic offices, a small puppy in his lap. He fondled the silky ears and knew he

should put the little dog back in its cage. He
should be doing a lot of things, like getting ready
to go home. He glanced at his watch. It was after
seven. He should have left an hour ago. There
was no pressing business. Rick had seen to
everything in the office and clinic before he left
at five thirty. One thing about Rick, hell or high
water, he left at five thirty on the dot. He had a
family and regular hours were a must. Sit-down
dinner was at six fifteen. By keeping regular
hours he had a good thirty minutes to play and
cuddle with his son. His family would always
come first. He had been honest, laid it on the
line with Griff and John, before he signed his
share of the partnership.

Griff stared at the puppy, wondering what
Dory was making for dinner. Six-course dinners
were beginning to take their toll on his waistline
and hers as well. Maybe a few hours of racquetball would do him some good. He'd call Dory
and tell her he had to work late. Homemaker
Dory would never understand that he would
rather play racquetball than be with her. And it
wasn't true. He just wanted some time for himself, time to work off some hostility. God, now
why had that word cropped up? What in hell did
he have to feel hostile about? Nothing. Not a
damn thing. That wasn't exactly true either. His
bank balance was precariously low. He was living
like a prince, or maybe a king, due to Dory's intense efforts, so he really shouldn't complain,
but he was going to have to. The rent and utilities were draining him. When the heat was
turned on his bill would triple. Dory's second-

quarter tuition would be due, the holidays were
around the corner, and he needed some new
clothes. A long talk with Dory was called for. If
not tonight, then by the weekend.

Still, he didn't carry the puppy to its cage.
This quiet time to himself was a balm. Everyone
needed some space. When two people lived together they had a tendency to smother one another. That was it, he felt smothered. How it
happened, how it got a foothold, he had no
idea. Dory really was Superwoman. She went to
class, worked on her papers at night, cooked,
cleaned, and still managed to have a social life
with Sylvia and Lily. If that was the case then why
did he feel smothered? Was there such a thing
as one person being too good to another? He
loved her. God, how he loved her. If he searched
the world over he could never find anyone he
could love more. Then why the dissatisfaction?
Why was he dragging his feet about going home?
Why did he want to play racquetball? Why?
Why? Maybe he needed a drink. He should call
Dory. He really should.

The black and white puppy yipped its displea-
sure when he was put back in the cage. "It's a
cold, hard world out here, little guy. Be thankful
you have a place to sleep," Griff said softly as he
shut the cage and turned off all but the night-
lights.

Griff drove past the racquetball club and
then made a U-turn and drove back. Cal Williams's car was in the lot; there was no mistaking
the ruby-red Ferarri. Cal could really give him a
workout. He knew he should call Dory. Instead,

he walked by the phone booth without a second glance.

When Griff walked into the kitchen a little after ten, he expected Dory to be fighting mad because her dinner was ruined. Instead, she smiled, laid aside the notes she was transcribing. He saw his dinner plate and silverware. "It'll only take a minute to warm in the microwave. Go along and take your shower. Would you like a drink?"

"Not really. How about a diet soda?"

Dory frowned. "I don't think we have any. Sylvia had the last bottle yesterday. How about some coffee or beer?"

"Ice water. I have to start watching my weight. All this rich food is going straight to my waist. That Sylvia really does watch her figure, doesn't she?" he asked, looking pointedly at Dory.

"Yes, she does. But, Griff, she's like a stringy hen."

"I never noticed," he said blandly. "I'm not all that hungry, so don't make much for me." He opted for the truth. "I played racquetball and picked up a hot dog with Cal Williams."

"Oh, is that where you were. I thought you were working late. Why didn't you call me? I would have waited on dinner."

Now. Now the fireworks would start. Instead, Dory grinned. "Who won?"

"He did. He's in shape. He noticed the weight I put on and ribbed me all night. Cut down, Dory, forget the pies and bread and give me salads and chicken." His tone was cooler and more curt than he intended. Dory's face fell. She looked guilty and frightened. God, why should she look *frightened*? "Hey, it's not the end of the world. I've always been weight conscious, you know that. You used to be too. Somewhere, somehow, we've gotten off the track. Let's get back on before we get to the point where it's hard to take the pounds off." He watched carefully for her reaction. There was none. She moved away from the stove and stared at him for a minute.

"I can fix you some chicken if you want. It won't take long."

"No. Just some salad. In fact, I don't even want salad. I feel bad that you cooked all this food." *And* spent all this money, he thought.

"It's no problem. If you're sure you don't want anything, I'll get back to my work."

Goddamn it, Griff thought as the needle-sharp spray attacked him. She made him feel guilty. Then he grinned. A tiff. They were having a tiff and what fun it would be to make up.

Dory was usually the first one in bed, her arms and body waiting for him. Tonight, she elected to stay in the kitchen to work. Christ, was she going to start holding him off when something didn't set right with her? He hated the thought. Hated the impulse that came over him to run downstairs and take her in his arms. Hated the thought that he would even go so far as eating the food he didn't want. He gave the pillow a vicious punch and then another. He rolled over and tried to sleep. He was still wide awake at three o'clock when Dory crept into bed. She lay so far to the edge he thought she would fall out of bed if she moved. He wanted to gather her in his arms and make love to her. Her stiff body told him she might agree but it would be on her terms. There was no giving in her this evening. Jesus. Women! He closed his eyes and eventually slept.

Warm tears soaked into the satiny pillowcase. What did I do, she cried silently. And he never noticed the scarecrow leaning crookedly against the front door.

Chapter Seven

It was raining hard the next morning when Dory woke. She crawled from bed and padded down to the kitchen. She put coffee on to perk and pulled out the toaster. If Griff didn't want her homemade cinnamon rolls then he could have dry toast with his coffee. She would eat the rolls herself and smear butter all over them. It wasn't an easy task to make cinnamon rolls from scratch and she refused to waste them.

The phone rang. It was Lily. "I can't possibly come to lunch today," she apologized. "I can't take the baby out in this weather and the morning news says this is going to keep on for the whole day."

Dory voiced her disappointment, but she felt secretly relieved. Lunch with Lily might have been nice, but there were other things that

needed doing today, and at least she wouldn't
have to rush home from the university to prepare a sumptuous lunch straight out of the pages
of *Woman's Day*.

Griff walked into the kitchen. He assessed the
situation of Dory sitting at the table lathing butter on the cinnamon roll and kissed her soundly.
"Oh, they look delicious. I'll have two with lots
of butter."

"No, you won't. You're having dry toast with
your coffee. I'm having the rolls." She smiled to
take the sting out of her words. "How did you
sleep last night?"

"Fine," Griff lied. Damn, he really wanted the
cinnamon rolls. "How about you?"

"Fine," Dory lied in return.

Griff gulped his coffee and reached for the
toast. "I think I'll eat this on the way to the
clinic. See you this evening. Remember, it's my
late night tonight. Do you have classes today?"

"One at ten and another at twelve. I should
be home by one at the latest," Dory replied, biting into the warm bun.

The minute the door closed behind Griff,
Dory tossed the rolls into the trash. She watched
the driving rain as she sipped her coffee. There
was no way she was driving out to Georgetown
in this weather. This was the kind of day you
cleaned out closets or baked cookies. But her
closets were neat, and if Griff was on a diet, that
left schoolwork or a book to be read.

She admitted she loved to snuggle in and putter around. A whole, entire day to snuggle and
putter. Maybe she would call Katy and Pixie and

see how they were doing on the article for *Soiree*. After she made the bed, that is, and cleaned the bathroom and rinsed the dishes and coffeepot. Then she would relax with a fresh pot of coffee and make her calls. Maybe it was time to see about the profiles. Katy was certain to ask how that was going and she didn't want to lie. On the other hand, she could do what all the other freelancers did, say she was *on top of it.* If the rain stopped, she could take a trip to Ollie's Trolley and see if the senator showed up. But that meant she would have to get dressed and schlepp out in the puddles. A girl could ruin her shoes doing something like that. Perhaps today wasn't the day to think about calling Katy or Pixie. Her eye went to the calendar by the phone. It was almost time to call Lizzie. Dory counted the large red X's and groaned. Where *had* the time gone?

Gay little notes penned by the office staff and Katy had been arriving with regularity these past weeks. For some reason they frightened her. She always tore up the notes and then was nervous and edgy for the rest of the day.

There was no point in calling Pixie either. Pixie would chatter on and on about what a wonderful time she was having as the star of a *Soiree* story. She really didn't want to hear about it.

You don't want to go to school; you don't want to get in touch with the senator; you don't want to call your friends; what *do* you want? A tired voice within her answered: "God, I wish I knew." Lately, she couldn't seem to make even the smallest decision about herself. She knew she should be hitting the books, attending the lectures, taking notes. She knew she should go on a diet and take off at least eight pounds. The number made her blink in awe. Eight pounds!

Maybe she should call Sylvia and ask her to go shopping. It was time to think about Thanksgiving decorations, and while she was at it, she could pick up some new knickknacks for Griff's den. The crystal unicorn he had admired in Neiman-Marcus.

I'll buy you a gift, a bribe if you will, and you be nice to me. Don't notice me for my lack of direction. Don't make me feel frightened. Don't ever do that to me again, Griff, she pleaded silently.

Something was wrong.

What?

Who to believe?

Sylvia? "Spend. Enjoy. Reach out, take it. Go for it."

Lily? "Snuggle in. Let's cook, bake and decorate. Be creative in your home. Forget independence. Forget the outside world, it's cold and cruel. Let Griff worry about it all."

Hide!

School?

It's hard. Work, work, work. Headaches. Nervous indigestion. Notes, always notes. More notes.

Take off those eight pounds. *Now.* Before it's too late.

Career. Once it was the most important thing in life. B.G. Before Griff. Griff said he understood. Everyone needed a hiatus.

Hide!

Hide from Katy, from Pixie, from the unseen senator, from Lizzie.

David Harlow!!!

The red X's on the calendar seemed to run together.

Was this the way it was supposed to be?

Aunt Pixie would tell her to clean up her act and straighten up and fly right. What did Pix know? She lived in a wine bottle.

Something was wrong. Was Griff falling out of love with her?

Was she falling out of love with Griff?

Never!

David Harlow!

The red X's.

Decisions.

Challenges.

Hide. For God's sake hide!

Griff.

Dory looked around, unseeing. Her heart was fluttering wildly. She could call Griff and Griff would make it better. Whatever it was.

No!

I can take care of myself. I have for years. I don't need anyone to take care of me.

Givvve meee aaa breaaakkk, the inner voice chided. If that's true, why are you sitting here doing nothing? A noncontributor.

The phone rang. Dory glared at it as if it were the enemy.

Dory didn't realize how cautious her voice sounded till she heard Griff asking her who she was trying to evade.

"No one. Why would you say such a thing?" Dory asked fretfully.

"Dory, I hate to bring this up, especially on the phone, but right now I don't have any other choice. The clinic needs a new centrifuge. If I put in my share, which I intend to do, my personal account is going to hit rock bottom. Now, we both agreed when we signed the lease for the town house that you were going to help with the finances. I didn't like it then and I still don't like it. You convinced me that it was the right move and I went along with it. The rent and the utilities are due in five days. I have a car payment to make and some payments on my charge accounts. If we can't swing the payments, then we're going to have to try and break the lease and move someplace cheaper. I told you that I wouldn't be taking a salary for the first six months and things were going to be lean. I'm sorry, Dory."

"But, Griff, I've been buying all the food and I did pay for all the extras, the chair for your den and the drapes and plants," Dory said in a shocked voice.

"Those were things we didn't need, Dory. I'm talking about the essentials. Didn't you hear what I just said? Once I pay this month's rent and pay my bills, I'm virtually wiped out. How would it look to John and Rick if I went back on my word and asked for an advance? I won't do it, Dory. I want you to think about this today, and we'll talk this evening when I get home. Dory, are you listening to me?"

"Yes, I am. And I'm shocked. You never told

me your bank account was so low. I thought you
had . . . what I mean is, I expected . . . oh, I
don't know what I mean," Dory fretted. She didn't
like this conversation. She didn't like it at all. As
a matter of fact, she hated this conversation.

When she hung up the phone she swallowed
hard. He was supposed to be taking care of her,
providing for her. God, what if she had married
him? If she had married him, would he have
said the same thing to her? Griff wanted money
from her. How cool and detached his voice was.
How impersonal. How goddamn impersonal.

She had spent at least three thousand dollars.
Maybe more. What more did he want? Hadn't
she knocked herself out making the town house
a home to be proud of? Hadn't she forsaken all
else to make Griff a comfortable place to live?
She had neglected school, her freelance work,
everything, to be what Griff wanted. Now, it wasn't
enough. He wanted more. He wanted her share.
Did he have any idea how expensive food was?
Did he think she liked running to the damn
supermarket every two days? Did he think she
liked all this hausfrau work? Did he think she
liked cooking and doing dishes? God, where was
the time for herself? And the gas, who did he
think paid for the fuel for the gas-guzzling SUV?
Some magical gnome who had an unlimited
supply of money?

It wasn't supposed to be like this.

"How *was* it supposed to be?" The inner voice
asked petulantly.

Dory sputtered. "Certainly not like this," she
said to the empty kitchen.

Rain beat against the kitchen windows, beating a tattoo as fast as her heart was beating. Her share.

She felt like throwing a fit. Anger, hot and scorching, coursed through her, the first honest emotion she had felt since moving into the town house. She stormed about the kitchen, beating at the appliances with her bare fists. Cups and saucers were swept willy-nilly from the table onto the floor. She kicked out at them. Her share! What was her share? Was it making a home? Doing the cooking? The shopping? Thinking of his every need? His every whim?

He accused her of not pulling her share!

Ignoring the mess, she raced up the stairs and pulled her suitcases out of the closet.

Run.

Hide.

Leave.

Go where?

Do what?

Her share!

Admit defeat!

Admit to being worthless!

Her share!

Griff's disappointment in her!

It wasn't supposed to be like this. Tears of self-pity rolled down her cheeks. She continued to sit on the edge of the bed, staring at her open suitcase. This was silly, childish. If she were Griff's wife, the suitcase wouldn't be on the bed. She wouldn't have thought of leaving. Theirs would be a marriage, not a partnership that shared expenses.

Marriage. Was that her choice? Was that little piece of paper the difference between a commitment and a financial arrangement? A man protected and took care of and supported his wife. With his lover he had every right to expect her to pay her share.

Dory admitted it wasn't the money. Money was only incidental. What hurt was discovering that all she had done, all she had accomplished in making a real home for the two of them was unappreciated. The decorations, the drapes, the plants . . . on and on she could add to the list . . . and it wasn't appreciated. The bills were due. She could give him the damn money, that didn't matter. It was knowing that all she had done was meaningless. Griff preferred to deal in hard facts and figures and remind her of broken promises.

The rain continued to beat its cacophony against the windows. At least they would get a good washing, she thought inanely.

The ringing phone demanded her attention. She ignored it.

Anger fought to the surface and she squelched it. More self-pity. Her world was falling apart. Nothing was the way she thought it would be. Not Griff. Not even herself. Nothing.

An inner voice warned her against taking rash action. "Slow and easy," it told her. "Think. You can handle this. Make a decision and stick to it. Do something, for God's sake! Anything, just do it!"

The phone shrilled a second time. "Hello," she snapped into the receiver.

"Dory, is that you?" the voice on the other end of the phone queried hesitantly.

"Katy!" Dory squealed. "My God, Katy, is it really you? I'm so glad you called. What are you doing? What's going on at *Soiree*? Tell me everything. How are all the girls? What's going on with the layout? How did Pixie do? Did the girls like her? Tell me the truth. I want to know everything. How's the weather in the city? Smoggy, I bet. How's your husband and the cat? Don't leave a thing out. You're calling on the WATS line, aren't you? Shoot," Dory said breathlessly.

"Is it that bad?" Katy asked.

"Yeah. Now tell me everything."

"Okay but first I called you with a few problems. I hope you don't mind. Let's get them out of the way first and then we can gossip."

"Hit me."

Fifteen minutes later Katy grumbled. "God, it was so simple. I should have been able to figure all of this out myself. I guess that's why you're you and I'm me. I'm telling you, Dory, you did this magazine a favor when you sent us your aunt. The place hasn't been the same since. She's got Harlow eating right out of her hand. I think she's lusting after him and making no bones about it. She's got to be the horniest woman I ever came across." There was open awe and admiration in Katy's voice when she continued. "And she isn't faking it either. Another thing I wanted to tell you. I sent some layout copy to you for your approval. Harlow says it doesn't go until you initial it. I thought that was swell. Do you agree?"

"Harlow said that? You aren't kidding me, are you?" She was feeling better and better by the minute.

"No way. He said this was yours and you have to pass final approval and he didn't care if you were residing in Nome, Alaska."

"Super," Dory said. Compliments from on high were so rare that when they did fall one had to be ready to catch and appreciate them.

"Pixie hosted a dinner party at the Sign of the Dove for all the crew and everyone from *Soiree* who wanted to attend. I might add that she had one hundred percent attendance. She's a trip. Harlow was so impressed with the check I thought he was going to pass out. I left at two thirty and the girls were telling me that the management stayed open till four to accommodate Pixie. I'm telling you, this place is like a morgue now that she's gone."

Dory laughed. Good old Pixie. She really did things up right and then tied a big red bow on them. She did leave her mark. "Tell me, what's with Lizzie?"

"Things are going great. She's delirious. She's really counting on you, Dory."

"I know. I'm working on it, Katy. Don't crowd me, okay?"

"Wouldn't think of it. Eileen is pregnant and is taking a leave of absence. Sandy is having a torrid romance with our new art director and loving every minute of it. Jamie is buying a cottage in the country and is going to renovate it weekends by herself."

"With those three-inch-long fingernails?" Dory laughed.

"That's what I said. She said they were false and she can remove them at will. It'll give her something to do on the train ride back to the city on Sunday nights."

"How's your husband and the cat?"

"In the order of importance. Goliath is fine. Eats two containers of Tender Vittles a day. He's getting so fat he can't jump up on the bed anymore. As for my other half. What could be new? Let's face it, the honeymoon has been over for a long time. I really hate the way he does the laundry. One week everything is pink, the next week, everything is blue. He refuses to separate."

Dory doubled over laughing. Katy was so good for her. God, how she missed everyone. "What else?"

"Well, one day this week a whole truckload of plants arrived and no one knows where or who they came from. No one remembers the name of the delivery company. When I tell you plants I mean plants. Wait till you see your office. The place is a damn jungle. I think Pixie sent them. Because . . ." Katy strung out her words, "she made a remark that she looked best among green things. At the time I didn't get it but I do now. She wanted to go *à la naturelle* with assorted flora and fauna. We covered her up a little and used some rental plants. Anyway, the place is a jungle. I have to pay someone overtime just to water them and spritz them every day."

There was a pause. Dory was too overcome to say anything.

"We miss you, Dory. All the girls said to give you their regards."

"I miss you all too. Say hello for me. And, Katy, thanks for calling."

"Any time. Thank you for helping me out. I was going crazy with all that stuff. You make it sound so simple. Sometimes I wish I were you."

"No you don't," Dory said softly. "Don't ever wish that. Be sure you say hello to everyone."

"I wish you'd come in and do it yourself," Katy grumbled as she hung up the phone.

Damn it, she did miss all of them. She really did. The brief workout on the phone was exactly what she needed. But was it what she wanted?

Dory lay back on the bed and let her mind go blank. Within seconds she was asleep.

Chapter Eight

Dory woke up an hour later feeling little better than when she had escaped into sleep. Her drowsiness gave way to self-pity when her eyes fell on the open suitcase at the foot of the bed. Groggily, she inched her way to the bottom of the bed and slammed the suitcase shut. The sound was almost terminal in the silent room. She fell back against the warm nest of the silken comforter, her eyes brimming with unshed tears. In some inexplicable way she was feeling threatened. Frightened. Afraid. And she realized that instead of trying to understand the reasons, she was trying to escape her roiling emotions. But if she couldn't feel safe here, in her home and Griff's, where would she be safe? If she couldn't handle her own emotions, she couldn't handle anything. So much for her brief high on Katy's phone call.

Impatient with herself, Dory slid from the bed. Perhaps she should give more thought to marrying Griff. It wouldn't be hard to manipulate him . . . What was she thinking of! Manipulate! Certainly Griff still wanted to marry her; he had asked her to be his wife months ago— before coming to Washington. If anything, he wanted her to marry him more than ever! She was the one with the problem, the indecision! Had she actually thought of manipulating him into marriage? She was aghast. She needed to get her head together. Needed to talk to someone.

She could call Lily. Lily was safe. Safe in her role as mother and as wife. Lily knew exactly what she wanted. And, she had her own little built-in insurance policy—the baby. Lily was as safe as if she were wrapped in a silken cocoon. There were no pressures on Lily to succeed. Lily never had to worry about failing, Lily was safe and Dory could be safe too. If she married Griff, she wouldn't be failing; she would just be quitting the game. There was no dishonor in that. Or was there? God, she just didn't know anymore.

She lugged the Gucci suitcase back to the closet. Angrily, she kicked at the red and green strip on its side. If she took it to the flea market, she could sell it and get enough money to buy groceries or maybe even pay the electric bill. Would anyone at the flea market even know what a Gucci suitcase was? How pleased she'd been the day she had bought it, along with its matching weekend bag. She had wanted it, so she had bought it, using over two week's salary to pay for it. She hadn't even given the price a second thought. It was enough to know that she had earned the money and could spend it as she saw fit. There was nothing wrong with wanting things. Permission wasn't required to buy it. God, how she hated the damn thing. On Saturday she would sell both the pieces. Lily would approve. Sylvia . . . Sylvia would sneer and ask her what she planned on packing her clothes in . . . a shopping bag? Sylvia had a complete set of Louis Vuitton.

November turned into a depressing month. All the glorious colors of autumn were long gone. The days turned cold and rain seemed to be a daily occurrence. Dory dreaded the coming of winter with the biting wind and icy sleet almost as much as she dreaded Griff's end-of-the-month lectures on spending.

Thanksgiving passed as just another day except for dinner at Lily's house. She had dutifully baked her pies and mashed the turnips as requested. She vowed to eat sparingly and then said the hell with it and ate as much as everyone else.

The digital scale in the mulberry bathroom said she was now eleven pounds over her normal weight. Just one pound over ten. Only three pounds over eight. Referred to in that manner, it didn't seem so ominous.

And always, no matter what she did, no matter how she tried to avoid contact with the kitchen calendar, she found her eyes clicking off the red X's. It was now dangerously close to the countdown when she would have to make the call to Lizzie.

Georgetown was a farce. She cut more classes than she attended. When she did do the reading, she couldn't remember any of it afterward. Oh, she made a pretense of poring over books and compiling long lists of notes. More often than not they were household lists and grocery lists. Griff never seemed to notice. He tiptoed around the kitchen if he saw her bent over her books and notebooks.

For some reason, Dory felt betrayed. Or was she the betrayer?

December made its entrance with a heavy snowfall. The mounds of white stuff depressed Dory. It wasn't till Lily called and suggested a trip to the evergreen farm to pick and chop their own Christmas trees that her spirits perked up. They bundled little Ricky into an apple-red snowsuit and started off. First, they stopped by Sylvia's house to see if she wanted to accompany them.

"Darlings, no one in her right mind chops down Christmas trees. It's . . . it's decadent. Your feet will get wet in all that . . . that snow. You'll catch cold and your hands will get chapped. Ridiculous! And, what about that child? What if he needs to nurse? I think you're out of your mind, Lily. Call Sears and have them deliver an artificial tree. They even come trimmed."

Lily grinned. "This is Ricky's first Christmas and it would be sacrilegious to have a plastic tree. Do you want us to bring you back some evergreens for trimming?"

"And mess up the house? No, thank you!"

"I wonder how she'd notice a few pine needles." Lily continued to giggle.

Dory sat contentedly watching the baby in his carseat. He was cute even if he slobbered all over everything, even if his shrill sounds made Dory wince. Motherhood. They did require a lot of work. Everyone wasn't cut out for parenting. Lily was the perfect mother who should have a houseful of kids to run after. Bottles and diapers and laundry. Babysitters and mashed food. She hated the idea. Still . . . maybe she could learn to adjust. Having one's own baby would certainly be different from watching someone else's. Your own flesh and blood. Griff's blood and her flesh. Her labor, her agony. Her sweat. Her stitches. Long and careful thought would be required before she made a decision.

Lily had borrowed the clinic van so she and Dory could bring back their Christmas trees. Now, fingers frozen and toes just beginning to warm from the van's heater, they were on their way home. Two trees and bundles of green boughs filled the van with fresh natural scent. Little Ricky sat placidly in his car seat, drooling onto the front of his Winnie-the-Pooh snowsuit. His sweet, warm head lolled as he nodded off to sleep.

"Lily, little Ricky is falling asleep and I know it's not his nap time. The cold air must have knocked him out. Do you want me to keep him awake so he'll sleep when you get him home?" After numerous days spent with Lily and her baby Dory was becoming quite familiar with their schedules and the way Lily liked to do things.

"Let him sleep if he wants." Lily concentrated on the road. "It really doesn't make much difference. Rick won't be coming home till late."

Dory raised her brows, looking at Lily quizzically. What had happened since they left the evergreen farm? Why did Lily seem so despondent? Or was it her own brand of anger? "I suppose you're dissatisfied when Rick needs to stay late at the clinic."

"That's a funny word, Dory. Dissatisfied? Don't you mean disappointed?"

Dory wasn't used to having Lily bring her up short. "Yes . . . yes, I suppose I do. Disappointed, then?"

Lily bit her lip, her pink, wind-stung cheeks making her chestnut hair seem more vivid. "I am disappointed in a lot of things." This she said quietly, almost solemnly, and Dory wondered if there was trouble in Lily's paradise. But Lily didn't seem to want to talk about it, and Dory was glad. She didn't want to hear that Lily wasn't safe. Out of the blue, Lily asked a question.

"Have you met the new receptionist-secretary at the clinic yet? I've been meaning to bring in one of my coffee cakes and get down there to decorate for Christmas. You know, just to bring the holiday spirit into the outer office. Little

Rick's pediatrician has these cute little felt angels hanging around the waiting room. I don't know who made them, probably his wife."

Dory was having difficulty following Lily's train of thought. Did she want to talk about Ginny, the new receptionist, or did she want to talk about decorating the office? The latter seemed safer. "If you want we could buy some of those Hallmark paper decorations, and I'll go down there with you to put them up. We could go when surgery is scheduled so the waiting room will be empty."

Lily nodded, concentrating on the road. "Well, have you? Have you met this girl they've hired?"

"No, but I've spoken to her on the phone. She seems very nice . . . I guess," she added when she saw Lily's features stiffen.

"When the baby was born Rick promised he wouldn't work past office hours," Lily complained. "I even heard him tell Griff and John myself. This will be the second night this week he's staying late."

"Do you want me to say something to Griff? Perhaps he and John don't understand how important your evenings are."

"No, Dory, don't say anything. I . . . I wouldn't want Rick to know I'm being such a baby just because he had to work late a few nights." Her mouth was drawn into a thin line as though she were biting back what she really wanted to talk about. "Hey!" She tried for forced brightness. "There's the stand where they sell the best apple cider outside of New York State! You remember,

Dory, I served it for Thanksgiving and everyone loved it. Let's stop."

"Sure. I love cider. I'll stay here with the baby."

Something was wrong with Lily. She was trying too hard. There were times, like right now, when Lily seemed almost frantic and just a shade too enthusiastic about her recipes and her decorating, not to mention her "happy, happy" home life. She seemed to be working overtime to convince herself that everything was wonderful. Or was she trying to convince Dory? Poor Lily, she was so vulnerable. How, Dory wondered, was it so possible for a woman to become so locked into family and home? She supposed she could question Lily, but Lily would say only what she wanted Dory to know, no more and no less. She would wear a stricken look and tears would come to her eyes. No, it was better not to ask questions of Lily. If Lily had a problem she would have to be the one to bring it up.

"Well what's it going to be, are we going to get the decorations for the office or not?" Dory asked as she sipped her apple cider.

It wasn't Dory's imagination. Lily's eyes took on a frightened look as she contemplated her answer. "No, I don't think so. When I mentioned it to Rick he didn't seem too interested. He said Ginny would do the decorating."

"But I thought you said . . ." Dory clamped her mouth shut at Lily's stricken face.

"I know what I said. The truth is, I wanted an

excuse to go to the office to take a look at Ginny. Sylvia said she's stunning. If Sylvia says she's stunning that means she looks like Gisele Bündchen."

"Sylvia exaggerates a great deal. So what if she does look like a model? What does that have to do with you?" Dory asked softly.

Lily turned to face Dory. "It has a great deal to do with me. It happened once before. I told you Rick was going to be late; this is the second time this week. That's the way it started the last time. Beautiful receptionist, handsome young doctor. Sylvia took it on herself to tell me about it. She also took it upon herself to have John fire the girl. Her name was Maxine. I never told Rick I knew. He was different for a while but he straightened out. That's why I decided to have the baby. I was so sure it would bring us closer together. I was so sure if I had a baby things would go back to the way they were before. I keep a spotless house, I cook wonderful meals. Little Rick is a delight to both Rick and me. I do everything a good wife is supposed to do. I think I'm reasonably good in bed. Rick certainly never complained. Everyone who comes to the house compliments Rick on what a wonderful wife and mother I am." Tears filled Lily's eyes as she stared at Dory. "If I'm such a wonderful wife and mother why does Rick have to look somewhere else? And he's looking. It's the same old pattern."

Dory stared at her friend, aware of the contented baby in his car seat. My God, Lily had actually had a baby to try and solve her problems. How awful for Lily. Playing Mother Earth wasn't her answer. Poor Lily. Men were such bastards. How could Rick do this to her? "Lily, I don't know. I just don't know. I assumed that everything was all right between you and Rick. You aren't sure of anything. You think he's doing something, but you aren't sure. Why don't you talk to him, get it out in the open? Tell him you know about the first time. It may not be true this time. Give him a chance."

Lily was appalled at the suggestion. "I could never do that!"

"Why not? Once the air is cleared you can go on from there. I know you love Rick deeply. Make a fresh start."

"I can't do it. I simply can't do it."

"What are you going to do, have another baby to make it come right for you? Are you going to depend on Sylvia to find out about this one so she can tell John to fire Ginny? You can't rely on babies to solve your problems. You have to work them out yourself, and silent suffering isn't the answer."

"Maybe not, but that's the way it has to be for now," Lily said in a cheerful voice. "I'm so glad we stopped for the cider. Rick likes to drink it in front of the fireplace before we go to bed. He'll be so pleased that I got it."

Dory had to physically shake her head to clear it. How could Lily turn on and off like that? From long practice she answered herself: Safe, secure Lily was frightened. Safe, secure Lily who thought she had Rick to support her and love her and give meaning to her life. If Lily could be insecure, where did that leave Dory?

When Dory arrived home from the evergreen farm she found a note from Griff on the kitchen table telling her he wouldn't be home that night and not to expect him until late the following evening. Something about a horse and a colt that was refusing to nurse. Dory hadn't realized she had been holding her breath till a long sigh escaped her with a loud swoosh. She would certainly have more than enough time to decorate the house with boughs of greenery. She was removing her boots when the phone rang. Kicking off one stout rubber boot, she hopped to the phone and caught it on the second ring. She fully expected to hear Sylvia's voice demanding to know if she was sneezing yet or had a fever. The breathless, squeaky voice left no doubt who was on the other end of the phone. It was Aunt Pixie. Pixie never believed in the social amenities. She got right to the point.

"I'm at the damn airport. Will you kindly tell me how in the living hell I get to the boonies where you live?"

"You're early, aren't you?"

"Only by two weeks. Will it be a problem? If it is, you're stuck with me regardless. Just give me directions. The cab driver hasn't been born yet that I'd trust."

Dory issued brief, concise instructions that she knew Pixie would never remember, "I'll have a hot toddy waiting. Shouldn't take you more than twenty minutes. You'll beat traffic by at least an hour."

"Never mind the toddy. I don't want any garbage clouding up my drink. You just get the bottle out and make sure you have a long-stemmed glass."

Dory laughed. "You haven't changed a bit. I'm dying to see you. Hurry and hang up and get here so we can talk."

Forty-five minutes later a whirlwind with six suitcases and a trunk sailed through Dory's kitchen. "I take it you're staying awhile," Dory grinned.

"Three days. I'm on my way to Hong Kong," Pixie said as she uncapped the squat bottle of Scotch. She poured the amber liquid into the long-stemmed glass and drank it neat. "What do you say we get sloshed?" she said, tilting the bottle a second time.

"Sounds good to me," Dory agreed, getting out a glass for herself. Pixie tossed her sable coat over the kitchen chair and Dory hugged her enthusiastically. "Watch the wig, watch the wig!" Pixie squeaked as she tried to adjust the precarious pile of red-gold curls.

"Oh, God, Pix, I forgot. Sorry. You look . . . great."

"I know, I know. A real pity you and I are the only ones who think so. People actually turn around and stare at me and it's not always with admiration." She sipped her Scotch approvingly. "Now that I've taken the edge off a little we can do some serious drinking. All they served on that miserable flight was Diet Pepsi. Diet Pepsi. I told that stewardess what I thought of that, let me tell you. All that saccharin. My God! A body isn't safe anywhere anymore. By the way, you look like something the cat dragged in, took a second look and then dragged back out. What'd you do, sneak back in when he wasn't looking?"

"Thanks," Dory said dryly. She sipped at her drink.

Pixie fumbled in her handbag and eventually found a pair of granny glasses. She propped them on the end of her nose and stared at Dory. Her mouth dropped open as she regarded her favorite niece. Her only niece. "Pudgy. God, I envy women who have the guts to be pudgy. I have to work at staying this thin," she said proudly as she stuck out a long, skinny leg clad in a white leather boot. Dory wouldn't have been surprised to see a pom-pom attached to the top.

"I know you do," Dory agreed as she watched the glass tilt again. There was no stopping Pixie. She drank like a fish and had no intention of stopping. She also smoked incessantly.

"What time will *Grit* be home. I'm anxious to see him. I'm sorry I won't be able to spend Christmas with you two but I got this offer"— her voice dropped to a hushed whisper—"from this gentleman I've been corresponding with and he invited me to come to Hong Kong for a visit. He makes shoes. Hand-made shoes. He's Chinese, Japanese, one of those nationalities. He said he has Western eyes. Shoes. Imagine, Dory. If he works out, we can get all our shoes for nothing. Just tell me what you want. Do you still have some kind of fixation about shoes? Or maybe it's a fetish."

Dory giggled. It was just like Pixie to go traipsing halfway around the world in the hopes of getting something free. It wasn't so much the shoes as a man that Pixie hoped to get.

"I'll be seventy-two next year. It's time I thought about settling down. I always liked Hong Kong. I can see me settling down over there. I'll get manicures and pedicures. Those people love to do that. I can have all the help I want. I don't think Mr. Cho lives in a rice paddy. He sounds well off. Anyone in shoes has to be well off—think how many feet there are in Hong Kong. My dear, you can count on me sending you a pair of shoes at least once a week. Isn't it wonderful?" she trilled.

Dory's mind raced. "Pix, reassure me. You didn't tell this Mr. Cho about your money and all those blue chip stocks. Tell me you didn't."

"But I did. I believe in honesty."

"Did you tell him about your drinking and smoking?"

"Bite your tongue. Do you think I want to scare him off? This is the closest thing to an offer of marriage in twenty years. I'm not a complete fool!" She emptied her glass with a loud slurp.

"What exactly is Mr. Cho going to bring into this relationship! Besides his shoes?"

Pixie's eyes glowed like marbles. "His body and his country home. I see you're skeptical. Let me put it to you another way." More Scotch found its way into her glass. "God, I have a headache. I know it was that damnable Diet Pepsi. As I was saying, my dear, I'm seventy-two years old. Life is whizzing by. Just whizzing. You as well as the world must be aware of my frailties, I've made no secret of them."

Dory tried not to laugh. "I try not to think of them," she said.

"Flatulence . . . that's the worst. God, it strikes at any time and any place. I have four partials in my mouth, and that horse's rear end that tends my teeth now tells me my gums are receding. Receding! On top of that, my skin has lost its . . . its . . . zap. It just hangs. This turkey wattle under my chin is not something I try to show off to its best advantage. I have varicose veins that reappeared at the same time my tonsils tried for a comeback. My boobs are not up and out; even after the last lift they're more like down, down, down. Just yesterday I counted my hair. I have thirty-seven strands. I'm addicted to booze and cigarettes. No one loves me but you and your mother, and I think she just pretends. Now, if you were me, what would you do?"

"Go to Hong Kong."

"Right. Right, that's exactly where I'm going. I do, however, have two traits that drive men out of their minds."

"What's that?"

"I'm not discriminating and I put out!"

Dory shrieked with laughter. Dabbing at her eyes and gasping for breath, she felt better than she had in months.

Pixie stared at the young woman across the

table. Something was wrong. This wasn't the Dory she knew. Not this frowzy-looking hausfrau . . . this creature clad in blue jeans and rubber boots. She glanced around the homey kitchen. Christ, the child had become domesticated.

"When are you getting married?" Pixie asked bluntly.

"It's not that I disapprove of living in sin, it just seems that with all this . . ." She waved her stringy arms about ". . . that you should have something that says half is yours."

"It's a rental," Dory said soberly. "What do I need half a rental for?"

"You certainly don't look like yourself, and I can see that something is bothering you. Want to talk about it? If you do, you better replenish this bottle; I think we just killed it."

"Yes, no . . . what I mean is yes, I want to talk about it, but no, not now, but before you leave, and I don't have any more Scotch. How about some wine? Neither Griff nor I are much for drinking. I didn't know we were so low. The wine is a good California chablis."

"As long as it's at least a month old I'll drink it. Remember the time we built the still on the farm? By God, I'd sell my soul for a bottle of that white lightning. *That* would certainly kill this headache."

Dory laughed. Pixie was just what she needed. The farm, as she called it, was a two-hundred-acre estate in upstate New York. The "we" she referred to was her fifth, or was it sixth, husband whom she had rescued from the clutches of the

law for running shine across the line as she was
driving through Tennessee in her Rolls-Royce.

"He did sing a mean ballad after a few sips of
our ambrosia. God, that was an experience. Pity
he had to die. When a man can't hold his liquor,
he isn't much of a man. I may be dissipated, but
I can hold my liquor. Mr. Cho says he's fond of
rice wine. I think we'll get along very well."

"Better be careful. You know what they say
about white slavers in those foreign countries.
Pray Mr. Cho isn't a procurer."

"I'm praying. Now, tell me how school is
going. I'm impressed, sweetie, that you decided
to go for your doctorate. It's about time someone in our family did something serious. I'm
sick and tired of carrying the ball for everyone.
All your silly mother wants to do is play golf and
get her nails done. I love her, she is my baby sister, but she doesn't know the meaning of the
word fun. Don't you believe a word she tells you
about our last visit," Pixie said, wagging a bony,
purple-tipped finger at Dory. Outrageous false
eyelashes fluttered wildly as Pixie made her
point.

"Let's not talk about that now. Later. With you
leaving, I just want to spend time with you before Mr. Cho gobbles you up," Dory said lightly,
hoping to divert Pixie from her questions.

"My life is an open book. I've told you my
news." Pixie's eyes were sharp and questioning.
"What is a safe topic of conversation with you?
The weather? What happened, Dory? Is this . . ."
she waved her bony arms again, ". . . is this a

mistake? Do you want out and can't find a way? All I have to do is look at you to know your world is upside down. What can I do? Is it money? Is it Grit, or is it you? Maybe you need to talk to your mother."

"It's Griff, not *Grit*. No, I don't need to talk to Mother. I'm working on it, Pix."

"How long is that going to take?"

"What?"

"For you to work on it? A week, a month, a year? Do you even know what it is you're working on? What is it, baby, you can tell me. We've never had secrets before. Don't close me out now." Pixie slapped her forehead so hard her wig tilted to the side. "Don't tell me you're pregnant."

"I'm not pregnant. I've been thinking about it a lot lately, though."

"Well, stop thinking right now. Parenthood is something to be taken seriously. It's not something you go into to make something else work. If things aren't working now, a baby will only compound the problem. Why don't we get comfy, slip into our lounging clothes and find something better to drink than this . . . grape water. I've had apple juice that tasted better. Do you have any vodka? How about brandy? I really don't want to open my trunk. Would you believe Mr. Cho demanded a dowry. Since he wasn't specific, I'm bringing my favorite drink that I'm sure he'll learn to love. A dowry yet, for God's sake. Did you ever hear of such a thing?"

"Sounds like a good idea. Would you like to

help me decorate the house?" Dory asked, pointing to all the evergreens dripping on the kitchen floor.

"I would not. Point me to the bathroom so I can get out of these clothes."

Dory showed her the way and then headed upstairs to her bedroom to change.

Pixie felt every year of her age as she watched Dory climb the stairs to the second floor. She disliked problems of any kind. How in the living hell could she go off to her fates while her beloved niece was having problems? She tried to look at it philosophically as she struggled to pull off the high, white boots. She rubbed her aching feet. She was getting old, and from the looks of things, she was also getting a few callouses on the balls of her feet. What next, she grumbled. She rummaged in her overnight bag for a Dior creation that swirled and swished when she walked. Now, if she just didn't trip and kill herself she would be all right. She wished she had remembered to ask Mr. Cho how old he was. The Oriental nature surely would prevent him from expressing comments about the ravages of time. If he refused to be a gentleman about the whole thing, she would simply pack up and leave.

She had three days to straighten out her niece. If she kept her wits about her, she might pull it off. Dory always listened to reason. She was bright, quick as a fox and razor sharp. At least she used to be. Now she appeared dull and listless. Oh, she laughed and talked, but all the

sparkle, all the life, all the zest was gone from
her. She had to get to the bottom of it. She also
had to remember to ask what the red X's on the
kitchen calendar meant.

Pixie rummaged some more in the cavernous
bag and withdrew a pair of beaded Indian slipper sox. She pulled them up to her knobby knees
with a flourish. She straighened her wig, patted
the curls into place and then added a spritz of
perfume that smelled like vanilla. She needed a
drink. The headache was still with her. By God,
that was the last time she was going to drink
Diet Pepsi and read a magazine on a plane. Why
couldn't that cheapo airline serve liquor like
everyone else? She gulped down three aspirins
and a sip of water. She coughed, sputtered and
cursed out the Pepsi Cola Company, along with
various cigarette manufacturers. Her language
was ripe, colorful, and to the point. She hoped
Mr. Cho would understand her penchant for
choice words. If not, he had a problem. There
were some things she wouldn't do for shoes.

Dory, attired in a flowing rainbow of silk, was
uncorking a bottle of brandy in the living room.
The fire was hissing and crackling and sending
sparks up the chimney. She wished Griff were
here to enjoy her aunt Pixie. Nothing was working right. She had been looking forward to the
Christmas holidays with Pixie and Griff, the people she loved best in the world. Now, it would
just be Griff and his mother.

Dory could feel Pixie's eyes on her, assessing
her, judging her. No, Pix would never judge her.

Assess her, yes, but she would never judge. She fixed a bright smile on her face and held out a three-quarters-full brandy snifter.

"The fire is nice," Pixie said, staring into the flames.

"That's one of the reasons I picked this place. Later I'll show you around the upstairs. There's a fireplace in the master bedroom. Cozy."

"I hate that word," Pixie grumbled. "Cozy is for old people who have to snuggle to keep warm or for youngsters who are necking in the backseat of a car. Cozy is not a word I like." She sniffed at the brandy and took a healthy swallow.

There was a hint of belligerence in Dory's tone. "I like to be cozy. I find it restful and . . . and . . ."

"Safe," Pixie said bluntly. "You're hiding behind words. I wonder if you're hiding from life, too, stuck here in this house. I want to compliment you on the bathroom. It must have taken you days."

"Weeks," Dory said grimly, not liking the turn the conversation was taking. Sometimes Pixie could get on her nerves. She didn't know everything. She didn't have all the answers. No one had all the answers.

"How's the freelance work going?" Pixie asked, watching Dory carefully.

"I haven't really started yet. I have a senator in mind. It's just a question of getting together at the right time."

"He must have been impressed when you asked him," Pixie said coolly.

"Well, actually I haven't asked him yet. I know where to find him when I'm ready. I've been pretty busy, Pix," Dory hedged.

"I can see that. This house just screams at you. It's so goddamn . . . homey it makes me sick. If you tell me you bake bread and cookies, I'm going to throw up."

Dory flushed but didn't defend herself.

Pixie got angry as she slapped her brandy snifter down on the cocktail table. "You aren't going to school on a regular basis. Don't lie to me, Dory. You aren't doing any freelance work. You and Griff seem to be having some problems. Just what the hell is it you're doing? I don't want to hear about this homemaking nonsense. I'm not knocking homemakers. I think they're wonderful if that's what they want. What happened to your creativity? When was the last time you used your brain? When was the last time your adrenaline flowed? When was the last time you bought a new pair of shoes, a new dress? A scarf, for God's sake? I want an answer and I want it now. If it means I have to give up Mr. Cho and Hong Kong, I'm prepared to do it. There's another fool out there waiting for me somewhere. You're the most important thing in my life, Dory. You're not happy. I saw that the minute I walked through the door. When was the last time you made a concrete decision?" She hated the stricken look on Dory's face, hated the brutal tone of voice she was using.

Dory shivered and hugged her knees to her chest. "I don't know, Pix. I just don't know. Somehow I got off the track. I don't know how to get back on. Help me."

"Oh, no. This is do-it-yourself time. I'm here to listen but that's it. In the end it has to be you who makes the decisions, the choices. I can help you pick up the pieces, but don't expect more from me."

"Are you telling me it's bail-out time?"

"Only if it's right and you're comfortable with it."

"That's just it, I don't know."

"Look, Dory, we all bottom out from time to time. If we didn't fail once in awhile, how would we know what it is to succeed? You have to do what's right for you. In here," Pixie said, thumping her thin chest. "There's a big world out there and you were part of it. This is another world, here in this house. If this is what you want, that's fine. If it isn't what you want, totally, then don't settle. Never settle, Dory. All your life I've told you not to settle. For if you do, you'll hate yourself in the end. We'll go into that some more later. Tell me about the friends you've made here."

Dory told her about Sylvia and Lily. "There were a few women I might have gotten to know better if I attended class regularly. That's it," Dory said defensively.

"That Lily sounds like Ms. Clean. Does she have a glass mobile too?"

In spite of herself, Dory laughed. "Just about.

She's a wonderful person, so is Sylvia. Neither of them really has anything in common with me, though. I tried, Pix, I really did. It wasn't right from the beginning. Griff admires both of them, for different reasons, of course. I was thinking about it last night. I think I tried to be both Sylvia and Lily to please him."

Pixie yawned. Why did women always want to please men? Why did they forever put themselves second? Why? Probably because as soon as a female baby could make sounds, da da pleased the father. We're conditioned, she thought grumpily.

"How do you feel about Griff now that you've been living with him?" Pixie asked.

"There was some adjusting to come to terms with but I did. I love him, with all my heart. What's even more wonderful, he loves me." It was true, he did love her. Even when he was preoccupied he would look up sometimes and smile at her. Her heart would flutter and delicious thoughts would course through her. "I love him," she repeated more forcefully.

"I suppose he's a goddamn thunderbolt in the bedroom too."

"You've got it."

"I've heard that diminutive Orientals have . . . scaled down . . . what I mean is their . . . they aren't fully as equip . . . have you heard that?" Pixie asked fretfully.

"It's probably some old wives' tale that started with a disgruntled woman to get even with some man. Worry about it when the time comes."

"You're probably right." Pixie's tone turned crafty. "I always found that when the New Year rolled around it was a good time to make decisions and get on the right track. New start, new everything. Diets are particularly successful because all the rich food of the holidays is gone. Expensive clothes go on sale. Bathing suits are out in full force and there's nothing to perk up a woman like a string bikini."

"Pix, you're about as transparent as cellophane. I appreciate what you're trying to do. I know my bottom line is coming up. I'll handle it, really I will."

"I have to believe that. You have my looks and my backbone. They've stood me in good stead for seventy-two years, and I can only hope they last as long for you. Soul searching is a precarious business. No one likes to look in the mirror and see anything less than perfection. "But perfect is just a word they threw into the dictionary. It's traits like truth, justice, honesty, the American way that are important when you look in the mirror. Those things show up." Dory wouldn't have been surprised to see an invisible cape appear with Pixie tossing it over her shoulder à la Wonder Woman.

"Are you hungry?" Dory asked, wanting to change the subject.

"Yes, but I'm not going to eat. How do you think I stay so scrawny? Not by eating, that's for sure. Well, maybe something to pick on. What do you have?"

"You name it and I've probably got it. I hang out in supermarkets a lot these days."

"Your mother told me I was as thin and flat as a swizzle stick. What do you think of that? She's jealous," she said, answering herself. "I'll eat anything as long as it doesn't have any calories."

"That limits things a bit. How about a ham and swiss on rye with brown mustard and a piece of homemade apple pie?"

"Love it, just love it. Can I help?" This was her chance to follow Dory into the kitchen and question her about the red X's on the calendar.

While Dory prepared the sandwiches Pixie trekked about the kitchen opening and closing cabinet doors. Neat too. She kicked at the evergreen boughs, shoving them into a corner, and peered through the glass on the back door. The cobalt sky was fast darkening. The snow had stopped, thank God. Snow was the enemy. A body could slip and fall and then they stuck pins in you to put you back together. She meandered back to the sink area. She forced a casual note into her tone. "What do the red X's mean?"

Dory stared at her aunt and then at the calendar. She'd known that sooner or later the foxy old lady was going to question her about it. Her voice was light as air when she replied, "I suppose you could say they're my bottom line."

"The big red circle, what does that mean?"

"I have to make a phone call on that day. That's the real bottom line. Here's your sandwich, Pix. I trimmed the crust off the rye since I know it's hard for you to chew."

"I knew there was a reason I put you in my

will. Did I tell you I have receding gums? It's tough to grow old."

"Pixie, you'll never be old. Not to me. You want to hear something funny? Every time in my entire life that I've been in a fix you've showed up. ESP, eh?"

"Not exactly. That mother of yours is the one you can thank. She called me the other day and said she thought you could use a good dose of me ahead of schedule. Said you didn't sound like yourself. That's the main reason I'm here."

Dory's mouth dropped open. "You mean that entire business with Mr. Cho was a put-on?"

"My God, no. I was going to just call you from the airport on my way, but when your mother said you needed me, I decided that Mr. Cho would have to wait an extra three days to ravage my body. That's what they do nowadays. They ravage and plunder your body. I read that in a romance book. God, I can't wait."

Dory stared at her aunt and then burst out laughing. "Pixie, you got guts."

"So do you. Now, get on your hind legs and put them to use."

Dory cleared the table. Pixie yawned and pleaded for a nap. "I think I'll have a nightcap first," she said, picking up the brandy bottle and carrying it into the den.

"Sofa bed's all made up. Just crawl in. What time do you want me to wake you up?"

"You know I die when I fall in bed. Don't ever try to wake me. I might be having one of those lascivious dreams I love. I'll see you later."

Dory flicked on the television. The evening

news was going off the air. What was she going to do with the rest of the evening? She knew from long experience that Pixie would sleep straight through till morning. The greenery. She might as well start on it. It would be nice for Pixie to see the house decorated before she left. It was a good thing she had her present. She would have plenty of time to wrap it before the older woman left. It was a gag gift, the only kind that Pixie would accept. A leather-bound journal embossed in heavy gold leaf. The perils and pitfalls in the life of Pixie Browning Baldeman Simmons Caruthers Ninon Roland Fallon. The salesman had stared at her in amazement when she told him yes, I want every word on the front. It had been hard to keep a straight face. Even harder when he told her how much it was going to cost. Pixie would love it now that she was going off on another one of her escapades.

It was after midnight when Dory swept up the last pine needle. The place really did look gorgeous—festive, bright, and cheerful. That's what the holidays were all about. The huge, red velvet bows on the staircase were magnificent. The garlands of greenery were fragrant and rich. Dory drew in her breath, savoring the tangy scene. She had always loved Christmas. She looked at the six-foot evergreen in the corner. That had been a job to get into the stand but she had managed. It used to take her father, her mother, her brother and herself to stand the tree in the tub that was used for just that purpose. She had done it alone. Alone, with no help. She had surveyed the scene, calculated the best way to get the screws into the thick trunk and then done it. True, she was scratched and her robe was almost ruined, but she had done it alone. She had put up a six-foot Scotch pine Christmas tree. Tomorrow, she would string the lights and put on the decorations. It wasn't till she was climbing up the stairs that it occurred to her that she hadn't wondered once how Griff was going to react to all the decorating.

It was womb dark when she turned off the last light and settled into bed. She smiled to herself in the darkness as Pixie's loud, lusty snores wafted up the stairs.

Chapter Nine

Dory fussed with the evergreen boughs over the fireplace in the living room, adjusting a bright red bow and shiny glass ornaments. Aunt Pixie sat curled up on the sofa, watching her, from time to time complaining about the "absolutely fattening" aroma coming from the kitchen as dinner simmered in expectation of Griff's arrival home.

"How does the house look, Pix? Think Griff will approve?"

Pixie snorted in her most unladylike fashion. "Dear heart, *you* are sleeping with the man. *You* should know what he likes and doesn't like, not I. Are you always so uncertain where this young man of yours is concerned?"

Dory winced. "Ouch! Right to the point, Pix. No, I know what he likes in bed well enough. I was wondering about the decorations."

"If he exhibits the same good taste as myself, he'll think they're atrocious. Don't you think you've overdone it, Dory?" Pixie's keen eyes circled the room, taking in the extravagant and, to her mind, tacky Christmas cheer. "If you were so set upon using poinsettias, why didn't you buy real ones? Silk is overrated, don't you think?"

Dory laughed. "I suppose you're right, but the real ones need so much care. This way, I'll be able to use them again next year."

Pixie raised an eyebrow and studied her niece. "Next year? Do you mean to say you intend to make a uniform out of those faded jeans and that fuzzy sweater you're wearing? God, Dory, will it take you a year to see what's becoming of you?"

Dory bristled. "What's wrong with me? What's wrong with a woman loving her home and her man and taking the best possible care of both? Honestly, Pix, sometimes you make me feel that if I'm not wearing an Albert Nipon original I'm no one at all! I've had enough of juggling a career and a private life. I'm happy! Leave me alone, okay?"

"And Griff?" Pixie asked. Obviously the thrust of her question was lost on Dory. Pixie wanted to know if Dory thought Griff was happy with these changes in the woman he had fallen in love with.

"Griff's wonderful," Dory answered, "and you know you love him. He's a terrific man and he adores you." Pixie sniffed. "I'm into old smoothies myself. He isn't one of those, what do they call them, those macho types?"

"Jocks? No. He's just a great guy. Levelheaded.

Warm and kind, loves his work. You barely met him in New York. You'll love him when you get to know him. Any guy who loves animals is okay. Animals have a sense about people."

"How can you say that, Dory?" Pixie demanded as she drained her drink.

"Very easily. It's true. Everyone knows that animals have a keen instinct and trust only reliable, likable people."

"Then how do you explain that Saint Bernard attacking me ten years ago when we were vacationing in Maine? I still think your mother sicced that dog on me."

"You were carrying the brandy bottle. All that dog wanted to do was lick your face. That dog was a real love. He was Mother's shadow for a good many years."

"Yeah, until he . . . never mind, your mother is a lovely woman . . . most of the time . . . like when she isn't minding my business. She's never approved of me. She's going to kill herself with all that golf she plays. What are we going to drink when this brandy is gone?" Pixie complained as she shook the empty bottle, "cough syrup?"

Dory tried to keep a straight face. Her mother and aunt's battles had been going on for years. "How about some vodka or gin? I have some bourbon. I think it's a hundred proof. Almost as good as your white lightning. You know something, Pix, you're *fast*." Dory grinned as Pixie trotted into the kitchen toting a bottle of bourbon.

"I hope this was a good year for bourbon," Pixie said, breaking the seal on the bottle. "I

never really got into bourbon. But when in
Rome . . ."

"I could have Griff stop and pick up some
more Scotch on his way home."

"What? And have him think I'm a drunk?
Never. I'll suffer with this bourbon." Dory watched
in awe as Pixie filled her wineglass almost to the
brim.

"He'd never think that, Pix. And if he did,
he's too much of a gentleman to say so."

"What kind of wine are you serving with dinner? And what is that mess you keep stirring?"

"Red. And this is stew. Very nourishing, lots of
vitamins. Crusty French bread and a cherry pie.
I baked the pie last month and put it in the
freezer."

"I can't eat all that," Pixie said in horror. "What
time will Griff be here?"

"Any minute now. Move over so I can set the
table."

"You mean you don't use paper plates? Who's
going to wash all these dishes?"

"The dishwasher. Don't worry, I remember
that soapy water makes brown spots on your
hands. I wouldn't dream of asking you to do
dishes."

"You're such a wonderful child," Pixie said,
tilting the bourbon bottle.

Griff arrived minutes later. Dory stood by and
watched while Pixie and Griff gave each other a
big hug.

"What are you drinking?" Griff asked. "Looks
good. How about making a tired man a Scotch
and water?"

"She can't. There isn't any more," Pixie said, sipping at her drink.

"Oh, I thought we had a full bottle. That's okay, how about some brandy?"

"There isn't any," Pixie said.

Griff nodded. "What you're saying is you drank the Scotch and the brandy, and if I want a drink, I better take some of this bourbon or that's going to be gone too."

"You got it. And when that's gone it's cough syrup for the both of us. I do like a fully stocked liquor cabinet," Pixie complained.

"I thought I had one." Griff grinned at Dory.

"That's right, you did, but you had nothing in reserve. That's the key word, reserve."

"I'll remember that. Where are you going with all those suitcases? Looks like the Grand Tour."

"I'm going to Hong Kong to get married."

Griff choked and sputtered. Dory wasn't sure if it was Pixie's declaration or that he had just happened to notice her fringed Indian slippers.

"Who . . . who's the lucky man?"

"Probably a gentleman of dubious nature. I haven't met him yet. Don't look so shocked. We've been pen pals for a while. He writes a mean letter, or at least that's what the man at the Chinese embassy tells me. He translates them for me since they're written in Chinese."

Dory filled a bowl with stew and set it in the middle of the table. A long loaf of crusty bread and a small crock of butter, along with a plate of fresh cut vegetables, were set on a mat near Pixie.

"I'll just pick," she said, filling her plate to the edge. "This girl is a whiz, a pure whiz. I had no idea you could cook like this, Dory. You must be very proud of her, young man."

Pixie made a pretense of sipping at her drink while she watched Griff's face. His eyes were blank and his face actually stilled. It was the first time she had ever seen that happen. A writer says such things in a novel, and the reader tries to imagine what a face looks like when it stills. Now Pixie was actually seeing it happen. Nothing moved on Griff's face. Then he smiled, but the blank look remained in his eyes. "Very proud. Wait till you taste the cherry pie."

"I have no intention of tasting the cherry pie. It's obscene to serve pie after a big meal like this," Pixie said as she ripped off a chunk of bread. "I can only eat the center or one of my four partials will come unglued."

"That makes sense," Griff said.

"I'll donate an emergency room to your clinic if you can use one. Do animals have emergency rooms? I want my name over the door. Is that okay with you?"

Griff swallowed hard, his eyes imploringly on Dory. Was the old lady so plastered she didn't know what she was saying or did she mean it? Dory kept on eating, refusing to meet his gaze. "I . . . I think that can be arranged. Our clinic is new and we could certainly use another room. Are you sure you want to do this? What I mean is, you don't have to feel you . . ." he floundered for words.

"What you're trying to say in a tactful manner, young man, is you think I'm blitzed and tomorrow I won't remember. Ha! I can hold my liquor and I get my liver checked once a month at the same time I go to the proctologist. At my age you can't leave anything to chance. When I told the doctor about these headaches he told me to stop reading. Eyestrain. So simple and I was so worried. This wine is terrible, Dory. Of course I'll remember. I love animals. Animals have a sense about people . . . don't they, Dory?"

"Have some more bourbon," Griff offered. Dory continued to stare at her plate.

"With stew? Goodness, a body could get sick doing something like that. Maybe with my coffee." Pixie leaned back in her chair and lit a cigarette. "Are you sure now that my name will be over the door of the emergency room? And the word 'Emergency' clearly painted on the door. That's a must. I love to do good deeds as long as everyone knows I do them. I never hide my light in a closet."

"That's under a bushel, Pix," Dory said.

"Whatever. I'll call a banker in the morning before I leave. Send me a picture. A colored one, and then another one when the first patient is treated."

"I'll do that," Griff gasped.

"I told you, Dory, I couldn't eat any of that pie. My God, there must be at least a thousand calories in one piece. Nuts and raisins, too. A small piece, I'll just pick."

When Dory carried the last dish to the dishwasher Pixie got up from the table. "I fear one of those damnable headaches is coming on. Dory, you should have stopped me from reading the *National Enquirer.*"

Griff was full of concern for Dory's aunt. "I have some strong headache pills. Can I get you a couple? I know what it is to get a headache."

"Good heavens, no. Medicine of any kind never touches this body," Pixie said. "I'll just take this bourbon with me in case I need something to make me sleep. You can always count on a good bourbon to put you to sleep. Dory, it was a wonderful dinner; even though I just picked I could tell. Don't get up, dear boy, these feet can still find the way." With a wild flourish she picked up the bourbon bottle and succeeded in knocking the crust off the cherry pie. She grabbed a piece of the crust to "nibble" on and made her way to her room.

Griff cleared his throat. "Tell me she's real. The truth now."

In spite of herself Dory laughed. "She's about as real as they come. She grows on you is what she does."

"Are you telling me she's serious about the emergency room?"

"She takes her 'good deeds' as seriously as she does her drinking. If I were you, though, I'd make sure her name is very big. Very big. It wouldn't hurt to make sure it gets in the papers. She's big on papers too. Especially the *National Enquirer.* She reads it from cover to cover."

"What say you and I have a drink in front of the fire? I have to unwind after that lady. She's a piece of work, your aunt. Or did she drink all the good stuff? What do you two have planned?"

Dory giggled. "Every last drop. I can make us some hot chocolate. There's some hot coffee

left. We're just going to wing it. Visit. Talk. Old
times, that kind of thing. Why do you ask?"

Griff rummaged in his pocket and withdrew a
thin envelope. "Here, I finally remembered to
pick up the theater tickets you wanted. Why
don't you and Pixie go. You won't miss me. The
two of you will have a ball."

Dory's entire body froze. How cool he was
being. How blasé. He didn't want to go to the
theater with her. Not anymore. Before he would
have gone simply to please her and pretend he
was enjoying himself. Was it too much effort to
pretend these days? And that look of relief on
his face when he held out the tickets to her.
Maybe she was being unfair. Maybe Griff was
simply being generous in giving up the tickets
so Pixie could enjoy herself. Don't think about
it now, her inner voice warned.

"What's it going to be, hot chocolate or coffee?" she asked brightly.

"It's not a drink I want, it's you. Come on,
woman, let's you and me snuggle up in front of
the fire and make wild, passionate love."

Dory linked her arm in Griff's. "Best offer
I've had all day. I'm going to hold you to that
wild part."

Griff smiled lecherously. "You're on."

"But not in front of the fire. Pix might hear
us. Up in our room, okay?"

"Okay." Griff's voice was husky and sexy and
his arms were warm and so strong.

Dory's eyes went to the unfinished dishes.
"Give me a minute and I'll be right up." She
pushed him toward the doorway. "Two min-

utes," she called after him, rushing back to the sink to rinse out the coffee cups and put the milk and pie in the fridge. One chore led to another and it was nearly twenty minutes before she climbed the stairs to their room and the softly glowing fire Griff had lit. He was sprawled on their bed, head cradled in his arms, fast asleep.

There was a sadness in Pixie's eyes when she said her good-byes at the airport. She clutched her Christmas gift tightly in mittened hands. "Pix, you're the only woman in the world who would wear mittens with a sable coat. I hope your first entry in the journal proves to be memorable," Dory whispered as she hugged the old lady, careful not to disturb the freshly curled wig. "Write. Send it to Mom's house and she'll see that I get it."

"Gotcha." Pixie kissed Griff soundly and waved airily to Dory as she bounded up the ramp behind a group of chattering youngsters.

Entering the town house the couple was assaulted with the scent of fresh evergreens. "I love it, reminds me of when I was a kid. I still can't believe you put that tree up yourself. You are absolutely amazing," Griff said, kissing her softly on the neck. "Hmmmmn, you do wild, wonderful things to me. Let's forget dinner and go to bed. We haven't been spending enough time together and it's all my fault. I didn't realize we were going to be so damn busy. Usually, when you open a clinic like ours it takes a good year to become established. I guess John's and Rick's fame has spread. I was the one who got that colt to nurse, though. There was a congenital obstruction in the pharynx, which required emergency surgery. Almost lost the little beauty. It was touch and go for a few hours."

"That's wonderful, Griff."

"Nothing like success to make you feel on top of the world. I could slay dragons right now or make love to the most beautiful girl in the world. I think I like girls better than slaying dragons."

"I should hope so. What say we shower together? You soap me, I soap you." Dory grinned devilishly.

"Now I know that's the best offer I've had in over a week."

"Has it been a week?"

"It has, but that's only if you're counting." It was a week. A week today, as a matter of fact. Dory couldn't be so caught up in her own world that she didn't know or care how long it had been. The thought bothered him and took the edge off his excitement. Dory's sexual appetites were as healthy and lusty as his own.

Their lovemaking was animal-like in its intensity. As he drifted off to sleep Griff felt vaguely cheated somehow. Dory lay wide awake. Why was it sex put men to sleep and awakened women? She lay quietly trying to decipher how she felt. Certainly not unloved. Griff had said the right words, done the right things, so why did she have to "figure out" how she felt? She should *know*. She should be feeling something, some afterglow, some invisible high that all lovers felt, that she used to feel. Instead, she felt . . . her mind sought for the right word . . . impatient.

Dory's last conscious thought before drifting off to sleep was that she envied Pixie and her free spirit ways.

Griff roused Dory when he finished showering. "Don't you have an early morning class today?"

"Hmmmmmm," Dory replied.

"Up and at 'em, tiger, let's go." Griff jabbed at her playfully. "We all have to work. Remember that old adage, 'He who does not contribute does not eat.' "

All semblance of sleep was gone. While his voice might sound playful, Dory caught the nuance that said it just wasn't so. "All right," she said, swinging her legs over the side of the bed. Her next thought came out of nowhere. "Griff, I'm going to take the shuttle into New York. There's one that leaves around twelve or so. I'll try to make it back tonight, but if I get held up, I'll return first thing in the morning." It was on the tip of her tongue to say she hoped he didn't mind. Instead, she left it as the statement of fact she intended.

Griff paused in the act of tying his dark tie. "Great," he said. "Have a ball and I think you should stay overnight. Don't worry about me, I can get something to eat from Ollie's Trolley on the way home."

Dory refused to think about Griff's exuberance as she showered. She would not think about it. No way was she going to touch that one.

D-Day. Red X day. Time to keep her word and

get in touch with Lizzie. Time to speak to Katy. Time for a trip to *Soiree*. Time to drag David Harlow out of the dark recesses of her mind.

Two weeks till New Year's. Two weeks and one day. The new year, a time to cast the old aside and bring in the new. Decision time.

An hour later the king-sized bed resembled a harem in disarray. Clothes and shoes were everywhere. Dejectedly, Dory sat on the edge of the bed. Nothing fit. At that moment she would have sold her body for a skirt with an elastic waist. If she started playing with moving buttons or half pulling zippers she would throw the line of the garment off. And her hair, God, what a mess. Freshly shampooed would do nothing for the old luster. How long had it been since she patronized a beauty shop and had a rinse, just for highlights? Ages. Lily's home barbershop could hardly be called a salon. She was a mess. Lord, even some of her shoes were tight across the instep. That was from running around in scruffy sneakers all day.

Eyeing the confusion all around her, Dory felt angry . . . and impatient. Angry that she had allowed things to get to this point and impatient to be on her way to the city.

A curling iron might help. Her fox coat, if she kept it on, would certainly camouflage her weight gain. Makeup would be no problem. She did look a little puffy around the eyes, but by the time she was ready to leave the swelling would be gone.

Pixie should be halfway to Hong Kong by now. The thought made Dory smile. Go for it,

Pix, because if you don't, there ain't no one out there gonna do it for you.

Dory had enjoyed the long talks she'd had with Pixie during her three-day visit. Not once had Pixie even attempted to tell her what to do. She listened and then prattled on about her own adventures and misadventures. Always her piercing gaze would lock with Dory's to be sure she was getting her subtle messages.

It was another hour before Dory returned all the clothes to their scented hangers and piled the shoes back in their marked boxes. She made the bed and straightened the bathroom. Makeup was applied swiftly and deftly; the curling iron whizzed through her hair to create a slight curl, which she misted with hairspray. She wasn't exactly like the old Dory but she could pass a quick muster.

Dory checked her purse for her checkbook, her wallet, and an ample supply of tissues. She wouldn't take an overnight bag. If she decided to stay in New York she would take a quick run to Saks and pick up a few things. The Christmas-gift check from Pixie, which was almost sufficient for a down payment on a house, was folded carefully. Citibank would applaud her when she deposited the check. Pixie's brand of security.

The thermostat was adjusted, all the lights off, the garage door open, the car warming up, the coffeepot unplugged. She felt an unexpected exhilaration as she closed the door behind her. Mechanically, she tried the knob to be certain it was locked.

Dory drove to the airport and parked the car,

pocketed the parking stub and walked to the entrance. Standing in line at the ticket counter, she impatiently watched the round clock high on the wall tick off the minutes. If things didn't speed up, she would miss the flight that was due to take off for New York in less than twenty minutes.

As the ticket agent completed arrangements with a traveler and the line moved forward, Dory suddenly became aware of someone watching her. Turning to her left, she focused on a tall, well-dressed gentleman, who was brazenly focusing on her. Dory felt a surge of sudden confidence. She knew the soft grays and silvers of the natural fox coat did wonders for her pale blond hair, and the bright raspberry silk blouse with its complementary wool tweed skirt offset the pink of her cheeks. Although her black Etienne Aigner boots were still feeling tight across the instep, they were the finishing touch to her outfit.

The man, dressed in a dark brown suit, with a luxurious overcoat of brushed suede, continued to stare approvingly in Dory's direction. It felt good to be admired and she warmed to a flush in spite of herself. She knew she would only have to give him a glance of encouragement and he would approach her. Not in the habit of picking up men in airports, Dory forced herself to look away. Was she so desperate for approval that she would resort to flirting with total strangers? Still, there was something about this man she recognized; she had seen him somewhere before; she knew she had. Where? Through the advertising department at *Soiree*? At Lincoln Center? Skating in Rockefeller Center? A touch on her arm.

"Excuse me," a deep masculine voice was saying, "I believe you dropped this." He held up one of her slim leather gloves.

Searching through her pockets, Dory realized he was correct. "Thank you. I'm always losing gloves. I suppose I should pin them to my sleeves the way Mother did when I was a little girl." Looking into his startlingly clear blue eyes, Dory felt her smile deepen. She realized with a certain alarm that this stranger was still holding the hand into which he had pressed her glove. He was tall, good-looking, and his obvious interest in her was flattering.

"By any chance do you have a few minutes for a cup of coffee? I feel as though I've been struck by Kismet." The blue eyes captured hers, making her heart race with excitement. There was a certain confidence about this man, as though he could instantly recognize what he wanted and could unerringly set his course for it. The words "charisma" and "power" kept bouncing through Dory's brain.

"I would like that," she told him honestly, "however, my plane leaves in a very few minutes. I'm going to New York." Now why had she told him that?

His disappointment was obvious. "Perhaps when you return to the capital then?" he asked, reaching into his inside jacket pocket to give her his card. "Please, call me. I've only just found you and you're flying away."

The ticket agent interrupted, "Can I help you? Miss? Did you wish to purchase a ticket?"

Flustered, Dory stepped up to the counter. "I'm sorry . . . I mean . . . I must go."

"You have my card, call, won't you?" A small salute and he was gone.

The ticket agent smiled warmly, noticing the situation between Dory and the handsome man who was now walking out of the terminal. In purchasing her ticket and rummaging through her purse for her American Express card, Dory never noticed that the business card he had given her had fallen to the floor.

On the forty-five-minute flight to New York Dory thought about her encounter with the stranger. It felt good to be admired. Just a bit of harmless flirting, she told herself, feeling slightly guilty about Griff, knowing that if she'd had the time she would have joined the stranger for coffee. Harmless flirting, she told herself. It was silly to keep thinking of the man as a stranger; he'd given her his card and his name would be on it. Suddenly, very, very curious about who he was and what he did for a living, she searched the pocket of her coat for his business card. It was gone. Lost. She had lost it, and some niggling fear told her she was losing her grip on more than just a card handed her by a stranger.

Chapter Ten

In the *Soiree* offices Katy welcomed Dory with open arms while the girls in the outer office hovered around, waiting for her to recognize them. She called each by name, pecked some on the cheek, smiled at others as she shook hands. God, it felt wonderful.

"Anyone water my plants? I'm into plants now." She grinned to a laughing Katy.

"Just like a jungle. When you move down the hall I'll be sure they follow you," Katy teased.

When. Not if. When she returned to *Soiree* was what Katy meant.

Dory felt smug as she accepted a cup of coffee from one of the secretaries. She smiled and thanked her. "What's new?"

"Not a whole hell of a lot. I was going to call you at least a thousand times but Lizzie forbade it. She said she made a bargain with you and that included no phone calls, except for emergencies. I managed. Not well, but I managed." Katy shrugged. "Your replacement . . . she isn't you. I want to transfer to your new offices with you. Can you swing it?"

The smug feeling stayed with Dory as she sipped the coffee. Hell yes, she could swing it. She would be the boss. If she decided to return, that is. Her visit seemed to convince everyone that that was her intention. Maybe she had been too hasty. She could have just picked up the phone instead of making the trip in person. She didn't want to rain on Katy's parade.

Was there such a thing as a creative high? A high brought on by friends and fellow workers. A business . . . a job . . . when had she last felt like this? So long ago she forgot what the feeling was like.

"How about some pastry?"

"No thanks. I'm dieting. Look and weep." Dory laughed as she opened the fox coat.

"My God," Katy said.

"That's what I said when I read the scale. Salads from now on, that's it. It really snuck up on me."

"Is Lizzie expecting you?"

"Not in person. A phone call, perhaps. She's here, isn't she? What's new with the adoption?"

"She's here. As a matter of fact she's been coming in at seven every morning to get caught up before she leaves. The baby arrives January first."

Dory's heart started to pound. She could feel the beginnings of an anxiety attack. God, not here, not in front of Katy, she pleaded silently.

Relax, get hold of yourself. It's your choice, your decision. Nothing has to be decided today. "But I thought . . ." Damn, why did she sound like she was whimpering?

"We all thought it would be another three months. What can I tell you? The mother delivered prematurely. The baby was in an incubator for a while. She may even get it for Christmas. We're all hoping. It's a girl, just what she wanted!"

A vision of her decorated town house flashed before Dory's eyes. Her first Christmas with Griff. Dinner with his mother. Lily and Rick would stop by. Sylvia would have them over for breakfast or brunch, depending on the condition of her house. Presents. Mistletoe and holly. Carols and church.

"Dory, this shouldn't mess up your doctorate. Remember, I checked it out . . . you can continue your studies at night at Columbia. It'll delay things a bit, but you're so set on achieving your doctorate, a few more months shouldn't make all that much difference. How's it going, anyway?" Katy asked cheerfully, as though it were a foregone conclusion that anything Dory tackled was soon accomplished.

"Oh, fine, fine!" Dory lied, feeling the old guilt about how she had let herself down.

Dory set her empty cup on Katy's desk. "I'll trundle along now and visit with Lizzie. I want to make the bank and do some shopping. I think I'll stay over at the Hyatt. Could you book me a room? If you're free, we could have dinner together. My treat. We have so much catching up to do. Do you think your husband will mind?"

"Mind? He'll be delighted. Tonight is his bowling night anyway. I'll stay late and catch up on some of my own work. Meet you in the lobby at seven. Is that okay with you?"

"Fine." Dory hugged her friend and waved to her coworkers. She was stifling in the fox coat, but she refused to take it off. If she was stupid enough to gain so much weight, then she would suffer for it. Wearing the heavy fur in the office was punishment enough.

Lizzie greeted her warmly, her shrewd eyes assessing Dory. "I would have settled for a call," she said softly.

"You look positively radiant, Lizzie. Katy told me the news. I'm so happy for you."

"I feel radiant. Hell, I am radiant, you're right. I don't think I've ever been so happy. Sit down, let's talk."

Dory let the fox slip from her shoulders. She waited for Lizzie to take the initiative.

"As I said, I would have settled for a phone call. But, don't misunderstand, I'm glad you came. Wanted a look-see, huh? Did you miss it?"

"Yes, I did miss it. Yes, I wanted a look-see, as you put it. And yes, I put on some weight. I'm dieting now. Nothing fits." Lizzie said nothing, her gaze sharp and pointed as she assessed Dory.

"I'm going to need an answer by Monday, Dory. I wish I could give you longer but I can't. I hope you understand."

"I do. I'll call you Monday morning," Dory said quietly. If there was ever a time for an anxiety attack, this was it, Dory thought. She waited. Nothing happened. She grinned at Lizzie.

Lizzie grinned back. "Bought any nice shoes lately?"

"I'm on my way to Saks right now."

"Dory, whatever you decide, it's all right with me. I want us to remain friends. I know you'll do what's right for you."

"Count on it. Make sure you send pictures of the baby."

"Count on it." Lizzie laughed.

"I'll talk to you on Monday."

Dory's first stop was Citibank. She cashed an astronomical check, deposited Pixie's check, and started out for Saks. She treated herself to a haircut, a manicure, and pedicure. Her next stop was the shoe department, where she bought four pairs of shoes and two pairs of boots. At the last minute she picked up a pair of naughty, feathery slippers. *I don't need them but I want them. That's reason enough,* she told herself as she got into the elevator.

Dory shopped till the store closed. She waited patiently for the doorman to get her a taxi. She could have walked; everyone in New York walked. But this was a day to pamper herself. A taxi ride was no big deal. She was all grown up now and could make her own decisions. *About time,* she thought.

Dinner with Katy was a pleasure. They sat for hours over wine spritzers and salad. They talked about everything and nothing but mostly about Katy's work and Lizzie's new baby. Eating was a time for relaxing, Katy said, and they could get down to the nitty-gritty when they got back to Dory's room at the Hyatt.

It was after ten when both women kicked off their shoes in the hotel suite. Dory ordered espresso and Amaretto from room service. It arrived within minutes. Dory added a generous tip to the waiter. Settled comfortably in the armchair, she faced Katy. "You're dying to know, I can tell. I don't know where to start. Everything is so mixed up. I'm so confused, I don't know which way to turn anymore."

Katy's friendly face showed concern for her friend. "A relationship is no different than a marriage. You have to work at it. Both of you. As far as I can see the only difference is that you can walk out without going to a lawyer."

Dory sipped at her drink. "It's not one of those he did this, he didn't do that, I did it all, things. It wasn't anything like that. I really think it's me, not Griff. I got off the track. My God, it got to the point where I was having anxiety attacks and I wasn't me anymore. I even went so far as to think I should have a baby. Thank God I had enough sense to know that was a mistake. A baby would only compound the problem."

"At least you're thinking clearly."

"Now, yes. And even now I'm not sure. I could have called Lizzie today the way I said I would, but at the eleventh hour I decided to come in. I needed to come here today. I haven't really made a decision. I have to talk to Griff."

"That's understandable. Did you tell all this to Lizzie?"

"Tell Lizzie! You must be joking. Lizzie read me like a book. She gave me till Monday and said I have to give her a concrete decision. She's being more than fair; she'll have her decision. Hey, Katy, this is my life we're talking about."

"Tell me about it, oh wise and wonderful friend."

"Don't you have anything to say, some advice to offer?"

"No way. I never stick my nose in other people's business even if they are my best friend. I want us to keep what we have. What I will say to you is get your priorities in order and work from there."

"I'm trying."

"Not good enough. You have to do it. Trying is for beginners. Jump in with both feet and do it," Katy said, swallowing the bitter coffee.

"I could screw up and regret it later."

"That's a chance we all take every day when we climb out of bed. You'll live with it because you have to. It's simple. You're going to do what you have to do because it's best for you. Can't you see that, Dory?"

How patient she was, this loyal friend. "It's easier to cop out and blame other people and other things."

Katy laughed. "I know all about that. I've been down some rocky roads and I weathered it. You will too. You're what we used to call 'good people' where I came from. Hey, have you bought any new shoes lately? What's the count?"

"Today I bought four pairs and two pairs of boots. I didn't buy any while I was in Virginia. I lived in sneakers. I'm going to burn them tomorrow when I get back. I detest sneakers. I hate them with a passion."

Katy had never seen such a wild look on Dory's face or heard so much vehemence in her voice.

"Hey, if sneakers aren't your thing, that's okay. Don't get hyper."

"See, see what I mean. It's coming out now. At home I held it in and was...I was... damnit, I was pleasant."

"There's nothing wrong with being pleasant."

"Oh, yes there is. Especially if you feel like yelling or voicing your opinion. Anger is a healthy emotion. Did you know that, Katy?"

"I should. I give vent to it at least a hundred times a day both here and home."

"I never did that in all the time I've been living with Griff. I was...I was just damn pleasant. I didn't want him upset. I wanted to make things perfect for him. I waited on him hand and foot. I made gourmet meals. I decorated that damn town house till I was blue in the face. I made it a place for him to be proud of. I put him first. I copped out on school. I copped out on myself, on everything."

"Is that what he wanted?" Katy asked softly.

Dory stared at Katy for long minutes. "I don't know. He accepted everything. He never argued or lost his temper with me. I made myself over for him. I did everything I could to make it work."

"But is that what he *wanted*?" Katy persisted.

"I don't know. I honestly don't know."

"Oh, yes you do. You know all right or you wouldn't be sitting here right now. It's easier to pick up the phone. But you made the trip. You left here a successful career woman. A woman who had her own apartment, was confident, had her own portfolio. How many times did I hear you talk about your small investments that you broke your back for? Every girl in that office would have sliced off her right arm for half of what you exuded. Just half. *That* was the woman Griff fell in love with and wanted to marry. Am I right or not?"

"Okay, okay. I think you're right. Love is love. Inside I tried to be the same person I was back here in New York. Just because I kept house shouldn't mean that I . . . oh, Katy, I screwed up. I know what happened. I tried to be all things. That person back in the town house wasn't me. It never was, even from the first day. I'm no Susy Homemaker. I'm me. Sylvia and Lily irritated the hell out of me. I put on a good front but I could feel myself churning every time I had to be in their company. God, I tried. I really tried. The more I tried, the unhappier I was. You're right. I turned into a caricature of myself. There were times when I would catch Griff looking at me as if I had sprouted a second head. I couldn't understand it. I thought it was what he wanted. I did everything to please him."

"You did everything but be yourself, the Dory he fell in love with. If he wanted a homemaker he could have hired a maid. He wanted you. The real you. The you that's sitting here now talking to me."

"The whole thing is a little hard to swallow. I wasn't fair to Griff or myself. I cheated both of us."

"There must have been some good times, especially in the beginning," Katy said gently. She hated the tormented look in her friend's eyes.

Better for her to see it, and help, than for Dory to go on and on and never make a decision. It was too easy to sink in, to say the hell with it. She should know, she had gone through the same thing a long time ago.

"Of course there were good times, wonderful times. I could never forget them. Never. But they're memories now, Katy. I sound bitter, I guess, but I want you to know I wouldn't change anything for all the money in the world. I needed that time with Griff and I think he did too. We'll both be better for it. It just didn't work. If I hadn't packed up and gone I would always have regretted it. Like Pixie says, Go for it, if it isn't right you'll know soon enough. That lady never steered me wrong yet. From here on in I have to do what's best for me. I have to get my life back. It's not going to be easy. I love Griff. Maybe I'll always love him. But I love other things too. I love New York, I love this job here at the magazine. I love that jungle out there, I love life. Maybe I do want it all. There's nothing wrong with that. I don't have to compromise, I don't have to give up things, I don't have to turn myself inside out to get it all. All I have to do is get my priorities straight. Right or wrong?"

"Sounds familiar, Dory. Familiar and accurate. You're on the right track. See what talking to an old friend can do for you?" Katy hugged her friend tightly.

"Thanks, Katy. You really helped me."

"Hey, you did it yourself. I just listened. Did I give you even one piece of advice? Did I say you were right or wrong?"

"You're right! God, I really did it all myself, didn't I? I figured it out. I've got it together. Well, almost. I have a few more hurdles but I can handle them. I might even have a setback but I know where I'm going. And before you leave I have to know how the profile and layout with Pixie came out."

Katy laughed. "It's going to be one of the best pieces *Soiree* ever put out, I can tell you that. The feedback we've been getting is fantastic. Pixie was so divine to work with. She asked about doing a follow-up next year—said she'd come all the way from Hong Kong—and she keeps questioning us about talk-shows. Talk-shows yet!"

"I'm glad Lizzie decided to go with it. Was it hard to get around what Pixie calls 'old age horny'?"

"Good Lord, no. It's a work of art. Exquisite taste, I can tell you that. That article generated so much interest, the entire board came to see the last shooting session. They loved Pixie, particularly after that bash at the Sign of the Dove. I sent you the last in-house release, didn't you read it? Harlow gave you full credit, two whole paragraphs as a matter of fact. He said, and this is a direct quote, 'We have Dory Faraday to thank for her insight and her courage in bringing this matter to our attention. It's a topic that most magazines would shy away from. Always being a front-runner, *Soiree* and the board feel that Faraday showed remarkable foresight in laying the groundwork for such a remarkable profile.' And he went on and on, giving you fragrant bouquets. I mailed it to you days ago."

"Not a word yet. I'll probably find it waiting when I get home tomorrow. When does it come out?"

"Spring issue."

"Send a dozen copies to Aunt Pixie in Hong Kong."

"What is she really doing over there?" Katy asked.

"She's doing her thing. She stopped by for three days before she left. She hasn't changed a bit. She'll live to be a hundred and enjoy every day of it. Griff loves her; they get along wonderfully."

"How could he not like her? She's one of the most remarkable women I ever met. Age certainly does have its moments. Give her my regards when you write to her."

"I'll do that. It was great talking with you, Katy. I missed you. I've missed all of this. I'll be in touch."

Katy wrapped her arms around Dory. "Any time. See you."

Dory drew the dead bolt and changed for bed. She'd think about all this tomorrow when she got back to Virginia.

Dory deplaned the following morning at National Airport. It was close to the lunch hour and the winter sun was glinting brightly through the long glass windows in the terminal. As she waited for the conveyor to deliver up her packaged shoe boxes her eyes kept swinging over the travelers. It was silly to think she might see the man she'd met the afternoon before, but she couldn't help herself.

Feeling more disloyal to Griff than she liked, she scooped her parcels off the conveyor and headed for the parking lot.

The town house seemed alien with its wealth of greenery. For some reason it irritated her. She adjusted the thermostat and hung up her fox coat. Annoyance cloaked her when she looked at the messy bed. She hadn't missed the littered breakfast table with the toast crumbs and empty coffee cup. Woman's work! she thought nastily. One leg of Griff's pajamas hung over the hamper. A wet and soggy towel was wadded up in the basin. One slipper was stuck under the door, preventing it from closing. "The hell with it!" Dory exploded as she made her way downstairs. She fixed a cup of strong, black coffee and sat down to drink it. When she was finished she would exercise for an hour and start to get back into shape. A salad for lunch and dinner and she would be off to a good start. Griff could have steak and salad. No more gourmet meals. No more a lot of things.

Four days to make a decision. Her eyes flew to the calendar. Four days. Ninety-six hours. Five thousand seven hundred and sixty minutes.

Griff. She had to think about Griff. If she went back, what would happen to their relationship? It was a known fact that distance did nothing for love. It did not make the heart grow fonder. Could she make it without Griff? Did she really want to go back? When she had left the *Soiree* offices she had stood outside, looking up at the office windows. She recalled saying, "This is where it's at." The words stunned her at the time and gave her food for thought as she made her way uptown to Saks.

If that was true, what about her time here with Griff? What did that count for? Was it a trial, a jumping-off point? Exactly what was it? A haven. A safe place to be for a while. Not permanently, but for a while.

When had "not permanently" become a part of her thinking? When she made the decision to take a leave of absence and return to school and move in with Griff, some secret part of her believed it was forever. It was to be a modern relationship that would eventually lead to marriage. She could admit that to herself now.

She loved Griff. Loved him heart and soul. A part of her would die if she left; this she knew as sure as she knew she needed to breathe to stay alive. But she needed more. There was no challenge here. She was making so little contribution to life. Her stomach churned with her thoughts. God, what should she do? How had she ever allowed herself to get to this point? Finding no answers, her eyes swept to the calendar and the red X's.

She was across the room to the phone in a lightning quick moment. She flipped the calendar to the back "note" page and punched out the number she wanted. Her breathing quickened as she waited for someone on the other end of the phone to pick it up. "Senator Carlin's office. May I help you?"

"Yes. This is Dory Faraday. Several months

ago *Soiree* magazine spoke to both you and the senator about doing a profile of him when the Senate offices adjourned for the holidays. I'd like to discuss a mutual date if he's in."

"As a matter of fact you just caught him. He's already packed to leave to return to New York for the holidays. One moment, I'll fetch him. He's talking to someone in the outer office."

An omen. It was an omen, she was sure of it. Dory's throat tightened as she waited for Drake Collins to come on the line. Even though she couldn't be seen, she brushed her hair back from her forehead and rubbed her index finger across her lips.

"Miss Faraday. *Soiree* magazine said you'd be getting in touch with me. I thought you'd forgotten." His voice was deep. A smile was in that voice, she could hear it.

"Senator, that's very amusing. I don't think the woman has been born who could forget you. If I'm to believe your press, you have charisma. That's the main reason I want to do this profile. You could consider it a public thank-you for all those breathless females who ran to the voting booth."

A low chuckle came over the wire, sending a chill up Dory's arms. "My first rule when taking office was never to get caught up in my own press releases."

Dory laughed. "When can we get together?"

"I'm free from the day after Christmas until the third of January when we go back in session. I believe my secretary gave you my home address."

"Yes, she did. I want to interview you on your

home turf and perhaps do some pictures of you both there and in Washington. And at Ollie's Trolley, complete with pictures of you and Nick. That's a must."

"Will it be a problem for you to come to New York?" Was that an anxious tone in his voice? Dory wasn't sure, but if it was, she liked the idea.

"No," she replied without hesitation, "Tell me, is there a particular lady in your life?" She held her breath, waiting for a reply. "Senator, I'm not asking for myself. If there is someone close to you, our readers would like to know. Pictures of the two of you together having lunch, jogging in Central Park, that sort of thing."

The low chuckle came over the wire again, but no answer to her question was forthcoming. Dory licked at her lips and smiled. "You're engaged and married to your career, is that it?"

"Now, you're talking my language. Until the right lady comes along we'll go with that. I'd like to chat with you longer, but I want to catch the shuttle. I'll tell you what. Let me get settled in, pick up a few groceries and I'll call you back tomorrow and we can set up a date. Have a nice Christmas, Miss Faraday."

"I will, Senator, and . . . enjoy your holidays."

Dory stared at the phone for long minutes after she replaced the receiver. It was a new beginning. Her first major decision since moving into the town house. It was something concrete, something she could get her teeth into. Something she wanted to do, damn it. Something she was going to like doing.

Picking up the phone once again, Dory

punched out the number for *Soiree*, catching
Katy just before she left for lunch. "Katy, I've
made contact with Senator Collins and now I'm
in a fix. Can you wire me everything we have on
him? If I'm going to appear intelligent on this
interview, I've got to know something about the
man. Express mail would get it here before
noon tomorrow and that'll give me a chance to
read it over."

Dory felt good. She'd gotten the ball rolling,
and all she had to do was follow along. It was
easy! Why had it seemed so difficult during
these past months?

The niggling voice Dory lived with questioned her about Georgetown. An excuse for
me to move here with Griff without the commitment of marriage, she answered it honestly. I'm
not ready for that doctorate, not yet. Maybe
never. Maybe next year, but it will be for the
right reasons. I have things to do, places to go.
I'm just not ready.

She certainly was clearing all the cobwebs out
of her mental closets today.

How she hated that kitchen calendar. The no-
tation in green lettering told her Griff's mother
would arrive the following day.

Esther Michaels was a lovely woman, a young,
fiftyish widow running a small advertising agency
and making a go of it. She and Dory had gotten
along well at their initial meeting, engineered
by Griff, in New York. The talk over dinner had
centered on the theater. Esther was into theater,

the ballet, and jogging. She was a rail-thin, gaunt woman, eating on the run and trying to nurse a peptic ulcer at the same time. Dory liked her because she was Griff's mother. Esther's eyes told her that she approved her son's choice. Dory was pleased when they left the restaurant, promising to meet again one day for lunch. It was the kind of promise all busy people make. Some day. Maybe. It wasn't important.

Dory felt annoyed that Esther was coming, but Griff had knocked himself out for Pixie. How could she do less? She couldn't. But, she admonished herself, I don't want to entertain her. Not now, when things are so up in the air, so uncertain. Surely Esther would notice the strain. She might comment and then she might not. She might prefer to let Griff and Dory handle their affairs in their own way without offering advice. She didn't want advice from Esther. From Pixie, yes. Pix would never steer her wrong. Pix could always see both sides of an issue, drunk or sober. Esther would side with her son. Dory knew that Esther wouldn't feel charitable toward her if she thought Dory was casting her son aside.

Her head ached. She rubbed at her temples trying to erase the nagging ache. If anything, it intensified. She could call Esther and tell her she would love to have her for a visit, for a day, but not for a full week. She couldn't handle a week. She would be lucky if she could get through a full day. That's what she should do. But would she do it? Her shoulders stiffened imperceptibly. Griff wouldn't like it if she changed Esther's plans.

I don't want her here. It's going to cause me emotional turmoil, and I have enough going on right now. A call to Griff would settle it. Dory would feel him out, see what he thought.

No, damn it! She wouldn't call Griff, or if she did, it would be to tell him her decision. If he didn't go along with it, that was his problem. Since it was she who would be with Esther most of the time, it should be her decision.

Dory reached for the telephone, punched out Griff's number and waited for the receptionist to put her through.

"Griff, I'm calling about your mother. I plan to call her today but I did want to talk to you first."

"Is something wrong, Dory? Look, if you feel it isn't convenient, cancel out. Mother will understand. Make it for later."

Damn, he was making it too easy. Besides, she didn't want later. She didn't want now, but she was stuck.

"That's just it, Griff. I don't want to make it for later. To be perfectly honest, I don't want to make it for now either. I don't think I can handle your mother for more than two days. Don't be angry. I'm trying to be honest with you. I didn't want to go ahead and call Esther till I spoke to you. She is your mother. But, you're going to be busy with the clinic and I'm the one who will have to entertain her. I don't want to do it, Griff. I can handle two days because I feel that's fair to you and to me. More than that I can't . . ."

"Dory, it's okay with me. You're right. Mom is demanding as a house guest and yes, you're

right, you are the one who would have to entertain her. The decision is yours."

"Then you aren't upset with me?"

"Of course not. I know what Mom is like. I understand, Dory," Griff said softly. "Honey, I'm
glad that you felt you could be honest with me
about all of this. Don't give it another thought."

"It's settled then. I'll call Esther now. See you
later, Griff."

It was done. Her second breakthrough. Her
second decision. Esther was coming for just the
weekend. Dory felt good when she hung up the
phone—good about herself. And ready for Esther.

She would have to clean the spare room and
change the sheets. She felt as if some kind, wise
person had given her a personal reprieve when
she yanked sheets and pillowcases out of a
drawer. A week ago she would have stewed and
fretted over the pattern and probably even ironed
the creases. Lily ironed permanent press. But
Dory Faraday's ironing days were over. When she
was finished she stood back to view her work for
neatness. She blinked. The orange and brown
zigzag pattern was almost blinding. These had
been Griff's sheets. He joked that he had bought
them on purpose so they would wake him up in
the morning. Esther would certainly be wide-
eyed.

Dory dusted the furniture with a tissue and
blew the dust off the top of the small portable
television. As she was leaving the room she contemplated the lint on the carpet. Instead of running the vacuum, she bent down sixteen times

to pick up the little bits and pieces of lint. Good for the waistline, she told herself.

When Griff hung up the phone, his mind went blank for a few seconds. The Siamese cat waiting for his gentle touch snoozed peacefully with the aid of a tranquilizer. Damn, his stomach felt as if it was tied in a knot. He didn't like the idea that the two women in his life might be having a problem. His mother could be a pain. If Dory felt she couldn't handle a lengthy visit he could accept that. Hell, he wasn't exactly looking forward to his mother's visit himself. He had to admit, though, that he was surprised by Dory's phone call. For some reason he had expected her to grin and bear it. He had never known her to dig in her heels and make a decision and then call and announce it to him. Suddenly he laughed. By God, that was exactly what she had done. She didn't ask—she simply told him. It was a good thing. He wasn't stupid. Dory was going through some personal turmoil now and Esther would only crowd the issue. Esther could do that without even trying. He loved his mother but—he grinned down at the sleeping cat—he did his maternal loving better from a distance.

The Siamese opened one eye and looked at the giant towering over him, then rolled over on his side and let the doctor examine him. All thoughts of his mother and Dory fled Griff's mind as he began his careful probing of the ailing animal. Dory had the situation in hand.

Chapter Eleven

Griff arrived home that evening ravenously hungry. For her. Dinner could wait, he told her with authority. Right now, there were needs food couldn't satisfy.

Dory flushed pink as he wrapped his arms around her, his cheek frigidly cold from the night air, whispering hoarsely into her ear, stirring new yet familiar longings within her.

Dory took Griff by the hand, leading him up to their room, her smile a promise. The fire in their eyes warmed the room as they watched each other undress, readying themselves for the caresses and kisses they hungered for, Griff lowered himself to the bed, gathering her into his arms, burying his lips into the hollow of her throat. Delighted little mewings sounded in her throat when she pressed her face into the furring on his chest, nuzzling at his nipples and feeling him shudder beneath her touch.

"Dory," he breathed, ragged and husky, falling back against the pillows, taking her with him. He found her eager mouth, returning her kisses with a bittersweet ardor. Hers were the softest lips he had ever kissed, and he believed he would never satisfy himself for their touch. His kisses wandered over the planes of her face, in the dimple near her chin, in the shining paleness of her hair.

His hands caressed her body, finding it beautiful as always, and he sighed with contentment as womanly curve fit against manly muscle.

Dory exerted pressure against him, forcing him to his back while she followed, her knees tightly clamped to his sides. She looked down into his adored face, feeling her love for him well inside her. Her long, silver-blond hair created a curtain as she bent to kiss him—long, loving kisses, meant to touch the soul and stir the senses.

Griff smiled up at her when he felt himself being taken within her. This was his Dory, the Dory he loved—always equal, sometimes dominant, sharing the best of herself, the most of herself, making him more a man because she was more a woman.

Their joining was loving, tender, and filled with joy. It had been too long since they had come together this way, equally, hungry for what each could bring to the other instead of that sorry, dispassionate surrender that was a poor balm for a sick spirit.

* * *

Sitting in the living room, sharing a glass of wine, Griff told Dory about things at the clinic and listened while she told him about her day in New York. The conversation went from acquaintances in the Big Apple to friends here at the capital.

"What did Sylvia do while I was in New York?" Dory asked. "I suppose she made a raid on Neiman-Marcus."

"Actually, Sylvia is down with the flu. John left early this afternoon to stay with her. He was joking that it's a good thing there are no emergencies at the clinic, otherwise it would all fall to me. Sometimes John and I regret the deal we made with Rick that he'd never have to work evenings. He always shows up extra early at the clinic, and he's no slouch on the job, so I suppose it all evens out in the end."

"Rick never stays late?" Dory asked, thinking of the last time she was with Lily and how despondent she had seemed. If memory served her, Lily had said that Rick would definitely be working late that particular evening. Dory also remembered the oncoming anxiety attack she'd suffered when she realized that if domestic, all-giving, Lily wasn't safe, then no one was. Safe. What a funny word, Dory thought as she nestled down into the curve of Griff's arm. Still, when she thought of making her decision and calling Lizzie on Monday, she wanted to actually crawl inside Griff, have him make the decision for her. She would like it if he would tell her what to do, take the responsibility away from her. Be one of those arrogant, chauvinistic men her mother was always reading about in romantic novels. Dory took another sip of wine, feeling it cool against her tongue. She hadn't told Griff about having to make that call on Monday and now she was glad she hadn't. This was one decision she'd have to live with the rest of her life, and it was one she was going to be totally responsible for. For the first time in a long while Dory finally felt good about herself. That didn't make the decision any easier, and she knew it, but she still felt good.

Dory was misting the fresh evergreen and the plants when she saw a taxi pull up in front of the town house and a mink-cloaked woman emerge, looking up at the house number. Griff's mother.

Esther Michaels arrived carrying a poinsettia plant that Dory could only describe as regal. Poinsettias were by nature full and leafy with bright scarlet leaves; Esther's plant grew straight up like a tree. She carried it as though she were the Olympic torch bearer. A Neiman-Marcus shopping bag and one from Gucci were clutched in her free hand. The taxi driver set her pullman bag down in the kitchen and waited patiently while Esther settled the plant and her shopping bags. She counted out the exact amount from a small change purse and added a skimpy gratuity.

"Merry Christmas, to you too, lady," the driver said sourly as he slammed the back door behind him.

"What was that all about?" Esther asked frigidly, honestly perplexed. "He gets paid by the company he works for, doesn't he?"

Dory eyed the large pullman. Just how long would Esther be staying? Maybe she was joining Pixie halfway around the world. The ridiculous thought almost choked her. This imperious woman would hardly acknowledge someone like Pixie, much less travel with her. Now, that isn't fair, Dory old girl. Esther is a lovely person; quit thinking these shabby thoughts about the poor woman. Nuts, she told herself.

"It looks as though you've been shopping," Dory said, hoping to ease the conversation into a light pattern, anything to get Mrs. Michaels to loosen up and make the visit bearable. Clearly, having dinner in the city with Griff's mother was quite different from having her come to stay.

"Christmas presents for you and Griffin. I do so like the holidays, and I'm so glad you invited me. I was afraid I'd be excluded from my son's Christmas," she said as she slipped out of her twenty-year-old mink that, unbelievably, was coming back into style because of its straight lines and wide Joan Crawford shoulders. "How is Griffin?" Esther asked as she removed her powder-puff mink hat and patted at her silvery hair. She looked lacquered, Dory assessed, and she would stake her life that Esther was a product of Elizabeth Arden . . . five days a week with pedicures thrown in. She was perfectly groomed from the top of her sleek French twist to the tip of her shoes.

"Griff's fine. He's working very hard to make the clinic a success. They all are, John and Rick included. Sometimes I think he does more than his share, but he's doing what he wants and what he likes best. That's what's important," Dory said quietly, mentally calculating the cost of Esther's Oleg Cassini suit. She'd been hanging around Sylvia too much!

Esther's look was sharp as she confronted Dory. She had just taken a really good look at the young woman. This couldn't be the same Dory she had met for lunches in the city, or could it? Griffin, dear boy, what have we here? Good Lord, Dory's cheeks stopped just short of being plump. Esther's eye skimmed down Dory's figure, focusing on the waistline, which was concealed beneath the lilac sweatshirt she wore. Was there a grandchild in the making? What did Griffin think of this? Where was the chic, the elegance, the success of Dory Faraday that had so attracted Griffin and had so pleased her?

Esther would not be a snob. Griffin hated snobbery. Still . . . this young woman, and she wasn't *that* young . . . something was definitely amiss. She could sense it. She hoped her tone was light when she replied, "Griffin has had this dream ever since he was a small boy. He's worked hard and I'm so proud of him. I do love winners, you know, Dory." It was on the tip of her tongue to ask if Dory's suspected pregnancy was a fact, but Esther bit back the words. She would ask Griff. She didn't want Dory to think that a grandchild was eagerly anticipated. It wasn't. And should suspicion become reality, Esther knew she'd be hard-pressed to hide her disappointment.

Dory nodded. She should be verbally agreeing with Esther, but it was hard to concentrate. Esther kept staring at her as if she were a bug on the end of a pin. She knew that in the past ten minutes she had failed miserably in Esther's eyes. She didn't measure up. She came up short. A lump settled in her throat. Damn it, why did people always have to judge other people? Why couldn't they just accept them?

Esther's tone became fretful. Lord, was she really going to have to stay here for an entire weekend? What *would* they do? The scent of the pine boughs and the giant tree was making her nauseous. Why couldn't they have had a plastic tree like everyone else? And all those decorations. God! Elves, gnomes, reindeer, and a lot of little stuffed mice. God! She forced a smile to her lips, lips that Dory knew were painted with a brush. The eyelashes came out of a case. Dory wished the bright blue gaze weren't so piercing, so probing. Lord, surely she wasn't waiting for confidences. The thought was so horrific, Dory almost gagged.

"Esther, would you care for a drink? Coffee? Soft drink? Brandy?" Damn, there wasn't any brandy; Pix drank it all. Please don't ask for brandy. There wasn't any Scotch either; Pix finished that the day she left. Her eyes tried to probe the liquor cabinet to see what there was. Vodka, gin, and some bourbon.

"Do you have any Diet Pepsi?"

Dory stared at Esther, Diet Pepsi. Of course, she would ask for Diet Pepsi. Pixie's experience with Diet Pepsi made her laugh aloud. Esther stared at her, frowning. "Private joke," Dory mumbled as she got up to get the drink for Griff's mother.

An hour later Esther said she felt tired and perhaps a warm bath and a tiny little nap might be in order. Dory almost killed herself getting up from the couch to show Esther the way to her room.

Back in the kitchen she sat with her hands propped under her chin. I don't need this. I don't want this. This visit isn't making me happy. And what are you going to do about it? her friend the inner voice chided. Not much, Dory grimaced. I'm temporarily stuck. After all, she is Griff's mother and I have . . . I want . . .

Damn, the holidays with all the pressures were getting to be a bore. The word startled Dory. A bore? It was true. Everything of late was a bore. And, I'm the biggest bore of all. The mental statement of fact did nothing for her mood.

When life and everyone in it was a bore there was only one thing to do. Dory stretched full length on the sofa. She pressed the ON button on the remote control. A soap opera sprung to life. Ha! And they thought they had problems. Within seconds, Dory was asleep.

The next two days were torture for Dory. Griff seemed to creep about, and Esther kept looking at Dory out of the corner of her eye. Dory couldn't wait for Esther to leave, and Es-

ther couldn't wait to be gone. Griff kept looking
at the two women in his life with puzzled expressions. Christmas Eve came and went with
carols on the television and the opening of gifts.
Nothing seemed to faze Dory. Christmas Day
was dinner and a scrumptious dessert that only
Griff ate.

Esther packed her bags while Dory cleaned
the kitchen and Griff watched someone's family
on television tell what their Christmas was like.
B-o-r-i-n-g.

When Griff returned from the airport, he
stalked into the kitchen. "If you don't mind,
would you tell me just what the hell is going on.
What went on here? What in the hell has happened to you, Dory?"

Dory stared at Griff. He had never spoken to
her like this before. Damn, put a man's mother
into the picture and it was a whole new ball
game. Was he taking sides?

"I wish you had warned me what a pain in the
neck your mother was. Two or three lunches
weren't enough time to get to know her. And
what gives you the right to talk to me that way?
I'm not your wife, you know," Dory said bluntly.

Griff slumped down on the sofa, his red muffler with the missed stitches, Dory's first effort,
still around his neck. His voice was soft, too soft,
when he spoke. "I know that. I mean about you
not being my wife. Even if you were, I had no
right to blast off like that. I'm sorry."

"I guess I am too."

"You guess, don't you know?" Griff said coldly.

"No, I, guess I don't know for sure. Everything

is all mixed up. I feel so confused, Griff. I've been wanting to talk to you for weeks now, but you're always busy or tired or something."

"What's that supposed to mean?"

"It means whatever you want it to mean. Something's wrong, Griff, can't you feel it? Can't you see it?"

"Something's been wrong for a long time. I've been waiting for you to get your act together so we could discuss it. I'm not that busy. Every time I want to talk to you, you're making bread or cookies or sewing or some damn thing. If you aren't doing that, you're on the phone with Lily or Sylvia. What am I supposed to think? The next thing you'll be getting headaches and backaches."

"That was a low thing to say," Dory snapped.

"It's true, isn't it? I damn near knocked myself out for your aunt when she was here. I had every right to expect you to do the same for my mother."

"I did. Is it my fault she doesn't want to go outside because her makeup will crack, and is it my fault that she has ulcers and can't eat regular food, and is it my fault that her last two accounts fell through, and is it my fault that I didn't know where her church was, a church that she attends once a year? Don't hang any guilt trips on me, Griff. The whole time she was here she kept staring at me as though I were something that should be under a microscope. I've had enough guilt to last me a lifetime. My aunt asked nothing of you; she didn't put you out, and she went out of her way to be extremely generous to both of us. If you didn't like her, why don't you just say so? No more guilt, you've given me enough trips that if I laid them end to end I could go to the moon. I've had enough!"

"So have I!" Griff yelled back.

Tears burned Dory's eyes. It shouldn't be happening like this. They should be talking it out like the sensible adults they were. She dropped to her knees in front of Griff and grasped both of his hands in hers. "I'm sorry, Griff, this is all my fault. This . . . this fight we're having is something that bubbled up and got out of hand. In a way, I suppose I subconsciously wanted it this way so I could . . . what I mean is . . . I thought it would make it easier for me to say what I have to say."

She drew a deep breath and held up her hand to silence him. "Please, Griff, let me say what I have to say because if I don't I may never get the nerve again. This was wrong for all the right reasons. I wasn't ready to make a commitment to you, either in a relationship or in marriage. I came here with you telling myself that I was going to go back to school. I wasn't even truthful with myself. Oh, in the beginning I believed it, at least for a little while. I copped out is what I did. With school, with you, and with myself. I tried to be like Sylvia because I thought that was what you wanted. Then I tried to be like Lily because I saw the approving way you looked at her. When that didn't work out, I tried to be a combination of both of them, thinking I read you wrong. What I didn't ever do was be myself. I'm not Susy Homemaker and I'm not a social butterfly. I'm me. I lost sight of that for a while. I'm not perfect but I'm all I've got and I have to get me back while I can. I'm not a loser, Griff. I don't even want to be a winner, I just want to be me. I have to go back and pick up my pieces."

"I know," Griff said huskily. "I know."

Warm tears trickled down Dory's cheeks. "I love you, Griff."

"And I love you."

"I'll only be an hour away. We can still see each other. I can write or call."

"I can do the same."

It was a lie and they both knew it.

"It took nerve for you to wear that *muffler* out in public, especially to the airport," Dory said, wiping at her tears.

"You're telling me. I lost track of the people who turned around to stare at me. Come here, Dory."

His arms wrapped around her. Her haven. Her warmth. Her security. She didn't have to let go. She could hang on and maybe some day. . . .

"No regrets, Dory," Griff said, smoothing the tangled hair back from her forehead. "You gave it your best shot and so did I. It wasn't meant to be . . . for now, anyway." There was a long pause.

"When will you leave?" Griff asked.

Without a second's hesitation, Dory replied, "In the morning. I'll stay in Katy's spare room till my sublet leaves."

Griff tilted Dory's head back so that he could meet her tear-filled gaze. "It's right for you. If you hadn't made the decision, I would have made it for you. I'm proud of you, Dory."

"Oh, Griff, I do love you. I hope I can handle this. Help me, please." She burrowed into his chest, her sobs racking her body. If it was this hard now, what was it going to be like when she got back to the city and was alone? Griff held her close, stroking her hair and her back.

He held her through the long night, his arms and back numb with the pressure of her body, but he didn't move. He watched the fire die down and then he watched the smoldering ashes. The twinkling lights of the Christmas tree were the only light once the embers turned to feathery, light dust.

As dawn crept up Griff shifted his weight on the sofa, his grip secure on the sleeping woman in his arms. "Almost time to leave the nest," he murmured.

His eyes smarted. From the smoke in the fireplace, no doubt. And the lump in his throat, his mouth was dry. The night had been long and his throat was parched.

She felt so good, so right in his arms. He had to let her go. She needed to go. He knew that one word, one look from him and she'd stay. He loved her too much to do that to her. In the end she would grow to hate him. He would hate himself.

"Time to fly, little bird," he said softly as he tried to move his arms. Dory stirred sleepily and then was instantly awake. She smiled. The first dazzling smile he had seen on her face since they moved here. His heart ached for what might have been.

"Griff, the tree, all the decorations . . ."

"I'll have one of the boys from the clinic pack everything away. While you get your things together what say I make us a going-away breakfast."

"Sounds good to me. Most of my things have been packed for some time. Griff, don't make more of that statement than there is."

"I won't." Griff's movements in the kitchen were sluggish. He hated what he was doing. He hated farewells. He hated good-byes of any kind.

Dory sat down to black toast and brown scrambled eggs. It was the most delicious food she had ever tasted. "Let's not make any promises or play any games, Griff."

"Agreed."

"We'll keep in touch. If you're ever in the city . . . if I ever find myself here . . . you know. Tell Sylvia and Lily I'll drop them a note."

"Gotcha," Griff said, forcing a light note into his voice.

A horn sounded outside. The taxi. Dory looked at Griff. "I didn't want you to take me to the airport. I wanted to leave you here, so I could think of you this way, not among strangers in a sterile airport. I have to go, Griff," she whispered, choking back a sob.

"I know, Dory love. You need to be back in your own climate, in your own environment. It's where you thrive, where you like yourself to be."

"I like to be in your arms, Griff. That's where I like to be. But it's not enough."

"I love you, Dory. Hurry, cab drivers aren't known for their patience."

"Griff . . ."

"I know, love. I know."

"I love you, Griff."

"And I love you. Move, damn it, or this is all going to be for nothing, and we'll have to replay it all when the next cab comes to get you." The sound of the horn pierced the frigid air outside.

Without another word, without another glance, Dory turned and walked out the door.

Griff stood by the window long after the taxi had gone. She was going back to her world. She was gone. He felt like hell. Probably a cold coming on. He was overdue.

Maybe he should go over to Rick and Lily's to have coffee and tell them that Dory was gone. Lily would be feeding the baby about this time.

Griff blew his nose lustily. For sure, it was a cold. What else could it be?

Chapter Twelve

Dory had put in her first week of work on the job and she knew she had made the right decision. Life was exciting again; she accepted her share of stress and plunged herself into learning Lizzie's managerial duties. Soon, she hoped, she would be able to blend those managerial skills with her own brand of creativeness, and her job would be innovative as well as challenging.

So what if this particular brand of happiness was paid for by crying herself to sleep every night? So what if her appetite was less than it should be and every pair of broad shoulders and head of dark hair she noticed in a crowd seemed to be Griff? She was coping. She was handling it better than she had expected. That was all that mattered, she told herself. As Pixie often said, "Everything in life has a price. The trick is deciding if you want to pay it."

The door to her office opened and in stepped David Harlow. "Katy said you'd need this coffee about now." He sat a cup that boasted "BEST BOSS IN TOWN" down on her desk. "You look tired, so I guess she was right. I stopped by to invite you out for dinner." There was a gleam in his eye as he appraised her sleek shining hair that brushed the shoulders of her mauve silk blouse. With a proprietary air, he reached out to smooth the pale blond strands.

Dory backed away. "Sorry, Mr. Harlow, I can't make it." She leaned back in her chair, sipping the fragrant brew.

"When we're alone you're to call me David," he told her, his tone oily. "How about tomorrow?"

"Busy, Mr. Harlow. In case you're not getting the message, I will call you Mr. Harlow." Dory placed the cup on her desk and stood up to face him.

She stood tall, smoothing her skirt over her hips. "Let me tell you something, Mr. Harlow. I am well aware of the fact that you have it in your power to remove me from the ranks of *Soiree*. Before I made my decision to return here, I knew that there would never be anything between the two of us, and I'm prepared to start over again somewhere else. I will not be compromised."

Harlow spoke as though he hadn't heard a word Dory had said. "What about dinner Saturday or Sunday? We can take in jai alai in Connecticut."

Dory shook her head.

"When won't you be busy?"

Dory flinched at his tone. This was it. "You're not listening to me, Mr. Harlow. It's time we understood one another. If you and what you're suggesting goes with this job, then you have the wrong woman. Oh, I could make all kinds of threats about going to the Civil Liberties Union or yelling sexual harassment, but I'm going to get on with my life, and I'm not going to let you get under my skin. I'll simply clean out my desk and be out of here within the hour. That, Mr. Harlow, is the bottom line. Take it or leave it." There, she had said it and she knew he'd been listening. And it hadn't been as difficult as she'd thought. She kept her gaze steady and waited.

Harlow grinned wolfishly and held out his hand. He was whipped and he knew it, and wasn't it said that discretion was the better part of valor? There were other girls, less dedicated women who could appreciate a man like himself. Oh, he knew he wasn't much to look at, but he also knew something else. Women were attracted to power. An Adonis of a janitor couldn't compete with the homeliest of men who held the three "P's": power, position and persistence. "Well, they told me you weren't a pushover, Dory." He grinned broadly. "This is only a truce; it doesn't mean I won't keep trying."

"Just so the record is straight," Dory told him firmly. "And also for the record, if you're Mr.

Harlow, then I'm Ms. Faraday. Got it?" She extended her hand for a shake.

"You have style, Faraday, I'll give you that."

"That's what they tell me. Time to get back to work, Harlow. Thanks for stopping by."

Harlow grinned. "Next time I'll make an appointment."

"Do that." Dory grinned back.

Harlow left her office, but he winked at her before he left. She wanted to throw something at him. He'd said the words and played the scene, but he hadn't believed a word of it. As far as he was concerned, Dory was simply going to take a little longer than other women. But even with her anger, Dory knew a satisfaction. She'd played by her own rules, and while she hadn't exactly had a complete victory, the ball was in her court. David Harlow would probably always be a thorn in her side but she'd cope. It was going to be rocky, but she'd been over rough turf before.

There was one more thing to do before she could sit back and relax with Pixie's letter, which had arrived in the morning mail. And then back to Katy's comfortable ranch house on the Island.

She flipped through the Rolodex till she found the number she wanted, then dialed and waited.

"Senator Collins's office. May I help you?"

"Dory Faraday, Miss Oliver. Is the senator in?"

"One moment please."

"Ah, Miss Faraday, it's a pleasure to hear your voice at the end of a long day, a very long day."

"Thank you." There was that smile in his voice again. "Senator, I really do want to apologize for not getting together over the holidays. I moved back to the city and managed to get myself promoted in the bargain. I think I more or less have things squared away here. How's your schedule?"

"Hectic. But, I have a farm in McLean where I go weekends. By pure chance I happen to have the next four free. I have to warn you, though, that could change at any time. For now, it's good for me if you could manage to get down here."

Dory's heart picked up an extra beat as she contemplated a long weekend with the man who owned such a wonderful voice. "I think I can arrange it. Would you like to start this weekend?"

"It's all right with me. Just tell me your flight number and I'll have someone pick you up at the airport."

"I'll get back to your secretary tomorrow, Senator. I'm looking forward to working with you on this project. I think it's going to be one of our better political profiles." As she spoke, Dory riffled through the files in the bottom right-hand drawer of her desk. Where was the envelope Katy had sent her with that material on Drake Collins? She had been so involved with making her decisions that she'd never opened it.

Her fingers found the mailing envelope and she pulled the tab to open it. Senator Collins was talking about bringing a pair of warm boots and heavy sweaters to the farm. She'd have to follow him around while he tended to chores and he planned to do some riding. Did she ride?

The contents of the envelope scattered out onto Dory's desk. There were newspaper clippings, Xeroxed copies of magazine articles in *Fortune, Business Week,* and *Time.* And an 8 x 10 black-and-white glossy photo, no doubt from the senator's campaign. Dory picked up the photo. Laughing eyes looked back into hers from a handsome face. Dory's eyes widened. The man at the airport. The senator was the man at the airport who had picked up her dropped glove and had wanted to take her for coffee! Little bubbles of excitement fizzed through her blood. There had been an instant attraction between them. She knew it; any woman could instantly tell if a man was interested in her.

"I'm counting on this article for *Soiree* to assure me of being a shoo-in on my next campaign for office," the senator quipped.

"We do have an astronomical circulation in your home state, Senator. If nothing else, you'll have the edge over your opponent."

"I'm looking forward to your visit. Till Saturday," Drake Collins signed off.

Dory sat for a long time staring at the phone. It was incredible, simply incredible. It would be fun to see if the senator recognized her from the airport. Fun. That was what she wanted right now. She still wasn't over Griff, and she didn't expect to be for a long, long time. She wondered what he was doing right now, this minute. She glanced at her watch. He'd still be at the clinic. Would he eat supper alone? With someone? Was he eating right?

Dory's shoulders slumped. She shouldn't be worrying about him this way. But love, when it died, died hard. And Dory still loved Griff, in a very special way. More special because Griff recognized her needs and was unselfish enough to think of Dory first. If anyone had had doubts or qualms about Dory moving to Washington, it had been Griff. He'd wanted to marry her. Perhaps marriage would have made the difference. There would have been a commitment. She would have had to think things through very carefully. Dory realized now that she had never burned her bridges behind her when she left New York. She had purposely contrived to keep a spot open for herself in case she wanted to return. But then, why had she left in the first place? Was it plain weariness of job and stress? Was it because she realized Lizzie would be leaving and she'd been the most natural person to step into the job? Did she think at the time that she couldn't handle the position? Was that why running away with Griff had seemed so important? And that was what it had been, running away, knowing that *Soiree* would welcome back its prodigal child.

She loved Griff, yet she had used him. In return for all those household chores and making a home, she had expected safety and solace.

And still it hadn't been there for her. No sooner had she arrived than she had begun to worry that Griff didn't love her, didn't admire her, that he'd admired other women more. She had expected to *keep* a home for Griff, but she had also expected him to *make* a home for her. Foolish girl. Why and where had she gotten the idea that all things good and worth having come to a woman only through a man? Griff hadn't changed, *she* had! Griff hadn't expected her to sacrifice, she had simply done it. He hadn't asked . . . she had simply given. And always he had appreciated it, but probably the whole time he'd wondered where his Dory had gone. The Dory he had known in New York and had fallen in love with.

"Griff . . . Griff . . . I let both of us down, didn't I?" She looked at the phone. She'd finally gotten it all straight in her own head and she wanted to tell Griff. Her hand fell back into her lap and she laughed aloud. Griff knew. Griff had always known.

Dory blinked back a tear, a smile forming on her lips. For now, she had found the place she needed to be, to grow. It wasn't the answer to everything in her life, but until she *wanted* to be somewhere else, it was home. And she was home free.

On to bigger and better things. Better things like a letter from Pixie. The airmail paper was as crisp and crackly as celery. Dory smoothed out the pages and leaned back, her feet propped up on an open drawer. It paid to be comfortable when starting one of Pixie's letters.

Dory, Sweet Child,

I know you must be chewing your nails wondering how I'm doing. In a word, super. That's as in s-u-p-e-r! Mr. Cho (he insists I call him Mr. Cho) and I are a perfect match. I've already filled the journal you gave me for Christmas. There was a tricky moment or two when Mr. Cho wanted to know why I had so many names. I glossed over the whole thing and he now thinks all Americans are crazy. Wealthy and crazy!

I'm marrying Mr. Cho on the second day of the Chinese New Year which is shortly after ours. He's a remarkable man. As you know, he demanded a dowry. He also demanded all my assets and said he would retire to manage them. We've worked up a written contract whereby he agrees to devote his entire life to me and to make you and me all the shoes we can hope to wear in a lifetime. (I had to fight for that one.) We both know I have a tendency to be flaky, but I have never been one to buy a pig in the poke. We did a little plea bargaining which is another way of saying I demanded a sample of his devotion. My dear, may I say it was one of the most heady experiences of my life. I worried for naught. I think even Mr. Cho was startled. We had a bit of role reversal when I had to wait for him for two days before he could get it all together. I loved every minute of it. I felt so . . . so . . . lecherous.

Mr. Cho is thirty-nine years old. I was a little surprised but he said not to concern myself, that age was only a number. He constantly tells me

I'm a work of art, meaning, I'm sure, that I'm a treasure.

Mr. Cho will retire officially the day of our marriage. The nuptial agreement has many little clauses and tacky little promises that I have no intention of honoring. I'm contributing seventy-five thousand dollars to the marriage. If Mr. Cho's eyes weren't almond-shaped, I think they would have widened in surprise. He considers that amount equal to being a millionaire. Aren't you proud of me? I never give all of everything except my body. Mr. Cho loves my wigs. He's now trying to figure out a way to keep them from slipping off my head. He loves to run his fingers through them. (Is that kinky or is that kinky?) On my arrival we both got blitzed, me on his rice wine and he on my Scotch. It was memorable.

I plan to take up residence in his house in Aberdeen. I'll have cards made up and send you one. Actually, the house is a shack. One of these days when I'm not too busy I may fix it up. Hong Kong is magnificent, and I do my shopping in Kowloon. Mr. Cho barters and haggles for me so no one loses face.

Under separate cover I'm sending you all the materials Mr. Cho requires for a mold of both your feet. Rush it back to me. I don't want him to get too lazy. Devotion is the name of the game, and if I'm paying for it, I want "our" money's worth.

I'd write more but Mr. Cho is suffering his third relapse and I want to make him some rum tea. These Orientals have no stamina. I can't even begin to tell you the trouble I had when I tried to explain the word 'performance' to him. Now he understands. That's why he's working on his third relapse. Just last night I had to tell him my bankers weren't going to be too happy if he kept caving in on a regular basis. Poor darling, every time I say, "up, up and away," he turns green.

Dory, dear child, I hope all is well with you and that you have made decisions of your own. I'm sending this letter to the magazine. I didn't want your mother getting hold of it. I can just see and hear her clucking her tongue and saying "that damn fool, he married her for her money." I know it's true and you know it's true, but your mother doesn't need to know. I can live with my decisions because for the first time in thirty years I'm happy doing what I want when I want. Amazing that I had to come halfway around the world to do it. Well almost, I do have to consider Mr. Cho and his . . . ah . . . slight deficiency. See if you can't get me one of those sex manuals that deals with staying power. Rush it airmail in a plain brown wrapper.

One last thing, Dory. After my seventy-five thousand dollar withdrawal, I signed my power of attorney over to you. I don't want those articulate bankers on my tail. Do whatever you have to do where my affairs are concerned. Take care, Dory, and please, be happy for me.

All my love and good wishes,
Aunt Pixie

Tears burned Dory's eyes as she folded the crackly letter. "Right on, Pix," she said softly. "Right on." There were many kinds of happiness, she told herself as she slid the letter into the desk drawer. Coming back was her kind.

How many times had she thought about Griff today, yesterday, the day before that? Hundreds? Thousands? At least. Why not call him? They'd had so much. She couldn't just cut it off. Why not call him and ask how he was doing? Why hadn't he called to ask her how she was doing? Because he was a man and a man didn't do things like that. Besides, she was the one who walked out. Before she could change her mind she dialed the number at the town house. Griff answered on the third ring.

His voice was just as she remembered and it did the same things to her it had always done. Her heart fluttered a little and her tongue felt as if it were stuck to the roof of her mouth. "Hi," she said brightly.

"Hi yourself. I was just thinking of you."

"Oh, how's that?"

"Because I just got done eating a casserole you had frozen. It was delicious. You left enough food to last me a month."

"I'm glad you're eating properly."

"So am I. How's things in New York?"

"Pretty good. I'm busy as hell but I love it. I got a letter from Pixie today. There's no way I can tell you what all she had to say. I could make a copy and send it on if you'd like to read it."

"I'd like that. Please, send me a copy. Jesus,

are you listening to the both of us. We sound so polite, so bland, so . . . so . . ."

"Like two nerds," Dory laughed.

"Yeah. I was going to call you but then I told myself you needed the time to get back into the swing of things. I want you to believe that."

"Why wouldn't I? You never lied to me, Griff. I think of you constantly. On the hour at least."

"I know, I do the same thing," Griff said gruffly.

"Look, what are you doing two weeks from Friday? I thought I'd come up and we could do the town or whatever you want. I could bring your things back then too. Lily said she would pack everything up this week."

"I'd like that, Griff, I really would."

"Okay, it's a date then unless Starfire foals that day. Can we leave it on that basis?"

"Sure. How's things at the clinic?"

"Great. We have more business than we can handle. Thinking of taking on a fourth partner. John fired Ginny today for no reason. Just out and out sacked her. Since he's the senior partner there wasn't much either Rick or I could do. For some reason it bothered Rick. By the way, Rick tells me Lily thinks she's pregnant again. He seems delighted and Lily of course is bubbling over with happiness."

Dory swallowed hard. "That . . . that's wonderful. What are you going to do about the town house?"

"I don't need this much room. It's pretty expensive. Lily said she'd get me an efficiency apartment so I kind of left it up to her. I can't stay here," Griff groaned. "There are too many memories. It's the wise thing to do."

"Yes." She hated to ask it but she had to know. "Are you . . . are you seeing anyone?"

"The only lady in my life right now is Starfire. How about you?"

"No. I've been pretty busy."

"I've missed you. You wouldn't believe the condition of the bathroom. You'd kill me if you saw it."

Dory laughed. "I wish I was there to see it."

"I know you do. This . . . this conversation isn't helping either of us, I guess you know that," Griff said hoarsely.

"You're right. I'll look forward to seeing you in two weeks. And Griff, if Starfire foals, there will be other weekends."

"See you, Dory."

"I'm counting on it," Dory said as she hung up the phone. A smile tugged at her mouth as she circled the date with a red pencil. Next to it she wrote in large letters: GRIFF.

If you enjoyed BALANCING ACT,
be sure not to miss Fern Michaels's new novel

THE BLOSSOM SISTERS.

*In a richly rewarding story filled with unforgettable
characters, #1* New York Times *best-selling author
Fern Michaels explores the enduring bonds of family
as one man loses everything—only to find the freedom to create a bold new life . . .*

Gus Hollister owes all his success to his feisty
grandmother, Rose, and he knows it. It was Rose
and her sisters, Iris and Violet, who raised Gus,
sent him to the best schools, and helped him
start his own accounting business. Rose even
bought the house Gus lives in with his wife,
Elaine.

But now, Gus stands to lose everything—his
home, his car, and his business. Worse, he's
alienated his beloved grandma, who tried to
warn him about Elaine's greedy, gold-digging
ways. Gus, blinded by infatuation, refused to listen, and now Elaine has locked him out of the
house he was foolish enough to put in her
name.

Heartsick and remorseful, Gus returns to Rose's
Virginia farmhouse seeking shelter. But it won't
be easy to make amends. Despite their pretty
floral names, there's nothing delicate about the
Blossom sisters. Unbeknownst to Gus, they've

also been running a very lucrative business from home and don't want interference. Yet family and forgiveness go hand in hand, and Gus isn't giving up.

With the help of close friends, new associates, and some very sprightly ladies, Gus begins to repair the damage he's done *and* help the residents of Blossom Farm begin the next phase of their business. He might even be finding the courage to love again. Because no matter how daunting starting over can be, the results can surpass your wildest expectations—especially when the Blossom sisters are in your corner . . .

A Kensington trade paperback on sale in May 2013!

Read on for a special excerpt.

Gus Hollister couldn't remember when he'd been so tired as he closed and locked the doors of his CPA firm. Well, yes, actually he could remember. It was last year at exactly the same time, April 16, the last day of this year's tax season. Not that it was totally over; he still had tons of stuff to do, extensions to file, but he'd made his deadline, all clients had their records, and he was going home. If only it were to a home-cooked meal and several glasses of good wine. Like that was really going to happen. But he was simply too tired to care whether he ate or not.

Instead of taking the elevator, Gus trudged down the three flights of stairs and out to the small parking lot. Exercise these days was wherever he could find it. He winced at the lemon yellow Volkswagen Beetle that was his transportation for the day. His wife had taken his Porsche, and he was stuck with this tin can. If only he were a contortionist, which he wasn't. Gus clicked the remote and opened the door. After tossing his heavy briefcase on the passenger-side seat, he struggled to get his six-foot-four-inch frame into the small car. He hated this car. Really hated it. He inserted the key in the ignition, then lowered the windows and stared out at the dark night, an anxiousness settling between his shoulders that had nothing to do with taxes and the long days and nights he'd been putting in.

For some reason he didn't think it would be so dark, but then he remembered that they had turned the clocks ahead a few weeks back. Regardless, it wasn't supposed to be dark at nine thirty at night, was it? But he couldn't bring himself to care about that either.

He was almost too tired to turn the key in the ignition, so he just sat for a moment, looking out across the small parking lot to the building his grandmother had helped him buy. A really good investment, she'd said, and she was right. He rented out the two top floors to other businessmen, and the rent money he received covered the mortgage and gave him a few hundred dollars toward his cash flow every month. He owed everything he had in life to his feisty grandmother, Rose. Everything. And they were estranged at this point in time because of his wife, Elaine. He wanted to cry at the turn his life had taken in the last year. He banged the steering wheel just to vent before he started the Beetle, put it in gear, and roared out of the parking lot at forty miles an hour.

Thirty-five minutes later, Gus untangled all six-foot-four of himself from the lemon yellow Beetle, a feat requiring extraordinary concentration and agility. Then he danced around, trying to work the kinks out of his body. The Beetle belonged to his wife. *She* looked good in it. *He* looked stupid and out of place sitting behind the wheel. Today, Elaine had been out job hunting, and she wanted to make an impression, so she'd asked him if she could borrow his Porsche. Every bone and nerve in his body had screamed out, no, no, no, but in the end, he had handed her the keys. It was just too hard to say no to Elaine because he loved her so much. Especially when she kissed him so hard he was sure she'd sucked the tonsils right out of his throat. When that happened, he could deny her nothing, not even his beloved Porsche.

Elaine had passed the bar exam six months earlier and was looking for gainful employment. *Or so she said.* For six months now, she'd been looking for a job. Citing the economy, she told him that all the law firms wanted were slaves, not a qualified lawyer who had graduated at the top of her class. That was the reason she hadn't been hired. *Or so she said.* She hadn't even been called back for a second interview by any of the firms. *Or so she said.*

Sometimes he doubted her and instantly hated himself for his uncharitable thoughts, uncharitable thoughts that had been coming more and more frequently as of late. His gut was telling him that something was wrong; he just couldn't put his finger on what that something was.

Gus reached across the seat for his briefcase, then closed and locked the Beetle. *God, I'm tired.* No one in the whole world could or would be happier than he when today, April 16, turned into April 17. He was a CPA, a damn good one if he did say so himself, and he had been working round the clock since January 1 to meet his clients' needs. He'd made a lot of them happy and a few of them sad when he pointed to the bottom line that said *REFUND* or *PAY THIS AMOUNT!*

Gus walked across the driveway, wondering where Elaine was. It was 9:55, and she wasn't home. The jittery feeling between his shoulder blades kicked in again when he saw no sign of his car. He frowned as he walked toward the back entrance of his house, the house his grandmother had bought for him. It was a beautiful four-thousand-square-foot Tudor. He shivered when he thought about what she would say when she found out he'd added Elaine's name to the deed in one of those tonsil-kissing moments. For months, he'd been trying to find the courage . . . no, the guts, to tell his grandmother what he'd done. He knew she'd go ballistic, as would his two aunts. None of them liked Elaine. No, that wasn't right either. They *hated* Elaine, they could not stand her. And Elaine hated them right back.

Elaine said his grandmother and the aunts were jealous of her because she was young and beautiful and had stolen his love away from them. He'd never quite been able to wrap his mind around that, but back then, if Elaine said it, he tended to believe it. With very few reservations. His grandmother and the aunts had been a little more blunt and succinct, saying straight out that Elaine was a gold digger. End of discussion.

The strain between him and his beloved, zany grandmother and dippy aunts bothered him. He had hated having to meet them on the sly, then keeping the meeting secret so he wouldn't have to fight with Elaine and suffer through weeks of tortured silence with no tonsil kissing and absolutely no sex. Elaine held a grudge like no one he knew.

He owed everything to his grandmother. She'd raised him, sent him to college, helped him by financing his own CPA firm, then helping him again by buying him the beautiful house that he now lived in. With Elaine. And, no prenup. His grandmother had never once asked him even to consider paying her back, even when he'd tried.

He loved her, he really did, and he hated the situation he was in. Tomorrow or the day after, regardless of how it turned out, he was going to have a come-to-Jesus meeting with his wife and lay down some new rules. Family was family, and it was time that Elaine realized that.

Gus opened the gate to the yard, and Wilson came running to him. Wilson was the one thing he'd put his foot down on with Elaine. She said dogs made her itch and sneeze. Well, too bad; Wilson was his dog, and that was it.

"What are you doing out here, boy?" Gus tussled with the German shepherd a moment before walking up the steps to the deck, which was off the kitchen. The low-wattage back light was on. He didn't need Wilson's shrill barking to alert him to the pile of suitcases and duffel bags sitting outside the kitchen door. *His* suitcases. Six of them. And two duffel bags. All lined up like soldiers. Next to the suitcases was a pink laundry basket with Wilson's blanket and toys. He knew even before he put the key in the lock that the door wouldn't open.

"Son of a bitch!" He looked at the hundred-pound dog, who was barking his head off and dancing around the pink laundry basket. The jittery feeling between his shoulder blades had grown into a full-blown, mind-bending pain.

The words *gold digger* flitted through Gus's mind as he tried to peer in through the kitchen window. The only thing he could see was a faint greenish light coming from the digital clock on the microwave oven. So much for that glass of wine; never mind a home-cooked meal.

"You shoulda called me, Wilson," Gus snarled at the dog. As though what he said was even possible. The big dog barked angrily, as much as to say, What do you think I'm doing out here.

"Let's check the front door." Wilson nudged Gus's leg, then slammed himself against the door. The envelope stuck between the door and the jamb fell to the floor of the deck. The dog backed up and sat on his haunches. "Aha!" Gus said dramatically as he ripped at the envelope. He held up a single sheet of computer paper toward the light.

Gus.

I'm sorry, but this just isn't working for me. I don't want to be married anymore. I'm going to file for divorce. I packed all your things, and they're on the deck, along with your dog. As you can see, I had the locks changed. I don't want to see you anymore, so don't come here, or I will file a restraining order against you. I'm keeping the Porsche to show you I mean business.

The signature was a scrawled large E.

"Son of a bitch!" Wilson howled at the tone of his master's voice. "And she's keeping my car! My pride and joy! Next to you, that is, Wilson," he added hastily. "How the hell am I supposed to take all my stuff in that tin can she calls a car? I damn well do not believe this!"

Wilson's shrill barking told Gus that he had damn well better believe it.

Gus sat down on the top step and put his arm around the big dog. His wife didn't want to be married to him anymore. But she wanted his house and his car. *Gold digger!* So, his grandmother and the aunts had been right all along. His thoughts were all over the map then as he tried to figure out exactly how and when it had all gone wrong. There must have been signs. Signs that he'd ignored. How far back? The start of tax season? Before? October, maybe? Elaine had been looking for a job for over six months, so that would take it back to October. What happened at that time? He racked his brain. Elaine wanted to go on a cruise, but he'd been too busy to go. She'd pouted for two whole weeks and only gave in when he bought her a diamond bracelet. November was a disaster, and they'd eaten out at Thanksgiving because all Elaine knew how to cook was eggs and pasta. He'd wanted to go to his grandmother's, but she had refused, so he hadn't gone either. A real man would have gone.

Then came Christmas. Elaine said Christmas trees made her sneeze and itch the way Wilson did. So, no Christmas tree. He'd had a hard time with that as he remembered how his grandmother and the aunts went all out for the holidays. Elaine had gladly accepted presents, however. Lots and lots of presents was what she'd said. And jerk that he was, he had complied.

He had mentally kicked himself and lost weeks of sleep because he'd kowtowed to his wife and not gone to see either his grandmother or the aunts for Christmas. Now, right this moment, he felt lower than a snake's belly. If possible, he'd felt worse on Christmas Day. Here he was, three and a half months later, and he still hadn't so much as spoken to his grandmother or his aunts. He really did have a lock on stupidity. His shoulders heaved. Wilson was on top of him in a heartbeat. Man's best friend. Damn straight. Right now, his only best friend.

"I'm thinking I need a lawyer, Wilson," Gus said, getting up from the steps. He swiped at his eyes. "Real men don't cry. Bullshit!" he said, swiping at his eyes a second time. Wilson howled his misery as he waited to see what Gus would do.

"Okay, my tail is between my legs, so the only game plan I can see at this point is to pack you up in that tin can, take you to my grandmother's, and beg her to let us stay there until I can get my head on straight. If I'm lucky, maybe she'll lend me that farm van of hers, so I can come back to get our stuff. Let's go, boy!"

Wilson ran down the steps and over to the yellow Beetle. He scratched at the door, leaving long gashes in the glossy paint. "Chew the damn tires while you're at it, Wilson!" Gus said as he opened the door. Wilson leaped in and tried to settle himself on the passenger seat, but his legs hung off the seat and actually touched the floor. He barked and howled in outrage.

"It's just for five miles, so relax. We'll be there before you know it."

Wilson threw his head back and let loose with an unholy bark that made the fine hairs on the end of Gus's neck stand on end.

Gus clenched his teeth. "Yeah, you're right, Wilson. We're going to be damn lucky if my grandmother doesn't kick our asses to the curb, and I wouldn't blame her one bit. I've been a real shit. She really pulled the wool over my eyes, Wilson. Meaning Elaine, of course, not my grandmother. I'm even worse than a shit!" Wilson whimpered.

Ten minutes later, they were at the turnoff to the Blossom Farm, which his grandmother had renamed after his grandfather, Brad Hollister, had died, and her sisters, Iris and Violet, had come to live with her. For the sake of simplicity, his grandmother had also taken back her maiden name, Blossom.

"Okay, get ready, Wilson, we're coming to the driveway. Look, this is serious, so pay attention. If it looks like Granny is going to kick my ass off her property, you have to step in and whine. However she feels about me, she loves *you*. You know what to do, so just do it!"

Wilson whined to show he understood his master's words as he tried to untangle himself. The moment the car stopped, he was pawing the door to get out.

Inside the old farmhouse, the three residents were gaping out the window. "Rose! It's either that gold digger or Gus! What are they doing here at this time of night? Oh, my God, lock the doors! Is the door locked? Of course it's locked, we always keep the door locked," Violet, Rose's sister squealed.

"We need to hide," Iris, the third sister, said. "Rose, you can't let him in even if he is your grandson! We can't let him find out what we're doing."

Rose Blossom peered out into the darkness. It was indeed her grandson and his dog coming up to the front porch. In full panic mode, she crouched next to her two sisters under the front bay window. "He knows we're in here. Something must be wrong," she hissed.

"Who cares?" Violet hissed in return. "If you let him in, we go up in smoke. Is that what you want?"

"Good God, no! We could go out on the

porch. I'll just tell him . . . something will come to me," Rose dithered.

"No, something will not come to you, Rose. I say we just hunker down and wait him out. Unless, in one of your stupid moments, you gave Gus a key. Did you, Rose?" Violet snarled.

"He's always had a key, you know that. I don't see him using it. We are, after all, estranged," Rose reminded her sisters. "Anyway, the key won't work because we have a dead bolt inside. All he can do is bang on the door. Let's just stay put and see what he does."

"Why is he driving *her* car?" Iris hissed.

"Maybe *she's* dead," Violet whispered.

"You wish. Highly unlikely, or we would have seen the obituary," Rose said.

Violet clapped her hands over her ears when she heard the first bang on the front door. Her sisters did the same. Outside, Wilson howled and barked, the sound loud and shrill enough to set the sisters' teeth on edge.

"My legs are cramping," Iris grumbled.

"Mine, too," Violet added.

"I know you're in there, Granny, so open the door. Wilson needs a drink. I'm sorry! I really am. Please, open the door!"

Winifred, the sisters' basset hound, took that moment to waddle up to the door. She barked, a charming ladylike sound that pretty much said, Welcome.

"Damn dog! Now for sure he knows we're in here," Violet hissed. "I really have to get up *now,* or I'm going to faint."

"If you're going to faint, do it quietly," Rose shot back.

More banging and more apologies ensued. The sisters turned a deaf ear.

Winifred turned and started to waddle toward the kitchen. "Oh my God, he's going to the back door. All he has to do is smash the glass, and he can open the door," Iris said, momentarily forgetting all about the cramps in her leg.

"Gus wouldn't do that," Rose said. But her tone of voice indicated that she wasn't sure if what she had said was true or not.

"He's not going to give up," Violet said. "That has to mean the reason he's here at this hour is important, at least to him. Maybe you should just open the door and talk to him through the screen door. Tell him you were just getting ready for bed or something. You and he *are* estranged, Rose. I don't think Gus is here just to make nice. Just open the door and tell him to make an appointment to see you. That way we can . . . you know, just let him see what we want him to see."

"That sounds like a plan. For God's sakes, do it, Rose," Iris said.

"Do I have a choice?"

"No, not really," her sisters said in unison.

Rose heaved a mighty sigh as she made her way through the dark house to the kitchen. She didn't even bother to turn on the light when she opened the door. She tried to make her voice as cold and unfriendly as she could when she said, "Please stop banging on my door, Augustus Hollister. Why are you here? What do you want?"

"I need to talk to you, Granny. It's important."

"Well then, young man, I suggest you make an appointment," Violet, the bossiest of the sisters, said coolly. "In case you hadn't noticed, we've retired for the evening."

"It's not *that* late. You guys are night owls. Look, I need to talk to you, it's important. If it weren't, I wouldn't be here, especially in that yellow sardine can that masquerades as a car." The desperation in Gus's voice were getting to the sisters, but they held their ground.

"Tomorrow afternoon around five fifteen will work for us. I hesitate to remind you, but you do have a wife. Shouldn't you be discussing *your* important business with *her*?" Rose asked, defiantly.

"That's why I'm here. She kicked me out, stole my car, and is threatening to get a restraining order against me. I need to borrow your van to bring my luggage here. Elaine packed it up and left it on the deck. She changed the locks on all the doors and said she'd call the police if I went back. Elaine does not want to be married to me any longer. So I need to stay with you until I can find a place of my own."